W9-AOE-783

A Last Resort

Also by Julian Rathbone

DIAMONDS BID
HAND OUT
WITH MY KNIVES I KNOW I'M GOOD
TRIP TRAP
KILL CURE
BLOODY MARVELLOUS
KING FISHER LIVES
¡CARNIVAL!
A RAVING MONARCHIST
JOSEPH
THE EURO-KILLERS

A Last Resort
... for these times

Julian Rathbone

MICHAEL JOSEPH: LONDON

First published in Great Britain
by Michael Joseph Ltd
44 Beford Square, London WC1
1980

ISBN 0 7181 1884 7

Set by Saildean Phototypesetters Ltd, Molesey, Surrey
and printed and bound in Great Britain by
Redwood Burn Ltd, Trowbridge and Esher.

The author and the publishers are very grateful
to Mrs Q. D. Leavis and Chatto & Windus Ltd.
for permission to reproduce extracts from
The Living Principle by F. R. Leavis

For nine months in 1978 I was the recipient of a Southern Arts Bursary during which I planned and wrote the first draft of this novel. I am most grateful for this assistance.

J.R.

"But Brinshore Sir ... the attempt of two or three speculating people ... to raise that paltry Hamlet lying, as it does between a stagnant marsh, a bleak Moor & the constant effluvia of a ridge of putrifying sea weed, can end in nothing but their own Disappointment. What in the name of Common Sense is to *recommend* Brinshore? – A most insalubrious air – Roads proverbially detestable – Water Brackish beyond example, impossible to get a good dish of Tea within three miles of the place – & as for the Soil – it is so cold and ungrateful that it can hardly be made to yeild a Cabbage. -Depend upon it Sir, that is a faithful description of Brinshore – not in the smallest degree exaggerated – & if you have heard it differently spoken of –" "Sir, I never heard it spoken of in my Life before, said Mr Heywood. I didn't know there was such a place in the World."

Jane Austen: *Sanditon*

I

SATURDAY NIGHT

We Make New Friends

1.

'BRINSHORE is not what it was, Frank – it's all right to call you Frank? I'm Jack, and Mrs Trivet is Tess, short for Teresa – what I said was, Brinshore is not what it was, there's no denying that ... '

'Last orders, please.'

'But still, er, Jack, it's a nice enough place to live in, you must agree ... '

'Oh yes nice enough place to live in. A nice enough place to *live* in – or I wouldn't have lived here all my life, now would I? Ha!' A broad grin was suddenly slapped across Jack Trivet's broad face, the *ha* a loud trumpet to go with it. 'Tess knows I wouldn't have lived in Brinshore all my life if it wasn't a nice enough place to live in, nor she neither, eh?'

'Jack. Mr Rigg has called last orders.'

'So he has, Tess.'

'My honour, I think... er, Mrs Trivet, what will you have?'

'That's very kind of you indeed, Mr Dangerfield. I'll have a Bell's, if that's all right with you.'

Afore ye go, thought Frank Dangerfield, but he said: 'And you, Mr Trivet, er Jack?'

'Well, I'll have a Bell's too, Frank.'

Frank looked round. Near them, and had been talking with them, were friends of Mr and Mrs Trivet – an elderly man, no not elderly but going bald and a little grey and with lines round twinkling eyes, called, Frank thought, Ern Copeman; and a young lad, about twenty, bleary with cracked lips, wearing a fisherman's sweater and cultivating a beard, called, he believed, Kev Rammage.

'Er, what's yours then?'

'Ern,' said Jack Trivet, 'Mr Dangerfield here wants to know what's yours.'

'Oh, nothing more for me, thank you Jack. You know I have to drive home.'

'Are you quite sure ... ?'

'Well then, if it's to be sociable, Mr Dangerfield, I shall have another half pint, and I hope the gentlemen in blue aren't looking.'

Ern had a dry, half-swallowed voice, an occasional stammer.

'And you, sir?'

Kev, the fisherman, hesitated. He had a pint glass in front of him, only two thirds empty.

'Kevin,' said Teresa, 'will also have a Bell's.'

In for a penny, in for several pounds, thought Frank, and turned to Mr Rigg.

'And for yourself, sir?'

'That's very kind. A brandy if you don't mind.' Mr Rigg had a white goatee and a white moustache with turned up points but nicotine-stained from the cheroots he constantly smoked, black-rimmed spectacles, white hair, wore a bow tie and was generally thought of as a gentleman. Consequently he was always *Mr* Rigg. He now leant confidentially across the bar. 'I think I should say that Mr and Mrs Trivet like to finish with doubles.'

'Of course, Landlord. And one of the same for me too.'

Three pounds sixteen.

THREE POUNDS SIXTEEN.

Frank was chilled. Not out of meanness, or a feeling of having been taken, but out of fear. Had he got enough? Yes, he had. Just. Three pounds forty-seven and a half.

'Water or soda, Mrs Trivet?'

'Nothing for me, Mr Dangerfield. I don't like to spoil a good Scotch.'

'Jack?'

'Water, Frank. Half and half.'
'Your good health, sir.'
'Cheers.'
'All the best.'

Ern Copeman, aging but still twinkling, drank his bitter; Mr Trivet and Mrs Trivet and Kevin sipped Scotch, and Frank, having lost some of his with too exuberant a squirt of soda, did likewise. Mr Rigg touched a drop of Martell, four star, V.S.O.P., to his lips and breathed the fumes in so they mingled with those of his Manikin. They were, taken in the same order, surveyor from the Council but did little surveying now, night-shift hand from TRICE (manufacturers of washing-up machines – *it'll all be done in a* TRICE), lady wife to the same, fisherman as aforesaid, teacher and head of art at the local comprehensive, and landlord of the Athlone Free House, Brinshore.

'Time please,' said Mr Rigg, and carefully placed his glass on the bar and his podgy beringed fingers beside it. Calling the hours was almost all his occupation – the actual work was left to a rather sullen barmaid whom Frank knew he should know – for should he not know every girl and youth in Brinshore between the ages of thirteen and twenty-two? All had passed through his hands or were still at school. But they always changed as soon as they left, and especially barmaids who tend to paint their faces and go in for elaborate hair-dos. Kev too he should know, but before he could place the lad Mr Trivet had taken up again where he had left off, for he was a persevering man and would not easily give up a subject once he had raised it.

'Now I recall, as I know Mr Rigg does, the Campbell Steamers which called at the pier like and made day-trips to the Island.'

Mr Rigg nodded and passed a stained finger behind the lens of his heavy spectacles to wipe away the rheum.

'And the Pavilion, where there was concerts, just down there to the left of us facing the sea, where until two years ago was a marquee, and now a plastic slide I cannot see any purpose for.'

'I suppose small children enjoy it,' said Frank. 'I mean it is a quite extraordinarily big slide.'

'The point I'm making,' said Jack Trivet, 'is that this town was once a resort. And now it is not. It's not a resort any longer.'

'It's a dump,' said Kevin.

'A joke,' said Ern.

'You still get a lot of day-trippers,' Frank persisted. 'Several coaches each weekend. And there's the caravan sites.'

'Have you noticed,' said Ern, 'how all the people on the coaches are geriatrics? Old people's homes on outings.'

'Yeah, hobbling up and down the prom, and asking where the toilets are,' said Kev.

'Which,' said Ern, 'the Council which gives me my monthly pittance has usually, in its infinite wisdom, chained up.'

'That,' said Mrs Trivet, 'is on account of the vandalism.'

'Of course,' said Ern, 'but what can you expect from coach-loads of geriatrics?'

'I blame the blacks. A lot of blacks come on the coaches too, from Brixton and such places,' said Mrs Trivet.

'I counted thirty-five blacks on the beach last Friday,' said Kevin. 'But they were all kids, I mean littl'uns. Some orphanage, I reckon.'

Frank sensed antagonism in the air – Mrs Trivet upset by Ern's joke about old people being vandals and a not total unanimity of opinion about blacks (he himself of course silently dissented from what Mrs Trivet had assumed was the consensus on the subject), and he was relieved when the pouty barmaid announced: 'Your glasses please, *if* you don't mind, let's be having your glasses *now*.' Dutifully he raised his, still only a quarter gone, but paused when Mr Rigg withdrew his cheroot and murmured in a gravelly voice, like dear old Jimmy James, all cigar and brandy: 'Don't hurry, Mr Dangerfield. A large Scotch shouldn't be hurried.' His own Martell was scarcely touched.

'From now on we are Mr Rigg's guests, is that not right Mr Rigg?' Mrs Trivet sparkled as she said this. She was good at sparkling, could do it at will, but usually meant it too. People, especially men, were expected to feel flattered when Mrs Trivet sparkled at them.

'You, Mrs Trivet, your husband of course, and any friend of yours, et cetera.' Frank felt the *et cetera,* accompanied by a movement of the end of the cheroot through an arc not more than three inches in length, was a shade dismissive, but accepted that he was now a guest in a public house, a guest of the landlord after hours. Not so the eight or nine others who were shooed out by the barmaid. She bolted the glazed door – frosted with florets and foliage – behind them.

Now, at last, Mr Rigg stirred himself. He set aside his cheroot, lifted the flap of the counter, and like a large barge emerging from a lock, guided himself carefully down the narrow canal between chairs and tables towards a door at the far end. He puffed a little and wheezed a little, and nudged a table as he went by. The bar they were in had once been the reception hall of the Athlone Hotel; the bars Mr Rigg was now on his way to – to check they were closed, check the tills, check the locks, and dismiss the rest of the staff – had been the hotel lounge and dining-room.

'This is a luxury,' said Frank, raising his glass. 'Drinking after hours. I feel like a gangster in a speak-easy under prohibition, waiting for the police to come blasting in.'

Ern, mandarin-like, his eyes almost invisible as he smiled, reassured him: 'No fear of that. Not with old Mr Rigg. I recall, and I've no doubt Jack does, the day a young bobby came in, many years ago now, and asked whose was the Jaguar on the yellow line outside. Mr Rigg just looked at him and said: "You're new here, aren't you?" '

'Ah, but Mr Rigg was a big man in Brinshore in those days,' said Mrs Trivet. Then: 'Here, Jane. I'll give you a hand with those,' and she lifted herself – a little awkwardly for she suffered with her back – off her stool. She moved, slowly, trim, even smart in appearance, between the tables collecting dirty glasses and bringing them back to the bar. Mr Trivet, Jack, collected and emptied the ashtrays. Frank wondered uneasily if he should join in but there was not enough work to make a third hand necessary or even useful.

Ern, to his left, spoke quietly: 'Well, young Kev, what's got into you tonight?'

'Bloody Council,' said Kev.

'Oh dear, have we been giving you trouble again? We're always interfering somewhere.'

'You only want cold running fresh water installed where we sell off the end of our catch, that's all. I ask you, how are we going to get cold running fresh water piped under the road, under the prom, through the harbour wall and on to the shingle. Cost hundreds. More.'

'Must plead not guilty to that one, Kev. Nothing to do with Borough Surveyor. Some clerk in Health must have found a ruling on it ... '

'All you lot are the same. It's all the same thing, I mean, isn't it?'

'I agree,' said Frank. 'Personally, I lump the whole lot together and call it the Department of Social Interference.'

'The Department of Social Interference, you're right Mr Dangerfield, that's it. The Department of Social Interference it truly is. And if they go on the way they are they'll ruin every last fisherman and that'll be a bleeding shame. Sorry Mrs Trivet, but it upsets me, it's bound to.'

'Don't apologise to me, Kevin. It's Jane I'm thinking of. No lady likes to hear language in her bar, it never does a house good at all. Isn't that right, Mr Rigg?'

Mr Rigg was chugging back the way he had come, but he ignored her, for he had a commission for his barmaid.

'Jane,' he said, 'go to the public and give Tim a hand if you don't mind. He's been very busy.'

He lifted the flap and came to rest against the inside of the bar. Jane squeezed behind him pouting more than ever, and clacked away on stiletto heels.

'She should never wear shoes like that while she's serving,' said Mrs Trivet. 'No way.'

Silently, and without moving his feet, so well-placed was he, Mr Rigg lifted each glass in turn and refreshed them beneath the Bell's optic. Oh dear, thought Frank, for he was now more than a touch muzzy, it'll be too bad if he asks me to pay, and he gave a little humph and a grin, but for himself only, the way people who are a touch muzzy do.

Ern was determined not to be muzzy.

'No, no thank you Mr Rigg, no more for me, I really must be off. A Scotch before I'm safely home would spell disaster I'm sure. Well, good night all.'

'I'll let you out,' said Jack Trivet, and followed Ern a little heavily to the door which he unbolted, held open, bolted again, before padding back to his stool.

'Shame about Ern Copeman,' said Mrs Trivet. But she was not taken up – all present either knew already what was a shame about Ern Copeman, or thought it was no business of theirs.

The lamps were out in the main room now – just a rose-tinted neon strip in the bar and a bulb beneath the red skirts of a large flamenco doll cast a limited glow on the bottles, glasses, dark polished wood and shiny fittings. Frank narrowed his eyes – reduced it all to shards of coloured light and admired it.

'Ern is a painter too, Mr Dangerfield,' said Mrs Trivet. 'I mean like you he paints pictures.'

Oh dear. She knows me. That means I must teach a son or a daughter. Trivet. At least three, may be four, large family – cousins, I think. One doing CSE, a girl in the third year ... but wait, could it be ... ? (his pulse ticked a little faster) ... now she was a great girl, a lovely girl, but gone two years? One and a half?

'Ah yes, Tess,' Jack Trivet was saying, 'but Mr Dangerfield, Frank, is a professional, see. Old Ern just does it for a pastime, a hobby like.'

'Hardly a pro, Jack. I shouldn't still be a teacher if I was.'

Mr Rigg showed interest, had perhaps identified Frank Dangerfield who was not a regular. Mr Rigg knew a little of most of what went on in Brinshore.

'Those your canvases in Johnny Manet's window?'

Frank assented.

'Very professional work, Mr Dangerfield, very professional. And professional prices asked too I should say.'

'Yes. But Johnny Manet hasn't sold either yet.'

'Nor will, I dare say. People here don't like the muck around them held up before their eyes. It's there without they buy paintings of it.'

Jack Trivet said: 'Now it's a shame, Frank, you couldn't have painted the front as it was. The old Assembly Rooms and the Theatre Royal just where that Leisure Centre's going up. I don't know what was wrong with the old Assembly Rooms.'

'They were losing money, that was what was wrong with them.'

'May be, Mr Rigg, may be. But will they pull down the Leisure Centre when that loses money?'

'They'll need dynamite if they do – the concrete that's in it,' said Kev, and rubbed his sad eyes with the horny palm of his hand.

'What people won't see,' Jack repeated. 'is that Brinshore isn't a resort no more. Not like what it used to be.'

'I can't see anything in this modern building,' said Teresa Trivet, 'no way can I see anything in it. It's not the same as the old way, now is it, Mr Dangerfield? I mean it doesn't have the same appeal, now does it?'

'No, Mrs Trivet, I don't think it does.'

'*Thank* you, Mr Dangerfield. Thank you.'

Clearly satisfied to have her opinion backed by a competent authority, she returned to her Bell's.

'In the old days,' said Mr Rigg – he had drunk nearly half his brandy, had lit another Manikin and was expanding – 'there were four live shows, *and* three picture houses in Brinshore. Now what is there?'

'Bingo and the Granada,' said Kev, without looking up.

'There was The Follies on the pier,' said Jack counting on his fingers, 'the Repertory', (he spaced the syllables carefully for since his teeth he had trouble with r's) 'at the Esplanade, and Gay Time in the Theatre Royal. Most years.'

Gay Time? thought Frank. What was *that?*

'So where was your fourth, Mr Rigg?'

'I include the Pavilion. Brass Ensembles. Concert parties with a compère. You recall the sort of thing.'

'Not really a show, though.'

'But *live*, Mr Trivet, live.'

Kev lifted his head. A grin, a little twisted, a little longing, showed beneath his beard. 'Molly won that prize at the Pavilion, didn't she, Mrs Trivet?'

Teresa was clearly divided by this – pride in a past triumph conflicted with doubt as to its acceptability in present company. Pride won, but only just.

'That's right, Kevin.'

'Proper little Shirley Temple she was in those days.'

'We liked her to look nice. She never lacked for good clothes.'

'What was it then Molly sang? *I Never Felt More Like Singing the Blues* – and what was the other?'

'You Are My Sunshine. She learned that off me. And Paddy Coleraine gave her a kiss, a certificate, and a box of chocolates, and his autograph. But that's all in the past now.'

'It wasn't the Pavilion,' said Jack. 'The Marquee. The Pavilion went when she was two and she were nearly four when she did that contest.'

Mr Rigg had sensed Mrs Trivet's doubt about the subject.

'And now Molly, Miriam's at university, I believe,' he said. 'A credit to you. Happy in it, is she?'

'Oh yes, Mr Rigg. And thank you for asking. She'll be pleased to hear you did. She came back today and would have come down with us but was tired. She's been studying very hard, but then she always did ... '

'Miriam Trivet. *Miriam* Trivet. Of course,' cried Frank Dangerfield, and fancied brass bands were again playing in the distance like they used to, flags waving, flowers ... 'You're Miriam Trivet's parents!'

'That's right Mr Dangerfield. I'm not surprised you remember her. For she always spoke most highly of you and still does. To tell you the truth, I've always been sorry she didn't stick to the painting and printing you taught her, I'm sure her best talents lay that way, but it was no use *my* saying anything on the subject ... '

2.

Ern drove his Escort carefully, as befitted a senior official in the Borough surveyor's department, and the police in their Rover 3500 did not take their eyes off the youths outside the Pier Disco to watch him go by. He drove on past decaying hotels, once hotels now flats with the stucco peeling, past the old Fair Fields now covered in heaps of brick, some of which were already houses and others of which soon would be, and so, mile by mile, four miles all but, all told, came to his own home in Merriedale.

And as he drove he thought of Frank Dangerfield and his paintings, well lit and well framed in Johnny Manet's window. They'd been there for three weeks and no sale, not one likely either, while he, Ern, the amateur, had sold *Land's End* a fortnight ago to a publican in Lewes for sixty pounds, not much less than the hundred guineas Manet asked for Dangerfield's pictures, and no commission off the price either. What would Manet take? Fifteen per cent? More like fifty.

And so Ern twinkled a little to himself as he carefully put the Escort round the Duck Pond – though when a duck was last seen there was anyone's guess. Pity about the elms – but there was no denying there was more light and space without them.

Frank's paintings he admired. Would talk to him about them some day. Very slick, almost too slick, beautifully drawn, the paint laid on like, like silk, and every detail of the shelter on the front, its broken windows and its graffiti, and the new Leisure Centre behind with its concrete and yellow brick and low tent-like roof as if it was trying to hide instead of standing proud like the old Assembly Rooms. Well, it was well painted, no denying that, but who'd want a picture of a vandalised shelter and a half-finished Leisure Centre? Whereas Land's End at sunset, with a yacht, its sails just catching the last rays and rosy with them, a heavy swell running and putting out into the Atlantic, that caught the imagination. And sold. People liked that sort of thing – even if, or even because the paint went on a bit thick.

Careful here turning into Woodcroft Lane – road narrow and dark – still only gas lights. Made a minute on it, what, five years ago? No, seven. Before the reorganisation. Got filed away, lost when they changed the councils over. It had been a good minute too, foresaw the problems created by the new estates, problems of flow, and the expansion of Woodcroft Primary, proper little bottle-neck when home-time came.

New houses over there behind the cypresses. Regency style. A bow-window, a varnished 'residential' door, a plastic 'brass' door-knocker and they put on five thou and sell them to clerks and schoolteachers instead of honest workmen who wouldn't want them anyway. Pine Croft Mews. Show-house. *Mews?* People are so stupid ignorant nowadays not to know what *mews* means. Whoops, careful, rabbit in the road. Must have come out of the hedge. Well, I saved that hedge. Dogrose, elder. Looks a treat this time of year. The Council wanted open-brick screen, the developers plain fencing. Why not leave the hedge, I said. Cost a hundred a year to keep up they said. A hundred a year for dogrose, elder, hawthorn and a bit of blackthorn, hazel catkins and primroses in spring, a hedge like that's an amenity, I say. And there's still rabbits in it.

Someone will be writing to the Council before long complaining his lettuce plants have been got at.

That's what people like Dangerfield with their cracks about Social Interference don't realise, thought Ern. That a fair bit of what we do is in response to busybodies amongst the rate-payers who can't leave well alone. Though I agree poor old Kev's got a legitimate moan, but I think I'll be able to scotch that fresh water tap, or anyway get the Council to pay after all, committee's sitting on Wednesday. Couldn't say anything about it of course, not even hint, he'll just have to worry about it a day or two more.

Here we are then. Merriedale. MERRIEDALE.

Ern carefully directed his Escort between high brick pillars and into the complex of estates known as Merriedale. First, the original Merriedale, a knot of wide avenues with well-groomed verges, shrubberies, and timber half a century old or more, and large detached houses built in twenties tudor and thirties functional; then three square miles of crescents and closes, denes and deans, meadows and meads, leas and leighs, dales and dells, parades and precincts with centres for senior citizens, play centres, health centres and a mobile community centre, and not an honest road or street amongst them. Getting on for a thousand acres of ranch-style, split-level, Scandinavian, regency, chalet-style, bungalow-style – on Merriedale you don't live in a house, houses are common. All had open-plan lawns, mostly bare of anything but grass and rose-bushes and a fenced-in scrap at the back for hanging out the washing. Dene after mede after lea of brick-coloured brick, concrete lamp-posts, blank walls, and laced-in, laced-up, lace-curtained windows.

Round Abbott's Mere Ern drove and recalled the residents' petition that one of his neighbours was getting up to have it filled in – a neat little pond with neat grass edges, carefully landscaped, once it had been the farm pond of Abbott's Farm and nearby had been the best blackberries for miles. Ern's mother used to bring them out from Brinshore, him and his brothers and sisters, one dead, one in Australia, one in Canada, and every late September their ghosts, his included, still stretched and fumbled, laughed and grumbled amongst spectral briars where now the Swiss-style chalets stood.

And so at last to his own three-bedroomed, with L-shaped luxury-sized living area, gas-fired all-through central-heating, double-glazed, in immaculate order (owner being a do-it-yourself man of professional training and ability), Scandinavian-style bungalow (which meant it had two roofs instead of one). His own because the mortgage was paid off, and the second mortgage too, raised for substantial additions to the original structure, all his, all his at last ... except it was his wife's also.

Ern parked the Escort on the two lines of concrete slab which doubled as run-in and boundary between his open-plan front and his neighbour's and got out as quietly as he could to open the garage door. Oh dear, the Greens have left their pram out again, but at least the kid's not howling, they'll be getting some sleep, and Dot Green certainly looks as if she needs it. Over the way cars parked, lights on, music – well some call it music, and very loud. Ern paused and cocked his ear, trying to make sense of the words ...

Ça plane pour moi
Ça plane pour moi

... that's French surely. But English too.

I am the King of the Divan

... daft words and far too loud.

Crash of glass and screams. Younger set of Merriedale. Wife-swappers, orgies, rumours only, much exaggerated no doubt, but his daughter went to one in her pyjamas last month. Said it was a Pyjama Party. All right if you're married, that sort of thing, Ern had said, and your husband doesn't mind, but his daughter paid no attention. They had met on the drive-in where he was now standing. They hadn't spoken to each other properly since her seventeenth birthday five years ago, the last day he'd spoken with either of them, his wife or his daughter. Life's been better since.

He pulled down the up-and-over behind him and walked round the car to the door at the back. Pitch-dark but he knew where every packet of seed and hank of raffia was, and so through the back door of the garage to where his back lawn, larger than most, had once been.

Because of a bend in the road, crescent, number twenty-eight had more space at the back than the others and now most of this was filled with a work-room, a tiny bedroom, a shower and a toilet – the rest being given over to tomatoes, potatoes, marrows, runner beans, cabbages, spinach according to season. The two extra rooms, built on to the garage but at no point adjoining the house, had been planned by Ern, given planning permission by Ern (rubber-stamped by a work-mate), and built by Ern even down to the plumbing (which had given him some trouble), and from the day the single bed had been delivered he had not set foot inside the main house – even paying for a man to retile the kitchen floor rather than do it himself at a fraction of the cost. Occasionally he would see, across the three-yard gap, his wife and daughter moving about, notice the flicker of the telly at night and hear their radio by day. For a time they had taken to staring blankly across at him, whether compulsively or by design he could not guess, and when they did he pulled down his venetian blinds. At work he was told his daughter had moved from the dentists where she had been a receptionist to Health and Social Security, and once he had seen his wife behind a till at Saintrose and he had hurried away without buying what he had gone in for. God knows what they did with the money – they already had two-thirds of what he earned.

He turned on the lights in his work-room and blinked, for they were bright – an unshaded bulb in the middle of the ceiling and two angle-poise lamps on the work benches. The room was fifteen feet by fifteen and carpeted wall to wall. One of the benches supported a power lathe capable of turning wood or metal. Tools hung on the wall above it and filled the deep drawers beneath it. It was Ern's conceit that he was self-reliant, a survivor. No disaster, holocaust or catastrophe was going to catch him out. When it comes, he sometimes said in the Athlone, it won't find me unable to manage, and he grew far more vegetables than he needed and forced them on neighbours, work-mates and pub acquaintances rather than give them to his wife.

'No, honestly, I mean it,' he would say, 'put me on a desert island and I'd be all right. I don't need anyone and no one needs me and I'd as soon be away from it all. Life on a desert island – that would suit me. Especially if I could generate my own electricity.'

The other bench was given over to Ern's hobby. Paints, acrylic and oil, brushes in pots, turps, linseed oil, acrylic medium, varnishes, charcoal, pencils, filled the shelves above it; canvases on stretchers (made on the work bench, of course) filled the space beneath it. On the neighbouring wall fifty postcards were pinned, seascapes and landscapes chosen for their emptiness, and these provided not the inspiration he needed but the appearances which would give his inspiration form.

His latest work, *Land's End II,* nearly finished, was on the ingeniously designed and carefully made bench easel. Ern turned the lamps to light it, reached down a bottle of Johnnie Walker and half filled a tumbler before topping up with water from the tap set in the corner between the benches, then perched on his stool in front of it and slowly drank his nightcap.

This painting was more sombre than the earlier version. The sun was almost gone, banks of black cloud lay across the horizon, the sea was dark and the land indistinct. A feeble glow from the distant lighthouse promised neither safety nor guidance. Only the two white sails of the boat, curved and neat like the wings of a tern, glowed luridly in the general gloom. Ern shivered. He wondered at the forlornness that informed his work, but wisely forebore to analyse it. He gulped down his whisky, turned out the lights and went through to his tiny bedroom.

Once in his pyjamas he paused for several moments in front of his shaving mirror – not out of vanity or narcissism but because the face he saw there was the only really familiar face in his life. The head was round and deep-browed, going bald on top, with black hair streaked with grey fluffed out at the sides. The widely-spaced eyes still glinted cheerily behind puffy lids; the mouth, before he removed his teeth, was small, and, so he had once been told, sensitive. A kind face but sad in repose. Ern understood what was tragic in his life, and yet was not so egoistical as to imagine that that he did not share the same problem with countless millions – he lacked opportunity to be kind.

With this familiar thought he performed the last ritual of his day. He turned a milled screw on the side of the milometer taken from the first car he had ever owned, a Morris Eight, and now set by his narrow bed. The number shown reduced from nine hundred and ninety-eight to nine hundred and ninety-seven – the exact number of days left before he could retire from the surveyor's department, Rifedale District Council, where, since local government reorganisation, his job had been reduced to a nothing of working parties and steering groups.

In the darkness the party continued across the road; the Greens' baby began to cry – nearer and louder than usual it seemed – and an ambulance wailed distantly, presumably on the road between Rifedale and Brinshore. Then, thanks to the whisky, Ern slept.

3.

Frank, because he was muzzy, was very careful about the way he crossed the road in front of the Athlone, but when he came face to face with the step surmounted by a heavy rail which fenced the prom off from the road he put one foot on the step and did a gate-vault over the rail, swinging his legs high in the air above it. Thirty-one and a half p jingled beneath him and eleven p rolled back over the edge into the gutter.

'Goddamn,' he said.

Fifty yards away the two young policemen in the Rover 3500 parked opposite the pier looked up, momentarily interested.

'Old Frank Dangerfield,' said one, easily identifying the very tall figure beneath the street light and recalling the thinning sandy hair and mottled white hands of his ex-art teacher.

'Who's he?'

'Taught me drawing, or tried to. At the Comp.'

'Didn't think it was P.E. the way he went over that rail.'

Their gaze went back to the knot of youths outside the pier, who, in turn, gazed back at them.

Meanwhile Frank, having given up his eleven p, negotiated the second rail by the shelter that he had painted, passed the three boats, Kevin's among them, and the hut where the fishermen sold off the end of their catch at the foot of the sea wall, and was now sliding, striding down the dully jingling shingle towards the wet brown sands.

The tide was out, right out, and he had to walk three-quarters of the length of the broken pier before he came to the water's edge. The night was clear, starry, a little chill for shirt sleeves, fresh anyway. Tiny black waves lapped up over the shiny sand, quick, close together – which Frank believed meant the tide had turned and was flowing, a fact he soon forgot. In front, distinguishable, a long line of deeper black, bumpy against the luminous black of the sea, stretched between him and the horizon and on the breeze, just a breath that ran with the tide, came the odour of seaweed. The Rocks. Far beyond, its source below the horizon, a light glimmed three times then shut off for a minute, then glimmed again and the Channel shipping moved out beyond it. Not a view with much interest in it, though Ern might have thought differently. Frank turned and faced the land. The fact was that while he shared with Ern a broken marriage, a talent for painting and a kind nature, Frank was quite a different person in every other way; and the difference showed itself most in this: Frank's unrealised instinct was to find inherent in the complex of a present that disgusted him factors that promised a better future; Ern longed for a landscape without people, without history.

The sea wall, masking what had once been a low fifteen-foot cliff, was an even white band dividing the darker broader strips of land and sky above from shingle and sand below. Very fashionable six years ago, thought Frank – with the right signature that sort of thing had fetched a thousand guineas and hung in the Tate. Well, it won't do now, not for me anyway.

He set his weight on one leg, his head on one side and

pulled the skyline of the town about in his mind. A rise in the middle with good timber. Clock tower and cupola of Trafalgar House. Very neat, but with windows boarded up and stucco flaking. Take it away and what will you have? A block of flats called, with developers' deference to the past, Trafalgar Tower – to match Denham Tower, already built on the other side of the pier. In front of it and below was the Town Hall which was a town hall no longer, the seat of local government having been moved (and Ern Copeman with it) to Rifedale. Yet still it housed in its long and numerous corridors section upon section of the hydra-headed, gargantuan-throated, insidiously growing, creeping menace of our old friend the Department of Social Interference.

Frank, irritated at the thought, took a large hand from his pocket and pulled his beard, then set himself on the other foot and his head on the other side. His gaze moved east; meanwhile the sea behind lapped and slipped, lapped and slipped like a puppy affectionate but shy, not sure of its reception, and the odour of seaweed drifted more insistently about his nostrils as the rock pools filled and gurgled and the rocks themselves slipped from view almost quarter of a mile behind him.

The Terrace – eight fine mansions, eight fine entrances with eight fine stairways and column-framed portals with iron rails set behind green benches and a gravel walk, access to the sea by shallow stairs cunningly set in the low cliff down to the pebbles where bathing machines awaited those who valued saline air and immersion, cure to a host of ills. A milliner's, a billiard room for the men and a circulating library for the gentler sex, and an hotel, to be called, with gracious permission, the Athlone.

No longer. Perched to the left, in isolation, yes, the Athlone, a light glowing dully upstairs where Mr Rigg no doubt smoked a last cheroot and sipped a last brandy, and twenty other windows, invisible to Frank on account not of his blindness but theirs. And to the right of the Athlone, what? A hole, a joke, a space where the other seven grand houses of the Terrace had been, a space that could not be painted. You can, Frank remembered, record corporate vandalism with a picture of a Leisure Centre, or a picture of a broken pier, but that space!

'Oh Great God in Heaven,' cried Frank aloud, directing his voice in the appropriate direction, and then: 'Goddamn and blast it,' as the sea sidled up to him and licked his ankles. He set off briskly in an oblique line and the sea wagged its tail and tried to follow him but the earth turned away and kept it on a tight leash. He jingled his coins and keys and whistled with ingenuous banality 'Oh I do Like to be beside the Seaside.' Not so muzzy now, he thought and neatly side-stepped a mound of sand and a hole left by a bait-digger.

The pier loomed above and ahead, an unlit pile of child's bricks set on stilts against the sky. Its centre was a small theatre, still beautiful but now a disco; the storms had knocked away the dome and the two towers that had housed the scene-dock. The same storms, twenty years ago, had swept away the centre of the pier proper with its small bandstand and café at the end, where the Campbell Steamers had tied up to take day trippers to the Island.

Frank stood beneath the glistening girders in the frontier land between shingle and sand. 'My Dad,' he said, 'my Dad was in charge of a gun, a big gun, right on the end of this pier. That was during the war, that was.'

The shingle rattled above him.

'Bugger off you great loony,' said a male voice, and a female one giggled.

'Oh dear me, I am sorry. I thought I was quite alone,' said Frank, and blushed in the darkness.

'Yeah. Well. So did we. So sod off now, will you?'

Something white glowed softly as the pebbles clinked again, then melted into the darkness – a thigh perhaps, now covered with a coat or skirt. Oh dear me. And Frank hurried on up the pebbles and back on to the front.

Fancy the Trivets being Miriam's Mum and Dad, he thought.

His flat was in one of the old houses at the bottom of the Chine. These had been the first tradesmen's houses, set between the village and the sea and to the east of the Terrace, before the High Street was built. Now they were cafés and boarding-houses with some flats, running to seed in most cases and no doubt doomed for the chop before long, which, the agent had said, gives them *character* – though a lot of people don't go for character these days.

No surprise this, since *character* included dark hallways, treacherous cracked lino and an ill-fitting front door at the top of the stairs; since *character* meant a kitchen done out in the same lino, a dirty stove, a square glazed sink, and a lethal gas water-heater; since *character* was a sitting-room and a bedroom furnished from the store in the alley behind the High Street (Houses cleared, free estimates, we pay cash), and the lot, since *character* is never cheap, at eighteen pounds a week. 'Well, it's the front Mr Dangerfield; that view over the Channel would come very high indeed if this was one of the new flats they're putting up,' and indeed it was the view that had clinched it for Frank.

Now he paused in the kitchen to pour himself half a glass of milk taken from the chipped old fridge, which growled in response. Then he walked through to the sitting-room, which doubled as bedroom as he used the bedroom as a studio. Here he threw up the sash and sat down in a low wooden armchair, really far too small for his large frame. A low stucco balustrade cut off the foreground but he could see the horizon and the end of the pier as he sipped his milk, and he could hear the whisper of the sea, and the lapping of the wavelets on the sand. Frank felt gentler now – things may be bad, he thought, and will get worse. But one day they will be better, oh yes.

Far off an ambulance wailed – somewhere in the town behind. Come from Rifedale. Presently the moon, a half moon, D-shaped so waxing, caught the waves that now listlessly broke above the distant rocks as the tide filled, and Frank dozed, the last inch of his milk forgotten.

4.

About five minutes before Frank left the beach Mr and Mrs

Trivet had passed by the street entrance to his flat. They then turned right up the Chine past the ornate drinking fountain (out of order), eight different marbles Jack Trivet would tell you, erected to commemorate the coronation of His Gracious Majesty King Edward VII.

'It's always nice to make a new acquaintance,' said Teresa Trivet. 'I believe he lives now in one of these flats.'

'Who?' asked Jack Trivet.

'Mr Dangerfield, of course. He's lived here three years now since he left his wife.'

They walked on past the Oasis Café and Jax Slax Boutique – walked slowly on account of Teresa's back. Really she should have had her stick, but she was too proud; really she should have had a taxi but a night-shift hand at TRICE keeps taxis for rainy days – instead she had the solid crook of her husband's elbow to cling to, with her thin sparrow wrist.

'I thought,' said Jack, with the care of one who wants to make a disputatious point without actually getting into a dispute, 'I thought you were acquainted with him already.'

'Only in a manner of speaking. I always saw him when I went up to school. Miriam spoke highly of him. He always spoke very highly of her.'

Being a night-shift worker Jack had been unable to attend Parent-Teacher Meetings. He used to say that if there were no advantages to night work other than the money, it would pay treble instead of time and a half.

'What's this about his wife, then?'

'I recall Miriam telling me, all her friends at school knew. It was in her last year there, no, I tell a lie, next to last. They've got a lovely house and children too, I think, the other side of the Downs, Pulworth way. But he's on his own here now.'

Ten more paces up the Chine.

'Those paintings of his in Manet's window. You don't need to know about art to see ... Better than colour photographs.' Jack used three or four rolls of colour film a year and knew what he was talking about. His pictures of the front somehow flattened out the background, made it smaller than it was.

Usually Teresa was in the foreground, always scowling. She never, ever smiled at a camera. 'But it's a funny idea to paint that shelter, rude words and all.'

'It doesn't do a man good to live on his own. No way.' Teresa felt that Jack needed occasional reminders of this truth, and others like it.

Carefully, Jack helping her tactfully at the curbs, they crossed the road at the top of the Chine and made their way up what had been a narrower alley, a continuation of the larger street. The road was still there, and the narrow pavements, but grass grew in the cracks at the edges between flags that were as familiar to them both as the backs of their hands. Stone, real stone flags, have a character that cast concrete and tarmac both lack. But where the two terraces of fishermen's cottages had faced each other across the road (tarmac over cobbles), where there had been scrubbed doorsteps with scrapers, plank front doors with polished knockers, upstairs windows so low you could touch their sills from the street, where these decent cottages had been there were now eight feet high chain-link fences set between concrete pillars. These fences – more suitable for protecting land lethal or valuable, or even a prison – were there to keep children or tramps off two narrow strips of wasteland where elder, willow, willow-herb and sorrel nodded over kitchen tiles – still dainty with ochre acanthus patterns on a maroon ground, one set of which Teresa had scrubbed, dried and polished every day for twenty-five years.

The Trivets rarely spoke during this stage of their weekly pilgrimage to and from the Athlone, though their mouths set in grim sour lines and Teresa clutched her husband's arm a shade more tightly. They might have headed a protest march thus – walking very upright, he heavy-built, solid like granite with grey wavy hair combed back, she with her immaculate perm; he in his Signal Corps blazer and shoes that reflected the single gas light, she in her amber trouser suit with topaz brooch.

The alley had been derelict for ten years, the planned development coming to nothing. Only the compulsory purchase order was effected – from a Miss Denham who lived sixty miles down the coast and who was glad to be rid of a property that was more trouble than it was worth. The far end debouched into a wide open space, one of several in the centre of Brinshore at this time, which the Trivets now walked across. To their right there was the new Health Centre – including Deaf Centre on Mondays, Disabled Centre on Tuesdays and Thursdays, Pre-natal Support Groups and Post-natal Support Groups on Wednesdays, and the Child Psychotherapy Unit on Fridays – all in a heavy, blank, concrete building with ramps and high walls and steel door-frames painted bright red, which, with its meaningless tower on one side, would have served better as a block-house against invasion than Frank's father's gun on the end of the pier, and would serve better now as a prison than as a place to see your doctor in.

To their left, across two hundred yards of empty tarmac, a thirty-storey block of flats rose above a new shopping precinct – the whole mess being what was once Denham House and its grounds. Four large cypresses and one cedar, now shading a paddling pool and swings, were all that remained of former glory before whose gates a narrow street of knocked-down cottages had tugged its forelock for a hundred and fifty years. Five trees and a name – for the flats were, of course, Denham Tower.

In the middle of the tarmac, by day a car-park, Jack Trivet paused, and passed his hand across the silvery ripples of his hair. 'Moon will be up soon,' he said. Then he turned his face inland for there was still a mile to go before they reached the council estate.

'Are you fishing tomorrow?' Teresa obscurely felt the moon was connected with tides and therefore with her husband's hobby.

'No. Haven't dug bait yet, have I? I'll be getting bait midday and I'll be fishing early Monday morning.'

They walked on. At the edge of the car-park Teresa asked: 'You'll meet me at the Little George then?'

'One o'clock. Half-past.'

Sunday lunchtime they usually spent in a pub much nearer where they lived. Always 'where they lived' – 'home' was a patch of chipped tiles and willow-herb behind a chain-link fence. For Teresa it was also a village in County Cork.

'Mr Dangerfield is quite a gentleman. I felt quite shamed in front of him when Kev made that remark about old people looking for toilets.'

Jack grunted – a noise perfected over the years to express his presence and nothing more at all, neither assent nor dissent, however qualified.

'Old people can find themselves very embarrassed by a lack of conveniences, and I don't think it's a matter for joking.'

Another twenty yards up a terrace with Edwardian bow-windows.

'I shan't tell Miriam that Kevin was there. After all he didn't ask to be remembered. Just brought up that ridiculous singing prize. She'll find him for herself if she wants to.'

'You were pleased enough at the time.' Jack referred to his daughter's tiny triumph in the Marquee. Teresa ignored him.

'I don't suppose she will though. I expect she's got a boyfriend at the university. Not that she'd tell us. Personally, I was surprised she went on with Kev after he left school and she stayed on.'

Jack fell back on his grunt.

'She'll be glad Mr Rigg remembered her though. I expect we'll go down together during the week to pay our respects.'

'She could have done that tonight.'

'She was tired. I didn't think she looked at all herself. Pale and she's lost weight. I'm sure she doesn't eat well at that place.'

'I thought so,' said Jack. But he wasn't agreeing with his wife. He stopped, head on one side. 'Ambulance. Can you hear it?'

'Now you mention it, yes I can.'

'Coming this way. Reckon I could hear it half the way from Rifedale.'

The siren, which had been intermittent, used only at important junctions, suddenly sounded much louder, almost on top of them. Then there it was, swinging round the corner three hundred yards in front of them, blue light flashing, divided windscreen between the white roof and the white radiator grill, then it was gone again, into a side street between the Trivets and the main road. They quickened their pace to the corner.

Half way down Alma Grove the ambulance had stopped, though its blue light still turned casting an ethereal light on privet and twitching lace curtains. Two neighbours, more curious or more concerned than the rest, stood in their doorways in dressing-gowns and curlers, with arms folded, and watched. Light from a front door, quiet advice and instruction – 'Steady now, two steps down ... let me get the gate open,' and two ambulance men wheeled, lifted, manoeuvred and wheeled again a laden stretcher up into the van. A third man walked beside them.

'That's Doctor Ferrit,' said Teresa.

'And that's old Trev Stevens' house, so I suppose that's old Trev.'

'Oh Jack. Is it really?'

'See that gate? He painted that new last weekend.'

'Should we go down. Marge'll need someone.'

'Wait a bit.'

Presently the folding ramp was hoisted in, the doors fastened. The doctor, tall, grey-haired, suited, watched the ambulance turn on a tight lock, and up past the Trivets it came again, lurched round the corner, and sounded off its siren right by them. Teresa put her hands to her ears.

'I hate that sound.'

They lingered a moment, undecided about what to do for the best.

Then: 'Doctor Ferrit's gone back inside,' Jack said. 'Look – that's his car the other side of where the ambulance was.'

'Marge'll be all right with Doctor Ferrit there. He's a good man.'

Still hesitating Jack said: 'I'll call by tomorrow on my way down to the front. See if she wants anything fetched.' Then: 'Nothing we can do.'

They pressed on, past lower, smaller houses – pebble-dashed, with timber facings. They passed a Chinese – almost the only lighted window the whole way.

'Do you want a take-away?'

'Not unless you do.'

She waited patiently outside while he ordered pancake rolls, prawn foo-yung, chop-suey, rice and chips. No sweet'n sour. They didn't like sweet'n sour.

Jack burped as he came out. 'Oops. Beg pardon,' and walked a little faster, get home before the foil containers lose their heat, get home to see the last half hour or so of the late film on telly.

'I wonder what it was.'

'What?'

'Trev Stevens.'

Grunt.

'I expect it was heart.'

Grunt.

'Of course they can do a lot these days, but I wouldn't be too hopeful. Not at his age. And he's been bad before.'

Grunt.

'If you see Marge tomorrow and it was heart, well, it's not fair to raise her hopes, you know. It'll only be worse when he goes.'

Grunt.

'She'll miss him.'

Brick buildings now, low box hedges, a wide green. The council estate. The Trivets' house in a corner of the patch away from the road, end of terrace, nice bit of garden.

Jack Trivet held the gate open for his wife then looked around and above him at the stars, and then at the half moon, just clear of the roofs at the other end of the road. Almost you might say he sniffed the air.

'Another nice day tomorrow,' he said. 'If you ask me.'

II
SUNDAY
Merrie Times in Merriedale

1.

AND so it was. And one of the first to appreciate its June loveliness was Ern Copeman, for he had reached that stage in life where sleep is not the important thing that it was – a condition aggravated by the fact that he slept alone and rarely went to bed more than rather tired, never downright fatigued. This last not out of laziness – lack of meaningful and fatiguing occupation was as serious a deprivation to him as lack of occasion to be kind.

Although he did not really want a paper he walked to the newsagent, saw that *The Observer* was not on sale (he assumed a strike), was satisfied to have an excuse not to buy, and so strolled home again.

At eight o'clock on a Sunday morning, even in early summer, Ern's crescent was a dull place, in spite of the swoop of martlets in the deepening blue of the sky and the fresh scent of the roses, still dewy. Two rows of bungalows (Scandinavian style) mirrored each other round the curve of the road, each with only two small windows on the reverse wall so if you came up from the precinct you were faced with forty almost blank brick walls. Army camps and open prisons have been designed with more verve. But Ern usually found something to grin at – his was a sharp sense of humour, zesty when undepressed, acetic otherwise.

At the end of the road the Browns had repainted their garage, doors and window-frames – the previous weekend they had stripped down the woodwork and undercoated it in greyish pink; now the top coats were on – the larger expanses in 'Matador', the frames in 'Petal Rose'. Against the Betty Uprichardsons and puce antirrhinums the combination was almost enough to turn Ern's mood to vinegar, but he took a grip on the fine weather and the martlets and mused instead.

He much enjoyed popular anthropology of the speculative sort – with Ardrey and Morris behind him it was not difficult to evolve a theory about the cheerful colours that assaulted his eyes wherever he looked. The colours, in presumably considered combinations, were aggressive, defensive/aggresive – the eye flinched from them. Ern had moved on and could now see 'Hot Sand' with 'Pampas', 'Fiesta' (a jolly orange) with 'Mango', and the Greens' house next to his own, done more to his own taste, in 'Moss' and 'Catkin'. All except the last said one thing loud and clear – 'Keep Out', 'Keep Off', 'I'm dangerous – like the spotted adder or the striped wasp I'll sting, bite, or poison you'; but the last, the Greens, with a parched lawn and no flowers said: 'I'm not here, please ignore me.'

Ern thought: I put it down to open plan. With nothing to hide behind but a lace curtain and frosted glass in the front door, nothing between you and the Intruder, the Stranger, the Hawker, the Hunter ...

A movement caught Ern's attention, a sudden scuttling movement out of a front door and round to a garage: little Gavin Blew, not four years old yet, pyjama top too small for him, printed over with Pinocchios, no bottoms at all, little bum still creased pink where the sheet had crumpled, getting his fingers under the up-and-over, heaving. Shall I help him? thought Ern, better not. Anyway, he doesn't need it – for Gavin Blew had created a knife-shaped gap into the darkness within and presently emerged dragging behind him a little wooden three-wheel scooter with plastic wheels. Kicking himself along with his heels he came down the drive-in, on to the pavement, and away past Ern whom he ignored. Ern thought it best to ignore him too.

Outside his own house he looked up and down the curve of the road – 'two-tier estate', he thought, recalling a sociological pamphlet they'd asked him to read at the office, 'second homes and last homes. And easy to see which is which. The last homes have gardens laid out like well-kept cemetries with roses in rows and rockeries that might have been made out of gravestones.' These belonged to Senior Citizens or those about to achieve that status, like the night-shift foreman from TRICE whose wife managed a shop. The second homes belonged to those on the way up, on their second, increased mortgages – store managers, solicitors' clerks just articled, teachers doing well, skilled workmen in electronics and surgical instrument making. Their front gardens were unwatered, toys littered the lawns, their garages had a second car – a fifth-hand Mini or Anglia for the wife while *he* went to work in a Datsun. Here and there boats died on trailers with flat tyres, unused symbols of spurious affluence. Bikes and skate-boards littered the drive-ins.

Ern turned up his own drive-in and heard a baby's gurgle from the pram on the Greens' lawn. Not quite believing his ears, he paused. Yes, the pram was shaking. He felt his blood go cold, the hair on his neck lift – it was not possible they were up and had put her out already – but the alternative was not possible either. He stood fixed, undecided, then after a quick glance at the blank laced-up windows, the curtains behind them still closed, tiptoed over to the pram and peeked in.

A five-month-old face, wrinkled, eyelids swollen, blinked up at him, a tiny bunched fist waved at him and knocked the plastic rattle suspended from the raised hood. There was a distinct odour of urine and baby dung – milky, farmyardy, a bit rancid. Dew still filmed the cover. An empty bottle with curds plastered round the inside lay near the baby's mouth. Well. Whatever. It's not my business, thought Ern. She's clearly well, clearly survived, they won't want to know I know, and he tiptoed back to his own territory. The infant, deprived of the face that had hung briefly above her like a moon, began to scream and he scurried faster into his garage and back to his rooms behind. But Ern was still concerned, and after fretting for a moment pulled a stool over to his work-room window and stood on it, thus giving himself a view that included half the pram. I'll give them ... ten minutes, he thought.

But before three had gone Dot Green appeared – twenty-five years old at the most, frowsy with Mogadon or Mandrax, stumbling, clutching a floral house-coat about her, pushing her hair out of her eyes, and peering round at the open-plan lawns, and the laced-up windows, all guilt and fear, an under-age Lady Macbeth. She fumbled at the straps that held the baby in the pram, gave up, trundled the lot through her garden gate and into her back-yard. Ern ducked, felt sure she hadn't seen him, and thus missed a sight which would have restored his humour – the synchronous return of Mrs Linden and Mrs Rose, two swapped wives, each to their own abodes ...

They crossed like trains on parallel tracks just outside Ern's house – Linda Rose and Rose Linden. The coincidence of their names, revealed at a Tupperware party two years before to shrieks of excited laughter from their neighbours, had made closer acquaintance inevitable. They were different: Linda Rose had been to a bad private school where she had won the javelin-throwing three years running and acquired a culture-varnish. She had long blond hair, and even at thirty-five with two sons and a daughter, was thought to be a beauty. Rose Linden was dark, younger, dumpier, with big boobs and thick lips. She came from Liverpool and had brought her vowels with her. Both were dressed in what they had worn at the Blacks' party the night before – a long hessian, tasselled affair that suggested a holiday in Tangiers adorned Linda's athletic frame; a gaudy floral, also ankle-length but cut very low so if you stood above and behind her and looked over her shoulder you could see just about all there was to see, enveloped Rose. Marks sold it as a nightdress.

'Children all right?' they said in practised unison as they passed right in the middle of the road.

'Fine thanks,' they echoed each other in reply, and both erased their jolly smiles as soon as they were back to back.

The Beauty's woven leather sandals slip-slapped up the concrete to her front door (done in a tasteful orange called 'Brandy Gold') where she sank carefully to her ankles, pushed the hair out of her eyes, and picked up the little crate of three gold tops and a pint of double cream for Sunday, and managed to tuck *The Sunday Times* and the *Sunday Express* under her arm as well. Rose had left the door ajar as usual so Linda was able to push it open with her neat foot, although her hands were full. The kitchen, she thought, as she put the milk and cream away in the cabinet-sized fridge, could be worse, though something smelled somewhere and dry crumbs shivered beneath her feet. Amongst other débris on the draining-board two heavy, chunky, frosted tumblers, unwashed, caught her attention – she sniffed them, and 'Blast. He's been giving her the armagnac again,' she murmured. She drifted into the L-shaped luxury sized living-room with dining recess to discover, as she expected she would, that the turntable still revolved in the music centre and the speakers hummed. She finger-touched buttons, the silent revolutions slowed but did not stop until she put her thumb on the disc to read the label. Golden Hits of Burt Bacharach. Let him put it away.

She sat down on a low mock-hide sofa with spongy cushions and looked around her as if she were new to the room and wondered if the contrasting wallpapers, some with a motif in gilt, were not a bit much, the gilt-framed prints of Breughels and Constables a bit dull, the aquarium with the gold fish immature ... perhaps if they got some, what were they called, fantails? The noises of the bungalow insisted. The fridge in the kitchen, the aerator in the fish-tank, then the lavatory flush. Who? A door opened and Stewpot of Junior Choice called a loud 'Byeeee', followed muffled as the door closed by the opening phrases of 'The Laughing Policeman'. Then: *Ha-ha-ha-ha-ha-ha-ha-ha, He-he-he-he-he-he-he-he, Ho-ho-ho-ho-ho-ho-ho-ho.* A door slammed open and she heard her husband's voice: 'For Chrissake shut that thing off, can't you?' The door slammed shut.

Silence. Linda Rose sighed, then, as tension gripped her

chest below her left boob, she began to beat the arm of the sofa rhythmically with clenched fist. This won't do. She stood up, pushed the hair back again and walked with very deliberate slowness to the bathroom, fumbled amongst the bottles in the cabinet (a light came on when she opened the mirror door), and found the Librium. Child-resistant container. To comply with regulations issued by the Department of Social Interference. Hold the cap normally. How the Hell is normal. Press down hard and unscrew at the same time. Should be press hard and screw. She grimaced, tried again. Nothing. She felt suddenly desperate – the crazy, stupid, *bloody,* bottle, slippery from the perspiration in her hand – and sat on the edge of the bath. You *need* a goddamn tranquilliser, she said aloud, to get this thing open; then hurled it, clatter, clatter, across the narrow gap. It bounced harmlessly, plastically, off the tiles and rattled away between the washing-machine (too big for the kitchen) and the wall.

As she put her hands to her face she caught a glimpse in the open door of another face, much like hers, straw blond straight hair, mouth puckered ready to cry, but thirty years younger, then it was gone.

Presently her husband stood there instead, tall, taller than her, fair short hair, eyes small and a little puffy, face pale, mandarin moustache, dressed, not unlike her, in an Arab long night-shirt, which did not conceal ... God, he's got an erection and she's only been gone five minutes.

'All right, Kid?' he asked.

'No. I'm bloody not.'

'Tina said you were crying.' He sat on the edge of the bath and put an arm round her.

'I've told you it's time we used her full name.'

'Bettina. What's up, Kid? Old George not been upsetting you, has he? You know I've always said we'll pack this caper in, just as soon as ... '

'No it's not fucking George. It's just my pills fell behind the fucking washing-machine ... '

'OK, Kid. OK. Cool it. I'll get them. There. Glass of water.

There. How many? Four? Sure? OK. Then back to beddy-byes for a bit, eh?'

In the bedroom she kicked off the sandals and stepped out of the Moroccan dress. As she shook back her hair she knew he was studying her, itemising her all over, especially her boobs and her bum, for signs of what Georgie had been up to, and his hard-on getting harder at the thought. She brushed up her hair, allowed herself to imagine the Librium were working already, felt nicer, and let her hair drop.

'Did he get it away then?' Tim invariably had to ask.

'Shan't tell. What about you?'

'Oh, no way at all. Usual story – one glass of brandy, touch of the low lights and the heavy breathing, and she crashes right out. Practically carried her here.'

Most Sunday mornings he said the same thing. She didn't believe it, didn't much care, supposed he was displaying some sort of gallantry.

'Rather a waste of armagnac. Why not give her the Stock?' She pushed up her hair again. 'So all you've got is a hangover.'

'That's right. And the horn.'

'And Kingsley Amis, the well-known novelist and contributor to girlie magazines says the best cure for a hangover *and* the horn is ... '

'That's it, Kid.'

From the room on one side of them the voice of Stewpot came up louder. 'And so for littleJimmy L ... can't quite read the name but it begins with an L, down in lovely Southset, near Brinshore, I love that place, I really do, with love from his Nan, 'cos he's getting a big boy and'll be seven on Monday ... ' Under cover of the noise Dorian aged twelve and Mark aged ten, sure now they wouldn't be disturbed, went back to what they had been doing before their father had pushed open the door and told them to turn down the radio. They were emptying the contents of fireworks, which Dorian had hoarded secretly since the previous November, into plastic washing-up liquid containers. ' ... it's a record

I'm playing for Jimmy in Brinshore, whose Nan loves him, and for Eric and Maud in ... '

'Sometimes,' gasped Linda, 'I almost believe what you say.'

'What?'

'About you and Rose.'

'Gospel truth I promise you.'

' ... and for little me too, and why not? Though why the guy calls himself *Plastic Bertrand*, I don't know.'

Ça plane pour moi
Ça plane pour moi

On the other side of the wall little Tina (Bettina, to her Mother) began to move everything she could lift. She piled it all against her door. There was a lot. Thirty-five dolls for a start.

Over the road Rose followed a similar routine though being more phlegmatic and younger did not get in a tizzy with her Valium; as she leant against her kitchen sink feeling the warmth of the sun on the nape of her neck and the sweat in the groove between her chubby buttocks which Tim Rose found such a comfort, she thought of herself as sleek, cat-like, and really rather happy to be back. *Her* wallpaper, *her* curtains, and above all *her* pictures, which were of ballerinas and clowns, were somehow cheerier than the Roses', not so grand perhaps, but cheerier. Anyway George was six years younger and wouldn't be on Tim's sort of salary for another ... when he was *they'd* be able to afford Tangiers instead of Benidorm.

Presently she wandered down past little Jimmy's room from which the sounds of heaving rhythmic laughter came – two people it sounded like, oh no it's that daft record and that daft boy is joining in, and so to her own bed.

Her husband, tall, with fair hair neatly trimmed, with a mandarin moustache, pretended to be asleep as she slipped in beside him, but she'd soon stir him awake, soon get him going ...

'Mum, Ma, Dada, Mum.'

'Jimmy, what is it?'

'I've got a music, Nana's sent me a music, she has a song for my ... it is, isn't it? my birthday tomorrow, Mum, Dada *listen, please* listen.'

They listened.

'Jimmy, go back to your room, there's a good boy.'

'But Mum, Dada, it's ol' Stewpot and he said Brinshore's a nice place ... Oh listen, can't you *listen.*'

Ça plane pour moi
Ça plane pour moi

The two women, each in their own homes but not too sure that it made much difference, remained sweatily entwined with their legitimate mates for at least an hour more until the church bells half a mile off roused them at last. Not that they minded the bells – George and Tim, Linda and Rose, shared the same joke about them. They were, they said, a heaven-sent facility to wake them up in time to be at The Club by midday opening time. How ever would we get up in time without them, they always said.

2.

Thus, while they stirred themselves at last to coffee and cigarettes, showers and grooming, those on Merriedale who had retired from getting and now recognised that there was more to life than spending, who felt that a Sunday wasn't a Sunday without church and were already in dresses and hats, suits and polished shoes with their smartest brooches and chunkiest cuff-links and had waited only for the bells to call them, now got into their Rovers, Toyotas, Princesses, Datsuns, Granadas and Allegros and slid almost noiselessly, so slickly clean and well-kept were their cars (a clean face is a sign of a wholesome spirit) to render unto God the things that are God's.

Amongst the whispering tyres and gently throbbing exhausts, the shine of polished bodies and the sparkle of spotless windscreens Miss Barnacle's invalid carriage – chugging and misfiring, blue fibreglass dowdy with several dents and tears in it – looked not a little incongruous. However, none of the good people who cruised beside her and past her resented her presence at all: Sunday service at Mudwick Parish Church without dear old Miss Barnacle would not be the same, though those who could not escape sitting near her sometimes claimed that her wrong responses took the edge off the spirituality of the occasion. However no one would have dreamt of saying this to her: her full name was Barnacle-Flavell, and half of this patronym she shared with the Dukes of Southset. Thus most in Merriedale tolerated her as an asset – a real lady amongst them, though most also thought 'Barnacle' an apt name: she was certainly a 'sticker', would never be moved.

And so to Mudwick Parish Church – Vicar: the Reverend Shamcall, B.Sc. (Econ.) – Sunday Services, etc., etc., Family Communion every second Sunday of the month at 10.45.

Oh *Blast*! thought Miss Barnacle, I quite forgot. No wonder there are so many cars about so early. She usually gave Family Communion a miss – her service was Matins at eleven on the other Sundays for which she arrived early to get her usual pew: much though she knew it was wrong of her, she did not *like* Family Communion. She now considered turning back but the thought of manoeuvring her sardine can (as she called it) out of the jam of cars filling the narrow lane behind her was too much, so she stopped (it would not be accurate to say 'parked') where she could. Then she stumbled, gasped and wheezed, paused for breath, stumbled, gasped and wheezed, refused proffered arms with 'No dear, quite all right, just get my breath ... I'll be all right,' until she made it to her pew in the cool interior. There she gasped and grunted another three minutes before setting down her leather (cracked) bag, smoothing her white (darned) gloves and her silk skirt (hem dropping) and finding the collect for the day in her prayer book.

Her father, a civil service commissioner, had made each of

his several children learn and repeat the collect every Sunday before breakfast.

'O God, the strength of all them that put their trust in thee, mercifully accept our prayers; and because through the weakness of our mortal nature we can do no good thing without thee ... '

Yes, covering the page with her fingers (oh dear, these gloves!) she still had it by heart, after seventy years or more.

Now she looked up, around her, at the little twelfth-century church, ignoring the whispering jostling throng about her, and thought to herself – Yes, how restful the green and peaceful the procession of Sundays after Trinity through summer, but, oh dear, he shouldn't have let them, those roses, quite wrong, like *sores* almost, I should have some lilies out by next week, perhaps I'll suggest ... though I'm not sure, ever since he converted the chancel into an Edwardian boudoir with those drapes, any flowers at all seem vulgar.

The bells stopped, the congregation shuffled and rose, the electric organ swung, yes *swung* into a syncopated jingle. Miss Barnacle turned off her deaf-aid and resolutely tried to remember the *real* tune, while all around her grinned at each other because of the missed beat as they sang: 'And therefore give us (bop) love.'

'The Lord be with you,' said the Reverend Shamcall, a tall, plump man, with shiny baby face, spectacles and thin lips.

'And also with you,' came back the cheery answer.

'And with thy spirit,' said Miss Barnacle.

And 'Thou that sittest at the right hand of God the Father,' said Miss Barnacle, while the rest said, 'You are seated at the right hand of the Father', and so it went on for the next half-hour, an awkward little counterpoint that most tried to ignore.

I believe in one God,	We believe in one God,
the Father Almighty,	the Father, the Almighty,
Maker of Heaven and Earth,	maker of heaven and earth,
And of all things visible	of all that is seen

and invisible ...	and unseen ...
And was incarnate by the Holy Ghost of the Virgin Mary, And was made man.	By the power of the Holy Spirit He was born of the Virgin Mary and became man.

But before the Creed came the sermon, and before the sermon the Gospel, which Miss Barnacle read to herself, preferring not to hear the New English.

'There was a certain rich man, which was clothed in purple, and fine linen, and fared sumptuously every day ... and ... Lazarus, which was laid at his gate full of sores, and desiring to be fed with the crumbs which fell from the rich man's table; moreover the dogs came and licked his sores.'

'There was once a rich man, who dressed in purple and the finest linen, and feasted in great magnificence every day. At his gate, covered with sores, lay a poor man named Lazarus, who would have been glad to satisfy his hunger with the scraps from the rich man's table. Even the dogs used to come and lick his sores.'

' ... and seeth Abraham afar off and Lazarus in his bosom. And he cried and said ... send Lazarus that he may dip the tip of his finger in water, and cool my tongue; for I am tormented in this flame.'

'And there, far away, was Abraham with Lazarus close beside him ... send Lazarus to dip the tip of his finger in water, to cool my tongue, for I am in agony in this fire.'

A sermon on this gospel should be interesting, thought Miss Barnacle, and looked round at the glossy, steak-fed faces, the silks, the leather, the fine worsted and the glint of gold, diamonds and sapphires. Let's see how the Reverend Shamcall is going to wriggle himself out of this one.

For Shamcall believed in butter. The best butter – and he knew, looking at those same shiny faces, which side of his bread the butter was on.

He came now to the chancel steps, spread his hands in a warm gesture of welcome, and said: 'Good day to you, friends', and something between a whisper and a rustle, a warm breeze through a leafy wood, came back at him: 'Morning, Vicar, and to you, sir, good day to you, sir' and so forth. Miss Barnacle sat upright, lips firmly closed, and waited. She found bonhomie impertinent wherever she met it, but disliked it most in church; moreover this gossiping from the chancel step was wrong – if the man really thought he was about to interpret God's Word, he should do so from the pulpit. God's Word deserved that much dignity. Shamcall pretended she wasn't there, as he had done ever since the bishop had shown him her letter about the new hangings behind the altar. Instead he concentrated on the wide smiling throng of rosy faces, powdered, lipsticked, neatly shaved, perfumed, cologned, and clean.

'And a lovely June day it is too, my friends, a day to lift our hearts on and give thanks to God for. Well, friends, today I'd like to say a word or two about something pretty central to that little story of our Lord's that I have just read to you, and that pretty central something is ... money. (This, thought Miss Barnacle, is taking the bull by the horns with a fair vengeance. How is he going to get off them?) Now, Our Lord in his wisdom was much given to these little tales, these parables, for this was the way to get his message across to the homely folk who were his first disciples, rough ordinary folk most of them with little time or taste for niceties or subtleties. He gave it to them direct, for it was the only way they would take it. So inhumanity, injustice, selfishness, abstractions difficult for simple people to handle, are presented as the Rich Man; the oppressed, the suffering, the needy, as Lazarus. He was not to know that this has led some people, some sincere, some perhaps less so, some perhaps even politically motivated, to see in this parable, this little story, an attack on money, on wealth as such, regardless of how it is used, but I cannot think this was Our Lord's intention.

'You see friends, and you will forgive me I hope if I appear to labour the obvious, money is a tool, a symbol, that's all, not in itself good, or in itself bad, but good or bad depending on how it is used. None of us here would be so silly as to say a bottle, for example, is a good thing or a bad thing – it is good sitting in a fridge filled with milk – it is a bad thing thrown by a hooligan at a football match. It's the use it's put to that makes it good or bad. Well friends, the same is true of money. The Rich Man in Our Lord's little story kept his money, dressed well off it, ate well to be sure, but, we may be equally sure, for that is the point of the story, kept it greedily all to himself, begrudged even the scraps from his table. Now this is not the right way to use money – neither wasteful spending nor miserly hoarding. My friends, look at it this way (and here Shamcall took off his spectacles which were gold mounted, and he smiled beatifically if blindly above the heads of his congregation): if we think of society as a machine, an engine, a complex affair of spinning shafts, driving cogs, turning wheels, each part dependent on the others, then money is the oil. Every engine and machine has to have a regular supply of oil to keep it running sweetly or very soon it will seize up and come to a grinding halt. Of course some parts need more than others, and there are some parts whose function it is to keep the oil safe, investing some where it does most good, keeping some against a rainy day, against a time when the machine may have to work even harder, put on a spurt as it were. And there are other parts, the moving parts if I may so put it, which need a constant flow of thin oil but in moderate quantities to keep them going at maximum efficiency, for as any engineer will tell you, too much oil on the moving parts can be as bad as too little. In short friends, and I can see I must be short for already one or two of you are looking at your watches and wondering if your pre-set ovens aren't a little advanced timewise, what I think Our Lord has to tell us now, in this so-called twentieth century, out of this little story, is not that money is evil, but that money used irresponsibly is evil. So I would ask us all, each and every one of us, good people, to spend a moment or two in silent prayer, and ask ourselves with all the sincerity our hearts can find – do we use our money responsibly? The answer will be different from last year or next year. Some may, when they face themselves honestly, feel that they have been a little self-indulgent recently, a little careless – too many fine clothes, too much rich food, that a little belt-tightening is in order now especially with the holidays round the corner. Others may feel, equally rightly, that in their case this is the time to relax a little, unbutton, buy the wife a new dress, the kids new bikes – in other words give that particularly finely adjusted and complex machine, the Family, a drop of oil to get things running smoothly again. Some may feel their reserves need building up – others remember that an engine that has too much oil is in almost as sad a case as one that is nearly dry. Friends, let us bow our heads in silence for a moment or two, each and every one of us, and examine the dip-sticks of our consciences – ask ourselves, as Our Lord asks us today in his little story – Do I use my money as responsibly as He, in His infinite wisdom and mercy, would like me to?'

Only Miss Barnacle's head, her deaf-aid long since switched off, remained resolutely unbowed.

'On Wednesday next, at seven-thirty, the Wives' Club are holding a barbecue, Mrs Fortescue has kindly offered her gardens for this occasion. Tickets two pounds to include steak and a glass of Beaujolais, so I'm sure you'll agree this is a bargain. Profits to go to the upkeep of our churchyard, apt to be sadly neglected at this time of year when our usual helpers have their own gardens to think of. On Thursday at three-thirty all are welcome at the Vicarage for our strawberry and cream teas, perhaps not such a bargain at fifty p, but the proceeds to a very good cause – CHAP, or Christian Help for Asian Peoples, an organisation which, since the coming of those poor Boat People, is in need of a drop or two of that oil I was talking about. And I've been asked to remind you of our annual flower festival at the end of the month which transforms our church into a veritable promise of paradise. The theme this year, for the usual trophies, is Works of Literature – each set piece should take as its inspiration the title of some famous work. And I'm sure if you find yourselves stuck for a title, the judges won't mind if I suggest a quick visit to the public library will set you on the right track ... '

The service went on.

'For thine is the Kingdom, the Power and the Glory,' said Miss Barnacle, loud and clear. 'For the kingdom, the power and the glory are yours,' they muttered about her.

'Almighty God we thank you for feeding us with the body and blood of your son Jesus Christ,' said Shamcall; and 'Almighty and everliving God, we most heartily thank thee for that thou dost vouchsafe to feed us, who have duly received these Holy Mysteries, with the spiritual food of the most precious body and blood of thy Son, our Saviour Jesus Christ,' said Miss Barnacle.

She left her pew during the last hymn – *Holy, Holy, Holy* also syncopated, so, she said, she could get her sardine can away before the mob came out and the turning and backing cars confused her and made her breathless – but really to avoid Shamcall's soft handshake at the church door.

A Volvo had parked close up behind her. Trying to get out she bumped its offside wing – she had a slight cataract in her left eye – and knocked a bit more of the fibreglass off the rear of her carriage. She didn't stay to see how the Volvo had fared though she knew she ought ... she was already in trouble because of bumping things, and couldn't face up to another incident.

3.

Ern, offering a dab or two at Land's End, heard the Rovers and Princesses returning, glanced at his watch, muttered a 'damn it', set down his brushes without properly wiping them, smoothed his hair behind his ears, grabbed money and keys and set off briskly for The Club. On the whole his present way of life, though just a stage, not permanent, a gap to be filled before his retirement, was not too bad a time, but one thing he did miss was Sunday Dinner. Even with his wife and daughter he had enjoyed it – a leg of lamb with onion sauce, beef with horseradish, a glass of Spanish Burgundy perhaps, and they knew he missed it. If he stayed in they clattered dishes, opened the kitchen window, let him see the steam billow out as they drained the cauliflower, let him hear the carving knife sharpened . . . .

The thing was to get to The Club at exactly two minutes past twelve – that way he got his corner stool in the bar before the mob arrived at three minutes past, but was not caught outside waiting for the bolts to click back, like the alcoholics who used to try the handles of the Little George back in Brinshore, opposite the house he'd lived in as a child. But this morning he had left it a little late – before he had got to The Club the Toyotas, Datsuns, Fiestas, Polos, and Fiats were already cruising past him and Charles Black said to Sandra Black: 'There goes ol' Ern, he's later than usual,' and Sandra Black said: 'I'm not quite sure I like your old Ern, there's something about him,' for Sandra knew he had rebelled, and Charles who knew it too said: 'Oh, old Ern's all right, wouldn't say boo to a goose.'

Mr and Mrs Brown, Mr and Mrs White, Mr and Mrs Lake said much the same as they purred by, and so of course did Mr and Mrs Linden and Mr and Mrs Rose.

By the time Ern reached The Club it was full and noisy and instead of his usual stool he had to stand in the middle of the bar to sip his bitter. He considered the garden, but knew it would be bedlam – Cis, Dinah, Veronica, Susan, Milly and Bettina would have taken over the iron tables with cokes, crisps and their favourite walking, talking dolls, while Gavin, Jonathan, Adrian, Jimmy, Dorian and Mark went 'bang, bang' in the bushes and secretly planned more serious mischief. He thought of The Lamb, but it would be just as crowded by now, and a mile and a half off anyway with chemical beer at the end of it, so he sipped his Gale's HSB and tried to ignore the noise about him.

A pub that serves Gale's beers can't be all bad, but The Club got near it. Once The Swan, once owned by old Mrs Rigg, then by Mr Rigg her son, it had been sold to Friary after the war, Friary had become part of Watneys and Watneys had found a large seventeenth-century building, once a farm-house, with a steady custom of five coarse fishermen and four bird-watchers a day, no sort of proposition and sold it to Charles Heard, who now lived in the Bahamas. He also owned the fields on which most of Merriedale was built a year or so later, and Ern knew very well how and why the Merriedale planning decisions had been taken, though he had not himself been high enough placed to receive any of the hand-outs.

Charles Heard's manager knew a thing or two as well – not least that Gale's HSB in summer and Winter Ale in winter brought in what he called the 'carriage trade', by which he meant Toyotas, Datsuns, Polos and the rest. And the manager's wife had the old dark-stained benches upholstered in wipe-over chintz, bought a lot of no-polish 'brass' and simulated black iron mantraps, axes, gridirons and the like together with a job lot of Victorian chamber-pots which she hung over the lounge bar where honest pubs hang their pint pots. They swept the sawdust out of the public bar and filled it with more 'brass', the nautical variety this time, and called it the Pilot Bar. Weekending yachtsmen used it, almost exclusively.

Ern hated The Club, but it was within walking distance and he loved Gale's beers. He drank in half pints and, in spite of the mob around him, went on drinking right through the two hours of Sunday midday opening. Sunday Dinner. The Lakes, the Whites and the Lindens were at one end of the bar; the Roses, the Browns and the Blacks at the other. The men sat on the wrought iron stools, the women took over the chintz benches behind them. Ern stayed in the middle, for the most part ignored. But he could not ignore the noise.

'Bob, how are you, pint is it? Charley, here's old Bob. Old Charley's on George Bernard Shaws with a touch of Worcester, well, I'm not surprised, I mean he was drinking his own wine cup last night, no one else was, eh? no one else was. Only joking Charley, marvellous party, really was. Bob, your lady wife, what's hers? Cilla? Campari with lemonade, right you are my love, and Sandra, where's Sandra gone, Charley we've lost Sandra, oh I see, she's off with the other lot and we've got Linda instead, well that's jolly. Linda? A sherry? A *sherry!* Come on. Here have a Pimms, my wife is, have a Pimms with me. Now Ted. You've got that have you? You have? That's marvellous, here we are then.'

This was Ossie White who stood out amongst the rest as a bit of a card – he was older, balding on top but smeared his dyed hair across the patches, and wore a jacket, a blue and white check, over crushed strawberry trousers. All the others were in knitted, short-sleeved shirts with crocodiles or panthers on the left breasts, all the others had shortish, razor-cut hair-dos, all the others had zapata or mandarin moustaches and their flares were white or fawn, and those who wore specs had them framed identically – in the fashion that Bamber Gascoigne used to affect. Not so Ossie White whose moustache was a military toothbrush and who blinked short-sightedly, and who had run for the Council as what he called an independent radical and had nearly got in too – trouble was people hadn't realised just what radical means. Some had thought it had something to do with socialism. 'Lord no,' Ossie had said. 'Look it up in the dictionary. It's to do with *roots,* old boy, *roots,* and that's what I'm on about.' Ah well, better luck next time. Ossie White owned a small chain of greengrocery shops in the south of London; all were run by Indians whom he bullied.

On the other side: 'Tim, you've set me up a pint I see, very civil. What do I owe that for? Keep on truckin', eh?'

'Bottoms up.'

'That's where I like' em!'

'It's all happening.'

'Dave. Meanin' to tell you. Marvellous colours you've done your place in. Rose has been on at me more than ever since she saw them. Thing is, what will you think if we come out the same?'

'Hang about George, hang about. I mean, you know, it's not just so the old shack looks nice we did those colours. Let you in on a secret, it's so we can recognise it – sort of identification facility if you catch my meaning. Now you follow suit and we're lost again, get it? Be always blundering into your place by mistake.'

Behind him the women. Their clothes and hair-dos were as different from each other as their mates' were identical, for each had a different message to get across, as – we went to North Africa for our holiday; my clothes may look casual but they cost more than what you got married in; a good cut is a good cut but a perm is just a load of curls; actually we're spending the afternoon on the boat. Their conversation naturally related to more serious matters.

'No, don't laugh, I'm quite serious about this, we had trouble with Jimmy, though I don't think he was quite as long over it as yours, but what we found worked was a musical potty. No, honestly, I'm not joking. When the poor little mite sat on it, it played the *Teddy Bears' Picnic.* No, I tell a lie. *Give a Little Whistle,* that was it. Well, I mean to say, we couldn't get him off it. I tell you what, I'll get George to get it down from the loft for you. George, GEORGE, oh it's no use when he gets together with your husband, they're like children, aren't they? Still, they're enjoying themselves.'

And the other women, the ones behind Ossie White. Muriel White, brassy, aging blonde, with a lot of sparkling jewellery: 'Well I won't hear a word said against Dorothy Green, not a word, I mean she's a real human being if ever there was, the first time I saw her, I thought there's a warm human being, if you know what I mean, but you see they *are* under pressure, I mean they must be, it stands to reason: he's only just qualified, and we all know what that means mortgage-wise and on the Crescent. Well quite, dear, that's just what I said to Ossie, not even properly qualified or else he wouldn't be studying with the Open University, would he? I mean since Ossie's gone into politics he's found out about things like that, and a teacher, just started, well honestly, they get nothing, nothing at all. Sorry dear? Oh didn't you hear? Well (voice dropped) it just happened as I was drawing the drapes this morning. Out came Dot Green on to her lawn, I thought to get the pram in, I mean it's a silly thing to do, I expect I've been as silly myself sometimes, I'm sure Ossie would say I have, but you won't credit this (voice even lower). The baby was still inside. Yes. Cross my heart, all night. Poor little mite. Well. A mother, especially a warm human being like Dot Green, who can do a thing like that needs help. Oh yes. She *needs* help ... '

Second rounds. Second half pint for Ern. Noise levels higher – almost now necessary to shout – to his left, Tim Rose: 'Well of course it varies on who you are, we all know that, but when you come down to it it's a question of matching men to machinery. That's what I said to him. I said, look James (he doesn't mind, we all call him James), it's a question of matching men to machinery. But do you know, he couldn't see it? Try as I might I could not get him to see it. Well you know between you me and the gatepost it can't go on much longer like this. I tell you, squire, the writing's on the wall and before long I'll be aiming off in another direction. Oh yes. At the end of the day I know where it's at. You see what he doesn't see – they're interdependent on us. Oh yes. I elisted the information, did my homework, checked the sums and without being technical squire, I can tell you it comes down to matching people to machinery, but could he see it? Could old James see it? Not he. I mean it's marvellous, isn't it. James Cheal, he builds up a firm like TRICE from scratch, from rock bottom, but what he doesn't really see, what he hasn't come to terms with me, is that there is competition, and it is breathing hard on our heels. Yes. Take my word for it, breathing very hard on our heels.'

Behind right.

'I mean I know she fits the same size as me, I'm not denying that, but I still say the difference in our figures is a whole world away. I mean you know what I mean. I suppose you can call it a question of style really, that's what it comes down to – mind you, I wouldn't like you to think I'm being stuck up about it. Oh no. No way. I've never been one to get on a high falutin' horse about that sort of thing – let her go down the Crescent in it one day and I'll go down in it the next, you know me Sandra, you know me Rose, my Dave has always said what he likes about me is I've got style, but no side, no side at all – no, it's not that. But that's what she thought and I couldn't get her to see it any different. Look

Linda, I said, I'd take that coat like a shot and I know you fit my size exactly, but that's not the point, it's a matter of style, I said. Of age. Well, she took that wrong right away, I mean some people are so touchy aren't they? and then when I was sorting the jumble for the school bazaar – you know I'm on the PTA committee – and there, there it was, that coat. Well, I thought, if it's not me, it's the jumble, and to tell you the truth we've not spoken since. I mean, Sandra, you know me well enough by now, and you do, Rose, you know there couldn't be a more neighbourly sort in the world, now could there?'

Third rounds.

'Must have a leak.'

'Have a short when you come back – what's yours, Ern?'

'Thanks-er-Tim. I've still got half a glass here. I'd really rather not just now.' Dear oh me, mustn't get caught up in these rounds, must be a fiver a time, poor Frank Dangerfield last night.

'Please yourself Ern, please yourself, Liberty Hall here.' Mean sod. Case of the paralysed right arm if you ask me.

'Darling, on your way see if the children are all right.'

'Of course, sweetie.'

'Ah hah, ah ha, newcomer. Just in time. Nick Green, what'll you have?'

But Ern saw despair on the young man's face and intervened. 'Just a half, eh Nick?' and caught Ted's eye just in time.

'That's right Ern, thanks a lot,' said Nick, much relieved. He wore a darned jumper, green corduroys, and had longish black hair that flopped about his forehead.

'Right, Ted. So that's two pints, a large Scotch for old Dave when he gets back, left his incontinence facility at home, eh? Hear that George? I say ol' Dave left his incontinence facility behind, yours working all right, is it? A cinzano with lemon for Sandra, a moussec for Rose, and a pink gin for Penny – hey Lindy, Kid, you're all right are you? Ossie taking care? Well done. Hullo, hullo, hullo, Dave back again, always good news is leaky Dave … '

'Not so this time, Tim, not so this time.'

'He looks pale. Ashen. What's the bad news Dave, hasn't fallen off, has it?'

'Eight cokes, two lemonades, and ten packets of crisps, that's what's the matter, old boy.'

'Aha. I get you. On your way to make sure it hasn't fallen off you get lumbered by the sprogs. Well, well, it serves you ... '

'Darling, were they all right?'

'Fine, sweetie, fine. Rose's Jimmy had mud in his eye, but a corner of the old hankie did the trick, and Linda's two lads are up to something in the laurels they didn't want me to see, but they had their flies done up so I don't suppose it was too criminal. Ours are putting their dolls together again for the third time, casualty ward they say, there's been a pile-up on the motorway. Good as gold.'

Ern and Nick Green.

'Cheers, Ern.'

'Cheers, Nick. Everything all right?'

'Yes, of course.' Suspicious look. 'Why not?'

'No reason. None at all.'

'Just thought I'd get out for a half before dishing-up time.'

'Of course. And why not? Dot all right?'

'Oh yes. Fine. Fine really. She's in with the er sprout, so I shan't stay long.'

'They're a tie at that age. They really are. But it all passes and in five years time you'll have forgotten it all.'

'Yes. Well. So they say. Still it does get you down. You know. No sleep. I mean ... Well, it'll be all right when the holidays come, I'll be able to do a bit more then.'

'Of course.'

Between them, silence. Everywhere else, bedlam.

'Going away then?'

'Well, no, not actually this year. I mean, you know, it is the seaside here, I mean that's why we came here.'

'No, I don't suppose I will either.'

Silence again between them. Nick stared in front of him,

very pale, moisture glistening in his eye. He is very tired, thought Ern, perhaps I've said more than I should. Not my business at all really. Better shut up.

'Well. I said I wouldn't be long, so I'd better ... '

'Yes, of course, Nick.'

'I mean next time it'll be ... '

'Of course Nick. Say no more.'

'Cheerio, then.'

*

When he got home Dot said to Nick: 'Did you see anyone then?'

'No, only old Ern. None of the women. Honestly, I couldn't Dot, you don't know what it was like in there. They were all shouting their heads off and looked half-drunk already.'

'Nick, I don't know what I'm going to do if I don't see someone. I've got to see someone.'

*

Fourth rounds: more on shorts now.

'Just a squirt then. Whoops!'

'Ted, Ted, where the hell has Ted gone? Ted I say – look this ice is a bit tired. Get us some fresh, there's a good ... Yes, I can see you're busy, but ... you know, I swear sometimes ... I mean, I suppose, well, it's typical in a way, isn't it? I mean if all you get is a sullen look when you ask for ice, then if you ask me the writing's on the wall ... Ah, Ted, good scout, well played, I say Tim, fresh ice here, Sandra, Penny, let me put some ice ... well, here we are then, bottoms up ... '

'That's where I like them.'

'But no, what was I saying before I was interrupted? Yes. Well. Now what I say is this. Maybe there's something wrong with me, maybe there's not, but I know I'm not alone in this. I'm not trying to be self-riotous, I don't mean to be self-riotous, but the way I see it is I value old-fashioned things like workmanship, a decent day's pay for a decent day's work ... '

'Ah there, there you have it Dave, where did you last see a decent day's work? I mean let's face it, let's have some light on the subject, when did you last see a decent day's work? I mean I'm all for a decent standard of living for each and every one of us, but we are entitled to ask for our money's worth in return, I mean that's fair, isn't it? I mean I'm not bothered if a chap wants a tea-break, and a coffee-break, and time and a half after forty hours, and an extra week's holiday. No, I'm not bothered. But only if, only if I'm getting him body and soul, all the way, for the time he *is* working. I mean that's it, isn't it? Am I right or aren't I?'

'Of course you are George, of course you are. I mean it's just what I always say. But what gets me is this. The average decent white British workman, on the shop floor, mark my words, on the shop floor, goes along with you. I mean we know, we *know* a Nip or a Kraut takes home twice the pay-packet and is five times more productive, the figures prove it, and your average white British workman would love to be able to do the same, he'd sell his soul to be able to do the same, but he can't, and we all know why he can't, we know who's stopping him. What I say is a man is a worker, and we're all workers, I mean if I'm not a worker I'd like to know what the hell I am, and a worker has one thing to sell. His labour. And to deprive him of the right to sell his labour on a free market to the highest bidder is economic suicide. And that's what these chaps are doing. I mean it's a real disgrace in this so-called twentieth century, let's face it, a real disgrace ... '

'Let's face it. There are things in this dear old country of ours that have got to be put right. I mean got to be put right. We're all agreed what they are, so why not, eh? Why not?'

'You're right Ossie. Along the line. But you tell me why not. I mean you tell me.'

'Well, look. You've seen the paper this morning. I mean it's a bloody disgrace. I mean people, animals like that, flaunting the law, have got to be locked up, I mean they have to be locked up. Two judges said so. Two judges said so and still they're free. I mean what if it was your lovely children they got their filthy hands on and worse? Well I know what I'd do if I could get my hands on them, as I said to Muriel this morning I know what I'd do to these sexual freaks who go for children – I've seen vets do it to porkers, and animals like that deserve just that. *Then* lock them up I say. Of course people like that aren't the root of the trouble. Oh no. But they are a symptom of what's wrong way down at the very roots of our society. That's where we've got to get, to the very roots, sort out the vermin, the pests, all the little grubs that are turning the very roots of our society from the once strong flourishing roots we once had. Sort out the evil grubs, then exterminate them – in a figurative way of speaking, mind you, I don't mean literally. But figuratively yes. Clean out the roots, plant again, then we'll have the old country on its feet again soon enough.'

'Well, squire, I don't honestly know I'd go as far as what you have been speaking with regard to, but the way I see it is we need strong government, and let's face it, while the unions have got the stranglehold ... '

'That's just it. That's just it ... '

'Just a minute Charles. Just a minute Ossie. I'm with you both all the way, all the way to the hilt. But what I don't see ... no, just a minute, just let me say this ... what I don't see is where you're going to get a strong government from until the people vote for it. And people won't, will they? I mean kids would never *vote* for a teacher with a big stick, now would they? And I mean, let's face it, for good or for ill we are a democracy. I mean that is the name of the game, isn't it?'

'So really, what you're saying Bob, if I'm with you, is it's a vicious circle. You can't win, can you? I mean it's as simple as that.'

'Now. There. That's it. If you two gents don't mind me barging in again, that is it. You have put your fingers on the spot that hurts. It is a vicious circle. And a vicious circle has got to be broken. It can be done. Other countries have done it. We have in the past. All it needs is determination, discipline, courage. DDC I call it. Not BBC which stands for Bumsuckers, Bolshies and Queers in my book, but DDC. Determination, discipline, courage. And not much either – just enough to stand up and be counted, say enough is enough, and get rid of what we know is wrong – repeal the homosexuality act, say no to the permissive society, tell the commies in the unions they can change their minds or go and live in Russia, see how they'd like *that,* and help, yes I mean *help* the blacks to get back to their own countries. That's it in a nutshell. . . .'

Fifth rounds.

'Come on girls, drink up, only ten more minutes, got to get another in if we can ... Well, what *about* the kiddies then? I mean what about them. They can wait ten more minutes, can't they? All right. ALL RIGHT· I said all right, didn't I? Ted. TED. T E D. Cokes, lemonades, crisps. You know. The lot. Jesus, I mean it's only once a week, isn't it? Now where was I, I'm sure all present will agree ... '

But there were fewer among those present than there had been, there being a sudden desire amongst them to spend pennies, Ern included.

Hardly had he unbuttoned, pleased to be away from the noise and shouting, and after his fifth half pint of Gale's HSB just a little muzzy, hardly had he unzipped than Bob Lake came and stood on one side of him, and Dave Brown came round behind him and unzipped on the other. Three worthy citizens quietly allowing nature to take its course while they read the graffiti: 'Necrophilia is dead boring; Snow White thought 7-Up was a drink until she discovered Smirnoff; the sun was setting in the west, she laid her head upon my chest, I kissed her, she bit me, I kicked her fucking head in; I thought Bognor Regis was the Last Resort until I came to Brinshore.'

Then shake, shake, shake, no matter how you shake your peg, the last lot's down your trouser leg, then, clean, upright, well-trained British as they are they queue for the cracked wash-basin, Ern last of the three and ignored.

'Great party last night, Bob.'

'Great party.'

'Charles and Sandra do us well, don't they?'

'I'll say.'

'Old Ossie been sounding off, has he?'

'Usual stuff, I pay no attention.'

'On about his roots, eh?'

'That's it.'

'I must say Bob, last night, you seemed to be about to have your evil way with our luscious hostess.'

Both were finished but stayed by the door as if reluctant to get back to the bar; Ern, now at the basin, and faintly curious, took his time.

'Well you know how it is at these dos. And that dress, I mean they were practically popping out, and that cut away down the back, I mean waaaaaarrrfff,' and he made a rude gesture, flexing his elbow with clenched fist.

'Don't know how you do it, Bob. I mean Sandra's not the first you've had on the side, not by a long chalk. I mean what have you got that I haven't. I can't see any difference between us.' This was unfair – his flares were grey, Bob's fawn, and Bob's moustache was more the mandarin than the zapata.

Ern got out his comb and began to slide it through the fluffy strands behind his temples. They continued to ignore him, though Bob Lake now lowered his voice and glanced over his shoulder at the door to the bar.

'Let you in on a little secret Dave, what I think gets the lid off the old honey-pot with regard to me. But keep it under your hat.'

'Go on then,' whispered too.

'I'm cut.'

'Cut?'

'You know. Had the Parky done on me. Vasectomy.'

Pause.

'Yeah. Well. Tell you the truth, so've I. Reckon most of us have on Merriedale, anyway those of us with a coupla kids.'

'Yes Dave old chum. That's very true. That's very true indeed. But, tell me if I'm right – when you're with a bird, I mean a bit on the side, you don't tell her that, do you?'

'And you do.'

'Every time. And you'd be surprised. First smooch we get into, I touch her up a bit, say nice things, and then that, and right away, no problem, she comes in closer and rubs her tummy up against me. No worry at all, always works. Tell a lie. Couldn't get a thing out of Linda Rose, but she's a bit toffee-nosed for my liking anyway.'

'Yeah, that's what my Penny says.'

'And she has it off with old George Linden.'

'I don't go for that, takes the edge off when it's all above board, I reckon. I mean when everyone knows. Anyway I reckon she reckons ol' Ossie White.'

'No. Get on.'

'Nuff said. But you just watch her, the way she goops when he gets going ... Hullo, George, how are you old son?'

'What have you two been up to then? Hanky-panky in the boys' bog, is it? Or a case of the paralysed right arms – Last Orders have been called, Dave ... '

'And I'm in the chair – scotch for you, will it be George?'

In the lady's loo Rose Linden said to Sandra Black: 'Honestly, I don't know what you see in Bob Lake, not really, I don't.'

And Sandra Black, who had big boobs, and a big bum, and was taller than Rose, and whose husband made more money than Rose's George, who, moreover, had had double gins in her last three cinzanos said: 'Because he has twice in his pants than what my Charles does, a real whopper. That's why. Now I've done it haven't I? Now I've shocked you.'

But you can't shock Rose Linden, at least that's what she always says, and now she put her hands to her mouth and emitted what might have been a whoop of delight.

Last orders had been called, delivered and paid for: one of the good things about The Club was that old Ted didn't hurry you drinking them – that was one of the advantages he said of having a house a bit out of the way like – the fuzz knew what sort of a clientele you had, there'd be no trouble with nice people like you lot from this end of Merriedale, so let's be sensible and take our time. Of course many people had gone and it was quieter now – you could hear the children screaming in the garden. Suddenly a crash, more a ringing sort of bang that ended on a grinding note, made everyone left pause.

'Whoops,' said George Linden.

'Shunt,' said old Bob Lake.

Dave Brown went to the window.

'Relax folks,' he said, 'coupla the yellow-welly brigade from the Pilot's Bar by the look of it. None of our lot. Dear, oh dear. Some poor wanker's run his Dat into a SAAB's tow-bar or the other way round and I'm afraid the Dat came off a very poor second.'

'Nasty, very,' said Bob.

Most Sundays someone in yellow welly boots, a weekending boat-owner, shunted someone else outside the Pilot Bar.

In the comparative quiet both Whites began to hold forth. Amongst the women Muriel White was saying, in a very firm tone, spacing her syllables carefully: 'Now I know, believe me my dears, I know many women believe, rightly or wrongly and they are entitled to their beliefs, that birth is a natural process. But what I do know is this. I had all my three by Caesarean, and my stitches were all in my tummy where they caused me no trouble. My two boys are at college and my girl is at a very good secretarial place in Town where they specialise for political work. So, I've told them not to worry. After three Caesareans, a hyster, a hyterestomeky has no fears for me.'

Among the men, and Linda Rose, tall, blond and beautiful, who peered over their shoulders from behind, Ossie was holding something like a court.

'Look. Look. I'll show you. But first let me tell you. Muriel and I, we went to Spain in the Volksy again this spring, like we always do. They're marvellous, those Volksies. It's a matter of tradition, see? They started right, and the tradition's still there. Anyway. What I was saying. This friend of mine in Town, you'll be hearing more of him as the movement gets under way, he told me of this shop in Alicante, in the old Josey Antonio, said it would interest us. So I did what he said. Well, I won't tell you all there was in that shop, but there was books, ornaments, little statues and jewels, but you'll get an idea of what it was like when I show you this ... '

He pulled back the lapel of his blue and white woven tweed jacket and pulled from it a pin hidden there, put his closed palm down on the counter and slowly opened it.

The pin was gold – at the end, neatly made in high-class enamel work, black, white and red, a tiny swastika.

4.

Ern walked. So by the time he was on the Crescent the Toyotas, Datsuns, Fiats and Fiestas were back in their drive-ways and the ovens had been opened. A smell of charred, dried flesh lingered over the open-plan lawns – shoulders rolled and boned, loin, leg, rump and rib, the choicest cuts. Outside the Browns, with their blood and pale blood colour scheme, he could hear voices raised with regard to the pre-setting facility on the oven. Penny Brown was accused of not understanding how it worked. Crash of metal as she threw the stainless steel carving platter into the stainless steel sink. Conciliatory noises. Finally laughter. Open up a Rich Mexican; heat up a Saucy Italian. All you need in this hot weather.

Ern opened a can of sausage and beans and ate it cold from the tin with a spoon, then poured himself whisky and water and lay down on his bed. It was too hot not to have the window open. Presently the smells of burnt dead animals faded and the noises of Sunday afternoon took over. The Senior Citizens mowed their lawns while their wives weeded and watered, or together they polished their spotless cars. The Blacks, Roses, Browns, Lindens and Blews (who had quarrelled with the Browns and so went to The Lamb Sunday lunchtime) brought out deck-chairs and the Sunday papers, inflatable paddling pools, transistors, and in the Blacks' case a portable TV. They mooched about tiredly, restlessly in shorts and bikinis, deprived by Anglo-Saxon dementia of the siesta they needed. The men for the most part went into their garages and played listlessly with power tools, retuned their car engines 'Brroooom, brrroooom', or filled glass fibre into the rusted sills of the old minis and anglias that their wives used as runabouts during the week. Indoors loaded, programmed, TRICE machines whirred away at the washing-up, the luxury models owned by the Whites and the Blacks with extra facilities for cut glass and silver: it'll all be done in a TRICE.

The children played with slightly exaggerated noisiness to begin with, nicely, good as gold, and very obviously in view, and then slowly trickled away down the service alleys behind the bungalows to the patches of wasteland which were forbidden to them, and their parents pretended not to notice that they had gone. Only Gavin Blew remained in sight, whining monotonously, for when pub-time came at noon he was nowhere to be found and his father had wasted nearly an hour of good drinking time, and was on the point of ringing the police, when he tracked him down to Abbott's Mere, a mile off – and there he was, throwing stones at the ducklings with his wooden three-wheel scooter lying beside him.

'It only goes to show,' said Sandra Black, who for all her easy ways with the fellows had her serious, socially responsible side as well, 'how right I am about that pond. I've got two hundred signatures and if I can make it two hundred and fifty I was told action would be taken with regard to it,' and the Blews said they would help her to get them.

On her lawn, stretched out on a lilo, her bra loose and the straps tucked into her armpits, Linda Rose turned over the colour supplement pages and eyed Ossie White, a hundred yards off, in bright Bermuda shorts now, sitting in a deck-chair beneath a sun-umbrella. He was reading the *Express.*

Lazy Sunday Afternoon, came from Rose Linden's transistor and Anne Nightingale's cheerful voice; 'brroom, brroooom', from the garage where Jerry Blew tinkered with his SAAB and listened to the final stages of Le Mans: Muriel White turned up David Jacobs on Radio 2 – she didn't like to miss the Concert Orchestra and Melodies for You on a Sunday, and she didn't see why she should be drowned out by the others.

But Rose Linden was nearest to Ern's built-on bedroom and *It's nothing but a heart-ache* drowned out even the Greens' baby squalling.

It's a bloody toothache, thought Ern.

Now the fourth Vietnam War, read Linda, the red caption printed boldly across the bottom of a picture of little yellow folk running and shooting in a swamp. Boring. Thumb-lick and over. *A Vietnamese patrol passes the body of one of the fifty Cambodians killed in the attack ... photographer Labbe rode to the front in a Ford Galaxie and noted American helicopters and jeeps ... They had no idea of what the fighting was about.* Thumb-lick and over. *The bottom oven will bake, roast and grill at the same time. The top oven is also a frozen food compartment.*

Powell slams pygmies who ignore race problems, read Ossie, *coloured births 37% in Ealing, 38% in Haringey, and 42% in Brent,* but the figures were already familiar to him, he had all the literature, and turned to *Lion Mauls Girl, 4, as She Poses for Photo* instead.

Charles Black, next door, had the news part of *The Sunday Times: Clara, a three and a half-year-old lioness, mauled five-year-old Kathleen Graham when she screamed with fright,* he read.

Word had got to Rose that Linda fancied Ossie so she now came on to her lawn, in her bikini, which did marvels for her big tanned bosom and very little for her dimply thighs, and settled down on her lilo after giving both parties a cheery wave. *KEEP YOUR HANDS OFF OUR CHILDREN, WE EXPOSE THE TRUTH ABOUT THIS PACK OF PERVERTS,* she read. The fourth pervert in looks a bit like my George she thought, or rather more like Tim Rose. If Linda goes off with Ossie, she thought, I'll have to find someone else. Was it true what Sandra said about Bob Lake, she wondered.

Eva Peron, idealised by the Argentinians will be played on stage by Elaine Paige, Linda read. Tall, blond – perhaps I'd look like that with my hair up and old-fashioned lipstick like Mother used to wear. *Not all of the many fantastic stories told about Eva Peron are true, but any of them could be true ...* but then it went on about the musical so lick thumb and over. More pics. *She became the most powerful woman in the southern hemisphere.* There she is with Peron. Handsome in white tie with a sash, blue and white. She screwed up her eyes behind her sunglasses and peered along at Ossie. Really, for his age, he's not in bad condition. Grey hairs on his chest. That pin.

Union bully boys got me fired, says go-it-alone Geoffery 18, read Ossie. *Eighteen-year-old Geoffery Lightfoot loved his job at a poultry-packing factory.*

A new-born baby found abandoned in a hedge on waste ground is being cared for by nurses at Eastbourne District hospital. Police are trying to trace the mother of the seven-pound baby who is being kept in an incubator, read Charles Black, aware that Sandra was now out on the lawn beside him with the review section. White satin finish shows off her body really well, he thought, get a hard-on even after all these years if I'm not careful. Can I get where I can see into Bob Lake's garage? thought Sandra, and gave a cheery wave at Linda Rose who was almost on a line between.

I WOKE TO SEE MY LOVER SHOT DEAD IN OUR BED read Rose and then shivered as she saw that the girl in question was actually called Maureen Rose. *Ordeal of Girl who lived in Terror of her Hitler Husband.*

I cannot imagine that Evita *will convince anybody,* read Linda, *that the tactics adopted by the Perons in the '40s and '50s form an acceptable political creed ... the political messages we hope emerge from the work are that extremists are dangerous and attractive ones even more so ... no country today can claim with confidence that it can't happen here.* Feelings about this hovered in Linda's head and an excitement that felt a little like sickness moved in her bowels. She verbalised: 'What would Ossie think of that?'

ONE SIMPLE QUESTION FOR EVERY CANDIDATE, read Ossie, then, *Should we hold a national referendum to decide whether to bring back the death penalty for terrorist killers and for those who murder in the pursuit of theft? ... The mass of the people have never been in any doubt on the matter. Every opinion poll shows a large majority for capital punishment.*

He had a fetish about Hitler and the Nazis, read Rose Linden, still on the ordeal of Maureen Rose, *he had a collection of uniforms, and books about them and used to say how he agreed about the concentration camps ... he had our four-year-old son goose stepping about the house ... he taught Carl words like Luftwaffe and Third Reich ... when he comes out I'll still be around. I'm afraid he might even come after me then. Prison is too good for Alan. Even death is too good for him.* At the bottom of the same page: *SKYLARK BOOK CLUB FOR CHILDREN ... Doctor Who, Wombles of Wimbledon, The Oxford Book of Children's Verse,* should we join that for Jimmy, she thought. Where *is* Jimmy?

These Macbeths are the most erotic ever, read Sandra Black, *the heat of their embraces even – no, especially – immediately after the murder, when they literally pant for each other, suggests a new meaning for Macbeth's references to 'Tarquin's ravishing stride': metaphorically he goes to violate Duncan as much as to kill him. This animal lust, and the vast amounts of gore on show (looking it must be said rather more like high-gloss Dulux than blood), are not the only reminders of the primitive darkness in this play ...* This is not the *Macbeth* I did for O level, she thought, and then wondered if the new paint on Dave Brown's garage was Dulux. He's going indoors, I wonder why, he's got a lovely tight little bum.

Her husband moved from a promising article on the *Spectrum* page headed *LOVE* which turned out to be a bore, to *WEAPONS – Why the bomb is not so special.* If you rate a broadsword's lethality at twenty, he discovered, a long bow at thirty-four and a flint lock at forty-seven, then on the same scale, a fighter bomber carrying nerve gas bombs comes out at 28,000,000 and a heavy bomber with cluster bombs at 150,000,000. They compare with atomic weapons rated between 660,000,000 and 18,000,000,000. We've come a long way in one hundred and fifty years, he thought. Sandra's fidgety today. Still bored he turned to the next column. *WINE. It'll be coming out of their ears.*

Linda Rose moved on listlessly from *Evita,* licking her thumb and over, licking her thumb and over. The back page held her up though. *Right now I'm on my final Superwoman book ... It's been like writing the Bible with no help from above,* she read, *but I think it's worth it ... I break at eight o'clock for breakfast and a bath. It's my first resuscitation area of the day ... Then I'll do my yoga, it's incredibly good for the concentration and gives me lots of energy ... I'm very athletic. I could do the Bridge Position straight away. The first time I tried it was like an orgasm so I did it five times more straight off. After Yoga it's back to work. I get a bit cross when people go on about coal miners. I may not be doing it underground but I bet I work just as hard – a sixteen-hour day including weekends ... my lovely publisher sent me some caviare the other day. Another treat comes from Fortnum and Mason, the most delicious chocolate cake in the world. I also need flowers around me . . . .* Do all writers work so hard, thought Linda. A dribble of sweat ran down her neck and between her breasts. I wonder where the children are.

Down the road Ossie, aware that Linda Rose was aware of him, gave less than full attention to *A SHABBY STORY. . . . In 1974 the Chilean government, whose air force is equipped with Hawker Hunter Jets sent the engines back to Britain for overhaul. They have stayed ever since in the factory at East Kilbride because two unions, the transport workers and the engineers do not happen to approve of the policy of the present Chilean government and will not allow the engines to leave. The Labour government, out of fear of its left wing and because of its lickspittle attitude to the unions has timidly acquiesced ... isn't this a disgraceful, degrading story? Harold Wilson said that the Labour Party is a crusade ... isn't it a strange crusade and a perverted code that can place Britain in the position of a thief who takes someone else's property and refuses to hand it back?*

Sandra had got to the small ads. *FOR HER Elegance Maternelle,* No, no more of that, she thought, *New catalogue of glamour leisure-wear in satins, nylons, and latex ... Rubber-wear sent by post.*

The explosion was small and almost inaudible at the distance.

How many mothers of children under five are chronically depressed? Charles read, *How many latch-key kids are there? How many fathers of children under five regard their domestic set-up as joyless, stressful? How many parents regret having children?*

A column of smoke, some black, some white, rose slowly and straight, up into the clear sky. About half a mile away.

'It says here,' said Sandra, 'we could have a swimming pool for a thousand pounds if we put in the hole. The kids would love that.'

'Yes,' said Charles, 'and so would everyone else's kids ... look at that. Just look at that.'

Soon the whole road was up, pointing, waving, excitement and friendliness on their faces as they tried to guess what was burning. The consensus had it that it was The Club, and Dave Brown, Bob Lake (in bulging shorts) and Tim Rose went off to see, just as soon as they heard the fire engines. Most of the rest followed and Ossie White took Muriel down in the Volkswagen.

Presently, up back alleys and across odd patches of waste-land, the children returned. Most were soon playing in their paddling pools and back gardens. One of these was little Jimmy Linden, who actually wandered into Ern's garden an hour or so later and stood watching him bedding out sprout plants. Ern didn't mind this at all. He liked to have someone to talk to, and he knew it annoyed his wife and daughter.

'I was on the trannie this morning,' said Jimmy.

'Were you?'

'Yes. No one knows but me, but I was.'

'What were you doing? Were you singing or just talking?'

This puzzled Jimmy. 'I wasn't doing nothing. It was ol' Stewpot.'

Ern vaguely remembered a past that had included Junior Choice.

'He played you a record, did he?'

'Yes. From my Nan. For my birthday. Tomorrow.'

'That was nice. What record was it?'

'I forget. It was in French a bit, so they said it wasn't mine.'

'Who said?'

'Mum. And Dorian and Mark.'

'But it was really?'

'Yes.'

'I believe you.'

'Did you hear it?' His face, which was smutty from the fire, brightened.

'No. But I believe you.'

'Can I put one of those in for you?'

'Of course.'

Together they stooped and kneeled above the string in the dusty earth, and Ern made a hole with the dibber.

Then: 'Jimmy,' called Rose Linden, over the gate. 'Jimmy, are you there with Mr Copeman?'

'Yes, Mrs Linden. He's here.'

'Oh Mr Copeman, could you bring him round here for me?'

This was an odd request, but Ern took the small boy's hand and did as he was told. As he got to the gate he understood a little. With Mrs Linden was a policeman and there was a white Rover 3500 patrol car parked in the road behind them. Jimmy went deathly pale, but he did not run away.

Ern stood there and watched the three go back to the Lindens' bungalow, and thus saw Nick Green pushing the pram up the road. Ern felt it would have been rude to duck back without acknowledging his neighbour.

'Oooof,' said Nick, quite cheerily. 'Well, she's asleep at last. Do you know how far I've been?'

'No idea,' said Ern, equally cheerily. 'To Rifedale and back?'

'No, no. But to the church. Hey, you know what? That fire. Half The Club's gone. I reckon I'll have to pay back that beer in the Pilot Bar next week, because where we were is burnt out. Lucky we weren't inside when it happened, eh?'

He parked the pram on the lawn, and rubbed his back. 'Well, must see if I can get some books marked before she wakes up.'

Ern remembered Nick Green was a teacher at the Comp.

Half an hour later Linda Rose, now in a loose dress, was sitting on the squashy soft mock-leather settee in her luxury-sized living-room watching a western on TV. Her two sons were on the floor beside her; her daughter was in her own bedroom piling up dolls against the door again. Tim was out: road-testing his retuned Dat. On the screen two fair-haired young men in jeans were fighting. One was on his back on a rock in a desert and the other was lying on top of him. Their you-know-whats must be touching, Linda idly thought. The one on top had the other's straight fair hair in his hands, and was banging his head on the rock.

The doorbell rang. Looking over her shoulder at the screen she sleep-walked out, pushing her hair back over her ears as she did. Up, would it look like Eva Peron?

In the hall she hesitated. Unmistakably the silhouette on the frosted glass of the front door was that of a policeman.

III
MONDAY
Back to Work

1.

THE tide was an hour and a half off full, wind nil to light airs, visibility half a mile but clearing, the time half-past six in the morning – the sun had been up nearly two hours but was only just shifting the mist it had itself created. Already the calm sea looked completed, heaving a gentle but generous swell up the last step of shingle, then contracting frothily back before stretching out again towards the land, green glass like slow lightning along the crests, then foaming back into its limitless self before coming on again, a giant cat, not mottled nor tabby but between the two, with white paws that sleepily it stretches out in front of it, then lets go slack. And like a sleepy, well-fed cat it dreamed of fish, was full of fish.

At least Jack Trivet hoped so. He braced strong round legs on neat feet, the left a yard lower down the shingle than the right, left hand on the butt, right a good yard higher up the handle of his eight-foot rod held in an arc tense like the horizon, the tiny weights and hooks baited with bleeding lugworm dangling way behind him. Then, not exactly at once but almost, moving in swift but considered progression, his weight moved on to his left leg, his torso swung from north-south to east-west and brought his heavy solid shoulders and his broad back through a quarter circle. The whole movement brought the rod to a line just short of the vertical above his head at which point the top section – cane mounted on glass fibre – whipped forward, adding its own spring to the already powerful drive of every muscle in his body. Following the lash of air, the sweet purr of nylon line running free, and free it seemed for far longer than it could, to a very distant plop a full one hundred and thirty yards out, the weights and hooks dropped through pale green to darker cooler depths to drift above the sands, and the fish like plates, gun-metal and gold on top, mother-of-pearl beneath, undulated above the rippling sands as the smell of torn lug exploded slowly out from the glinting hooks.

Above and beyond this the mists moved – violet, rose, gold, lilac, silver, grey and white as the air stirred and the sun lifted; amongst them, just heard from the land if, like Jack, you knew what to listen for, the lap of water on clinker-laid planks, the occasional deep squeak of leather-bound oars in wooden rowlocks as Kevin Rammage moved invisibly from buoy to buoy over the rocks where his lobster pots nestled seventeen feet beneath. And way beyond, more audible than the boat, the lightship moaned three times then was silent, three times a minute, and Miss Barnacle-Flavell three miles down the coast felt reassured – she'd listened to 'Moaning Minnie' as she called it through misty summer dawns for twenty years and at such lovely silent times felt that after all, another twenty, which would still leave her just short of her hundred, might not be a bad thing, even in a world that included the Reverend Shamcall and the Department of Social Interference.

Presently a steady crunch of shingle behind Jack Trivet brought his head round and without surprise he saw, coming along the beach towards him, his cousin Arthur King. Arthur was taller, greyer, sparer than the fisherman; older, in fact not long retired, with lachrymose eyes and a droopy lip. Through most of their adult life Jack had not had much to do with Arthur, who had been a factory inspector, which Jack suspected might encourage him in airs, but recently had felt drawn to him – 'Old Arthur's all right you know,' he'd say to Teresa sometimes – and liked to pass the time of day with him on the beach or in the Little George. Quite often they met on the beach, for Arthur had a metal detector and came out after fine weekends to pick up what the trippers had left, or, more likely, what their scrambling and scraping had brought up through the shifting shingle and sand from ten or twenty years below.

At five yards he grunted. Jack replied with a grunt and turned his eyes back to where his line broke the glass skin of the sea like a long long silver needle, still more than a hundred yards off. Arthur set down his detector, took off his earphones, and pulled out pipe and pouch.

'Any luck?' he asked as he fingered tobacco shreds into the bowl.

'Not yet.'

'Nor me.'

'Still time. It's an hour off high tide.'

'Oh yes. But past the best for me. Shan't be able to get down later when it's out, see. Promised to take Joan over to Langley.'

'Ah.'

Jack smiled his grim secret smile. He'd learnt to drive in the war, kept up his licence, but had never bought a car. He took Tess over to Langley twice a year in the bus. Most of his mates with cars did the trip once a month for the shops were better in Langley, and spent money corresponding.

'Clearing.'

'Yes.'

'But forecast not good.'

'No. Breaking up a bit now. But we've had a good spell. Reckon it'll be overcast by noon.'

'Yes.'

Arthur sucked on his pipe.

'That young Kevin Rammage out there? Looks like his boat.' He wiped his eye and narrowed it. 'Yes that's young Kevin, I reckon. Reckon he does well this time of year. The Silver Fish Fork guarantees his lobster catch at two pounds a pound.'

'And sells it at seven.'

'Well, that's true, that's true.'

Arthur smoked on.

'Miriam's back, I hear.'

'Yes, came back Saturday.'

'They get long holidays.'

'She has a lot of reading to do. And she's going for a job at TRICE – in the office, that is.'

'Well, she's a good girl, Molly.'

'We're satisfied, Tess and I.'

'Every right to be. She's done well.'

Jack wound in, the line flinging off drops as it tore like a dressmaker's blade through the silk towards him, then weights and hooks broke the surface and were presently dangling between his careful fingers as he baited up again. There's something down there, he thought, I'll try slipper limpet, I knew I'd felt a nudge or two, something's having a nibble. See if I can drop it just a yard or two short – but he *said* none of this. Look a fool if he talked and then caught nothing. Arthur watched and smoked till he'd cast again – just where he wanted. Jack could land his hooks on a plate at a hundred yards, but again he never said so. What was the point of saying so? *He* knew he could do it.

'Sad about Trev Stevens,' Arthur said, once Jack had put the catch up on his reel. The implication was too clear to be questioned; the news dropped like a large stone into deep water, a shock first, then its fall gradually slowing till it settles rather than lands in the sand that rises briefly in clouds around it.

'Gone then.'

'About six o'clock last night. Marge was with him. They told me down at the Granby.'

'In that, what do they call it? Intensive care unit, was he?'

'Yes. But they call it a centre now, don't ask me why.'

They both thought of poor old Trev Stevens with tubes and wires plugged and inserted into him, a nurse watching the flickering lines on the screen in the office outside. Like on the telly. Then the lines slowing or disturbed and Marge hurried outside while they pulled the screens round and requests for the specialist went out over the tannoy for everyone in the hospital to hear. Of course Marge hadn't been with him, not actually. Only before, and after for a sight of him before they wheeled him away.

'Funeral's Thursday. Out at Mudwick, by request.'

'He came from Mudwick. Born in one of them cottages near the church. On Thursday?'

'Afternoon I believe. They're sending flowers from the Granby.'

'I'll tell Tess. She'll want to go.'

Soon Arthur knocked out his pipe, gave a nod and received a nod, put up his earphones again and set off once more, weaving back and forth over the high tide-line of wrack, weed, and cuttle-fish bones. Jack fished on and fifteen feet above him, and a hundred yards to his right, just over the fishermen's hut and their winch (rarely used since they mostly went out at high tide and returned with it), sat Frank Dangerfield. He had two small pads of water-colour paper and a travelling set of water-colours, very neat, very small in a japanned black metal case with fine squirrel brushes mounted in silver and silver capped. His grandfather had taken them to Afghanistan and back and Frank valued them highly, as highly as anything he owned.

He worked hard with concentration complete but scarcely noticed, converting with precise but unverbalised thought his perceptions of the shifting colours of the heaving sea – bottle-green through blues and plums to distant mauves, and of the mists rising into a sky that had glowed with the softest palest peach along the horizon and now was turquoise above the mists, worked hard converting these perceptions into washes of coloured water, drying fast but not fast enough, which is why he took two pads. Every colour but the browns he'd used and was now annoyed when a tiny adjustment to a wash was marred by a trace of unwanted pigment from the cube next door – two hours was enough, and he felt drained, exhausted. A bad thing with a day's teaching ahead, and an Academic and Policy Meeting at the end of it, but he felt he'd be quite pleased with the four small sketches he'd done in the time. And so satisfied that the last patch of tinted water had dried to a soft and rosy flush where the mist came between sea and sky on the last sketch, he began to pack up.

Out at sea, nearly a mile out over the rocks, Kevin pulled

in his sweeps and the clunk of heavy timber on timber carried back to land. He hauled on a lanyard and the little motor fired and died, he pulled again and this time it caught – pop, pop,pop,p,p,p,p,p; his boat lurched as he got back to the stern sheets to take the tiller, and then settled as he turned the prow to the pier, clearly visible to him now. Beneath sea-wet sacks three brown and purplish-brown lobsters and two brown and purplish-brown crabs contracted legs and heaved themselves about on top of each other, and, distressed at the new and ominous vibrations, strained in despair to open claws Kevin had bound with twine when he lifted them first from his pots. Under other sacks a large plaice flapped for the last time and settled with three others, three bream, two squid, and a small conger eel he'd taken off the trot line at low tide in the dark. He'd be lucky to get a tenner for the lot, which was a poor return for a night in a boat; he'd be lucky to find buyers for the squid and the eel at all.

Jack on the beach lifted his head at the sound of Kev's boat and as he did so his line went taut; he struck, then feeling the weight let it run, then struck again. This time the pressure was not so great, and he began to wind, carefully at first then faster, his rod bending like a circus master's whip arched above his head, then the line snagged again and he knew it was a sole, digging its nose in the sand as they do, then on again until suddenly the rod flicked straight and the large fish exploded out of the water, twenty yards out, comically flapping and spinning before smacking one last time into its element, a large flat-fish, as big as a dinner-plate, as big, as big as a posh serving-plate for carving on.

Jack didn't bother with frills, had no gaff or landing-net, but he got it in safe, four pounds if an ounce, while above him Frank stayed to watch and Arthur, three hundred yards down the beach also paused, took off his earphones, and shook his head at his cousin's luck – something of a byword in Brinshore this – four pounds still pulsing, gun-metal and gold on top and mother-of-pearl beneath, pulsing, gasping and flapping until he stunned it with a stone.

Presently he was on his bike, pedalling slowly up the still

streets back to the council estate and his bed, his prize wrapped in newspaper in the carrier behind him with his bait box, and his dismantled rod strapped to his crossbar, and as he pedalled he thought: 'Two good meals there, even with Molly back, and new potatoes out of the garden with mint and butter, and new-picked peas if there are enough yet.' He sighed with pleasure. 'Not a bad end to the weekend, not a bad weekend at all,' and he whistled to keep out the thought of the five night shifts ahead.

Out at Merriedale everything was going forward in the jolly bustle of getting the old man and the kids off to work and school – sunshine breakfasts, snap crackle and pop, oooh those honey-bears watch out they don't steal them, washed down with a fizzy, tangy pill in a glass because modern foods are not always designed to meet the dietary needs of the body (did your gums bleed when you brushed your teeth?); cracked wheat and malted grains all in the first light granary bread; break into fresh ground and soluble solids of pure coffee; 'Mum, MUM, M U M I want G R E E N M I L K!' Well, that can be arranged – dip the rim of the glass into green food colouring then into granulated sugar, pour a small measure of peppermint essence, top up with ice-cold milk and think of green pastures, enjoy a natural pinta, you know the way it is ... you wake up one morning, look in the mirror and decide it's time for one of you to say good-bye to a little surplus weight. From then on you come up against more than your fair share of temptations. Not the least of which is the dreaded sugar-bowl. And it's right here that Sucron scores, ladle it into your tea – from high in the mountains of Ceylon where the sun seems to shine for ever, a soft breath of magic, serve it in modern smoked glass elegance.

Isn't that a pleasant new one? You hear all the new sounds on Radio One and of course lots of good disc jockeys to bring those sounds your way throughout the day ... Digby Richards there, a new one on RCA, a number entitled Whisky Sundown, *forty-four and a half minutes past seven o'clock, time you got your head out of the sheets, if you're early at work you can laugh at the others.*

Linda Rose this morning was making a very special effort with the children, that is with Dorian and Mark, because a little something told her they ought to look extra smart and nice, well you know the way it is. I mean if news had got to the school of the fire and who started it, Oh God it was like a cold clammy hand moving inside her stomach every time she thought of it, where the FUCK are the Librium.

Tim Rose moved about quietly, making no demands, dear Tim, trying not to get in the way or be a nuisance, trying almost not to be there, for Christ's sake Tim, say *something.* You'd think someone had died in this house.

Dorian and Mark, twelve and ten, watched pale and expressionless, little Mark with his thumb in his mouth, bless him, as their mum burst into tears for the sixth time since that nice policeman called yesterday evening, and: 'Well, of course this will have to be taken further,' he'd said when he'd got most of the truth out of them.

On with the DLT breakfast show, and as I mentioned earlier on, we decided it's not just enough to in fact say hello to people going to school at the moment, particularly at the moment because most people are taking their O's and their A's, there is a method by which Radio One can assist you to pass your O levels and A levels or at least to put you in the right mood to go in and take those exams so we now present our history paper this morning so I hope you're paying attention becai e it could all help you and as I said just before the last record it could put the mockos on your exams, right, the history paper which today consists of no less than three questions begins now . . . .Here we go. Ah, the first question. Are you seated? Come on now stop mucking about, now siddown a minute, that's it, er, you got pen ready. Question one. Approximately how many commandments was Moses given, to the nearest five ...

Tim's gone at last, and Dorian with him in the Dat, now there's only Bettina and Mark to get to the Woodcroft Primary. As always she stopped the Mini outside Rose Linden's to pick up Jimmy, for it was her turn this week, they took it in turns week and week about to do the Woodcroft Primary run.

Rose met her at the door in her free and easy kaftan direct

from exotic Thailand, her plump honest face shiny with spots on her forehead, which she ought to do something about, thought Linda, in spite of all her troubles. But she was like that, Linda was, always ready to give others a thought even at the worst of times.

'Oh Linda, I'm awfully sorry,' said Rose, smiling as sweetly as a wormed apple, 'but Jimmy's gone already.'

'Gone? Why?'

'Well I wasn't sure you'd be going today, not after everything, you know? So when I saw Penny Lake getting out her Morris Minor ... '

'He's gone with Penny Lake.'

'Yes, you see ... '

'Oh, there's no need to say any more.'

Back in the car Bettina asked where Jimmy was, for they were in the same class, and quite close pals for boy and girl who don't much mix at that age, but her mum was crying again, because on top of everything else she knew she'd finally broken friends with Rose Linden. She wouldn't answer so Tina and Mark just put their thumbs in their mouths and sat like that until they got to school.

Frank had a car, a beat-up, fifth-hand, ten-year-old Morris Oxford, but unless it was pouring or he was late, he usually walked. His route took him through what had once been the posh part of Brinshore, built for commuters when the railway arrived, but the large, expansive red-brick villas had been converted into flats and the stockbrokers, lawyers and businessmen had departed to greener pastures. As he walked, his mind fidgeted at the part of his job that he currently felt worst about – The Living Past of Brinshore.

This had started a year ago – an idea put up by the head of history, who was a careerist and an educational pace-setter, that is a man ready to climb on to several passing bandwagons at once, the sort of fads the Schools' Council and the Department promote. The fads in this case were the mixed syllabus, cross curriculum one, the mode three internally marked Certificate of Secondary Education one, with a touch of the environmental studies, a pinch of the social studies, and a fair measure of child-centred learning and a dollop of team-teaching too. The whole greasy stew added up to a two-year course for the 'less academic' fourteen- and fifteen-year-old kids, ending in examination in three subjects at once – history, art and geography, at CSE. At first Frank had allowed his department to be pulled along, at one time had even felt it wasn't a bad idea, but now, after teaching it for a year, he found it made him very angry indeed.

At first his disquiet was provoked by the realisation that what his colleagues demanded from the art department was not 'the disciplined ordering in visual terms of the pupils' perceptions about the reality of Brinshore past and present' that the wordy syllabus had asked for, but what he now saw was at best illustration, but really window-dressing, nothing more. The photographs they took, the lettering they practised, the neat line-drawing he encouraged against the prevailing wisdom of the splash and express yourself school, the glazed and fired models of the old Assembly Rooms, all ended up as peripheral decorations to the wordy, plagiarised, misspelt 'projects' put out by the other departments, or were used to tart up displays whose centre-pieces were meaningless demographic maps or flow charts.

But now he felt there were more radical objections to the whole enterprise than the mere misuse of the talents and skills that he on the whole successfully and with a certain amount of joy on both sides drew out of his pupils. As yet he couldn't express his understanding of what was wrong in a way that matched his feelings, and certainly not in a way that would get through to anyone else, but it was intimately connected in his mind with the corporate vandalism that went on on the front and elsewhere in the town. It was connected with the pier dying on its last fifty yards of rusty girders, the destruction of the lovely stucco that had graced the front of the Theatre Royal, and the Leisure Centre shaped like a tent and built in brick the Council said was sand-coloured to match the sands but which was, to Frank's eye, more the colour of dried-out dog-shit. It was all to do, he felt, with denying the existence of the past in the present; the past was being converted, processed into history; yesterday was shifted into a dimension of its own quite cut off from today, put like an ape in a cage where you could say of it: how interesting, how quaint, were we really like that once? Didn't we do well.

This Monday, until break, he would be in the space between the foyer and the library where normally ferns, polished parquet, and cases of silver cups reflected the reality of the school behind as accurately as similar furnishings in the reception area of an undertaker suggest the real nature of his business. There he would be erecting a display intended to capture the history of sea-fishing in Brinshore from 1700 to the present day, and the thirty adolescents, most of them now turned fifteen, whose work it was, would run up and down the corridors between the art studios and the foyer, and make a lot of noise; that is unless they all went off to the lavs, the boys to smoke and the girls to gossip and comb their hair. He hoped they would. A bad start to what might be a bad week, was his final thought as he turned into the school gates, and narrowly escaped being run over by young Nick Green, in his very old Triumph Herald, black hair flopping in his eyes, pale, washed out, and terrified of being late.

2.

Brinshore school had a past that still somehow informed its present: three large buildings, long but none more than three storeys high, bore witness to it. Two of them were decent brick in thirties modern, two storeys and mirroring each other exactly, and linked by a central square tower with a clock. At the foot of this tower were the main offices, the headmaster's in the centre, and the foyer. These buildings had first been the Girls' and Boys' Elementary Schools, then the Girls' and Boys' Secondary Moderns, then the Brinshore Secondary Modern Mixed. There were still three teachers in the school who had taught in all of them, and one who had even been in the old mixed elementary down in the town, now demolished.

Behind was the third building, a low structure, mainly glass and aluminium, but fancily textured in the blank spaces, dating from the booming sixties – which meant there were carpets or parquet flooring, stainless steel fittings in the loos and scandinavian-style coat-hangers and lockers; which meant that the roof leaked after ten years and the parquet was rising. This had been built as a primary school sharing the campus, but had been converted in 1972, when Brinshore went comprehensive, into a new science block. The expense of this conversion had been enormous – nearly twice the cost of the original primary.

Now nearly two thousand children and young people streamed in through the wide gates and across the tarmac, the males dressed in heavy blue jackets and baggy grey trousers, the girls in white blouses and shiny blue skirts – combinations which were in both cases obscene for what they did to the appearance of young limbs and torsos, obscene for the bright warm June morning. Amongst them came almost a hundred teachers in cars, on bicycles, and a few on foot, tweed jacketed, suited, bloused and neatly skirted, loaded with brief-cases and marked exercise books and exam papers, cheery with greetings for each other, kind but firm with the children who loitered, pushed, ran, dropped litter or for whatever other reason deserved reproach.

The lord of all this, an enterprise in terms of numbers involved and capital invested, equal to or larger even than TRICE, was Leo Arthur Harte, B.Sc. (Chem.), a fact the Local Education Authority proclaimed on a large board outside the gate. Someone else, an authority of another sort though no less local, had added in black felt tip 'is a shit'. Frank assented to this though his own sobriquet for the man was HAL, the initials reversed. The joke was based on the computer in *2,001, A Space Odyssey,* the computer that was benign, all knowing, had a rich calm voice, played chess with its human inferiors and beat them, but which was not in the end infallible and which, when threatened, turned into a paranoid homicidal psychopath.

Our HAL, in the shape of a little man, very neat, with wavy

silver hair combed back and a silver moustache, now stood on a patch of lawn near the entrance most used by the teachers. It was his rule that all teachers should be on the premises by eight forty-five, asking for an unpaid fifteen minutes Frank grudged – for no reason than that it was presented as a rule and not as a request. He therefore did his best, as far as he was able for he refused to wear a watch, to time his arrival for eight-fifty.

You could set a watch by HAL's greetings to his teachers. Between eight-thirty and eight-forty he smiled: 'Good day to you, Paul; fine morning Jane (he always used Christian names, and often got them wrong); it's lovely as early as this at this time of year, isn't it?' Between eight-forty and eight forty-five he was brisk: 'Morning Bill, nice weekend? Morning Mary, there's a letter for you in your pigeon-hole,' and so on. HAL personally sorted the mail – it was one of the many ways he received inputs relevant to his staff, some of whom foolishly used the school as a letter-box for personal mail they didn't want to receive at home. He rarely opened the letters, but could deduce a lot from them: this one is having an affair, that one has applied for a post elsewhere, and so on. From eight forty-five there was rarely any greeting at all, just a nod, and if occasion served, a 'request' as: 'Frank, old chap, that boy, that tall one, forget his name, he's just dropped a chewing-gum wrapper, be a good chap and call him back, will you?' Frank ignored these requests if he reasonably could, though in spite of himself felt a quite potent respect for HAL's obsession with litter. 'Old chap' was a warning: Frank used to say 'if HAL calls you "old chap", duck.'

Head and shoulders above the rest then, including HAL, sandy hair balding, melanin mottles on his bare crown, fair moustache and beard vaguely reminiscent of turn of the century royalty, Frank moved like a camel through the throng collected outside the door nearest the art studios, and passed through. 'Morning, sir, morning Mr Dangerfield, get out of the way, can't you see old Dangerfield wants to get through.' Frank was irked as usual by the fact that the children were not allowed in until the bell went. Yet the doors were unlocked – why didn't they just storm the place?

Down corridors still quiet he went, past class-rooms with windows on to passages so anyone, and that meant HAL, could see in, to the suite of three studios and a pottery room that was his own domain. Young Pet Rogate, dark-haired, in a pink nylon overall which came below her hem and so faintly suggested that she had nothing on underneath, moved about in the pottery room putting out balls of clay. She was very skinny, a fair teacher though shrewish, and married to the head of English. Frank occasionally fancied her quite strongly, but she was wet as well as shrewish so he had stopped at flirtation in spite of the exigencies of his celibate state. This morning he merely called a greeting over his shoulder and passed on.

He unlocked his own studio, a large airy room, darker than it should have been, but good enough. He was soon immersed in getting together pictures, models, drawings, neatly lettered cards that were to go up in what HAL called the display centre. The title of this exhibition was *The Living Past of Brinshore's Oldest Industry: Fishing.* That was a good one Jack Trivet caught this morning, he thought, and was annoyed he could not name it – plaice, sole, lemon sole or Dover sole, were there any other flat-fish?

Around him were wide tables, set in horseshoes not rows: against the walls large hardwood chests of drawers holding papers and cards of all sorts, at the far end a heavy hand-press, a silk-screen printing apparatus, and wall cupboards full of cutting tools; to his side he had two large walk-in cupboards, one full of paints – tempera, water, oil, inks and dyes, the other converted into a dark-room; from the girdered ceiling hung prints – on fabric and on paper and photographic, and on all the remaining wall space were drawings, paintings and more prints – many of quite startling professionalism, and a few with insight too. Behind him where he had had the roller blackboards taken out were shelves stacked with a junk-shop collection of *trouvailles* – skulls, human and animal, vases, ornaments, feathers, stones

– flint cores from the Downs, rocks glistening with crystalline excrescences, and fat round pebbles from the beach – shells of course, conch down to scallop, and weird pieces of sea-bleached wood. The air, after the weekend, tasted faintly of turps, linseed oil, ink, paraffin. Frank thought it was a good place, a place very much his own creation, built up from the unprepossessing hangar he had inherited from his predecessor four years before.

A bell rang, several bells, voices and feet stormed down the passages. 'Can we come in, Frank?' He scarcely looked up. 'Of course Christine,' and in twos and threes fifteen sixth-formers drifted in, young ladies and young men, most turned seventeen. This was Frank's tutor group – the ones he was meant to register twice a day, keep records on, provide what was called 'pastoral care' for, a term which he knew to be a euphemism for social interference. Christine, who was plump and motherly, and rather disapproved of Frank, did most of this for him. She now took the register. Probably next year, her last year, she would be head girl; then, thought Frank, she would be even bossier.

Still, she called him Frank, against her will, but because seven or eight of her colleagues, most of them boys and led by a black revolutionary called Martin, scoffed at and abused anyone in the group who called him 'sir' or 'Mr Dangerfield'. This group, in this and most of their activities, had Frank's support and sympathy. He had theirs too – for had he not fought to get Martin reprieved from a sentence of suspension passed on him after he had organised a sixth-form sit-in? This had been a protest against the way personal testimonials were kept secret from them, and especially those on applications for places at universities (UCCA forms). The sit-in had achieved nothing, but the sentence on Martin was commuted – instead he had to write an essay a week for four weeks on titles relating to the Responsibilities of the Individual to Society.

This Martin, a thin youth with slightly protuberant eyes that tended to be red-rimmed, for he read a lot, and was doing very well academically, now came and stood near Frank, watching him work.

'Frank,' he said at last.

'Martin.'

'Frank, won't you come to Assembly with us this morning?'

'I think not Martin.'

This was a source of contention between them. Frank almost always skipped Assembly; Martin and his friends resented strongly having to go. Frank insisted they should – to keep the peace, especially with Mr Paul Anderson, the tyrant who ran the sixth-year office. Frank feared an old dispute was about to reappear.

'I'd rather like you to, Frank.'

This was a subtler approach than the usual hectoring he received on the subject, and he looked up, but a little warily, for at the back of his mind was Martin Bright's history, as recorded in his file. His father had left Paddington when Martin was small and had subsequently been killed in Angola. Mrs Bright trained and later worked as a social worker but had been so harassed by the West London Police, on account she supposed of her political activities, that she had applied for rehousing under an overspill scheme. This had brought them to a tiny flat in Brinshore and no hope of work other than as a school cleaner. At least the police now left them alone, though she found that to be ostracised by her white neighbours was almost as difficult to bear. There were no non-Europeans in Brinshore other than the Chinese in the take-aways and the Paks in the curry-house. Martin, however, was accepted and even liked by many in his age-group, and that was enough for her.

'What's this all about, Martin?'

'You know those essays I have to do.'

'Yes. You're behind on them and want me to plead for you. You think my presence at Assembly will soften Mr Armstrong's heart.'

'No. Not at all. The fact is I handed in rather a good one on Friday. So good in fact, Hitler Armstrong said he was going to read a shortened version to Assembly this morning. I think you ought to hear it.'

'Is this a joke, Martin?'

'Oh no, Frank. Not at all. It's called "Reflections of a Young Man on the Choice of Profession", and it's *very* improving.'

Frank sensed a plot, suspected the essay contained ironies too subtle for Hitler Armstrong to detect, yet broad enough for some at least of the assembled sixth and fifth years – the result could be cataclysmic, giggles blossoming into shouts of laughter, Armstrong discomfited to the point of apoplexy, yes, thought Frank, he should be there in case of repercussions.

However, the essay turned out to be painfully dull.

A depleted upper school – many were doing O's and A's, just as DLT had promised – began to shuffle and cough after the first minute or two as Hitler Armstrong droned on. He was a small man with fair close-cropped hair, a linguist, and a distinguished squash player who had strong views on clean living (good) and socialism (bad). Above all he was a man ambitious to be a Headmaster, he was consumed by a desire to be a Head.

After a brief introduction explaining what he took to be the genesis of what he was about to read, but out of respect for the wishes of the author not revealing who had written it, he began in a dry monotonous voice: *To man God gave a general aim – that of ennobling mankind and himself, but he left it to man to seek the means by which this aim can be achieved; he left it to him to choose the position in society most suited to him, from which he can best uplift himself and society . . . .*

Frank was already lost – mention of God embarrassed him, his reaction was to assume boredom.

... serious consideration of this choice therefore is certainly the first duty of every man beginning his career. One should not leave such an important matter to chance.

The text bored on – the Deity in the form of conscience would be our guide, our parents and teachers too, ambition for its own sake should be guarded against, also brilliant opportunities that might not be fulfilled or fulfilled too easily.

However, having made our choice, other considerations might affect us, over which we would have less control.

... *but we cannot always attain the position to which we believe we are called; our relations in society have to some extent already begun to be established before we are in a position to determine them. Our physical constitution too must be considered, let no one scoff at its rights.* Here Frank noticed Gwyn Davies, across the gangway from him, suddenly lift his head and frown, then draw in breath, and finally begin to listen with real concentration, head on one side. This Gwyn Davies taught history, avowed himself a Marxist and had probably remained unpromoted as a historian as a result, in spite of phenomenal exam successes. He was small, puckish, Welsh, and nearing retirement.

Self contempt is a serpent that gnaws at one's breast, sucking the life-blood from the heart, and mixing it with the poison of misanthropy and despair. An illusion about our talents is a fault which takes its revenge on us ourselves and even if it does not melt with the censure of the outside world it gives rise to more terrible pain in our hearts than such censure could inflict. and then, later, *a profession that gives us no assurance of worth degrades us, and equally we shall as surely succumb under the burdens of one which is based on ideas that we later recognise to be false.* Come, thought Frank, that's a bit near the knuckle, and looking sideways realised that Martin in the row in front was actually looking back at him. This was disconcerting – Martin's views on education as indoctrination were crude but often struck home, and Frank was annoyed to feel a blush on his neck. He turned his attention back to Hitler Armstrong still prosing away on the dais in front; he was coming now to a peroration which obviously affected the little man, standing there in all his smug awareness of his own perfection. Almost his voice broke.

But the chief guide which must direct us in the choice of a profession is the welfare of mankind and our own perfection. If a man works only for himself, he may perhaps become a famous man of learning, a great sage, an excellent poet, but he can never be a perfect, truly great man. But if we have chosen the position in life in which we can most of all work for mankind, no burdens can bow us down, we shall experience no petty, limited, selfish joy, but our happiness will belong to millions, our deeds will live on quietly but perpetually at work, and over our ashes will be shed the tears of noble people.

Well, thought Frank, a plot there is – for one thing I'm sure of is that Martin never wrote that himself, so who did? However, HAL's sudden appearance, almost genie-like in its unexpectedness on the platform beside Hitler Armstrong, distracted him.

'What a wonderful start to the week,' cried HAL, and clapped his hands – supposedly to express enthusiasm but in fact to pull back the almost lost attention of the audience. 'Excuse me Mr Armstrong, Paul, but when I hear something like that, I really do feel I must put my oar in.' He took Hitler Armstrong's arm in playful bonhomie, spoke as if in confidence but so all could hear, 'You, Paul, know as well as anyone how much I believe the secret of running a good school is delegation, and how little I interfere in areas where I am confident the chap in charge is doing a good job, as I know you are, but,' and here he turned back to the Assembly, 'when I hear something so inspiring, so sincere, so ... *apt*, then I feel I have to endorse, and be seen to endorse it. The fact that what we have just heard came from the pen, the mind, dare I say *soul* of one of you young people in front of me ... no, never fear, I shall respect the confidence already placed in Mr Armstrong, I shall not ask him who was the author ... then I know we are not doing such a bad job here, no matter what carpers and critics may say. Young men, young ladies, I shall keep the example of what I have just heard before me throughout this week, especially as it is a week of preparation for our careers event and I recommend you all to do the same ... ' with this he sprang lightly down the steps off the stage and moved swiftly and purposefully to a big glass door half-way down the hall. Hating himself for doing it, Frank leant forward and touched the shoulder of the boy in front of him, and indicated the door to the boy's puzzled face. Just in time it was opened for HAL to pass through, but it was a near-run thing.

'I'm asked to remind you of a disco to be held in the sixth-form coffee bar next Friday,' Hitler Armstrong began, as the tattoo of his master's glossy brown shoes receded up the passage beyond, 'a chance to invite and meet ex-pupils just down from university and college ... '

HAL's twinkling brogues now took him on what he called to himself his 'early morning patrol' (through potentially hostile territory), though to his staff he called it 'checking that education is properly under way again'; this took him up and down several corridors with shiny brown composition floors, cream and green painted brick, with large windows and glazed doors opening on to and into class-room after class-room after class-room. The first area, normally occupied by fifth- and sixth-formers, was deserted – they were still in the Assembly he had just left, or already in the girls' gym for exams, but quickly he was amongst those principally used by third and fourth years who had begun their first lesson a full twenty minutes earlier. Because the hall was no longer big enough to hold all the assembled top two-thirds of the school at once, a complicated system operated, annoying to everyone except HAL who had devised it, by which Upper School (fifth and sixth years) and Middle School (third and fourth years) had long assemblies on chairs on alternate days Mondays to Thursdays and a short one all together but standing up on Fridays. This meant that the first period for those not in Assembly lasted a full hour instead of forty-five minutes, but it also confused the dual functions of teachers – as tutors they should be with their tutor groups in hall, as teachers it might be that they should be in their class-rooms if the first class of the morning was in a different 'school' from their tutor group. When this arose they were meant to stay out of Assembly and take their classes – unless, like Frank on this particular Monday, pressured by Martin Bright to hear his essay, they forgot.

That this had happened HAL was made suddenly aware as he came to the corner of the corridor that led down to the art and craft suite. Voices were raised.

'If you can't wait quieter for Mr Dangerfield I'll send the lot of you to Mr Harte, I mean the lot of you.' This was young

Mrs Rogate, the pottery teacher, in the doorway of her studio at the end of the corridor, shouting, almost screaming, at a group of large, tousled, blowsy adolescents who were hectoring her back. 'I most certainly will not let you in. That door stays locked till Mr Dangerfield comes.'

'But Miss, please Miss, Sir said, bollocks to ol' Lah-di-dah.' This last, based like HAL on Mr Harte's initials, was the less offensive nickname most pupils had for him. When he heard it HAL did not hesitate. He turned on his heel and was off as briskly as he had come, only noting as he went that Frank Dangerfield would have to be pulled up about this – the man, though undoubtedly a good teacher, was getting slipshod about details, details which may not seem too important on their own, but that was what running a large school was all about, attention to detail ...

His retreat took him round two sides of a quadrangle laid out to a neat grass and with shrub borders, strictly forbidden to pupils at all times, and so into the maths corridor. Here education really was going forward, and he slowed his step to observe it. In the first classs-room, with a group of third years, normally the worst disciplined group in the school, old Mr Trim, tall and lean like a heron, slightly stooped about the shoulders like a heron, was up by the blackboard expounding the mysteries of modern maths. 'Right,' he was saying, 'I don't need to tell you there are two ways of solving this one – an old one and a new one, a quick one and a beeeee silly one.' The class joined in with well restrained delight on the 'beeee silly one'. 'And those in their wisdom up there', Mr Trim raised his eyes to the ceiling, 'have directed me to demonstrate the beeeee silly one.' As he lowered his eyes they met HAL's through the interior window. The older man's went expressionless and held HAL's for three seconds, and it was HAL who flinched away. Mr Trim was the surviving teacher from the old elementary school down near the Chine, and would retire at the end of this present term, having refused to take the option of giving up at sixty. Only, or almost only HAL would be glad to see him go: the head of maths also found him impossible – not because old Trim could not teach modern maths, he taught it as well as anybody, but because he would not give up criticising it to both pupils and parents at every opportunity.

The last corridor back to his office tool HAL past the English suite and then the library. English, like art, was a subject HAL felt ill-at-ease with – aware of imponderables, shifting standards, the unquantifiable, the less than exact, the danger of not altogether justifiable heaving to the surface. A dispute some years ago with the previous head of English about bad language in school texts had led him to insist that an unbowdlerised edition of *Romeo and Juliet (The bawdy hand of the dial is now upon the prick of noon)* be withdrawn, and this in turn had brought on him a rebuke from the General Certificate Examining Board.

Today all seemed well in this area. In the first room the new head of English was taking a third-year group through *Animal Farm*, a book HAL had actually read and of course whole-heartedly endorsed. Napoleon=Stalin, Snowball=T-rotsky, Mr Rogate wrote on the board and the children laboriously copied down the nôte.

In the next room young Nick Green was reading aloud from an old small red cloth-bound book, the sort of set that has been knocking about English class-rooms for half a century. The girls were attentive, either watching Green with open-mouthed wonder at his dramatic prowess or following, some with their fingers, in the text. The boys were more restless, but not yet a nuisance. On the board HAL read the following:

> Imagine you are a neighbour of Silas's – how would you react to his fostering of Eppie? How would you try to help him? You may imagine the story is happening NOW if you like.

This also pleased HAL – although he felt the title was a bit long it seemed to him to be a very good example of the sort of involved, relevant approach to the teaching of English literature that it was at this point in time politic to encourage.

He knocked, politely.

'Ah. Nigel. May I come in?'

A shadow of incomprehension passed across Nick Green's face, then was replaced by the slight, shy smile he kept for the middle-aged and elderly – especially when in positions of authority. Usually they found it quietly charming.

'Of course Sir, of course.'

Were they going to stand up or would he have to tell them to? But HAL saved the day by waving down the two or three who were struggling to their feet.

'No, please let's have none of that. If I was with a visitor, then yes, but it's not my intention to interrupt the flow of education, you just get on with what you were doing while I have a word with Mr Brow ... Green.'

Since what they had been doing was listening to Nick this presented a problem, but Nick was sharp-witted enough to see it.

'Yes. That's right. Four G One just carry on reading to yourselves where I left off.'

In low tones, but audible even at the back of the class, HAL uttered banalities about how well Green was settling in, what a fine book *Silas Marner* is, and so on. Then as he was going, hand on door, he turned and raised his voice, added a venom to it that was copied from the bullying sergeant of his first few weeks on National Service.

'You there. Back row. Three in from the window.'

'Who Sir? Me Sir?

'Yes, you Sir. Stand up when you speak to me. Name?'

'Trivet Sir. James Trivet.'

'Right James. Now the first thing I want you to do is straighten your tie. Good. That's better. Quite a good-looking boy when he's tidy, don't you think Mr Green? Now, if you don't mind I'd like you to bring Mr Green the book you were reading. Not *Silas Marner,* I think.'

The Confessions of a Taxi-Driver arrived in Nick Green's hands.

'Nigel, old chap, if I was you I'd put this James Trivet up in front in future and keep an eye on him. If he's like his sister he'll be a clever lad and do well. Shame to waste potential. Millicent's at university now, James, is she not? Well, boy, speak up.'

'Please Sir, Miriam Trivet's my cousin not my sister.'

HAL's glare quelled the giggles and returned to Trivet who was pale and quelled enough already. Clearly he was merely inept, not insolent.

As HAL set off down the corridor a subdued chatter broke out behind him, the flow of George Eliot's prose and Nick's not uninspired rendering of it, quite destroyed.

His last port of call was the library – a source of less adulterated self-congratulation to him than almost anywhere else on the campus. For a start, all but the sixth were excluded from it during class hours so it was very rare indeed that he came across any of the anxiety-causing embarrassments that met him elsewhere – insolence, graffiti, minor vandalism, incompetent or even subversive teaching; but mainly he felt warmed here because it was the only place in the school that post-dated his appointment.

The first library had been gutted one week after his arrival, the night after he had publicly caned four fifth-year boys, to show, he said, who was boss. Since that day he had left caning to the heads of years, chaps he could depend on. Still, the whole episode had been an object lesson, he would say, in how things can be so disposed that good comes out of evil. The new library was magnificent – a large, airy octagon, with a gallery reached by spiral staircases, all done in stone, oak and stainless steel, with black, mock-leather chairs. From the outside it stood out like a tumour against the clean if boring lines of the rest of the block. Inside it was, HAL thought, a fit temple to wisdom, knowledge and education. The powerhouse of the school, was his favourite description of it. He rather hoped that when he finally retired (he was fifty-six) the L.E.A. would have it named the Harte library.

Today, with most of the upper sixth doing A levels, there were only three girls there, just released from Assembly. Each looked up blankly when he opened the door, and went back to her books when she saw who it was.

At last, safe back in his office, his 'early morning patrol' accomplished with minimal loss of face, he planted himself in his big leather armchair behind his large desk with blotter and gilt ballpoints stuck in a marble slab, and set his mind firmly on what he called the real graft of his job. This was never a moment he liked. He had opened the mail at eight o'clock and his very competent secretary was dealing with it; his in-tray was empty, so really was his desk diary. Academic and Policy Meeting at four o'clock. Visits from the Science Adviser and the Youth Employment Officer – but the heads of science and careers would deal with them after he had welcomed them. In his sunny room filled with the scent of roses picked from the senior mistress's garden, the furniture well-polished, the glazed bookcase unblemished by finger marks, Brinshore Comprehensive seemed very far away. From his window he could not see any of the buildings, only the council houses across the road. Indeed, set off the foyer and surrounded by smaller offices, and in spite of the fact that it was at the centre of the whole, there was no room actually further from any of the class-rooms than this one. He even had his own private toilet.

HAL sat in his chair, listened to the very distant hum of two thousand children being educated, and blankly wondered what to do with himself. 'Where to begin' was the way he put it.

Then the intercom on his desk purred and gratefully he flicked a switch.

'Brinshore Police on the line for you, Mr Harte.'

'Thank you Mrs Stevens, put them through.'

'Mr Harte? Inspector Harris here.'

'Ah Ian. How good to hear you, old chap. Have a nice weekend?'

'Yes, thank you, sir.'

'What can I do for you then?'

'Well, there was a fire out at Mudwick yesterday afternoon, out at The Club, you know? Far side of Merriedale. It seems pretty certain one of your lads was involved, also his brother and a friend from Woodcroft Primary ... '

'And you want the low-down on them, before you decide what to do about it?'

'That's it, Mr Harte.'

'Right you are, Ian. Can do. Let's have name, address and so on.'

'Dorian Rose is the one you've got ... '

HAL pulled pad and pen towards him, a happy smile playing over his face. This was just the sort of work he felt equipped to deal with.

So absorbed was he that he hardly noticed the subdued shufflings and whisperings outside his door as Four CSE Three, those of them who were not smoking or gossiping in the lavatories, helped Frank Dangerfield carry through to the intermediary space between library and foyer, the display centre, the material that added up to *The Living Past of Brinshore's Oldest Industry: Fishing.*

However, once he had rung his head of lower school and been told that he would have to wait until the end of the first period before Dorian Rose's file could be sent over, HAL did notice the noise and went out to see what was going on. Frank, on his knees and more camel-like than ever, surrounded by a dozen or so bulky, bulgy adolescents, was putting the finishing touches to the 'environment' they had together created.

'I think it looks great, Mr Dangerfield.'

'Really great.'

'Eh, Sir, Mr Dangerfield, why don't you put that lobster-pot like round to the left, I mean right a bit, then Maureen's picture of them skates'll be seen better.'

'That's a very good idea, Karen. I expect Maureen put you up to it, but it *is* a good idea. There Maureen, that's better, isn't it?'

'I didn't ask her to say that Mr Dangerfield.'

'Of course you didn't. I'm sorry I said you did, but anyway she was right, I love your picture of the skates.'

'Eh, Mr Harte, Sir, don't *you* think it's fab, I mean real great? I think it's lovely.'

Silence fell on the group as they all realised their Leader was among them. HAL took his time – he knew that on occasions like this the right comment was important, and anything too quick, too glib would be distrusted.

Out of mobile display boards, hung with fishing-nets strung with briny slabs of cork they had created a wide, deep cave cunningly lit with display lighting; on the walls were pictures, prints, drawings depicting fish, fishermen, boats, gear, and tackle. Pushed well out to the periphery, flow charts and graphs expressed obscurely what could have been said succinctly in words and figures, namely the steady decline since 1900 of the fleet from twenty-five boats to four now. In the centre of the back wall was a blow-up of a coloured print of the west beach depicting fishermen in round black boaters, and their wives in shawls hauling boats through the breakers, and mending nets. Under it, written with excellent broad-tip penmanship, HAL read: 'This print was made in 1840 by W. B. Cooke. Note the Athlone Hotel in the background with the Terrace, now demolished, behind it. To the right and inland the group of fishermen's cottages that made up Chine Street. These too have been pulled down. Jack Rammage, 4CSE3, was born in one of these ... '

'Very nice, very nice indeed, Mr Dangerfield,' said HAL, elbow supported in one hand, chin in the other, with index finger against his cheek. 'Where did the original of that print come from?'

'I'm not sure. I suspect it appeared in a magazine about watering places; on the back is what I take to be a puff for Eastbourne. I found it framed in a bric-à-brac market down the coast, but George and Sam here did the blow-up, and a jolly good job they made of it.'

'They did indeed.' HAL's eyes moved to the foreground. On a board set at a slope and covered with contact paper simulating marble, were parsley and ferns, two squid, one dab, and a small conger eel – the very centre of the display.

'I say those are good, now I really admire those, they look absolutely real.'

The silence intensified. HAL bent forward to touch the

glistening dab and a large bluebottle buzzed off, confusedly knocking into the hot lights above.

'They are real,' said Frank. 'Jack Rammage got them off his brother Kevin this morning.'

'Ah yes. The Rammages. Well, boys and girls, it really is a magnificent show, a magnificent show. Now if you'd all make your way quietly back to your classroom, I'll just have a word here with Mr Dangerfield, and he'll be along with you promptly. Quietly, I said QUIETLY.'

When the last raucous voices had faded down the corridor he put his hands in his pockets and jingled keys and small change. 'Frank, old chap,' he said, 'I'm sure I don't have to tell you this, you've been here long enough, but those Rammages need watching. Simple fisherfolk, salt of the earth, but not adaptable to modern ways, not adaptable. A dying breed, sad in a way, but one mustn't be sentimental about the past. In the meantime that boy Rammage needs watching!'

'I think I understand you. I've absolutely insisted that he changes the fish every day. If you prefer I'll ask him to take these away at four, and not bring anything tomorrow.'

'I think that would be better. Perhaps you can knock up some real models to take their place.'

'I don't know. Perhaps an empty marble slab would after all be the best comment.'

'Yes well. Whatever you think best, old chap.'

Still jingling HAL began to move back towards his office. 'Splendid Assembly this morning, old chap, I saw you there.'

'Yes. I ... I think one of my tutor group was ... er, involved, so I went along.'

'Martin Bright? Well of course you mustn't say so. Anonymity to be protected. But I gather it was one of those essays he was asked to do. Jolly good. Another success I think, a potentially awkward customer straightened out. Still – it's a pity your class had to make a row while you were there, but I do understand you wanted to hear it, old chap,' and he let himself into his office, leaving Frank angry amongst the ferns of the foyer.

Later, because he wanted someone to talk to about it, and

because he had to go into the town to the bank, he took Pet Rogate with him and went to the Athlone. Usually she stayed in her pottery room over lunch eating yoghurt and apples, so she wasn't missed, not by her husband anyway.

Back in his executive chair behind his polished desk HAL pulled the Dorian Rose file towards him. The head of lower school had clipped a note to it.

'Can't understand this, Leo,' he read. 'Dorian is quite one of the best. Always well turned out. Good worker. Top stream. Good report from Woodcroft Primary. Father in management at TRICE, Mother has a tuchaclass. Case for the shrink, not the court, if you ask me.'

With a practised eye HAL leafed through the folder. Good attendance. Excellent punctuality. Commended twice for good work already, though still in his first year. He turned to the digest from Woodcroft Primary. Similar story, but severe reprimand in the previous year for what the Head there had called gross cruelty to animals. He wondered if he should give Woodcroft a tinkle about this but decided against it – Mr Edwards was just a wee bit of a crank about some things, sound enough for the most part, but apt to put on shorts and a tweed hat and tramp about the marshes looking at birds or march down ancient rights of way to keep them open. Gross cruelty to animals would be biased to say the least – probably some harmless prank with a cat was involved, nothing more. As a child HAL had had good fun with an airgun shooting sparrows and frogs.

The connection with TRICE was more interesting. He put his fingers together and mused. Good relations between TRICE and the school were always good policy. After mapping out his approach he flicked the switch on his intercom.

'See if you can get Mr James Cheal for me,' he said.

While he waited he began to make notes on his pad for his opening remarks at the after-school meeting on vocational education.

'He's not at TRICE, Mr Harte, they told me to try Belmont.'

'Do that then, will you?'

His notes turned to doodles – a circle with spokes, lines off the ends of the spokes at right angles to them. All right for some, he thought, spending their Monday mornings at the posh golf club on the Downs.

'Cheal here.'

'James. Harte here from Brinshore School.'

'Harte. Pleased to hear you. What can I do for you?' The voice was deep, just a little roughened, a Rolls Royce in need of a service, though the accent was plebeian. HAL imagined the large whisky and soda on the bar.

'Well James, it's not so much help I want as advice.'

'Advice I don't charge for, so go ahead.'

'We've a boy in a spot of trouble here, and I'm not quite sure how to proceed. Since he's the offspring of one of your chaps, I thought I'd find out what views you had on the matter – I mean you'll know the background better than I do.'

One of your chaps meant the board or management. Probably management – the board's kids went to private schools, in fact the same was true of all but one of top management.

'Name of Dorian Rose,' supplied HAL. 'Son of one Timothy Rose.'

There was a moment's silence though HAL fancied he could hear the chink of ice on the edge of a glass. 'Yes. I've placed him. Tim Rose. *Assistant* personnel manager. But wife's quite a looker, with a tuchaclass. Well what's the kid been up to?'

'Set fire to The Club yesterday afternoon.'

Deep laugh at the other end. 'What, that snotty place the other side of Merriedale? He should be decorated.'

HAL laughed heartily in reply.

'So Harte. What are the choices?'

'Well, James. According to the book he should go to court. Juvenile of course, so there'll be no names in the papers but these things get around and the parents will be upset. Apparently a younger brother is up the same er, creek, as well.' HAL knew Cheal had a taste for rough language. 'And the court will only ask for social workers' reports and one from the child psychiatrist, and so on, and the thing will drift into limbo. Now I think I can fix it with the er, police,' HAL couldn't bring himself to say 'fuzz' – some things were sacred to him, 'not to take him to court if I guarantee to get the reports for them, by-passing the court, if you see what I mean.'

'You do that, Harte,' came the voice, and then the click of the phone as Cheal, Chairman, one third owner and creator of TRICE, millionaire from Alma Terrace back of Chine Street, who had gone to school with Jack Trivet and had been taught there by old Trim, hung up on him.

HAL raised his eyebrows at the intercom, then smiled, pressed a button.

'See if you can raise Inspector Harris again,' he said. All in the day's work, he thought.

Between five and fifteen minutes past four the heads of this and the teachers in charge of that, the senior masters and the senior mistress, the liaison teacher for so and so, and the co-ordinator of the other, all in all about a third of the total staff of Brinshore Comprehensive assembled in the sixth-form coffee bar and arranged themselves in the seats that had been set out in rows for them. The careerists sat in the front, the dutiful in the middle, the dissidents and young at the back. Frank put himself near the back, next to Gwyn Davies who had been head of history in the old Boys' Secondary Modern, and still should be, but was now liaison officer with the L.E.A. In-Training Centre at Rifedale. Although not acquainted beyond the bounds of the staff-room, Frank liked the small, neat Welshman whose hatred, and therefore understanding of neo-imperialist corporate capitalism was so intense and so deep that his pupils passed O and A level at a rate unequalled by any other teacher in the school. 'It's on account I know the system so well, I know exactly what they want the kids to say, see?' was his explanation, and it was probably true.

'Tell me, Mr Davies,' said Frank, as he sat down, 'why are these meetings called Academic and Policy Meetings?'

'You want me to tell you why these meetings are called Academic and Policy Meetings?'

'That's right, Mr Davies.'

'I'll tell you then, boyo. It's on account of all discussion of policy is purely academic.'

'Boom, boom.'

'Well, I didn't see you at dinner today, then.'

'No. I had to go to the bank. Had a pie and a beer at the Athlone on the way back.' And had an earful of how Pet Rogate wasn't getting on with her husband as she used to, and there they were sitting in front.

'That way ruin lies. The kids'll smell it on you, you know, they always do. But particularly I wanted to see you.'

'You did?'

'On account of that essay read at Assembly this morning, read by Mr Armstrong and endorsed by no less a person than Lah-di-dah himself.'

But a voice called from the end of the room: 'Right ladies, right gentlemen, we'll begin if you please,' – the deputy headmaster, a kind man, aged well beyond his years. At this time of year he was a recluse, working fourteen hours a day, trying to concoct the timetable that would run from next September. However, it was his job to quieten any rabble HAL might choose to address, and he came out of his hole to perform this and similar tasks.

'Tell you later,' said Gwyn, but he forgot and never did.

HAL rose and went first through a series of notices – disco for sixth-formers, past pupils, staff and guests next Friday, heads of departments are asked to remind colleagues to be punctual and to set a good example themselves, to keep their record books up-to-date, to pay their dinner money, to collect dinner money, to sell raffle tickets, to report cases of vandalism promptly so steps may be taken, to wipe their noses when necessary, blah, blah blah.

'Right then. The main item on today's agenda is vocational education. Now I've deliberately left this very open, in future discussion we'll narrow it down in whatever ways appear appropriate. Today I am just concerned to initiate what I hope will be a far-and-wide-ranging enquiry, by thinking aloud in front of you, that's all I'm doing, just thinking aloud, and then throwing the subject open so we can see what lines are emerging. Well. Not long ago the Prime Minister gave us the benefit of his wisdom on this subject, and I think got quite accurately near the nub of the matter when he said, and I quote, "there is no virtue in producing socially well-adjusted members of society who are unemployed because they do not have the skills." What I think he was saying is this. Education is double-faced (Whoops, thought Frank, and grinned at Gwyn Davies). On the one hand it's about productivity, educating kids for the sort of jobs the country needs them to do, on the other it's about social adjustment. Well, today we're talking about the first. Forgive me if I seem to philosophise now, but I don't think the two are really inseparable. Our society is a society of boundless opportunity and we should be proud it is and ready to fight to keep it that way *(The imperialist state maintains itself on a war-footing and forces potential competitors to do likewise,* thought Gwyn). Let me try to get down to grass roots to show you what I mean. This afternoon, not an hour ago, while reassuring myself that education was taking place (sycophantic laughter from the front rows at this chestnut), I came across three boys loafing about by the lockers near the changing-rooms. Clearly after games they had escaped the eagle eyes of the PE staff, no fault of yours old chap (a nod to the Head of PE), and in the chat I had with them it emerged that each and every one of them had academic or career problems. Well of course I noted down their names and what they had to say, and I might add that the lesson they were cutting was physics, and their year head and tutor will be getting a memo from me in due course so their files can be brought up-to-date, so in this particular case an apparently negative event has been turned into some positive use. . . .

'But what I am driving at now is this. Every which way you look at it those lads were already up against the frustrations that face those who for whatever reason – lack of need aggression, lack of need achievement in what is essentially an achieving society – have set themselves low targets, seem doomed to under-achieve. For there is no doubt that in all the bewildering array of opportunity our society offers, it does promote aspirations – be they holidays abroad, new cars, and cultural aspirations too, I don't exclude those, which initially require high performance, or at least mean or median performance at school. Now I believe that it is out of these frustrations that many of the social ills our society is heir to arise – and this is where I make the connection between social adjustment and productivity. A lad whose productivity will be low, who knows already it will be low, is already going to be deeply frustrated and is likely to turn out, no matter what we do about it in the line of pastoral care, youth counselling, careers advice (social interference, thought Frank), and so on, a bad'un. Let me sum up so far. What I feel we have to do is give our customers the requirements they need to get the jobs which will enable them to fulfill their legitimate aspirations. (*The radicalisation of the working class is counteracted by the development and satisfaction of needs which perpetuate the servitude of the exploited,* Gwyn recalled.)

'Let me put it another way, still thinking aloud of course. As I see it, the way our curriculum is structured at the moment, it is a dual system, as I said before. On the one side we have the graft of technique, of defined bodies of knowledge to be mastered in subjects like maths, physics, metalwork, domestic economy, business studies – all with the end in view of giving the kids the skills they need for productive lives, or at any rate of providing the basics on which these skills will later be grafted. On the other side we have broadly speaking the arts and what I would call the non-productive, and I mean no disparagement, creative crafts which give our customers the means, the skills if you like, to enjoy the good things our society provides in leisure time. In this connection, let me say, in parenthesis, how pleased I am with the way the new CSE courses in TV Appreciation, History of Pop, and the Living Past of Brinshore are going. And I do, at this moment in time, especially recommend those of you who have not already done so to visit our design centre to see

Frank Dangerfield's latest creation in that sphere. Frank, old chap, I take it the Rammage boy has removed the nuisance he contributed? (Frank, angry and blushing, nodded assent). Splendid. Where was I?

'Now what I feel is this: we should seek ways to bring these spheres closer together. You see, those three lads I was having a barney with this afternoon could not relate them. On one side was education for work where they felt they had already failed: when they left they would get poorly rewarded jobs, with little status, or no jobs at all; on the other, limitless means of enjoyment and pleasure. One of them for instance agreed with me that colour TV was a good thing to have, he would have one when he set up house on his own. Of this he was certain. It had not occurred to him that even the excessive unemployment benefit now available would not run to such a luxury. What I tried to get across to that lad was this: only by learning the skills necessary to fulfill his aspirations would he earn the right to enjoy his stake in our society which is the due of each and every one of us. I think he took the point.

(*Stability under late capitalism is ensured by fostering a sense of having a vested interest in the existing system to the point where it becomes part of the instinctual structure of the exploited,* thought Gwyn.)

'Now I've been tossing those ideas about in my mind for some time *(since eleven-thirty this morning),* and I freely admit my first thoughts were very crude. I put them to you now in all humility to save any of you who may be as dull-witted as me from making fools of yourselves, as I may be now, in the lively discussion I'm sure will ensue. First, I don't think we can relate education for production with education for leisure or social adjustment by any mechanical system of rewards or punishments – e.g. by giving the high achievers in maths or physics extra art or pottery, and the low achievers less until they've done better. Nor can we initiate an intensive campaign of moral teaching on the lines work is a duty, you've got to pay your way. Not that I don't believe in this, of course I do, it is the corner-stone of my ethic, and should be of our customers too, indeed is of many of them, but there's been so much of this talk about, politicians and the media, such an overt approach has become counter-productive.

'Let me put before you the sort of lines I do see development taking place on. What I would like to see, especially for those of our customers who are under-achieving, is more courses like the Living Past of Brinshore, more courses that cut across the curriculum, that seek to unite the dichotomy that splits it at the moment. I'm just talking off the top of my head, but why not link basic electronics to the TV appreciation course, the technology of car production to our course in beginner driving and car maintenance, why not insist on getting the kids to *use* basic chemistry and physics in a practical way to discover just how, really how a pottery kiln works? What I feel is it's our place in society to make people feel at home in it, to appreciate and use to the full all it has to offer, to get people to see that the dichotomy between work and leisure is a false one, that they are entirely interdependent one with the other ...

('This smacks of Marxism, doesn't it?' whispered Frank. Gwyn frowned: 'Of course it bloody doesn't.')

' ... let me put it crudely to finish with. What our kids have to understand, really understand so it is a lesson properly learnt, is the basic truth: that only by contributing to the making of colour TV sets, in however roundabout a way, do you earn your right to enjoy them.'

(Gwyn remembered: *The stage where people cannot reject the system without rejecting themselves is the triumph and end of introjection.*)

The deputy headmaster, in his spurious role as chairman, now rose. 'Before colleagues express their views I would like to say one thing. No courses of the type suggested can get off the ground next September. The basic outline of the timetable is taking shape, and I'm not putting it back in the melting-pot now ... '

More obsequious laughter, led this time by Mr Harte himself.

The discussion that followed was indeed lively. The head of

lower school maths, a woman, attacked Mr Harte for not concentrating on the real root of the problem – the unequal opportunities for vocational education open to girls.

The head of sociology saw the role of his department as one peculiarly, indeed uniquely, equipped to provide the nuts and bolts of the sort of courses the Head was proposing.

The head of religious knowledge took exception to the Head's dismissive approach to moral education.

Frank began a short talk on how the potters he most admired, the Japanese masters of the late nineteenth century, had learned their skills from a centuries old tradition of peasant-based craft, not from a thermometer or by understanding the chemical reactions that took place in the kiln, but he was tired and frustrated after a long day and he sat down before he had finished. He was also put out by the unrestrainedly adoring look he was getting from Pet Rogate, in spite of the fact that she was sitting next to her husband. One voice whispered: you're making a fool of yourself with her; another said: what the hell.

The head of science, the head of maths and Hitler Armstrong, all ambitious men, rose to repeat in even less comprehensible jargon the very things that HAL had already said. Two working parties were set up to meet weekly until the end of term when they would report their findings at the final A and P meeting of the school year. The meeting closed at five forty-six precisely.

3.

AT five forty-six, or thereabouts, the atmosphere in the Trivets' kitchen was sour – as it usually was at this time. Miriam Trivet was at the stove, Tess in her chair by the fridge with a cup of tea and a cigarette. New potatoes and peas simmered.

'Move yourself, Mum.' Miriam opened the fridge, lifted out a covered plate. 'How shall I divide these? There are four fillets, but they're huge.'

'Let's see.' Tess peered through cigarette smoke, poked at the fish with her finger. Earlier she had been a little tipsy, now she was tired, her legs and back ached, she was on the edge of a hangover. 'That's just like your Father. *I* don't know what he means us to do with them.'

'Oh come on, Mum. It's not his fault if the fish he catches don't divide up into convenient helpings.'

'Well, I don't know. You please yourself.'

'How about if I do one for him, and half each for us?'

'He said it should do for two meals.'

'Well that way it will, won't it?'

'I suppose so. I don't want much.'

Miriam lifted the frying-pan out of the oven and sliced fresh lard into it.

'Have you any breadcrumbs or egg?'

'He usually does them in flour.'

Since her back went Jack had done much of the cooking.

Miriam found the flour and dredged two fillets, the other two went back into the fridge.

'These won't take long. Do you think you should call him?'

'He'll come when he's ready.'

Miriam shrugged.

'They'll spoil if they're put on one side to keep warm.'

Tess watched her daughter as she pushed the fillets about in the pan and felt a glow – affection, pride, appreciation – in spite of her depression. Miriam was a good-looking girl, well would be if only she'd take a bit of trouble, have her hair done instead of leaving it straight and long, wear a proper dress instead of that old jumper and jeans. She was clever too. And sensible. Tess vaguely felt that the cleverness came from her, the sense from Jack. She always said she had no idea where the looks came from but to herself admitted that this daughter took after Jack.

'It's nice having you back,' she said. 'We've missed you.'

'I was only away eight weeks this time.'

'It seemed longer.'

'Well, I came back before I should.'

'You won't be in trouble, will you?'

'Oh no. All the lectures and classes have finished. It was just staying on for parties and silly things like that. I couldn't be bothered.'

'It'll be nice to have someone to go out with in the evening.'

Miriam put down the skillet.

'Look Mum, I'm not going out drinking down the Little George every night; a, I can't afford it, and, b, I shan't have time, especially not if I start at TRICE next week. I'll sit in with you here, and we'll be company, but let's leave the George and the Athlone for weekends.'

'That's a fine prospect then,' said Tess, 'you studying and me watching the telly each night.'

The clink of china on the stairs, and the door opened. Jack came in, heavy-footed, carrying cup and saucer, dressed in vest and work trousers, bleary, hair tousled.

'Just in time Dad. These are just about ready.'

He grunted, put down the cup and saucer, went to the sink and rinsed his face.

'Shall I dish up then?' Miriam asked as he dried himself.

'Yes. Do you want a hand?'

'No. You sit down. I can manage.'

Capably Miriam drained the potatoes and peas, holding the saucepan lids against the pans with a cloth, lifted the fish on to warm plates, spooned out the vegetables, filled a kettle for the washing-up and put it on a low gas, then sat down between her parents.

'There we are then,' she said brightly.

'Very nice Moll,' said Jack.

'Fish is never the same from a shop, is it?' said Miriam.

Tess pulled a face at her plate, irritated by the mutual admiration society of which it seemed she was not a member. 'Don't ask me, Miriam,' she said. 'Your father never lets me buy fish.'

'Don't need to, do you?' said Jack. 'The potatoes and peas come from the garden too.' He poured himself another cup of tea.

Presently, when they were all but finished, Tess lifted her

head – like an animal, suspicious and wary in its den, Miriam thought.

'Door,' she said. 'There's someone at the door.'

'I'll go,' said Miriam, and squeezed behind her father who was now fiddling with the radio on the table, retuning it from Radio One to Radio Downland.

'It's two men, from work. They want to see Dad.'

He grunted, went out into the hall, shutting the door behind him. Wife and daughter could hear voices from the front door, not words.

'What's he up to now?' said Tess. 'I never know what your dad's up to.'

Miriam began clearing the dishes on to the draining-board.

'Leave them until he's had his wash.'

She sat down again.

Presently Jack came in, sat down, fiddled with the radio.

'What was that then?' asked Miriam.

'Bill and George. They do the job me and cousin Bob do, but on the day shift.'

'What did they want?'

Jack looked quietly pleased, gleeful. He was pleased too that Miriam was there to hear what he had to say for Tess refused to listen to anything to do with work.

'It's about this job we've been on the last three months. There's an overhead loop, see, moving round the benches. It's for assembling this bit of the motor like. Well, there's a coil, difficult to explain exactly, but as they go by I have to thread over, well like three washers really. Now the agreed rate is sixty an hour, see, six hundred a shift, but the charge hand had Bill and George adding a bit of cladding today, said it could go with the last ring without any extra effort. Well, they weren't going to have no truck with that but there wasn't much they could do, see, and it's a carry-on getting in the union, so they just did one in three or one in four wrong like and when the charge hand went for them they said it came from having to do the extra in the time.'

'And they want to be sure you do the same.'

'That's it.' He chuckled. Tess stared out of the window and

shook her head dismally – one day he'd be fired, then where would they be. No hope of her going back to work with her back.

'I thought you were a machinist, Dad.'

'Not since I lost the top off my finger. Since then I've been doing a bit of this and a bit of that.'

'Did you get compensation?'

'Oh yes.'

'But don't ask him how much,' said Tess, 'because he won't tell you.'

This time Jack stared blankly out of the window,

'I reckon you ought to get it for your skin trouble too.'

'May be. But they can't show it come from work, see.'

'Oh come on.'

He got up, moved heavily to the sink. There he washed, put on a shirt, carefully combed back his hair, left hand following the comb in easy rhythm, head on one side. Before the war, when Tess, newly over from Cork, learning the hotel trade, had fallen for him, he had looked like James Cagney. (Two married daughters there were, older than Miriam, one in Langley, the other in London.) When his hair was done he spread cream cheese on crackers, put them in a plastic box, snapped an elastic band over the lid. Finally he mixed up orange squash and water and put the bottle with the box in an old bit of towel.

He poured himself a last cup of tea and sat down again. Slowly and carefully he smeared ointment on three fingers (two on one hand, one on the other) which had skin sores that wouldn't heal, wound finger stalls over them and plastered them down using a roll of Elastoplast and scissors. He managed all this quite deftly. Then he finished his tea.

At last he put on an anorak, kissed wife and daughter, and let himself out. They went into the front room to watch him cycling down the road. At the corner he turned and waved, they waved, and he was gone.

'You know he said he does six hundred of those things in a shift,' Tess said. 'Well, he does it in half the time. Then he has a nap and later he reads the papers; they get them early, sent up from the station.'

'Well, I'm glad it's like that,' said Miriam, with all the firmness she could get into her voice.

Twenty minutes later Frank was sitting on the edge of his old chipped bath while the lethal gas-heater roared and water gushed from tarnished taps. He opened a letter he had found waiting for him when he came home. The writing he thought he knew but he had not seen it for some time. He turned to the back. All the best, Max (Flash). Interested he returned to the beginning and read:

> Dear Frank,
>
> No use beating about, how are you and all that crap. Here's the thing. I've landed this wheeze of a job from Southchester City Council leisure department. They've just gone Labour again, by one seat, and they're starting this Art for the People project and I'm in charge. The idea is this – street theatre (of course), community poetry magazines, and a whole load of ideas for visuals – community photography, collective murals on blank brick spaces, play sculpture, lots of ideas, you'll think of more. I'm to get together a team, and I want you on it.
>
> Of course carpers will say it's crap to give the conscious ones something to take their mind off the revolution, but it needn't work like that. Anyway, it'll be better than what you're doing now – stuffing talent through the exam system and emasculating it on the way.
>
> One thing though. My budget is derisory. I have fifteen thou for salaries, and I won't be able to spare you more than three. So what? You can live on that, no problem.
>
> Think it over, give me a ring by the end of the week. OK?
>
> All the best, Max (Flash)

Frank turned off the water. In silence and steam he mused, suddenly very bitter, almost in tears. Three thousand? He was sending more than that to the woman who kept his daughters on the other side of the Downs, the bitch who was still his wife.

Still. Good old Max. They had been students together and for a time Max had taught with him at Brinshore but had left after a row with HAL.

Frank crumpled up the letter, tossed it into a corner, and climbed into the bath. The water lapped and swished and made the background silence worse. He got out of the bath, padded wetly into the room he used as a studio, picked up his radio, and returned to the bath. As he lay back, knees well crooked for the bath was far too small, and longed for the tension and frustration to soak out of him, hundreds of children all over Brinshore and thousands even millions everywhere else were beginning their homework (Imagine you are a neighbour of Silas – how would you react to his fostering of Eppie?), some disc jockey or other on some station or other lowered the pick-up of Ian Dury's single:

I could be a driver of an articulated lorry
I could be a poet I wouldn't need to worry
I could be a teacher in a classroom full of scholars
I could be the sergeant in a squadron full of wallahs
What a waste
What a waste
What a waste

and Frank smiled at the beat, the energy, and tapped to it on the edge of his bath, and the kids put down their pens for a moment and looked out at the golden evening.

HAL, driving his B.M.W. towards Rifedale where he lived, frowned and returned; Nick Green settling down to mark books asked Dot to turn it off but then put it on again when he heard the baby was bawling; Linda Rose went into Dorian and Mark's bedroom, picked up the trannie, took it into the kitchen and dropped it into the waste-bin where it continued to play:

I could be a lawyer with stratagems and ruses
I could be a doctor with poultices for bruises

I could be a writer with a growing reputation
I could be the ticket man at Fulham railway station
What a waste
What a waste
What a waste

Miriam washing up with the evening sun pouring on her through the kitchen window and blotting out with its glare the narrow rows of back-yards that stretched for half a mile in front of her, mouthed the words which she already knew, tilting her head from side to side so her long tresses swung and bounced to the record:

I could be the catalyst that sparks the revolution
I could be the inmate of a long term institution
I could go to wild extremes, I could crawl and die
I could yawn and be withdrawn and watch them all go by
What a waste
What a waste
What a waste
Because I chose to play the fool in a five-piece band
First night nerves every one night stand
I should be glad to be so inclined
What a waste
What a waste
But I DON'T MIND . . . .

And at TRICE, through the whirring and the clanking, the whining, grating and pulsing, the music came as Jack and cousin Bob settled into the first hour of their shift threading washers on to a coil and misplacing every third and fourth bit of cladding and Jack wondered darkly at the absurd and shameful conspiracy he was part of, the conspiracy between manager and producer in a commodity-based society. After midnight some of the younger lads would watch a blue film on an eight-millimetre projector set up in a store-room, three card brag would be underway elsewhere, but Jack would try to doze beneath the harsh neon lights and in spite of the racket and the hot dry air. Outside the night would go chill and black and the dull hours would trickle away – three o'clock, four o'clock, five, until the *Sun* and the *Mirror,* the *Mail* and the *Express* came up from the station:

What a waste
What a waste
What a waste
What a waste.

IV
TUESDAY
Miriam's Day

1.

BACK straight, not a hair out of place, leather handbag on the floor beside her, Tess sat at a table in the Copper Kettle and wondered uneasily what to order if the waitress noticed her. To the casual, even to a careful observer she did not look out of place at all in her amber trouser suit with its topaz brooch, and a fine silk scarf round her neck – and none of the blue rinses and pink rinses with painted nails at the end of arthritic fingers which flashed diamonds when they stirred their coffee and jangled gold charms when they lifted their cups to drink, gave her more than a passing glance. Yet she felt ill at ease – late morning coffee was not her scene, she told herself, and shook her head, no way at all was it, and she wondered again what on earth had possessed her to say she'd meet Miriam in the Copper Kettle when Miriam had suggested Fratelli's coffee bar.

'Just a coffee please dear, er white.'

The waitress came straight back, put down a cup two-thirds full of black coffee, a small foil tub, hermetically sealed, and a bill for twenty-five p. Tess looked at it all with something not far off misery and returned to staring longingly at the bus-station across the road.

Then, yes. There she was, the sun bright on her hair and her face, a quick glance left and right, then striding almost trotting across the road with a big smile, and a wave as she got near enough to see her mother.

The blue rinses and the pink rinses looked up and thought: what a nice gel, so fresh and unspoilt; the waitress recognised her from school, cracked her face, and said: 'Hi Molly, coffee is it?' and Tess relaxed at last. Perhaps the Copper Kettle wasn't such a bad choice after all – certainly it had more style than Fratelli's.

She watched Miriam peel the top off the foil tub and add cream to her cup and she followed suit, to the manner born.

'Well, pet, how did you get on?'

'Oh I got the job all right, but it was a laugh, I can tell you. Do you know what? They gave me a test, I ask you, read this passage then fill in the gaps, and some arithmetic, I swear it was all a lot easier than the eleven plus. Really! It was. And they gave me half an hour for it, in a little room all on my own, I'd finished it in five minutes, so I took it in to them. Well really. I wasn't going to sit there for twenty-five minutes not doing anything. It would have been all right if I'd taken a book.'

'Did you see anyone?'

'Oh yes. But it wasn't the Mr Stanwyck you said it would be. All I got was the *assistant* personnel manager, ever such a funny man, well quite nice and all that, but he seemed an absolute dumbo to me. Really! Complete twit. Timothy Rose, it said on his desk.'

'I don't think I know him. What's he like?'

'You've not missed much. He's tallish with one of those neat hair-cuts, and a silly moustache coming down each side of his mouth. He started off calling me Miriam Trivet, then Miriam, then he asked if I could operate a photocopier, and I said if it was like the one at the university library then yes, and if it wasn't I was quite capable of reading the instructions. I think it was then he started calling me *Miss* Trivet. And you know what? This'll make you laugh.'

'What?'

'Well just about then, after the photocopier bit, guess who came in.'

'How should I know?'

'Jimmy Cheal.'

'No!'

'Yes!'

'And did he recognise you?'

'Straightaway. Just like that. "You're Miriam Trivet, aren't you?" he said. And I told him why I was there, so he told Mister Timothy Rose I was to have the job and then he took me into his office and gave me a gin and tonic. And mum, honestly, it was *huge.* The gin I mean. He just went on pouring and pouring, even after I'd told him to stop. There wasn't room for more than half the tonic there was so much gin in the glass. He asked after you and Dad and asked to be remembered to you, and I told him that I thought Dad's skin complaint was from work ... '

'Oh Molly, you didn't!'

'Of course I did. Why not? And he said he'd get the firm's doctor to look at it, so some good'll come of that I expect. Then when I left I went out through this Mister Rose's office and he went all hurt on me and said why didn't I tell him Dad went to school with Mister Cheal, so I said it wasn't one of the questions on his form, but if he felt it was important perhaps he should know too that Dad's on the night shift in the motor assembly room and the school was the old Alma Street Elementary.'

'I hope he didn't think you were being cheeky.'

'Well, what if he did? Anyway he wasn't exactly Prince Charles as far as his manners went, but just silly and a snob. And wet too. Hey, I don't think much of this coffee, do you?'

Tess warmed happily to her daughter, looked round at all the blue rinses and pink rinses, stuck-up lot she thought, and wondered how she might prolong the pleasure of it all.

'No, I agree,' she said, 'the coffee isn't as good as it should be. Shall we move on somewhere else?' and she insisted on paying for both of them – fifty p for two cups of bad coffee, I ask you.

On the pavement Miriam took her arm. 'Well, Mum, where would you like to go?'

'Well, we could go along the front, it's such a nice day. And then, if you like, stop off at the Athlone for a pie or a sandwich.' She said this a touch anxiously, was ready to concede if Miriam objected because she really was enjoying herself and didn't want to spoil things, but Miriam too was enjoying herself and to Tess's relief said: 'Yes, why not. It's time I looked in at the old place and saw Mr Rigg and the others.'

'They always ask after you,' said Tess, now full of satisfaction.

They walked slowly, for Tess could never now go more than slowly, down the High Street and into the Arcade. Here Miriam pulled up for a moment and shook her head.

'I'll never get used to it.'

'No. I don't suppose I will.'

'It's like having a tooth out, feeling the gap with your tongue. Worse really. Like having a limb off I expect.'

'I suppose it is,' said Tess.

The end of the Arcade, with its cast-iron and glass roof, looked on to blue sky and fresh white clouds, sea deep blue then patches of emerald with white horses, and in the foreground, a descending slope of mud and rubble where once the Assembly Rooms had stood. It was also like, Miriam thought, a surrealist picture – sea, sky, and clouds naturalistically painted but appearing in a totally unexpected context. As they neared the end of the Arcade the awfulness of the Leisure Centre, ochre brick and scaffolding, came into view on their left.

'Did you hear about Princess Mary?' asked Tess.

Miriam had, but knew her mother wanted to tell it over again.

'She came to lay the stone, just when they were starting it, and she was wearing a turquoise-coloured coat and one of those hats. Well, you should have seen the rain, and only planks over the mud. One of the Council, he was holding the umbrella, slipped off into the mud, right over his ankles. And when she'd done that silly bit, you know, tapping it with a silver trowel, pretending she'd done the work, do you know what she said?'

'Go on tell me.'

'She was angry, they're not supposed to show it, but she

was angry. She said: "You'll have to ask me back to see it when it's finished" and then she got back in her shiny black car and they drove her off.'

They crossed the road and Miriam helped Tess up the steps on to the promenade.

'Come back when it's finished,' repeated Tess.

There was a breeze, the tide past full was still well up, everything fresh and sunny – seagulls sailed on the breeze and a little tern come from its nesting place on Mudwick Marsh, hovered swallow-tailed just the far side of the breakers, swooped, recovered, hovered and swooped again, came up with a sprat and winged purposefully back along the coast to feed its chicks.

'Will they be open yet?' Miriam asked.

'Oh yes. We've been on summer hours since last month.'

'All the same we've plenty of time. Let's sit down and enjoy it.'

They sat in the vandalised shelter on a bench so scored with graffiti that none were now legible, and with their necks unprotected from the breeze since all the glazing had long since been shattered.

Arseholes, bastards, fucking cunts and pricks Tess avoided reading, aerosoled on the wall above her head. Still, the view over the sea was fine, apart from the ruined pier.

'Mr Dangerfield did a painting of this shelter and the Leisure Centre behind,' she said. 'It's in Johnny Manet's window but no one will buy it I'm sure. He even put in the dirty words.'

'I'd like to see it.'

'Well. It's a funny sort of picture. Perhaps we'll meet him today. He sometimes has lunch at the Athlone.'

This wasn't strictly true. The day before had been the very first time Frank had done this, but Tess felt wary of admitting that she had been at the Athlone only twenty-four hours earlier.

'Does he?' said Miriam. 'He always used to have his dinner at school. I'd love to see him again though. He was a dear, and an awfully good teacher, I loved him. I'd love to talk to him again, I feel I understand a lot of things he used to go on about so much better now. Does he still have that funny beard, like Edward the Seventh?'

'I think it's an attractive beard. It suits him.'

'He thinks it makes him look arty, but really it's just old-fashioned.'

'It suits him,' repeated Tess.

They stood up and Miriam took her mother's arm again. In front of them, almost opposite the pier, the Athlone stood – four storeys, grey, with wrought iron balconies, but the end wall facing them was a giant blank, as if a cheese-wire had sheered down it, a blank save for the words painted boldly across the smoothed cement.

The Athlone Hotel
Free House

The seven large houses that had completed the rest of The Terrace hovered as ghosts in Miriam's mind above ...

'What on earth's that?' she exclaimed.

'That? Oh that. Didn't your father tell you about that? He's always on about it.'

'No he did not. But what is it?'

They stopped and Tess leaned on Miriam. Where, two months before, there had been rubble which an earth-mover had nudged about as if it meant to go on doing just that day after day for ever, were now seven or eight mounds, each about five feet high with heavy wooden barriers, made, one might think, from sleepers torn up from an abandoned railway, placed between them. The mounds were part turfed, part planted with small shrubs, but the grass was already brown, and the shrubs looked dead. Litter lay in drifts along the footings of the barriers.

'Well, what is it?' Miriam repeated.

'They said in the *Post* the lumps are like the waves on the other side of the prom and the wooden things the breakwaters. Like a mirror. And you can sit behind the wooden things and be out of the wind.'

Miriam looked out over the sea, still running deep blue and

green, though the sky was filling now with greyer clouds, and then back over the humps.

'But they're so, so ... tatty, so drab. Ugly. And that's the best they can do instead of The Terrace. Well. I don't know. I really don't know.'

'They said it was temporary.' Much though she hated the humps, Tess now felt defensive about them, apologetic in the face of Miriam's scorn.

'Molly Trivet. How nice to see you.'

'How nice to see you, Mr Rigg,' and to the publican's delighted surprise she stood tiptoe on the polished brass rail below the bar, and was thus able to lean across and peck him on his silvery, bristled cheek.

'Well, Molly,' he said, 'the first one's with me. What'll you have? It'll be a Guinness for Mrs Trivet, I'm sure, but for you?'

'I've already had a gin and tonic with Jimmy Cheal this morning, and I suppose I shouldn't mix ... '

'Important company you keep. If I know Jimmy Cheal it'll have to be a large gin and not too much tonic,' and he nudged the optic with her glass three times.

'Oh come on Mr Rigg, you'll have me sloshed, I've never been sloshed before midday.'

'Well it's half-past twelve, you know. How did you come to be drinking with old Cheal so early in the day?'

'She went for a summer job, Mr Rigg, which she got of course, and Jimmy saw her there, and being the gentleman he is gave her a drink. Just as you have.'

Mr Rigg ignored most of this – he did not like being lumped in the same social bracket as Jimmy Cheal. 'Well Molly. But why work at TRICE? I'd have given you work here, you know that.'

'I couldn't work pub hours, Mr Rigg. Otherwise of course I'd have preferred to be here ... '

They chatted on and quite soon the bar began to fill up, mostly with businessmen, shopkeepers and travellers having a ploughman's and beer, a sandwich with whisky and just a splash, until soon there was quite a racket and Miriam's head began to ache. It was the smoke too, a smoky atmosphere always put her out of sorts. Two of Tess's cronies joined them, made a brief fuss of Miriam, insisted on kissing her, and then ignored her to chat with Tess. Most of the conversation was about illness and hospitals, about poor old Trev Stevens and Marge his wife, funeral at Mudwick Church Thursday, let's see that's the day after tomorrow isn't it? afternoon, well yes I am going, Marge asked me to, but usually I don't go to funerals.

Then in the mirror behind the bar Miriam saw Frank Dangerfield, sitting in a window-seat behind her eating a pork pie, with a pint of bitter at his elbow. He was leaning forward and listening – politely even intently, and Miriam shifted on her stool to see who his companion was. The pottery teacher, Mrs Rogate. And a stupid first name, yes. Pet. What was Frank Dangerfield doing with her, having lunch in a pub? She was married to Mr Rogate who had taught her one third of her A level English course – a silly opinionated wet who wore his dark hair frizzed out in an Afro and had made an awful mess of teaching selected Tennyson. In short, he deserved Pet Rogate, and Frank Dangerfield did not.

Miriam put her head on one side, tried to hear what the woman was saying. She was leaning forwards towards Mr Dangerfield, talking quietly but very quickly and intensely, smoking and blowing the smoke in his face. Miriam suddenly felt sure she was saying how misunderstood she was, how her husband didn't take her seriously, stuff like that. Her painted fingernails were chipped; there was dry clay in her hair, and she was ridiculously thin. Miriam felt a sudden wave of distaste and anxiety that quite shocked her. Now she hoped Frank would not notice her, that her mother would not notice Frank.

'Well, Moll, that's a long face. What you got to be miserable for?' She turned, feeling a lightening of her heart, to face Kevin Rammage, who had come up on her other side and was standing with both large red hands on the bar, and looking at her out of kind blue eyes set in his brick-red face with a new beard coming.

'Kev. Kev, Oh how nice to see you!' she covered his hand with hers, he pulled it back to put his arm round her shoulders in a shy, clumsy embrace.

'What are you having then, Moll?'

'Just tonic, Kev.'

'Go on have a gin in it.'

'Honest Kev, I've had far too much already.'

'Come on Moll, for old time's sake. And the top off a bottle of Guinness for Mrs Trivet.'

'Very kind of you Kevin, I won't say no.'

'There we are then.' The barmaid had drawn him a pint, he drank a third of it, wiped his moustache on the back of his hand and said, 'Well Moll, how's things then?'

'All the better for seeing you, Kev. I was just beginning to cop one. Hey, I like the beard!'

They chatted on while he had a pasty and she had a warmed through steak pie, and he had another pint. After a time she noticed he kept rubbing his eyes in the balls of his hands.

'Kev, you look exhausted.'

'Well, I was out in the boat all night, didn't get in till gone ten, and I've not been to bed yet. In fact Moll I think I'd better be off now, or I'll just fall off my stool.'

'I'll come with you for the walk. Mum's not going to move till gone chucking-out time and I've had enough. Mum, I'm going for a walk with Kev but I'll be back at three to see you home.'

'Now don't you worry about me pet, I'll be quite all right. I can get the bus back, just as I caught it down, so you please yourself and I'll see you at home.'

Followed by Kev, talking over her shoulder to him and being careful it was the shoulder furthest from Frank Dangerfield, Miriam made her way through stools and tables to the door.

'Bye Mr Rigg, thanks for the drink.'

'Bye, Molly, don't leave it so long before you come again.'

'I won't Mr Rigg, 'bye Jane.'

Even the pouty barmaid had a smile for her.

'Good God,' said Frank Dangerfield, 'that's Miriam Trivet going out, and I never spoke to her. Oh blast, what must she think of me?'

'Who is it?' Pet Rogate looked round. 'Oh yes. The Trivet girl. She was talented, wasn't she? As I was saying, it's not that he doesn't value my work Frank, he really does, almost too much I sometimes think, it's more that he doesn't really seem to connect me with it, I mean me, Pet Rogate, do you follow me or am I being silly?'

'No, no. I follow you. Clear as daylight and not silly either. Look, there's Miriam's mother, I'll have to have a word with her, and we ought really to be off if we're not to be late . . . .'

2.

Hand in hand Kev and Miriam strolled gently up the almost deserted High Street towards Trafalgar Park and the house on the far side of it where Kev had a room.

'You're still in the same place then?' Miriam asked.

'Oh yes. Yes. Same old place.'

'Well it's not a bad place.'

'No. Not really. Not bad. Landlord wants to put the rent up again. But I suppose I'll stay.'

'And the bed's still broken?'

Kevin blushed, shook his head. 'No Moll. No. I'm afraid not. I'm afraid I mended it.'

'Oh Kev,' Moll laughed and tossed her hair back. 'You said you'd never have it mended, never, not till I married you.'

'Well. It got worse. Honest Moll. The mattress was slipping down the gap between the frame and the wires. Anyway, Moll, I don't reckon really we'll be getting married now you're at College and all that.'

She squeezed his hand, touched at his kindness and tact, removing the chief cause of possible tension between them.

'No Kev. Anyway not till you learn to swim. I'm not marrying a fisherman who can't swim, keeps his boots on in the boat, and doesn't even have a life-jacket.'

'I can't bother myself with those things. I tried once but it was a real nuisance. Reckon I'd have strangled in the tapes before it saved me from drowning. It was like those jackets they put on loonies in the films and they're to stop you moving at all, aren't they ... ?'

She let him ramble on, knowing he was chatting himself away from the awkward topic he had so brusquely settled, too brusquely for him, she now realised. He hadn't been quite as ready as he had sounded to release her from a promise made three years before, through a storm of giggles, when the bed broke.

He was interrupted by a string of minor explosions, like a toy machine-gun, and an invalid carriage bumped into the curb beside them, bounced off, came in again and halted with a final backfire. The near-side rear wheel mounted the pavement leaving the carriage tipped at an alarming angle towards the middle of the road. An elderly, indeed old lady with a large beaky nose, rapped on the window and pointed with her thumb behind her. Kev knew what was wanted, went round to the back of the carriage, stooped, took a breath, heaved, and dropped the misplaced wheel on to the road.

'Thank you very much, Kevin.' The lady had now opened the sliding window and was leaning towards them. Her voice was loud but breathless, the accent and tone those of someone well-educated sixty-five years earlier. 'I won't get out you know, it makes me wheeze, but seeing you here I thought I'd have a word. Is this your young lady?'

'Er, yes. Yes. Miriam Trivet. Moll, this is Miss Barnacle.'

'How do you do? Let me see, you must be Jack Trivet's youngest gel. I knew your grandfather, he used to do my garden when times were bad and he was out of work. And your poor father, I remember, was a prisoner of war. Your grandfather used to talk about him, and we used to try to get parcels together for him, though I never knew if he received them. I've always said Brinshore is a small town, and so it still is for I don't count those awful Mudwick Estates. Well, my dear, what do you do for a living? I hope you're not relying on this poor boy for a livelihood.'

'I'm at university, Miss Barnacle. Southchester.'

'That's very good. I'm pleased to hear that. You'll know the Flavell Concert Hall there of course. That came out of my great-uncle's bequest. No credit to him – he should never have made so much money, quite a wicked thing to do and only right most of it should go to such a good cause. Your father and mother must be proud of you. Now Kevin, what's the latest news with you?'

Miriam stood back and Kevin took her place at the window.

'Well Miss Barnacle, I'm afraid there's no more news at all.'

'That's not necessarily a bad thing. It may well mean that second thoughts are after all in train. You wrote as I advised you to, did you?'

'Yes, Miss Barnacle, and like you told me I got them all to sign it.'

'Good boy. Well done. And there should be a letter in the *Post* on Thursday from me. It's the only way. Keep up the pressure, keep on nagging and once in every five times they give in.'

Old Miss Barnacle now slid her window shut, putting far more effort into it than was really necessary, and with similarly exaggerated movements turned on the ignition, pressed a starter, revved her engine in a cloud of blue smoke, let it die on her in a succession of backfires and then repeated the whole process. This time she got away, jerkily, and as she reached the middle of the road remembered to put on the indicator to show she was pulling out. Flashing thus she swerved round the opposite corner and was gone.

'What on earth was that?' asked Miriam.

'Old Miss Barnacle. You know Miss Barnacle.'

'It's the first time I've actually spoken to her. Why is she picking on you?'

'It's on account the Council want to make us put a fresh water tap where we sell off the end of our catch.'

'On the beach you mean? That would cost hundreds, wouldn't it?'

'Easy.'

'And dear Miss Barnacle is helping you resist.'

'That's it. Well, she means well. But it won't do no good. There's some law about selling fish in question, see. It don't matter a lot really. It's never more than a pound or two, the end of the catch.'

'But in a year that could be as much as four hundred pounds. And you sell it cheaper than the shops, don't you, old people get their fish off you.'

'That's right. There's five or six old biddies come regular and they couldn't buy fish at a fish shop, that's for sure. Mind, I reckon they feed most of it to their cats.'

'Good luck to them if they do.'

'Good luck to the cats.'

They walked on in silence for a while. and thus came to the end of the old town, that is the end of the first early nineteenth-century speculation. Opposite the whitewashed gates to Trafalgar House and gardens a modern block, ten storeys high, rose out of a pond of congealed tarmac, dwarfing the old timber beyond.

Kevin gestured at it.

'Joyce Copeman works there,' he said. 'You know, old Ern Copeman's daughter. Lives out at Merriedale but used to be opposite the Little George, up your way.'

'I thought she was a dental receptionist. Well, I know she was. She worked for my dentist.'

'She packed that in. She's with the Social Security now.'

'I was in the same class in the fifth year.'

'Yes. I know.'

'I couldn't stand her. Nor she me I expect.'

'That's right.'

'Kev. You've not been seeing Joyce Copeman have you?'

'Well. I'm not a monk, Moll. And there have been one or two, not just Joyce. But I always wish they were you.'

Miriam made no answer to this, felt a bit cold about it, but gave Kev's hand another squeeze to show she wasn't upset.

'Shall we go through the Traf then,' asked Kev, changing the subject.

'What, and over the wall the other side, like we used to?'

'Yeah. I still always do. No one's ever stopped me, and it's half the distance.'

They went through the big gate-posts stepping over the low iron chain fastened to prevent cars driving in. A notice advertised brass bands twice weekly in July and August and gave the prices of admissions to Pets' Corner and Playground. All were three years out of date and bore the old Brinshore U.D.C. arms instead of the Rifedale logo – a wavy line beneath a hump signifying, it was supposed, Downs and sea. Large evergreen oak trees closed over them for a short spell, then opened into wide lawns with cedars and a bandstand facing a largish regency house – square, plain, whitewashed, its only ornaments a Doric portico and a small clock tower with a cupola.

'It'll be Joyce Copeman then I have to see tomorrow,' Miriam said as they crossed the lawn. 'I've to see them, oddly enough, about my dental fees; they should give them back to me because I'm a full-time student.'

'Department of bloody Social Interference. That's what old Frank Dangerfield called them the other night.'

'Where was that then?'

'Round the Athlone. Saturday night.'

'He seems to be there a lot now. He was there just now.'

'I never saw him. Didn't he speak to you then?'

'No. Never recognised me.'

'Oh he would if he saw you. We reckoned he fancied you, remember?'

'That's silly, Kev.'

This was said sharply, and silence fell between them for a moment, but still Miriam felt she should make amends for any offence to Kev however trivial or slight.

'That Mrs Rogate was with him, so I don't expect he was ready to be bothered with the likes of us.'

'Never took much to her. She used to go all shrill and piercing when we threw clay about. Daft woman. Hey. How about a choc-ice?'

This was also part of an old pattern, neglected for over two years for they hadn't gone on long – with her A levels she hadn't given him the time he wanted. Now she didn't know quite how she felt, as he carefully rehearsed their old progress from the front to his room – part warm, part flattered, but also nervous, and even irritated. She sat on the low bough of the cedar (as she always had) and waited – the sun had gone in, she still had her headache and had just said to herself: 'No, this won't do. This is not really on,' when he reappeared, face moody and frowning, head shaking slowly as it used to do when they quarrelled.

'What's the matter?'

'They're bloody shut. That's all. All boarded up. I reckon they don't open no more except weekends.'

'Oh well. We can sit here for a moment. I still feel tired, and you must be exhausted.'

He shrugged heavily but sat beside her, big hands loose between his corduroy trousered legs. There was a clumsy patch on one knee that bothered her quite sharply – for a time she had done his mending and she was neat, meticulous with a needle. He continued to frown and shake his head, then flapped a hand at Trafalgar House. From this close they could see where the whitewash was flaking, how its windows too had been boarded up.

'And they're going to knock that down,' he said, 'along with everything that's half good in the town. Say it's no use for anything and cost of upkeep, and that. They even say it's dangerous. How can an old boarded-up house be a danger?'

Miriam knew all about this – inquiries, petitions, committees, Friends of Trafalgar House (Hon. Treasurer, Miss Hilary Barnacle), had been a continuing feature of Brinshore life for many months. But she said nothing, let him go on. She was used now to being treated as someone who had been away for years, though her university terms were never more than ten weeks and she came back for occasional weekends. Still, she was moved at his concern, passion even; wondered if it was to do with the fact that his home life had been a broken and troubled one – which was one reason why no one objected when he left school at sixteen, took a room on his own, and his uncle's boat. His uncle had drowned – he hadn't been able to swim either, always kept his boots on at sea, and took no life-jacket. Perhaps Brinshore was Kevin's family, and he hated to see it go for that reason. Though, she reflected, her father felt as strongly on the subject, but said less. Well, it upset her too. Particularly it upset her when Chine Street went, more than she ever let on, for her mother's sake. Tess had nearly had a nervous breakdown – heartbreak was the old name for the complaint – and Miriam had hidden her own feelings.

Presently Kev stood up and took her hand, and they moved into the woods behind the house. They passed round a small pond with a large rockery at the back of it planted out with exotics, some of them subtropical. Frogs plopped off giant lily pads and dragonflies flitted sideways. A donkey eeyored over to their left and Miriam recalled the little monkeys with sores, the parrots that were always in moult, and a llama, ignored by the two goats and a shetland pony it shared a paddock with, utterly wretched in its loneliness.

Twice they crossed the track of a miniature railway and both times Kev took elaborate precautions to ensure Miriam would not be knocked down by passing trains.

'That train used to run along the pier,' Kevin said. It was what he always said.

An hour or so later Miriam stood in front of Johnny Manet's window and looked at Frank's paintings. The one of the shelter and the Leisure Centre was the one that took the eye with its arseholes, bastards, fucking cunts and pricks, but after five minutes or so she preferred the one of the pier. The mutilated structure was more telling, a torso without head or limbs, but the memory supplied them. But would it if you weren't familiar with what it had once been?

It had not been a problem getting away from Kevin's. She wasn't too sure what had happened – perhaps he had sensed her reaction on coming into a room that even after two years should have been familiar to her. But it had not felt familiar. It was more scuffed and dusty than it had been, the furniture looked older and shoddier than she remembered. There was a pull-out from *Penthouse* over the foot of the bed, and a dark hair (Joyce Copeman's?) in the soap-dish of the sink. A postcard of Millais' *The Reapers* which Miriam had given him was still stuck in the frame of the tarnished mirror, but the corners were cracked and curling.

For a moment they had sat on the edge of the bed. Then, 'I'm getting in,' Kev had said.

'OK.'

'I have to be up again tonight.'

'Do you?'

'Yes. I bloody do.'

'You don't ... '

'I don't have to swear. But the ten or twelve quid I'll make tonight, if some rotten bastard hasn't stolen me trot line or nicked the little ones out of me pots, I can't do without.'

'All right, Kev. I understand.'

'Do you?'

'Well, I try.'

'I have to pay insurance now. Self-employed. And back payments on the years I didn't know I was meant to. And the engine needs an overhaul.'

'All right, I do understand. Really.'

While this had been going on he had stripped down to his underpants baring a body white as it had always been, rather unhealthy looking in contrast to his face and hands – and now he pushed yellowish feet between the sheets. The frame, in spite of his repairs, creaked.

For some time she had sat there, trying to tell from his breathing whether he was really asleep or not, then had squeezed his hand, felt no pressure in return, and so let herself out.

Now she stood in front of Frank's paintings feeling for her unusually indecisive. The day had turned cloudy, even chill, there seemed to be nothing attractive in view, nothing she particularly wanted to do. She knew she ought to go home, help her mother prepare the second half of the sole, but it was already half-past four, her father would be up before she got back, the atmosphere would be sour – perhaps worse if her mother had had too many.

Then again – there was nowhere else to go.

In the foreground of Frank's painting of the pier were the four fishing boats and the tiny hut where gear worth stealing was stored and where the end of the catch was sold off. The boats were numbered, black on a white square and Kevin's – LS33 – was there. LS for Langley-by-Sea, the nearest place that could claim to be a port. She wondered if Kevin knew it was there, if he would be interested.

Miriam. Miriam Trivet. Come on in and have a cup of tea. You look as if you need it.'

In the doorway of the shop stood Johnny Manet, and Miriam again felt her heart lift.

'Why not, Johnny?' she said.

'Why not indeed. It's just brewed, soon find you another cup.'

She followed him through the shop – artists' materials, prints, framing samples and small articles of pottery, fancy work, knick-knacks, classier than the souvenir shops, much more expensive, and really no nicer. At the back was a small well-lit office, furnished in stainless steel with a pillar-box red filing cabinet and a pillar-box red typewriter. An artists' supplier's calendar featuring classic but erotic nudes (June was a Bonnard – gold flesh dappled with lemon yellow, rosy nipples, greens and violets in the shadows) hung on the back of the door.

Manet found a smoked glass cup and put it on the tray with the one already there and filled them from a transparent teapot. He was about forty, had long sandy hair, but was running to fat, a fact he tried to hide behind a loose machine-embroidered jerkin with wide sleeves and no waist. Below he wore bottle-green jeans and rope-soled shoes.

'So Miriam,' he began after he had sipped his tea, 'what are you up to these days?'

She explained.

'But why not work here? My shop is yours, you know that. Why work for a capitalist pig like Jimmy Cheal – hasn't he enough of the good things of life already, without you adding beauty, grace and charm to his hideous factory?'

'Come on Johnny – you'd pay me half what I'll get at TRICE, and for longer hours.'

He shrugged: 'When times are slack you could paint those lovely flower pictures you do, and make pictures out of pressed flowers again. Both sold well. I'll commission you – fifty per cent asking price and I'll frame them out of my share; it'll be a commission, no need to talk about sale or return, they'll all sell. I'll take ten a week all summer, for five pounds minimum I'll sell them, so that guarantees you twenty-five pounds a week – with ten more for helping at busy times in the shop. Will Jimmy Cheal give you thirty-five a week?'

'Yes.'

'But work in a factory? No one does that unless they have to.'

'It's not in the factory, it's in the offices. There are people there I know, I'll enjoy it.' She realised now he was serious, making an offer, and this embarrassed her.

He sensed this, changed the subject.

'So. You were looking at Frank Dangerfield's pictures. Which did you prefer?'

'The one of the pier.'

'So do I. And I think I might sell it. Trouble is, the buyer wants one of the pier as it used to be to go with it. But if I ask Frank to do one, what will happen? A very rude answer.'

'But it's not necessary. You can almost feel the old pier in Mr Dangerfield's picture.'

'That's what I told my client. But she won't listen. The thing is, Frank did the pier as it was, back in '55, he was only fifteen, but he did a really nice job on it – somewhere between Monet and pointillism, very nice. Frank says a vicar in Yorkshire has it, sold it through his sister who was working there at the time.'

'I never knew Mr Dangerfield was in Brinshore all those years ago.'

'No? Well, it's an interesting story. His father was

R.N.V.R., Royal Naval Volunteer Reserve to you, and was in charge of the gun on the end of the pier. Did you know that? There was a gun on the end of the pier. Well Frank was born about then, and his father liked the place and came back to live here from, I think 1947 to 1958, then they moved. And that's why Frank came back here too. He liked the place.'

'He must be mad.'

'Well. It's not the place it was.'

'That's true.'

They drank Earl Grey.

'Could Mr Dangerfield make it as an artist?' Miriam asked, more for want of something to say than anything else.

'You mean as a straight easel-painter? Lord, no. No way. It's not that sort of ball-game any more. Apart from anything else he's been out in the sticks too long. Oh, he'll make a few quid each year, and would make more if he sold his water-colour sketches – they're a bit Turnerish, you know? – but he has some silly fetish about not passing off unfinished stuff. But never more than a few quid. And he has a wife and kids to support, you know? And the wife is bad news, I can tell you, very bad news.'

Miriam felt irritated. She didn't want to hear about Frank's wife. She finished her tea.

'Well, Johnny, I must ... '

'But I have ... '

'Mr Manet, Miss Barnacle-Flavell is here to see you.'

These last three came almost together, the third from the assistant in the shop below.

'Goddamn,' said Johnny, 'I'm afraid I'll have to see Miss Barnacle. She expects it. No, don't go yet, just let me see to Miss Barnacle. Do you know her?'

'Yes ... '

'Everybody knows her. But you don't want to see her, so just wait here, till I'm through with her. I won't keep you long after that, I promise you.'

Johnny Manet padded out and Miriam heard him welcome Miss Barnacle and heard her wheezing, breathless replies, then their voices became indistinct as they moved into the front of the shop. She sipped her tea, found it a refreshing relief.

On the desk was an illustrated catalogue: The Fine Art-Ware and Reproduction Co., she read. Wholesale only. It was open at a page illustrating wall plaques. *These metal plaques meticulously finished in copper-style satin finish with gilt trim are each embossed with reliefs derived from the finest achievements of our European heritage, and chosen for our unique collection by acknowledged art experts.* Van Gogh's Sunflowers; a Modigliani Nude; a Raphael Madonna. Miriam turned a page or two. *Now everyone can enjoy the vibrant colours only the Great Masters knew how to mix, enhanced to their original splendour or even beyond, by the miracle of new XL photo-reproductive techniques and new metal-lustre inks.* Renoir this time – a fat nude that literally shimmered from the additives in the colours. She turned again. *Be the first supplier in your town to cash in on the more relaxed attitudes prevalent today – accurate and finely detailed reproductions in simulated marble or bronze of the classical sculptures the museums never dared to show . . . .*

'Well, for once she was pleased,' said Johnny as he came back in. 'Just a framing job, but she let me choose the frame, so she liked the result. Do you know she once bought five of your pressed flower pictures? She still asks me if I can find some more like them – says she'll use them for Christmas presents – so you see what I mean, I can sell them.'

He sat down behind the small desk, reached for his cup and found it was empty.

'Shall I brew up some more?'

'No Johnny, no thanks. I must be off.'

'Well, if you must ... Hullo, been looking at the catalogue? Those are rather fun, aren't they? Here, let me show you.'

He pulled open a filing cabinet drawer and pulled out a small statuette made in white plastic with an oily finish. It represented two naked wrestlers, one held upside down by the other, both gripping each other's penises.

'A laugh really, aren't they? Do you think I can get away with them in Brinshore? Why not, eh? Have you seen the seaside postcards they do now? *Far* worse than they used to be, and no one objects to them.'

Miriam got away as soon as she could.

3.

When she got back she found her father sullen, and her mother wretched and angry. She had woken him too late, and burnt the fish by leaving it in a covered frying-pan while she tried to tell him, her speech a little slurred, about what had happened during the day. Jack found most of this bad news, as Johnny Manet might have said. He did not feel quite comfortable at the thought that Miriam would be starting at TRICE next week, and he wasn't pleased to hear she had been hobnobbing with Jimmy Cheal. Tess had told him too that Miriam had left the Athlone with Kevin Rammage and had not been seen since. He liked Kevin well enough but he felt sure that in the nature of things she went to bed with the lad, and therefore worse might follow. Finally he was annoyed she had arrived late for dinner – normally it didn't signify, but when there was fish he had caught ...

After he had gone Tess was apologetic, wanted to make amends. 'We'll stay in tonight,' she said, 'you have your work to do, and later there's a film called "Will Shakespeare"; I expect you'll want to see that.'

Miriam turned from the window where they had been waving to Jack and glanced down to the low glass-topped table where the *TV Times* lay. A wet-looking man in red doublet and white lace flexed a stagy-looking foil; from beneath a mop of carefully frizzled, boyishly untidy hair his eyes glowed with the sort of blank penetration that advertisers use to suggest passionate fun, a come-on. *The Playboy who became the world's greatest writer,* she read, and THE SHATTERING OF AN IMAGE.

Drums, solemn march music – much brass, woodwind, modulating to atmosphere music, overlaid now by a rhubarb chatter in stage cockney, knocking and shouts of 'Will, Will Shakespeare, Shake Who? I'll shake you my fine caterwauler, go on be off with you.'

Major creative writers, Miriam read from the book on her knee, *are concerned with a necessary kind of thought ... The thought in question is antithetically remote from mathematics; it involves a consciousness of one's full human responsibility, purpose, and the whole range of human valuations.*

'Aren't you going to watch this?' her mother asked.

'May be,' she replied, but did not look up. Tess raised an eyebrow but said nothing more. She knew Miriam had to read a lot of Shakespeare at Southchester, had read a lot at school, in fact had bought the complete works with sixteenth birthday money; but she had always had a mind of her own, it had never been any use arguing.

A man from Stratford was searching for Will. Found him. Shakespeare said: 'How fares my family', and referred to his wife as a she-dragon, looked sad to hear that his little son Hamnet was missing his father, called for the barmaid: 'Kate, my pretty Kate.'

'This is pretty awful stuff, Mum,' said Miriam.

Tess leaned forward, back very straight, hands on the wooden arms of her chair, a cigarette in the left, a glass of Guinness in the right. 'I think it's rather good,' she said.

Miriam tried to get back into her book but the dense argument, the thick texture of the sentences, the hard, bright, well-wrought structure she knew it to be dissolved, in the presence of the telly, into slowly swirling mud. Her attention drifted willy-nilly to the box. A courtier was talking to an older man whose appearance signalled 'statesman'. They were not discussing Shakespeare now but Marlowe and the scene flashed back to an earlier conversation between Marlowe and the courtier. Marlowe said: 'He had the right to sell his soul if he got a fair price for it.' The courtier scoffed: 'What did he get for it? The lascivious mouth of Helen of Troy. I could do as well with Joan my serving wench and still live in hope of salvation.'

'He got the only two commodities worth striving for,' Marlowe answered. 'Freedom to inquire and knowledge to reward the inquirer.'

Commodities, thought Miriam. *Commodities?* Now Jove in his next commodity of hair, send thee a beard.

'Who wrote this stuff?' she asked.

'It's in the paper,' said Tess, without looking away from the picture.

Miriam looked at the *TV Times* cover again. *John Mortimer Writes,* it said. THE SHATTERING OF AN IMAGE. Well, she thought, but *whose* image?

'Knowledge is power,' said the courtier, now back with the statesman. 'As Secretary of Her Majesty's Secret Intelligence, wouldn't you agree with him, uncle? Knowledge gives us power, isn't that so?'

The old man rumbled back impressively in a C. P. Snow voice: 'In a long life I have found it so.'

In disgust Miriam returned to her book, but the last line had been a curtain lowerer. A bright girlish voice chirped in its place: 'There's a really delicious new orange drink I want to tell you about. New Bird's Appeal. Remember the name. New Bird's Appeal. Mmmm. It's like freshly squeezed oranges. So this morning I didn't need my orange squeezer. Watch.' Then a bright young man's voice: 'Hey – it *does* taste like freshly squeezed oranges. It's *really* great.'

We must cultivate a more adequate notion of thought, Miriam read, *and that means cultivating the practice. There must be practised thinking that brings in consciously, with pertinacious and delicate resource, the un-Cartesian reality underlying language and implicit in it; what is inexpressible in terms of logic and clarity, the unstatable, must not be excluded from thought. This ... is the importance of creative literature.*

Meanwhile Marlowe was recruited to the secret intelligence of our great Protestant Queen; King Philip, a spider in a closet, sent *his* spies to swarm in every priest's hole and confessional in England (a confused metaphor, for spiders *attract* flies, they don't send them out, thought Miriam), and young Will joined the players as a cock-crowing extra in *Doctor Faustus* and met Marlowe, to whom he said: ' "Bring me my coach, my chair, my jewels" – that's a fine death line for the Queen in *Tamburlaine.*' 'Oh, I'm glad something meets with your approval,' said Marlowe. 'Well, I was moved when I read it. It had some *truth.*' The actor/manager intervened:

'We have so much gunpowder left over, what d'ye say to a chronicle-historical, I've got it! The wars of York and Lancaster. I shall play that saintly monarch, Harry the Sixth ... ' and faded out on solemn music suggesting an inspirational moment.

Miriam again attempted to read, then gave up for a time. Marlowe spied, and then was locked up to finish Henry the Sixth. Shakespeare unlocked the door and went in, looked over Marlowe's shoulder. Marlowe said: 'The scene is Temple Gardens. The barons are quarrelling. Before they pluck roses they ask Lord Warwick to choose between them.' Shakespeare said: 'Lord Warwick? He's speaking the part of my own county.' Marlowe said: 'What luck! You can help me.' Shakespeare took over. Mystic music. Temple Garden scene played with misty edges. Cheers. Voice over: 'You've leapt from the barnyard to Parnassus in one jump, ambitious rooster.'

A rooster *leaps?* wondered Miriam.

'New Kellogg's Rise and Shine now tastes as good as orange juice . . . .'

Then Steed in a helicopter.

'He used to be in that programme,' said Tess.

'The Avengers.'

'That's right.'

Cars raced about beneath the helicopter.

'That's Milbrook proving ground,' said Steed, 'and if you're a Vauxhall car it's hell down there, especially in weather like this. Just look at that Scimitar. Its sheer enthusiasm sees it through. The Viva can't resist a challenge, still bouncing back for more, the Cavalier revels in tight corners, and that Cavalier Coupé must be doing over a hundred, no problem. And it's no problem for you to see your Vauxhall dealer, put a Vauxhall to the test,' and the helicopter soared away.

Miriam realised that her attention had been really held by the energy, however frenetic, of all this, and reflected ruefully. She went out into the kitchen, spread spread on bread and poured a glass of milk. When she came back Tess had started on her second bottle of Guinness, and Marlowe was instructing Shakespeare to write a scene in which a father unwittingly kills his son, having first ascertained that Shakespeare loved his own son. Then Marlowe's murder, done nastily (sick naturalism intended to suggest *real* life), was cut into actors playing the scene: moral or message – Shakespeare knew about life when he wrote. Shakespeare said to the landlady or bawd: 'He led the way and we followed like sheep. Well, he's dead. He is the dead shepherd.' Marlowe's voice over: 'I'm dying? We're all dying, some quicker than others.'

'Well, that's true,' said Tess.

Miriam read: *'Modern English' represents drastic impoverishment; the assumptions implicit in it eliminate from thought, and from the valuations and tested judgements that play so essential a part in thought, very important elements of human experience – elements that linguistic continuity had once made available. Actually up to the present (let us hope it may still be said) a richer continuity has been maintained than 'modern English' gives us. It has been maintained (and to maintain a language is to develop it) because we have so long and so rich a literary tradition. I mean by tradition something living – it exists in a public that lives with it ...*

And 'The Dead Shepherd' came to an end with the return of the Stratford yokel, who, when the playboy asserted he was now a playwright, said: 'Oh William Shakespeare, what terrible lies you do tell.'

Miriam said: 'I'm going to bed.'

'I'll just finish this,' said Tess, meaning her third Guinness, 'and watch the news. It wasn't very good after all.'

'No.'

'I thought the bit about the Catholics was silly. Cheap.'

'So did I. And not only the bit about Catholics.'

In bed she put Leavis aside deciding he would have to be read closely and noted. She picked up *Little Dorrit.* Merdle cut his throat and Physician went to the baths. *Where he was, something real was,* Miriam read, *and a half grain of reality, like the smallest portion of some other scarce natural productions, will flavour an enormous quantity of diluent.* Her mind wandered back over the day. Kevin now in his boat with his boots on; Kevin in his bed exhausted and a black hair in his wash basin. Frank Dangerfield with Mrs Rogate, his paintings in Johnny Manet's window; and she wondered if Miss Barnacle had kept any of her pressed flower pictures. The frightful rubbish in Johnny Manet's shop, and the awful catalogue. A half grain of reality will flavour an enormous quantity of diluent, Miriam thought, but it's an awful ocean of diluent we're floundering in.

Soon she slept.

V
WEDNESDAY
Day of Social Interference

O7.22

FRANK padded about his shabby flat, the brown lino chilly to his large bare feet, clutching round him a flannel dressing-gown which was too short and exposed his blue-veined calves. It had been a bad night and it was a lousy morning – the night plagued with dreams of his two daughters, wide-eyed and accusatory, and of course three years younger than they now were, for in his dreams they kept the age they were before his life with their impossible mother became intolerable; the morning dull and chill with low cloud and raw moisture off a sea grey and flat, nudging at the base of the shingle, but listlessly like an old old woman faced with three steps that she'd really rather not climb.

He turned from the sash-window and punched the button of his trannie which was on a low bookcase above his Phaidons and Thames and Hudsons, and padded back to the kitchen, down two steps, and filled a greasy kettle over the stained glazed sink and set it on a misplaced gas-ring over uneven jets of flame. *My Beloved Spake* sang soloists and chorus on Radio Three, and Frank, who never could understand what all the fuss about Purcell was based on, padded back up into the living-room, stabbed the trannie into silence and drifted back to the window.

A level art today, he remembered. Unprepared Project Design. Seven-hour paper; candidates may bring in packed lunches. A choice of three subjects, inventiveness and interpretation rewarded as well as technical proficiency. Candidates may choose any appropriate media, but work submitted will be in pictorial form, though may include sketches of three-dimensional objects, blah, blah, blah. What a load of cod.

He had six candidates and would be shut up all day with them. Not a bad day really. He could take a book. But there would be no opportunity to chat up Pet Rogate – not that is unless her third years played up to such an extent that he would *have* to go in and sort them out. He thought about her. They would have an affair. The first three or four times at least would be fun – she so small and thin, bird-like, he would try to get her to go on top, bring herself off on him, if he held out long enough ...

The kettle whistled and he moved away from the window and the grey sea – just as well, I would have been wanking in no time following that train of thought, and why not, though better not standing in a window overlooking the prom and the shingle, surprising how many there are about as early as this even on a dull morning.

He sat in his kitchen chair and masturbated, legs wide, coarse dressing-gown falling away on either side of him and was surprised at how soon he came and how much there was, catching it in a Kleenex; then moving more slowly, more languidly, certainly a shade more cheerfully, drank tea too sweet and ate bread layered with butter and marmalade so thick that a gobbet slid off and landed on his thigh. Tremors of disgust stirred in him, but he suppressed them ruthlessly – he wasn't going to let residual feelings of bourgeois guilt spoil his efforts at improving the shining hour, no way.

After breakfast he stripped off the dressing-gown – he slept naked in summer, wore an old shirt in winter – and sponged himself down at the kitchen-sink with the geyser roaring and filling the air with half-burnt fumes, pleased he could bend and stretch with so little effort and affectionate towards his cock, now snugly detumescent. He padded, leaving wet footprints on the lino, first to the lavatory and then back to the front room where he dressed slowly while *Goddess, Goddess, e-e-e-excellently bright* was sung by Peter Pears from the trannie and Barry Tuckwell's French horn hallooed in pursuit through the forests of the night; Goddess excellently bright Frank warbled as he stamped downstairs to the outside front door and picked up off the mat three letters which he took back up to his kitchen table.

Inland Revenue.

'With reference to your tax return filed with us on the first of this month we note that you have declared no income from sales of paintings etc. in the year ended 5th April last, although our records show that in the three years preceding you declared income from this source. With regard to what may be an oversight on your part we enclose a further Tax Return for your completion and draw your attention to paragraph eleven, page two of the Tax Return guide, headed Subsidiary Earnings and paragraph forty-five' blah, blah, blah.

Dentist.

'We remind you that you have an appointment for your twice yearly check-up on Tuesday 28th June at 4.15 … '

And the third was a real shocker.

'In the County of Southset Petty Sessional Division of Rifedale, COMPLAINT has this day been made to me by the Rifedale District Council that you being a person duly rated and assessed in respect of the rates set forth below have not paid the whole of the said sum. You are therefore hereby summoned to appear on Wednesday the 21st June at 10.30 o'clock …

TOTAL AMOUNT TO BE PAID £174.70

The BITCH, Frank swore, the FUCKING BITCH. She gets two-thirds of my salary and now this. The FUCKING BITCH.

He sat at his deal table, head in palms, elbows on the table, and with his free hands stirred the papers about. Only a week's notice because the bitch had been sitting on it for two weeks before forwarding it to him. But I haven't got one hundred and seventy-four pounds, he thought. I haven't got it. Then he swept the lot to the floor and spoke aloud: 'This', he said, 'is the Day of the Department of Social Interference. This is Social Interference Day.'

08.47

Mrs Lucie Shiner sat at her desk in the social workers' office in what had once been Brinshore Town Hall, and planned her day's calls, using the system of priorities the department had devised to make the best use of her time. She found she had two CIII(PI)s out at Merriedale, the kids who had set fire to The Club – not children at risk but they got a high rating because they had the suffix PI, police intervention, so something had to be done soon. She then leafed through her card-index, and found a CIV in the very same road. 'Well, that is convenient,' she thought brightly. Mrs Lucie Shiner was always bright, indeed had been noted for it on Open University summer-schools. Baby left out in its pram all night, unconfirmed. With confirmation the case would have got a CI rating. And now, didn't she have an EV out that way? Yes here we are, that Miss Barnacle-Flavell and her invalid tricycle. Not a high priority but time it was sorted out before the old bag – dear old soul, I mean – killed someone with it.

Cheerfully Mrs Shiner checked off reference numbers and found the right files, cheerfully she patted her immaculate bun and smoothed her immaculate skirt. Cheerfully she waved a goodbye to her colleagues and went out to her sparkling Mini in the car-park. Mrs Shiner loved her work – service was the name of the game, controlled, rationalised service, meeting lovely people and helping them sort out the nasty little wrinkles that get into even the best run lives.

09.02

As Mrs Shiner left Brinshore Old Town Hall, Ern Copeman arrived in his office in Rifedale District Council and set about completing two campaigns of interference of a more personal nature. In his tray were papers giving notice of two meetings. He skimmed through them.

REDEVELOPMENT OF BRINSHORE FRONT
Second Stage – Steering Group
Meeting at 11.15, 14th June, Room 216
AGENDA:

1. Access to Leisure Centre Site
2. Referral of Athlone Hotel scheme

The fact that the steering group was to rubber-stamp the referral, *sine die,* of the Athlone Hotel scheme was a measure of how far he had been successful. It had been a long business, ever since, in January, Town Planning had put out a confidential outline that would involve the demolition of the hotel following compulsory purchase. Working stealthily, using his knowledge of how contracts had been awarded for the Leisure Centre, playing on a retired colleague's susceptibility over the development of Merriedale many years ago, and even letting it be known just what Mr Rigg's relations with the police had been when Mr Rigg was a big man in Brinshore; in these and other ways he had persuaded enough people that Planning's outline was not after all in the best interests of the rate-payers. A quick show of hands was all that would be needed this morning and the Athlone would be saved. Ern felt warm at the thought of this, decided that a carefully worded press release was in order, realised that it would probably make the weekend edition of the Brinshore Post.

He turned to the second sheet.

BRINSHORE FISHERMEN: WORKING PARTY
Meeting at 3.15, 14th June, Room 216

AGENDA:

1. Consideration of Councillor Mrs Liza Cheal's proposal made in committee on 7th June last. (See attached copy of relevant minute)

This would be easy, thought Ern. Jimmy Cheal's sister-in-law had a lot of pull. At least two of his colleagues would be glad to please her by giving council policy a nudge over a matter as minor as fresh water facility; all he had to do was point out to them where their real interest lay.

Thus and in many similar ways Ern turned the non-job that had been left to him after the Local Government Act into an interesting and stimulating game. And he was useful, he felt sure, a mole in the corridors of power, discreetly influencing decisions in the real interests of the people.

09.18

Poor Linda Rose couldn't settle to anything that morning, no way. She slopped about her lovely bungalow in her house-coat, more a wrap-around really, floral satin it was, a cigarette between her long fingers, and her lovely hair loose about her shoulders, and, to tell you the truth, just a touch greasy. She wasn't dressed because dear Timothy had taken the kids to school – she had told him that she still couldn't face the other mums, not after the way Rose had treated her on Monday. The thing now, she thought to herself, was not so much *where* to begin, as whether it was worth beginning at all – I mean what's the point of it all, she thought, what *is* the point, looking at the saucepans in the sink and the plates and glasses, greasy too, smeared, splashed with milk-shake, much of it all covered with a fine film of burnt toast dust where Timothy, dear Timothy had scraped away without looking where he scraped. Sodding toaster on the blink, he'd said. Really she just could not get up the energy to empty the TRICE and refill it with this lot, she really couldn't, I mean, when all's said and done, what *is* the point?

The radio offered some help, an answer even. Have you noticed how often things work out like that, I mean like now for instance, how just when Linda was asking herself *what's it all for,* it just happens there's an answer on Radio Two? You've got to admit there's more to it all than we let ourselves acknowledge, when you come down to it, when you really bother to notice things like that. Anyway, here is what Linda heard on the radio at just that moment in time.

'... the centre from um in the end ... is only ... er, brings unhappiness, and um there is SO much evidence for this, the spoilt CHILD who wants it all his own way and ends up TOTALLY unhappy to people who are adults who just really THINK of THEMSELVES and what they can get and their world centres around themselves it's CLEARLY, it leads from this to er unhappiness so I think we just try and explain that the real sense of fulfilment and even happiness in a long-term sense comes from GIVING and SHARING and we're right back to Christian love, aren't we?'

But poor Linda was just not open to this sort of suggestion at that point in time, and as the music came, sort of zithers and guitars punctuated by tinkly bells, she not only moved away from the trannie but told the gentleman who had been speaking to sod off.

She drifted down the passage and into her boys', her lovely boys, her boys' room. The bedclothes were all everywhere, toys, books (not many), pieces of grey plastic from put-it-together-yourself kits, dirty clothes, and God knows what else, *everywhere.* Linda stood in the doorway and smoked and ash trickled off her cigarette in a little wormy shower and she didn't really notice. What she did notice was the corner of a poster flapping down, its bit of Blu-tack still adhering, and without thinking she moved in to put it up. Something crunched beneath her feet – black plastic, either Dorian's Instamatic or the joke camera that squirts and belongs to young Mark, I'm not going to see which, she thought – and she pushed the corner up and pressed the Blu-tack to the wall.

War Planes of Word War II – The Luftwaffe

This room stinks. It actually stinks. But I'm not going to sort it out. I've told them I won't. I'll do the washing and the ironing, right enough, but they can sort it out. There's got to be a start made somewhere, and with her finger she traced over the insignia on a Heinkel's tail and murmured: 'Ossie White is right. I mean a start has got to be made somewhere, that stands to reason,' and she wondered if she had the nerve to go round to his house and tell him so, offer herself to the Movement.

Back in the kitchen the radio posed a different question in whining contralto: *If I were a flower, blooming in a bower, would you take my loveliness, enjoy it for an hour? Would you keep me for the day, keep me safe from sorrow? I'll give you all my loveliness, if you give me your tomorrow.* I'll give you *anything,* if you give me your tomorrow, thought Linda, her mind still on Ossie, and she shuddered.

A piano tinkled away into silence then the rich, warm, lovable, Irish voice came through, speaking you'd think to Linda and no one else in the world at all: *Desist woman, it's well you know I'm promised to another. It's twenty-five minutes past nine and here's a letter from George ... a mention for my lovely wife Shirley, it's our ivory anniversary, our fourteenth, ah, ah, you and Shirley, fourteen years together and nary a cross word, give her quite a lift if you could give her a mention and wish her all my love, for fourteen years of love she's given me, and the two sons she's presented me with, Richard now ten and Jason who's eight ...* '

And Linda turned away from the rich, warm, lovable, Irish voice thinking *she'd* been presented with two boys, Dorian aged twelve and Mark aged ten, and if she could present them to anyone else, anyone else at all, at this moment in time, that would be fine with her, just fine.

The chimes – bing-boing, bing-boing – and she went to answer them. Perhaps it's a randy milkman, she thought. But on the step was a little lady with slanty specs and her hair in a bun, and busybody written all over her.

'Mrs Rose? Hullo. I'm Lucie. Lucie Shiner, from the Department. May I come in?'

'It's to do with Sunday, isn't it? With what happened on Sunday. At The Club.'

Mrs Shiner looked at her clip-board, and glanced up with a lovely smile.

'Yes it is, Mrs Rose. But you'll soon see there's nothing to worry about. May I come in?'

'I'm not worried,' and Linda led her into the dining recess, and sat her at the table – a large one, crimson-stained beech, modern design. Let her see the Constables and the Breughels in their gilt frames, the classy Japanese music centre, the coloured glass vases and ornaments, let her see we're Middle Class, she thought.

And really she needn't have worried, for although Mrs Shiner was a pert little thing who gave quick little glances at everything, mentally ran a finger along the bookshelf (six volumes from the Arts Guild Book Club) looking for dust, and would, Linda thought, know this place again, so inquisitive was she, she had, after all, come with quite good news.

'You see Mrs Rose, what's really important, what really matters is to find out just why Dorian and Mark started this fire. And we believe we'll get to the root of that by making as little fuss as possible. In our experience the more the kiddies are frightened out of their wits, the more they'll sort of clam up. I mean this *is* what we find.'

And Linda nodded, wondering what was coming next, and what was coming next was this – would Mrs Rose be willing to take her kiddies along to the Child Psychotherapy Centre to see Dr Naylor-Prim, and let him have a word or two with them? He was a lovely man, so kind and gentle, and once the police and the court had seen his report, that would probably be it, especially if Mr and Mrs Rose consented to follow whatever course of treatment he recommended.

'Treatment?' said Linda, suddenly alarmed. 'You're saying my boys are ill, aren't you?'

'Oh Mrs Rose, I'm not saying anything of the sort. How could I? I haven't even seen them ... '

But you've seen their mad mother, and that's enough, thought Linda grimly.

' ... but no, I'm sure they're not *ill.* Not *ill.* Anyway Dr Naylor-Prim will know what's wrong I'm sure ... Now let me see, he can fit in an appointment on Friday at three-thirty, if you collect them from school, Mr Harte does know the appointment is being made, yes, he'd like you to go along too ... '

'And if we do this that really may be the end of the matter?'

'Oh yes, that really is quite likely.'

'That would be a relief. Yes it would.'

'I'm sure it would. These little crises seem so awful at the time don't they? But they blow over you know, you'll all be laughing at it in six months I dare say. I can say then you'll go?'

'They say there was fifty thousand pounds' worth of damage.'

'Do they really? Dear me what they do get up to, don't they?'

And Linda showed her to the door. As she shut it and turned back to the kitchen, feeling all tense and nervy again and wondering if she should have another Librium, her ear tuned back to the radio and the rich, warm, lovable Irish voice which was actually saying, at that point in time: *Ah pull yourself together woman, for goodness' sake, things could be worse, couldn't they? It's five minutes to ten o'clock, time for one more record and what better way to go than with the hit-song from* Evita?

Linda looked out over the lawn with its broken doll's pram and rusting climbing-frame to the brick wall, bushes, featureless grey sky beyond, lit another cigarette and inhaled very deeply, enjoying the momentary dizziness and nausea.

The strong soprano sang and Linda stood a little taller, held her chin up.

The song lifted itself to its familiar climax. Linda put down her cigarette, pushed her hair back and up behind her ears.

Her eyes glistened, she looked very brave . . . .

Don't Cry for me Argentina

10.08

Noises, varied and all faint, but contrasted by distance: nearest at hand gentle breathing, occasional sighs and sniffs, the rustle of paper, the susurration of an eraser and the whispering sweep of a hand brushing rubber crumbs to the floor, the louder squeak and knock of a chair-leg pushed back or pulled in; in the distance girls on the playing-field shrill and clear; nearer occasional cars and a lorry; and nearer still but still distant Pet Rogate's voice also clear and shrill like an offstage Bach trumpet above the rumble of Three N next door. Frank sat on his desk, head in the air and cocked on one side, foot swinging, and listened.

He wondered – shall I get down and have a look around, see what they're up to, whisper encouragement and so on? No. They've hardly had an hour, indeed one boy and one girl have only just really settled in to anything, keep as quiet as I can now and let them get on with it. That bloody summons. Nearly six hours to go, concentration will be a problem later, let them keep at it as undisturbed as possible while they're still fresh.

He glanced down again at the question paper though he had already read it often enough to know it by heart. Choose one. Design a sculpture for your school playground; design a t-shirt suitable for the town or village where you live; design a package suitable for a new brand of chocolates. A brief written outline may be appended to describe materials, method and dimensions where these are not clearly implied in the finished drawings. Not bad really, Frank thought. A little dull, but fair. Well, the customers seem quite happy now, after a shaky start. He looked down the studio at six heads (four girls, two boys, one blonde, one red-head, two darkish brunettes, two pretty, two plain – and two male) bent over cartridge paper and drawing-boards.

Steve would probably come up with something interesting and Barbara too (Babs they called her, poor girl); plump Di would be doing the chocolate box and something with flowers no doubt, oh well, she was competent – I really must not go nosing amongst them, must let them get on with it. 10.09½, God this is going to be a long day, and he crossed his legs the other way. I suppose I shall have to ask for the morning off, that's going to be fun, please sir, I've been summonsed ...

He made himself think about candidates from previous years. Miriam Trivet. She did a lovely entry. A record cover for a new group had been her choice; a dangerous question he had thought, too many precedents to choose between, too many blind-alleys to get stuck in. But she had taken the question head on, called her fictional group The New and done a sketch of about a hundred eggs, harshly lit, almost monochrome but with hints of colour, the eggs laid out in steep surreal perspective and two or three cracking as if about to hatch, and just one chick showing, bright orangey-yellow, a foetal head and beak, eye still shut, pushing out into the open. The New. She should have gone to Art School instead of reading English at ... where? Southchester. Yes, Southchester – where that rogue Max Flash wants me on his daft Trotskyite project. Still. Miriam Trivet.

The door at the end of the studio thumped open and Frank jumped, an oath or a rebuke dying on his lips as he took in HAL's silvery hair, bright suit and twinkling brown shoes coming past the candidates towards him.

'Hard work afoot here, I see.' To Frank it seemed like a bellow. 'Small group you have.'

'A level, Mr Harte.'

'Of course.'

'I mean really A level. I mean they're actually doing their exam.'

'Yes, yes I can see that.' He was up at the desk now, and dropped his voice ostentatiously. Nevertheless Frank was sure that until then, the Head had had no idea that a public examination was under way.

'This the paper? Hmmm. Yes. Yes. Very good, very good of its sort.' He continued in a loud whisper which Frank feared would be even more irritating than his blustery opening. 'Of its sort mind you. But I sometimes wonder if we don't turn out too many chappies and lasses skilled at this sort of thing – overcrowded profession, leads to disillusionment and so on. Of course, as you know Frank, I'm not against teaching art as such, oh dear me no, far from it. But I feel the emphasis should be just a little less on the vocational, on the technical, know what I mean? Of course I'm just thinking aloud, and you'll tell me if I'm wrong, but the point as I see it is to give the customers something meaningful to fill their leisure hours with, going to be a growing problem with the new technologies, silicon chips and all that, we must all recognise this, wouldn't be doing our job properly if we didn't. No, as I see it, the emphasis in arts teaching should be on creativity and self-expression, as a means to social adjustment.'

He moved off down the long wall behind the candidates looking at the hundreds of pictures pinned there, nodding and tutting as he went. Hating himself for his meekness Frank followed, but refused to add to the disturbance by replying. HAL paused in front of a batch of meticulously shaded pencil-sketches of racing-cars blown up from newspaper photographs. 'Now correct me if I'm wrong, but while I admire the skill and discipline that's gone into these, isn't there a case to be made that over-emphasis on technique might stifle the kiddies' interest, put them off it all? A case if you like for more enjoyment, more self-expression?'

After all Frank rose.

'Art has nothing to do with self-expression,' he said, firmly and too loudly. The boy Steve, at the end of the row and nearest to him looked up suddenly from a mop of black hair, a grin on his face, then went quickly back to his work. He appeared to be drawing, with great care and accuracy, a large life-belt; Frank vaguely wondered why.

HAL was nonplussed. 'You'll have to convince me of that,' he said.

Frank turned away, confused and angry with himself for being drawn – particularly in front of six of his best pupils, during an exam. He knew work would stop now until HAL went; he knew HAL had nothing to do, no particular reason for going. He pulled at his Edward VII beard. 'Surely art is to do with discovery, with finding out. And one needs technique for that, as surely as the sciences do. Oh, I don't mean finding out about oneself, I mean about reality, about truth.'

Girls' voices approached on their way to a gym lesson – to be held on the field since their gymnasium was used for O and A level written papers throughout the month.

'Ah yes,' said HAL, 'but now you're talking of the few, the very very few, the men and women of true genius.' His voice took on a note of false reverence, like a guide's in the Vatican. 'And they will find their way, we may be sure of that, and the rewards they deserve in an open society like ours. But for ordinary mortals like me and you Frank, it's enough we should give our kiddies the means to earn a living and the means to enjoy their leisure in socially acceptable ways. That's the way it is, every which way you look at it. And I know that in your heart of hearts you're with me on this.'

Frank looked firmly out of the window, eyes above the heads of the girls going by, eyes above their goose-pimpled thighs twinkling beneath green briefs, knickers really.

'No. I'm not,' he said.

Steve spluttered behind him. Then a girl's voice beneath them came loud and clear, just the other side of the glass.

'Miss, when we going to have proper gym again? It's too blooming cold out on the field on a day like this and it's making my tits stand up.'

The spluttering spread amongst the candidates.

HAL moved away from the window, his face a hint ruddier than it had been.

'Well I mustn't stand about gassing all day Frank, interesting though our little chats always are; what I came to see you about is this. Young Bright.'

'Yes?'

'I'm afraid he's really put his foot in it with Paul Armstrong this time and suspension looks to be unavoidable. I'd like you to come along and thrash it out with us, you being the boy's tutor. Get some sense into him if we can. Now when are you free?'

'I'm not free today at all. Not even for lunch. I have to stay with this lot.'

'I'll organise a relief.'

'I'm afraid the rubrics say there has to be an art teacher here.'

'Mrs Rogate will be free. If she isn't I'll get her freed. After break she will relieve you.'

At last HAL headed for the door. To ease him on the way Frank got there first, opened it for him. But curiosity got the better of him.

'Headmaster. What has Martin done this time?'

'Martin? Oh you mean Bright. He didn't write that essay Paul Armstrong read out at Monday's Upper School Assembly.'

'No? I thought it was dull. Dull for Martin I mean.'

'Dull or not. He didn't write it.' HAL's face was now pale again and completely expressionless, small grey eyes cold and fixed on Frank's above him. 'Apparently it was written by Marx. Karl Marx.'

Candidate Steve did not splutter this time. He whooped. HAL went quickly. Frank shut the door and turned to face five young red faces, all exploding at last, one of them nearly hysterical. Only plump Di, doing the chocolate box, remained impassive.

'I really don't see what the fuss is about,' she said.

11.20

'National Insurance Contributions and Benefits, General Enquiries, Please Enter', Miriam read. She pushed the swing door and found herself in a large room with a counter at the far end, four tubular chairs against the counter, and fifteen more in three rows of five in the middle. The floor, black vinyl tiles, shone; the walls, painted cream, glittered; and the ceiling, set with acoustic tiles, seemed designed to amplify every noise so everything that was said at the counter, however quietly, could be distinctly heard in every corner of the room. An oldish lady in a grey coat and a black hat had arrived just ahead of her and was already at the counter. A girl of Miriam's age, but with black hair piled on her head and a lot of make-up on her face, came in behind the counter. With some distaste Miriam realised the girl was Joyce Copeman. She stayed as near the door, as far from the counter as possible and wondered whether it would not be better to wait in the foyer until the old lady had been dealt with.

'Would you care to take a seat?' Miss Copeman called.

'I'm the only person on counter today so there'll be a wait.'

Reluctantly Miriam moved into the room and took one of the chairs.

'Now what can I do for you?' Joyce Copeman asked the old lady.

'Well, it's not me. It's me husband.'

There was a silence. The old lady sniffed. Miriam could see that she clutched a tiny slip of white handkerchief.

Joyce Copeman was brisk. 'I see. Well let's have *your* name first, if we may.'

'Stevens. Margery Stevens.'

Of course, thought Miriam. I should have recognised her.

'I see, Mrs Stevens. And your husband's first name?'

'Trevor.' The old lady sniffed again.

'I see, Mrs Stevens. Now what's the trouble with Mr Stevens?' Sniff. 'Out of work is he? Unemployed? Had an accident? Ill?'

Sniff.

'He's dead.'

'Oh I see. Mrs Stevens, what you need is a Death Grant. I'll get you the form.'

Platform heels clacked away. Mrs Stevens, alone at the counter, turned her head. Tears glistened on her cheeks, then a smile flowed on to her face. 'It's Molly Trivet, isn't it? Jack Trivet's girl.'

'That's right Mrs Stevens. I was sorry to hear about Mr Stevens.'

'Well, he didn't feel much they said. He went very peaceful.'

'It was so sudden though.'

'It was. We was just sitting there, watching the film, the late night one, and suddenly he said to me, "Eh Marge, I do feel queer ... " '

Platform heels clacked back.

'Here we are Mrs Stevens. Now if you'd like to glance through this N149 and then fill in the BD1, I'll just see what this lady wants.'

'Oh come on Joyce. You know me.'

'Goodness. It's Molly Trivet. Well. Kev Rammage said you were back. What can I do for you? I'm sure you've not just dropped in to see me.'

Miriam took a breath: 'Last October I had dental treatment, and at Christmas an abscess, and together they were classed as two lots of treatment. I paid the dentist ten pounds. I don't suppose you remember but you were working there then. Anyway, the University Education and Welfare Office at Southchester says that as a full-time student on an L.E.A. grant and no other income, I'm entitled to free dental treatment.'

'You should have filled in an F1D at your dentist. And got him to sign it.'

'I did. It was you fetched me the form.'

'And sent it here with the receipts.'

'I did.'

'And you haven't had your money?'

'No.'

'Well perhaps you're not entitled after all.'

'No. That's not it. What happened was this. You sent back a letter, I mean the people here did, with a certificate of entitlement, but also asking for the receipts.'

'So you didn't send the receipts.'

'Yes. I did send the receipts.'

Deadlock. The two girls, both faces wooden, stared at each other across the counter. Joyce Copeman gave way. 'I'll go and get your file,' she said, and clacked away again.

Mrs Stevens looked up. As she spoke she shook her head from side to side and the tears seemed to be flowing faster.

'I can't do this. I can't make head nor tail of it, I really can't. Trev used to do all this sort of thing.'

'Shall I have a look?'

'Oh would you, Molly? I'd be so grateful.'

The explanatory pamphlet was six sides of green print.

'Look,' said Miriam, 'don't bother with this now. Take it home and read it when you feel better. Let's just fill in the form now. Particulars of deceased. I don't suppose it matters if I do it, so long as you sign it.'

'Does it say anywhere how much?'

'No, Mrs Stevens, I don't think it does.'

'The Funeral Directors gave a quote well in excess of a hundred pounds.'

'I don't suppose you know his national insurance number, do you?'

'No Molly. Not off-hand.'

'You're still in Alma Grove?'

'Yes dear. Number eight.'

Clack, clack, clack, clack.

'Here we are then, Molly, Miss Trivet. I've got your file – oh I see you two are getting on all right, aren't you? Very nice, I'm sure. As I say, here's your file and no receipts in it.'

'Could I see the file?'

'No, of course you can't see the file. It's confidential. No unauthorised person can see Department files.'

Miriam felt anger swell, like a balloon slowly filling.

'How can it be confidential to me. It's a file *on* me. It can't be confidential.'

'But you're not authorised, are you?'

'Surely I'm authorised to see my own file.'

'Ooh, I don't know, I'm sure.'

There was a pause. Then Molly said: 'Is there a Supervisor? Someone else I can see?'

'There's Mrs Jones. But she's busy.'

'I'd like to see her.'

'I'll go and find out.' Clack, clack, clack away, then clack, clack, clack, clack back again to pick up the file she had left between them.

Mrs Stevens looked up, more tearful than ever.

'I don't know the year he was born. I know his birthday. Next month that is, but I don't know the year Trev was born.'

Miriam took her hand. 'How old was he?'

'He must have been fifty-nine. Yes. That's right. Because he talked of how some folk in some jobs retire at sixty but he being just day shift at TRICE still had six years to go.'

'Well, that'll do. See, it says: "Or age if date of birth

unknown''. Now let's see. Did Mr Stevens have any other income, other than TRICE. Like a war pension or anything?'

'Oh no. Nothing like that. All we had was his wage packet. Until they took to paying with those cheques.'

'Did he leave a will?'

'No. I'm sure he didn't leave a will. What would he leave a will for?'

Miriam went quickly through the rest of the form. Mercifully little of the rest applied.

'I don't suppose you've got your marriage certificate with you?'

'My lines? No. They're in the sideboard drawer at home with all that sort of thing. Trev looked after all that.'

'Well, I don't think it matters. Look it says if you haven't got all that, you should still fill in the form and leave it here. I expect they'll write if they want anything else.'

Clack, clack, clack, clack.

'Here you are. Mrs Jones told me to give you this.'

Miriam took a small slip of paper. Under the Department heading, reference number and so on she read:

> Dear Madam,
>
> With regard to your enquiry, the receipts for dental charges disbursed by you were forwarded by this department to the Family Practitioner Committee at Rifedale for the necessary refund. I therefore suggest you contact these people at the address below.
>
> Yours faithfully
>
> A. Jones
>
> Family Practioner Committee
> 157 Spithead Road
> Rifedale

'So I've got to go to Rifedale?' she said.

'Looks like it.'

'But it'll take an hour and two buses.'

'Yes. Yes, well.'

Mrs Stevens intervened: 'Miss. How much is this grant?'

'Thirty pounds and it'll be three weeks before you get it.'

'But the funeral's tomorrow. They'll want paying before three weeks.'

'Funeral Directors are very accommodating.' Joyce Copeman turned back to Miriam and gave her a grin like an open razor. 'Pity it's not down the coast, init? Then Kev could give you a lift in 'is boat.'

11.36

Frank peered over Steve's shoulder. In the circle of the life-belt the boy was carefully pencilling in a drawing of Brinshore's broken pier – he must be doing the t-shirt for your town or village, Frank thought as he moved away to answer the door. It opened before he got there. Pet Rogate – pink nylon coat, dark hair tied back, so thin you felt you could blow her over or crush her to your bosom, shower hot kisses on her upturned ...

'I've been asked to relieve you, Frank.'

'But I don't want relieving.'

A frown drifted across her face. 'But Lah-di-dah wants to see you.'

'That man's name is HAL. Yes. He did call by and say something like this would happen. I shan't be long, I don't suppose.'

He gave her a wink, nearly chucked her under the chin as he passed because he longed to touch her, and then he was gone – loping down the corridor, hands in pockets, singing to himself *Goddess, goddess, e-e-e-e-excellently bright.*

In the display centre he suddenly caught a whiff of a most unpleasant smell – he paused, head up, sniffing to catch it again, but it was gone. Fishy it had been but worse than fishy. Well, the Rammage lad had long since removed the fish from The Living Past of Brinshore's Oldest Industry display, so that wasn't the cause, yet the odour came again as he tweaked a bit of net back into place, and adjusted one of the lights. Then he went past the rubber plants and the ferns outside HAL's private lavatory and into the foyer, knocked on his master's door.

Tableau. 'When Did You Last See Your Father?' HAL behind his desk, Paul Armstrong sat across one end of it, Martin Bright standing in front of them. Oh dear, thought Frank – well, I won't let them make me part of some ghastly tribunal if I can help it.

'Frank. Good of you to come. Pull up a chair.' HAL, very serious, waved at two high-backed chairs against the wall. Frank swung not one but both out and planted them more or less side by side behind the boy. He sat in one and motioned Martin into the other, crossed his long legs, put his head on one side, and smiled.

'What can I do for you, Headmaster?' he chirruped.

HAL reddened, Hitler Armstrong paled, the muscles in his face setting, his eyes widening. Both looked to Frank like bad carvings, or rather masks. That was it – tribal masks designed to inspire awe and even fear in the simple-minded, but wood really, just painted wood.

'This is a serious matter Frank.'

'Go on Headmaster.'

'Young Martin here has admitted to playing a very silly hoax on Mr Armstrong. And Paul and I are inclined to take a really very serious view of the matter, very serious indeed.'

Frank glanced at Martin, made a comical grimace, and said: 'Tut, tut.' Then more loudly: 'Could you put me in the picture, Mr Harte?'

'I think you know the background – young Martin presented to Mr Armstrong an essay entitled "Reflections on a Choice of Career." Mr Armstrong assumed it was the lad's own work and read it out as such at Upper School Assembly. It now transpires that young Bright was not the author. That's it in a nutshell, isn't it Paul?'

'No Headmaster, it is not.' Hitler Armstrong leant forward gripping the corners of the desk and Frank could see his knuckles whiten. The man was in a rage – a cold, controlled, but nevertheless savage rage. 'The author was Karl Marx. Bright has put it about that it was Marx. Has deliberately made it known. So. I am now held in ridicule as some sort of Marxist, and you too, sir, since you publicly endorsed it from the platform. I haven't finished. This ... plot is the word, this plot was considered, planned with malice, and should be punished accordingly. This boy is a troublemaker. He was set these essays because he is a troublemaker. Now he must be punished as a troublemaker, seen to be punished, made an example of.' The angry little man sat back in his chair, head shrunk between his shoulders, and passed a hand across his lank greying hair, icy eyes fixed on the black boy who continued to keep his own gaze on a point about a foot above HAL's head in front of him.

HAL said: 'What do you think of all this, Frank?'

'Storm in a teacup,' said Frank, with boisterous cheerfulness, then aware of Hitler Armstrong's reaction, moderated his tone. 'Please don't think I'm minimising the offence, I can see it does make you look a bit foolish, but basically it's a jape, a joke, that was the intention, I'm sure. A laugh. That's all.'

'Mr Dangerfield, as head of sixth year I have to keep a sense of discipline alive in young minds, keep a proper respect for duly constituted authority that alone will make them the good citizens it is our duty to turn out. To do this I have to be respected. My job depends on respect, and this young whipper-snapper has maliciously plotted to injure the respect that is the *sine qua non* of my job. Unless we want anarchy he's got to be seen to be punished severely.'

HAL put his fingertips together. 'Just what have you in mind, Paul?'

Armstrong again smoothed down his lock of lifeless hair.

'Suspension for the rest of this school year. Readmittance in September only on presentation of a written statement of intent to behave himself.'

'Oh come on,' cried Frank. 'This is ridiculous. Martin's trying to get to university. You're robbing him of six weeks of A-level teaching that could well cost him a grade, or even two or three, off his final results ... '

'I'm not *robbing* him of anything.'

'But that is just what you're doing . . . .'

'Gentlemen, friends, colleagues. Hard feelings. I understand but we must be rational about this. I'm inclined to take a median view. With Paul I go along as to the seriousness of the offence. With Frank I take a less serious view of young Martin's intention ... '

'Why don't you ask him what his intentions were,' Armstrong spat. 'Go on, ask him.'

The school seemed very far away as it always did in HAL's room – nothing to be heard but the rumble of a lorry beyond the high chain-link fence. Martin kept his slightly protuberant eyes on the point above HAL's head but about the corners of his lips there was now a hint of a grin.

'Well Martin. You heard what Mr Armstrong said. What was your intention?'

The eyes came down, the grin broadened, white teeth in the dark face, but, Frank thought, a nice grin, not malicious. 'I don't see why there's a fuss. Sir. I borrowed the essay because I had a lot of ... real work to do. Mr Rogate wanted an essay on Keats. Mr Davis one on the Chartists. Both by Monday. So I took a short cut. You know Karl Marx was only a year older than me when he wrote it and I didn't know he'd read it out.'

'Mr Armstrong, *if* you please.'

'I didn't know *Mister* Armstrong was going to read it out. And afterwards it seemed, well, dishonest really, to let people go on thinking I'd written it. So I told everyone, you know, in the sixth-form coffee bar and that, whose it really was. I'm sorry if it's caused Hit ... Mr Armstrong to be upset. Is that what you want me to say?'

'There, that's the point,' Frank spoke quickly. 'I mean Martin didn't *know* it was to be read out, couldn't have known.'

But Hitler Armstrong was smug now, spoke slowly, emphasising each word. 'I told him on Friday I was going to read it out on Monday.'

'But he didn't know when he wrote it. Well. Copied it out.'

HAL put his fingertips together again, adopted a judicious tone. 'We've heard views from all concerned. Admirably put. And I understand the feelings involved and they do everyone credit. That is, they do Mr Armstrong and Mr Dangerfield credit. It's up to me now to decide what is to be done. But before I do, I want Martin to be quite clear about one thing. I am not motivated by the reputation of Karl Marx. No way. In his time he said much that was wise. But times change. We know now his views on materialism for example were exaggerated. I mean there are such things as spiritual values, life is not all economic forces, that view does not do justice to fully human needs and, ah, aspirations. So. I am taking a serious view of this, Martin, not because the name of Marx comes into it, but because, every which way you look at it, there was deception ... '

'But Sir. I put that right. I tried to anyway ... '

'I would prefer it if you didn't interrupt me, Martin. You've had your say and I am in full possession of the facts. Martin. I'm suspending you for two weeks to start next Monday. You may return to school on Monday the third of July but I shall require a declaration of intent to work and behave in the way we require here. Now you may go back to your studies.'

Martin stood up, gangly in grey flannels and ugly blue jacket, put his chair back against the wall. At the door he turned.

'Thanks Frank,' he said, and his white teeth flashed.

Frank stood up, and looked down from his height at the tribal masks. Little men, he thought. 'I must get back. Relieve Mrs Rogate,' he said.

Armstrong looked up at him balefully. 'That boy is incorrigible. A troublemaker. And I think his UCCA reference should reflect the truth about him.'

'Eh?' asked Frank. 'Am I following you?'

'I don't know if you are. Headmaster, you have Bright's file there. Please read again his UCCA reference. After all, it does go out over your signature.'

Frank recalled that the whole business had started because Bright had organised a sit-in to protest that pupils should see the reports sent by the school about them to the University Central Council of Admissions, reports that accompanied what were in effect applications to go to university. He also recollected that Bright's report was a glowing one, praising his academic promise, recommending him highly. Frank had written it himself, basing it on reports from Bright's subject teachers – HAL simply signed it.

Armstrong waited until HAL put the form down. 'Now Headmaster, my contention is that our credibility as a school depends on universities and colleges believing our reports. Bright will be accepted on that as it stands. At university he will be a nuisance, probably a leftist since he is already reading Marx. I think that reference should be done again and include this time a proper objective account of his activities, of his attitude to authority and to society. That way our credibility will be maintained.'

'Count me out.' Frank was now very angry. 'Count me right out. I'm having nothing to do with this.'

HAL looked up at him. 'All right old chap. No need for you to stay. You have your work to do.'

'Are you going to re-write that UCCA reference?'

'Come, come Frank. UCCA references are ultimately my responsibility. I know your views, I think, and I will bear them in mind. Now, as you said, you must relieve Mrs Rogate.'

'There's nothing more for me to say then.'

'Not really, old chap.' HAL turned to Hitler Armstrong, pointedly excluding Frank. 'Bright's clever, but there's bad blood there. No father you see. And immigrant too, doesn't really understand our ways yet ... '

Plenty to say but nothing that can be said, Frank realised, turning on his heel. Vindictive little squirt. Both of them, vindictive little squirts, and he stormed back down the corridors to the art studios. When he got there Pet Rogate melted away ignored, and annoyed at being ignored.

His candidates put up with him striding about and banging things for ten minutes before complaining. Then he cooled down a little and looked at their work. It seemed to be coming on nicely. Across the top of Steve's life belt the word BRINSHORE had been lettered in; pencilled in the lower half, beneath the drawing of the pier, were the words *The Last Resort.* This tickled him, went some way towards restoring his good humour, though he felt he should have done more for Martin Bright, but what could be done he could not for the life of him see.

Then he remembered the rates demand, summons rather, that he would have to ask for time off to answer it, and that he would have to answer it for he did not have one hundred and seventy-four pounds, and HAL was not now going to look favourably on requests from him for time off. So he would end up losing a day's pay. He sighed and puffed and began banging things again until again the candidates turned on him and shushed him.

12.02

Things went well at Rose Linden's – she was the sort of woman Lucie Shiner got on with and she readily agreed that little Jimmy had been little more than a bystander when the other two boys tried to blow up The Club. After a good old chat it was now time to get on to her third call. Still in the same road, so that was convenient.

Bing-boing, bing-boing.

'Mrs Green? My name is Lucie Shiner and I'm from the Department. May I come in?'

Dot Green looked out, framed by the opening.

'I didn't ... you never said you were coming.'

She was young, with mouse-coloured hair, long, and a pasty face. Her jeans and old jumper were grubby, and she looked very, very tired. 'What's it about?'

'It's not *about* anything. I had another call to make in the road, and our records show you have a new baby here and it's a month since the Health Visitor came, so I thought I'd drop by. But if you'd rather I made an appointment ... '

'Oh no. Now you're here you may as well come in. But I'm not *ready* for you.'

She led the way past the kitchen which was steamed up

and filled with the noise of a spin-drier at work and into a living-room that was in shape and size the same as Rose Linden's. But the furniture was different, a G-plan three-piece suite, the rest second-hand, and several yards of pine-plank shelving filled with books, mostly paperbacks, very few ornaments, and two unframed posters – all these indicated a student marriage of not more than two years' standing. There was a pile of un-ironed clothes on the dining-table and breakfast things – Swiss-style cereal – still uncleared.

'Would you like a coffee or something?'

'Not unless you're having one. I had one at my last port of call.'

'Oh I'm always having one. So you might as well.'

Dot went into the kitchen. She wasn't long there, no longer than it takes for half a pint of water to boil in an electric kettle, but long enough for Lucie Shiner to nose about the living-room.

'Who's doing the O.U. then?' as Dot came back with two cups.

'Right. That's my husband. Nick. It's daft really. I mean he's only been qualified a year. But he wanted to be a lecturer. In a college, you know? So he's started doing this. Reckons on getting a leg up with another degree, you know?'

'I got where I am through the O.U.,' said Mrs Shiner with simpering modesty.

'Really? Right.'

She pushed a sugar-bowl towards the visitor, who smiled negatively and dropped one of her own sweeteners into the muddy liquid. 'I started with *Handicapped in the Community,* and went on to *Growing-Up in Tower Hamlets.'*

'Do you want to see Leila?'

'Leila?'

'The baby.'

'I'll have a peek before I go, but there's no point in disturbing her. Is she asleep?'

'I suppose so. She's in her pram, in the back garden.'

Lucie Shiner stirred away. 'Good little sleeper, is she?'

'Oh marvellous. Bloody marvellous. In the last week I've had eight hours' real sleep. I tot them up. She sleeps. Oh yes. She sleeps. But not when I sleep. Right?'

'That can be a problem.'

'Right. It can. Sometimes she screams if she sees me. If I go near her. That really upsets me, you know? I mean, that's not right, is it?'

'And it's getting you down.'

'Right, it's getting me down. Sometimes I wonder if she's really mine. If the hospital didn't screw it up. Switch mine for someone else's. I didn't see her, not properly, for a week. Of course I'm all screwed up about it now. I shouldn't say these things. I mean in hospital they were wonderful, really wonderful, you know? But really she's never really seemed like my baby, right?'

'Oh I'm sure she is Mrs Green, I'm sure she is. You mustn't give way to these ideas. I'm sure they're fantasy. It's quite a common scenario, you know, at least this *is* what we find, and it wears off as you settle down. I mean you must realise you're in a changing ongoing situation, with its different phases, and you're in a sticky one just now, but it will change.'

'Just a phase?'

'That's right.'

'Right.'

This, thought Lucie Shiner, is really a case for the T.L.Cs. Accordingly she added sweetener to her voice. 'Lovely coffee this, just what I needed. But that's not to say you shouldn't have all the help you can get. Have you seen your doctor recently?'

'Post-natal check-up, the last. Ten days ago. He stuffed his hand up me, you know? all rubber gloves and vaseline, and said I was fine.'

'Yes, I'm afraid some doctors aren't just quite as sympathetic as we'd always like to family problems,' giving another touch of the T.L.Cs.

'I don't know. I didn't tell him about any problems. You can't tell your doctor your kid cries when you want to sleep and sleeps when you have to be awake, can you? I mean that's not what doctors are for, right? He'd just give me a little yellow pill, a mother's helper, and I'm not getting into that scene.'

Oh dear, thought Lucie Shiner. Residue of lower middle-class ethic here. Doesn't approve of pills. That's not going to make it easier.

'Well now. You attended a pre-natal support group, I suppose.'

'Right.'

'Where was that then?'

'In the mobile community centre at Mudwick.'

'And a post-natal support group?'

'No.'

'Why not?'

Dot Green held her temples for a moment then pushed her fingers back through her mousy hair. For a moment her eyes flashed quite wildly and Lucie Shiner felt a tremor of alarm. Perhaps the T.L.Cs would not be enough. Usually, she found, a back-up was needed, psycho-chemotherapeutic, support groups, or both.

'Why not, dear?' she repeated, her voice now pure saccharine.

'Because it's a *mobile* community centre, and after it got vandalised in Mudwick, they moved it to Woodcroft, right? by the primary school, and that's ten minutes' walk this end, then fifteen in the bus, and the buses run once every two hours, so it's a minimum of an hour's wait at Woodcroft before I can get back. All carrying a screaming baby because she's too small for a push-chair and the pram won't go on the bus. That's why not.'

'That does make it a bit difficult.'

'Right.'

'Still. We must see what can be done. I'll make one or two recommendations, drop a line to the Health Centre and so on.'

She jotted down some notes on a clip-board.

'You're making a report on me. You've got a file on me.'

Again the alarm signal, but Dot Green had said this very calmly, there was even relief in her voice.

'Well, just enough to remind me who you are, nothing sinister in that, is there? Now shall we go and see Leila?'

'Leila?'

'The baby. That's her name, isn't it?'

'Leila. Right. Yes, you'll want to see her.'

They went down the hall – empty apart from a second-hand chest of drawers, and uncarpeted, and out through a patio door into the tiny back garden. Sheets patterned with orange sunflowers hung from a line in the grey air above a large glossy baby carriage, a present from doting grand-parents. Leila was as she should be – asleep on her front, no pillow. There was, however, a half-full bottle with the teat an inch from her mouth beside her, and a dribble of saliva and curds on her cheek. This is not the moment to criticise, thought Lucie Shiner, we'll leave that go for the moment, but I must remember to make mention in my report.

'She's lovely, isn't she? Isn't she lovely then? Right if I pick her up?'

'Do you have to?'

'I've had two of my own you know.'

'Right. Go on. I don't mind. Be my guest.'

Lucie Shiner picked up the baby, cradling its head carefully – though it was already supporting itself quite well. No visible bruises. She pried with her fingers – Leila began to whimper – she's thin, judged Lucie Shiner, but not under-nourished. She chucked and cooed: 'Who's a lovely one then, who's a lovely one,' and jogged the baby which stopped whimpering, gurgled instead.

'There, there,' said Lucie Shiner. 'A touch of the T.L.Cs. That's all. Costs nothing and goes a long way.'

'T.L.Cs?' asked Dot.

'Tender Loving Care,' said Lucie Shiner and laughed in her friendliest, brightest, most *open* way.

'Right,' said Dot.

Mrs Shiner handed Leila back to her mother.

'Well, I must be off,' she said. 'I've got at least one more call to make. Just keep up the T.L.Cs and I'm sure you'll get along fine.'

'The T.L.Cs. Right.'

Leila began to whimper. By the time they were back at the front door, with Dot standing on the step holding the baby, Leila was howling.

She howled as Mrs Shiner crossed the open-plan lawn, and howled as she got into her Mini, and her howls rose even above the noise of the starter.

Mrs Shiner gave them both a wave as she let in the clutch.

Wonderful what a touch of the T.L.Cs can do.

15.32

HAL washed his hands in his private basin and sniffed. Somewhere there was a most unpleasant smell. Not strong, but very nasty. And this wasn't the first time he'd caught it. He pulled on the IS towel machine and dried his hands. I must remember to speak to the caretaker, he thought, but as he went out into the foyer he was confronted by his secretary and what he thought were four of his sixth formers, though if they were, then they were disgracefully un-uniformed. Reprimand rose to his lips, but his secretary checked him.

'Headmaster, these are the student teachers. I told you they were coming today.'

'Ah. Ah, yes, Miss Barratt.'

'They'll be on teaching practice next term and are here for a preliminary look round.'

'Quite. Jolly good.'

'You especially said you'd like to talk to them at half-past three.'

'That's right, Miss Barratt. Well come along, come along, come into my den all of you, I think we can find enough chairs, sit yourselves down, sit yourselves down. That's fine, that's fine. Well. Well now. It's my custom, on these occasions, to spin together a few strands of homespun wisdom, practical tips and so on. All the theory, and much of it very fine stuff, though some a bit airy-fairy, you'll get down at the college. But here we have our feet on the ground, and next term that will be true for you too. Feet on the ground. Practice. The practical business of teaching. That's what it's all about, isn't it? The name of the game.

'But before we go further, let's hear what your special subjects are. English, very good, and you're doing English too? Art, I see, and another for art. I see. Two doing English, and two doing art.

'Good. Good. Let no one undervalue the contribution of your disciplines to society at large, society as a whole. There's no doubt, and here I quote from the findings of the Multi-Disciplinary Assessment Conference I attended last year, that the importance of the creative, self-expressing side of the curriculum has been escalated enormously in recent years, and rightly so, for its contribution to social adjustment. I mean no one can deny that social workers of all sorts, and I include teachers in their pastoral role, are worked to the hilt, to the hilt, and there is always a backlog of unfinished work breathing on our heels. But that is just patching up, picking up the pieces. It's back to the roots we have to go, and that is where your subjects play their role.

'Let me put it to you this way. I'm a practical man. A pragmatist. I don't claim to be able to handle concepts; indeed I tend to distrust those who say they can. It seems to me that conceptual thought often charts the course to a foregone conclusion. What I like to do is the reverse. I start with the facts, day-to-day experience, and work from there, and that way I know where I stand, and I'm ready to defend my conclusions to the hilt.

'Let me give you a for example. Last Monday I had a phone-call from the police. The Super actually, I count him as a friend. You see, for good or for ill this is a comprehensive school, we cater for all sorts, and we're bound to have some villains as well as a sound majority of good citizens. But this time I was surprised. Three lads, one from here and two from Woodcroft Primary, set fire to a pub on Sunday and did a fair bit of old damage. Now our customer from among these lads comes from a good home, mother middle class, father in a management situation at TRICE, so when the Super rang up I was able to say to him, leave this one with me old chap, it's not in your parish.

'And why did I do that? Because I could see clearly what these lads were up to. Look at it this way. Setting fire to a building is an act of frustrated self-expression and so clearly what these boys lack at home is socially acceptable means of and opportunities for self-expression. The youngest kiddie should be making things in his own way – out of washing-up liquid containers, old egg boxes, the possibilities are endless, and bringing them to his mother for her loving appreciation. The older boy, the one who is already here is no doubt already learning skills of a more advanced sort here in Frank Dangerfield's admirable department, but do his parents know this? I shall have them up here and explain to them where they have unwittingly failed their own children in failing to provide the sort of facilities at home that we lay on at school. In the meantime these boys will not be chivvied by the police, I have the Super's word for that, nor will they become part of the backlog of our overworked courts. On Friday they see the County Child Psychotherapist, a wonderful man, and out of what was a very negative situation last Sunday, by pulling together school, police, social workers *and* parents, a positive outcome will be brought about.

'But only because we have caught these customers young. Here's another example where things may not work out so well, because it's too late. Cropped up today – practical instances to make practical points. Boy in the sixth year. No names, no pack-drill. Broken family, mother alone, courageous woman, school cleaner, but no background, you see, and he's turned out a bad'un. Mind you, he's clever. No two ways. A very high achiever, but not to put too fine a point on it, a cheat. When asked to write a punishment essay, he plagiarised, took someone else's work and submitted it as his own. Now what I believe that lad has lacked is the discipline that comes from a disciplined approach to self-expression.

Creative work, work that encourages real self-expression must be structured, must give the kiddies prescribed limits within which they can fulfill themselves before it will properly perform its dual role of giving them the satisfaction that is their due as real human beings and keeping them off the streets, for let's face it, call a spade a spade, that's what social adjustment comes down to, every which way you look at it, that's the name of the game.

'So that's why we structure creative work here at Brinshore Comprehensive. Walking round the school the other day, making sure that education was taking place, I came on two fine examples of what I mean. Young Nigel Green, probationer, English, you'll meet him, set this for work on *Silas Marner,* a fine little book by one of our greatest writers. Where is it, I made a note of it, here we are. "Imagine you are a neighbour of Silas's – how would you react to his fostering of Eppie? How would you try to help him? You may imagine the story is happening NOW if you like." Now that's a fine example of how we try to encourage a creative response to great literature, a structured creative response, allowing for structured, creative self-expression. And another example you can't fail to have noticed on your way here is our little exhibition "The Living Past of Brinshore's Oldest Industry", a fine example of the creative processes harnessed to other disciplines, given a place, a *function* in the *whole* context.

'Of course these views I hold are not shared by all. We had a chap here some years ago, and, I make no bones about it, I'm glad he left, Max Flash his name was, a Jew I think, not that that matters. Anyway this Flash character had some very high-falutin' ideas about art, saw it as a way of turning over everything we respect, hold most dear, the very bulwarks of our society. Used art as a tool to propagandise the kiddies. He was an ideologue, you see. That was his trouble. Well I'm sure none of you will be wanting to try anything of that sort here. School is the place for laying foundations, not undermining them; for giving the kiddies the structured base they require, the stability they want. Then, when they are adults, let them question things if they must, but from within the structure, if you follow me.

'That's all from me for now. We'll meet again next term, when I know you'll come dressed appropriately. Not for me, you understand, it's the customers themselves that expect it. You'll find your heads of department splendid people, Mr Rogate and Mr Dangerfield, but if you have any problems they can't solve, well the buck stops here, my door is always open.'

16.03

Hilary Barnacle-Flavell was drafting a letter to *The Times.*

> I wonder if your readers share my distaste, moral and aesthetic, for two publicity campaigns currently being run by two public bodies: I refer to the Department of National Savings and the Open University. Both vulgarise and cheapen the greatest achievements of our civilisation and link them with motives of blatant self-interest. In the current issue of the *Radio Times,* there is an offensive advertisement in which one of the great last self-portraits of Rembrandt is used to promote the National Savings Certificates Retirement Issue. Worse is that for the Open University. Beneath a headline in heavy type which reads *After Working All Day for Somebody Else Do Something Important for Yourself,* a succession of paragraphs in brutal prose which jokily shifts from the whimsy to the mock serious, outline some of the courses provided by that institution. The whole is illustrated with cartoons whose poverty of response is matched only by the prose. The arts for instance are represented by a nude lady with a fig-leaf being painted by a man on whose canvas a fig-leaf only appears. Mathematics – beneath a headline 'Making Maths Add Up' – are illustrated with a crude drawing of Albert Einstein reduced to a comic character operating a pocket calculator.
>
> It has been well said that the more one extends higher education, and especially in an age of techno-

> logical aids and open universities, the more insidious becomes the menace to standards and the more potent and unashamed the animus against them. Unless standards are maintained somewhere the whole community is let down and the only place where standards can be maintained is the university properly conceived. The real university is a centre of consciousness and human responsibility for the civilised . . . .

She paused – aware she was wandering from the point. That was the trouble these days: there was so much to be said, so much prodding to be done, so many people who ought to know better were falling away, one often did not know where to begin. Or in this case, she thought wryly, finish.

Then her doorbell rang.

Hilary Barnacle set aside her pen, pulled herself up from the heavy old desk she had been writing at, and made her way slowly past chairs, tables, bookcases, a glazed cabinet filled with bric-à-brac and collector's pieces, and so into the hall where a grandmother clock on the wall marked off the seconds with a heavy tick. The only other noise in the house was her breathing which was a heavy whistling gasp by the time she reached the door. She waited for it to improve, but it didn't, and she didn't like to keep people waiting outside so she fumbled with the latch and got it undone.

A small dark-haired woman glanced up from a clip-board and smiled dazzlingly.

'Miss Barnacle-Flavell?' she said, 'I am Lucie Shiner and I'm from the Department.'

'Ah yes. Please come in.'

'May I?'

'You must excuse me. My breathing. Please go on ahead. I shall be quite well directly.'

'What a lovely house you have. So many pretty things. And so many books. Some of them look quite antique.'

'Won't you sit there. By the desk. And then we'll have everything to hand. Yes. Many belonged to my brother of course. He was High Commissioner in Bhorguida-Dhu. But quite a lot are my own choice. Now Mrs Shiner, what can I do for you?'

'Well really, Miss Barnacle-Flavell, it's more a question of what *I* can do for *you.*'

Dear me, she's determined to be *bright,* thought Miss Barnacle.

'It's about your trike, really, that I've come, and to see if we can't fix up something, perhaps, well really just a little more suitable.'

'Oh dear. Well I do rely on it, you know. Entirely. I should be lost without it. I know it's an ugly thing, and smelly and noisy too, but it gets me about. I should be lost without it.'

'Yes, of *course,* Miss Barnacle-Flavell. But we do wonder if you've looked at all the alternatives. You see we *are* phasing them out bit by bit – as you say they *are* noisy, and of course they're not entirely safe either. Well, this *is* what we find and I think you've had experience of that too.

She has in mind my two accidents. Well, I expected trouble, but not from this quarter. From the police, yes, but is the fact I bumped a milk-van and a lamp-post really a Department matter?

'... so shall we just have a look at what the Department can do to replace the trike? Now you should have had a letter from the Minister and the leaflet N1225 and Form MY58 through the post.'

'Should I? I expect I did.' Miss Barnacle's breathing was now as normal as it ever was, and her responses brisker. 'But you know I never bother with all that. I leave the tedious things for my nephew. He comes over from Langley every now and then.'

'Well, let's just have a look, shall we?'

'Mobility Allowance. New option for Vehicle Scheme Beneficiaries. And what's this? A personal Message from the Minister for the Disabled. You know Mrs Shiner I do find this sort of thing impertinent. Diminishing as well. I mean, do they really think they can fool us in this way?'

'Oh I'm sure there's no deception intended.'

'I am not speaking of deception, Mrs Shiner. I am referring to the fact that this letter is presented as if it had been written on a typewriter and signed by this Alf Morris man in person. And it hasn't. And to assume that I or any other registered disabled person might believe that it has, is to assume that disabled people are fools.'

'Oh Miss Barnacle, I'm sure I don't know about that sort of thing. But shall we see what it really says.'

'If we must.'

'Well then. It's really all quite simple you know. What it says is this. There has been a change in the law ... and many thousands of disabled people are now entitled to the mobility allowance of seven pounds a week.'

'Taxable?'

'Yes. It says here it is taxable. Now. If under the old vehicle scheme you have a tricycle or a car or a private car allowance, now you can have a mobility allowance instead.'

'Instead?'

'Yes.'

'I can have seven pounds a week instead of my sardine can?'

'Yes.'

'I thought that's what it said. Where are my other glasses? Here. No, those are the reading ones. Yes, here. Eyesight going. Deaf too. Now, that's better. Mrs Shiner, it would have to be taxis. Seven pounds would get me in and out and in to Brinshore. But not back again. I'd have to stay in an hotel till the week came round again ... Oh never mind.'

'But Miss Barnacle-Flavell. Why go into Brinshore at all? You can use the seven pounds to pay someone to do your shopping for you. Or to take a taxi half a mile to the Merriedale Precinct, and you could do that as often as three times a week I should think.'

'I don't go *shopping* in Brinshore.'

Miss Barnacle peered across the room. Beyond a copper jug – brought back from Africa after her stint housekeeping for her brother the High Commissioner – she could see through a French window her madonna lilies just bursting their buds. They would be ready for Sunday ...

'How would I get to church?'

'I'm sure we can arrange a lift. I'll get in touch with the

Young Wives for you, there's sure to be somebody goes by. Mudwick Parish is it? There, I've made a note of that. Now let's get back to the letter.'

'Must we? Glasses. Other glasses. Here we are. Right then. Read away.'

'It says here ... "Moreover they can switch to the mobility allowance without a medical examination and without any age limit". "Without" is underlined.'

'Is it really? So it is.'

'So there'll be no problem there.'

'Problem?'

'With your eyes.'

That's it, thought Miss Barnacle. She knows I had the wrong glasses on when I hit the milk-van. How did they find that out? I never let on. Not even to the milkman. Such a nice man.

'I don't go *shopping* in Brinshore,' she repeated.

'No, Miss Barnacle.'

You stir up people like that Rammage and the other fishermen. You are chairman of the Friends of Trafalgar House. You are second cousin of the Lord Lieutenant of the next county. For your age you have a psychological disfunction towards need autonomy, and your need affiliation is misdirected. You are a silly old woman and you ought to be put down or locked up. That clock – like one of those beetles, death-watch is it? How can she live here with all this old stuff round her, she doesn't seem to have a telly and doesn't she ever put the radio on? Something to cheer things up a bit. There's no bright colours anywhere – no wonder she's always out driving that death-trap all over the place.

'Then you don't really need the trike, Miss Barnacle-Flavell. I mean it's not a necessity, is it? You don't *need* to go to Brinshore three or four times a week.'

'Oh reason not the need,' said Miss Barnacle who found reasons to go into Brinshore five or six times a week.

'Eh? Beg pardon?'

' "Reason not the need: our basest beggars Are in the poorest things superfluous: Allow not nature more than nature needs, Man's life's as cheap as beasts" ... '

'I'm sorry. I don't quite ... '

'Shakespeare, dear. King Lear.'

The clock ticked.

'Shakespeare's lovely, isn't he? I mean did you see that Macbeth on telly the other night ... Such a lovely actor he was.'

'I watched five minutes and then switched off. The way the lines were spoken was a disgrace. Anyone who did not know the play well, and there must have been some considering the way things have been allowed to slide in our schools, would have been very hard put to understand it at all.'

'Oh, but Shakespeare's not really for understanding, is he? I mean really when you get down to it, it's the beauty. And the drama. I mean it's like poetry really, isn't it?'

A terrible feeling of fatigue and despair filled the old lady, so for a moment she feared she was going to make a fool of herself and cry.

She pulled herself together: 'Well, well. Now just what is it you want me to do?'

'Oh Miss Barnacle-Flavell, *I* don't want you to do anything. You're a completely free agent in this. But we do feel all things considered you'd be better off with the mobility allowance than with the trike.'

'I dare say you're right. I dare say.' Hilary Barnacle breathed as deeply as she was able. I will not weep, she said to herself. I will not weep for this silly philistine woman, for people who cannot understand *any*thing. I will not weep for myself – I had really much better not drive about any more.

'Well then. There must be a form to fill in,' she said at last.

'That's right. The MY58. If you tell me the answers I can do it and all you'll have to do is sign it.'

In less than five minutes it was done.

'They'll come for the trike in a week or so, I expect. And you'll get the order book through the post. Orders cashable for four weeks at a time at any Post Office.'

If I can get to one, thought Miss Barnacle.

'There's no need to come to the door. I can let myself out.'

But that wasn't the Barnacle way. She got to the front door on Lucie Shiner's arm and then held her – the social worker thought it was so she could get her breath back, but she had something else to say.

'Mrs Shiner. You are a public servant. Most of my family were public servants. My grandfather, Ferdinand Barnacle worked for the Department in his day. Do you know what he used to say about it?'

'I'm sure there wasn't a Department of Social ... '

'Oh no. You're quite right. In those days it was called the Circumlocution Office. In fun, that is. I forget what its real name was. But Grandfather Barnacle used to say the Department was there with the express intention that everything should be left alone, that its method was to be a windmill grinding immense quantities of chaff, and because of it nothing ever got done. And that was how it should be.'

Mrs Shiner waited. She had no choice – the old lady's hand, a little claw-like with arthritis, was fastened on her wrist.

'Well my dear. Times change. Still the grinding of chaff, but now you seem to *do* things as well. You seem to *get in* everywhere.'

'I'm sure we wouldn't be doing our job if we didn't.'

'I dare say not. I dare say not.'

At last Mrs Shiner could get to her Mini. Silly old bag, she thought. After all, she can hardly be badly off living in that place.

And there she was wrong. Hilary Barnacle had never worked. Not, that is, for money. She had kept house for her brother, who was a homosexual, once he had reached a position in the Colonial Service where a hostess to entertain for him was regarded as essential. When he retired they bought the house and lived there for a year before he died, having been hounded to suicide by a Sunday newspaper. As his sister she did not qualify for a widow's pension. Her income came from annuities whose value dwindled and which was swallowed in paying a man to garden for her and a woman to do the heavy cleaning. Any that was left went to charity or on presents for her numerous great-nephews and -nieces. On food she spent less in a week than Mrs Shiner spent at the hairdresser's.

When the lady from the Department had gone, Hilary Barnacle-Flavell stayed in her hall for a moment or two and looked with pleasure, as she often did, at a pressed flower picture she had bought at Johnny Manet's and which she had liked too much to give away. She would miss her visits to him. She would miss chatting with people like Kevin Rammage, and that delightful Trivet girl – fancy coming across her after all these years. She would even miss the other old biddies who called themselves the Friends of Trafalgar House. She sighed, told herself to pull herself together: she had letters to write and she had better do them – while she still had the means to get to the post.

16.25

157 Spithead Road was an Edwardian semi-detached villa set in what had once been a residential road behind the new Council offices of Rifedale rural district. Although these offices had been custom-built following the Local Government Act, and although three old Town Halls had, by that act, become theoretically redundant (those of Brinshore, Langley and Rifedale itself), the Department in all its manifestations had still been forced to acquire property to put further roofs over its operations. In Spithead Road at least six large houses had plain boards in government green or government grey in what had once been their front gardens – now only the shrubs remained, the rest laid to easy-to-keep-up tarmac. The back gardens were filled with mobile huts, the file repositories and typing-pools serving the houses themselves. If Ern Copeman had put in a request for permission to erect such a hut in his own back garden instead of the expensive and permanent brick attachment that he now lived in, he would have been refused; and the refusal would have been typed and filed in one of these huts.

It was not to a hut at the back that Miriam addressed herself, but to an imposing Edwardian portico. Set on pillars of polished brown stone, the heads of Shakespeare and Milton supported a limestone lintel which was carved in art nouveau lettering with the words *Empire Villas.* The wide entrance had glossy tiles and a glazed door, flanked by stained-glass windows. A painted board, screwed to the frame beneath a tarnished brass lion's head knocker announced: *Family Practitioner Committee. Please Enter.*

Miriam pushed the unlatched door, which, though heavy, moved with an inert ease that suggested fine engineering, and found herself in a wide, deep, dark hall. Stairs climbed away from her into gloom, wide stairs with wrought iron and oak banisters on one side and oak panelling on the other. They were uncarpeted now: only two brass rings screwed into each step and a blank of unpolished wood between them showed where the runner had once been. To the left of the stairs, at the end of the hall and lit by another window with a stained-glass border, a man was working. He was smearing a black glutinous substance on the floor and beside him, leaning against the oak panelling, was a roll of cheap carpeting. Only the distant sound of a typewriter and a voice murmuring monotonously as if dictating suggested that there was anyone else at all in the house. Four large heavy doors with porcelain handles effectively shut these noises away from the listener in the hall.

'There's enquiries behind you,' the man on his knees in front of her said.

'Oh. Oh yes. So there is.'

There was indeed. Just inside the door she had missed a small window cut through the wall and the panelling; it had a narrow sill on which was screwed a cheap plastic bell-push. *Enquiries. Please Ring for Attention.*

Miriam rang. The bell sounded loud and harsh, but brought no answer. She peered through the window and saw a tiny office partitioned off from the rest of what must have been the large front room. There was a chair, a small switchboard and a telephone.

'Tea-break,' said the man at the end of the hall. 'They knock off as far as enquiries are concerned at four-thirty, but they've taken to having tea a bit earlier like.'

Miriam pressed the bell-push again and kept her finger on

it while she counted ten. Silence returned, lengthened. She was about to try a third blast when the door inside the little office opened and a middle-aged, grey woman in grey cardigan and grey skirt came in.

'You're a little late you know. We don't take enquiries after four-thirty, you know.'

'It's not quite half-past.'

'Very nearly.'

'But not yet. And I've come on the buses from Brinshore and I don't want to have to come back again tomorrow.'

'You could write, you know.'

'I want to get this tidied up as quickly as I can. I felt a personal visit might help.'

'You'd better give me your name and address.'

Miriam did so.

'What's it about then?'

'I am a full-time student on an L.E.A. grant. I qualify as having a low income. I want to claim back money I paid my dentist six months ago.'

'You've left it a bit late.'

'I have not left it late. I first wrote about this in January.'

'I see. Well, I'm sorry but really this is a Department matter. You should go to the Department.' The Grey Woman looked at Miriam's address. 'In Brinshore.'

'I have just come from the Department in Brinshore. They said that they have sent the receipts I gave them there to you here. They said I should see you about it.'

The Grey Woman blinked through her grey spectacles.

'I'll see if we've got a file on you.'

She dematerialised, and then the large door nearest the enquiries window silently opened and she rematerialised in the hall.

'I won't be a minute,' and she floated noiselessly up the stairs until the gloom at the top breathed her in and she became part of it.

Miriam had *The Living Principle* with her but there was nowhere to sit. She did not accept boredom readily, and though sometimes shy she was a sociable person. She moved down the hall. The man who was working on the floor was about thirty, looked fit and vigorous, wore a check shirt and jeans. He was now running a sort of short-toothed comb over the black substance he had smeared, pushing it into the corners, levelling it, and leaving it with a uniform pattern of shallow ridges. Working thus he had obscured about one third of a pleasant floral pattern of stylised carnations and acanthus leaves laid out in white, ochre, terracotta and blue tiles.

'What are you doing?' she asked.

'Laying this carpet.' He pointed to the roll of cheap floor covering. It was a sick sort of shade on the yellow side of red. Blood Orange, a label at the end announced.

'But there's nothing wrong with the floor.'

'Nothing at all. Good for another hundred years if you ask me.'

'And it's pretty too.'

'Yes, very nice. Old-fashioned like, but nice. And the same's true of the floorboards in the other rooms. They're quality, I can tell you. Close fitting. Solid. Well, solid's not the word – not a furniture mark on them nor even a stiletto heel.'

'You're doing the whole house?'

'The whole house. Except under the copier upstairs. That's too heavy to lift so I go round it. Upstairs they're having High Veldt. It's a sort of cross between dirty yellow and dirty green. Not my choice. Colour of duck shit.'

In spite of her studenty appearance the carpet-layer had identified Miriam's origins. He talked to her openly, without false concessions to her sex.

'But why are they doing it? What's the point?'

'Oh there's a good reason. Be sure of it. What it is is this.' He lowered his voice, conscious that if the Grey Woman returned she might not approve of such free talk with one of 'them', the public. 'Each establishment like has its own estimate of running and maintenance expenses. If they don't use it up in one year, financial year that is, they get less next year.'

'I should have thought they'd have tried to aim for that. I mean, aren't they meant to be cutting public waste?'

'Yes, well. That's not how their minds work like, is it? Fact is I should have done this before April the first but I was doing the same up the hospital, much bigger job that, but they fiddled it by saying because the order was in in March it was all right, it could come out of last year's portion, if you see what I mean.'

'Do you know what it's costing?'

'Of course I do. I'm the contractor. Me and my brother and two fellas as works with us like. This'll cost 'em eight hundred quid. We wanted to do it for seven but no, they said eight. Twenty-five we got at the hospital and the same story – lovely black vinyl floors they had there, not more'n six years old.'

'Two thousand five hundred pounds.'

'That's right.' He prodded the black stuff. 'Fixer's just nicely on the turn so I have to get the covering down.'

Miriam watched him. He worked briskly, neatly – trimming the material to an exact fit in the corners and along the wall; then he went back to his large can of black stuff and gave it a stir.

'Just time for another length before they chuck me out,' he said.

The Grey Woman stood at Miriam's shoulder.

'There's no file, you know, in your name here,' she said.

'What does that mean then?'

'It means we never got your receipts here.'

'Where are they then?'

'Are you sure they had them at Brinshore?'

'It says in my file there that they had them and that they sent them here.'

The Grey Woman blinked. 'They never got here.'

'Where are they then?'

'Must have been lost in the post.'

'So what do I do now?'

The Grey Woman shrugged.

'Go back to your dentist and ask for duplicates,' she suggested.

Miriam took a deep breath.

'This place is crazy,' she said. 'This place is really crazy.'

The Grey Woman blinked. The carpet-layer, on his knees again, looked up and grinned.

'That's right, my dear,' he said. 'You tell her.'

17.32

Ern Copeman hummed to himself – *In an English Country Garden* – as he drove his Escort home to Merriedale from the Council Offices in Rifedale. The sky was clearing now; there was the possibility of a sunny evening ahead. Perhaps he would tidy up his early peas, lift a root of new potatoes, or after all stay indoors and make a start on an idea for a painting that had come to him during the day – a picture of an old aeroplane, a Gypsy Moth or something of the sort, seen from below, wings tilted, flying into a stormy sunset. No land in it, no sea. Just the sky and the aeroplane. Or better still make it a sunrise.

Then a half pint or so at the Athlone, or The Club – what was left of it. You had to laugh though, think of that, three kids messing about with fireworks left over from the fifth of November, and half a pub gone up in smoke. And they say youngsters lack initiative these days.

The Athlone's the place though, he thought as he waited at the level crossing, and he gave himself a broad wink. The Athlone, saved for posterity – well, for my time anyway.

It hadn't been easy. Ever since the plan for pulling down the pier had been cleared – and there was no point in fighting that, the old structure was too far gone – the Athlone had looked to be doomed. But over six months Ern had dropped a word here, sent a minute there, queried this committee's findings and asked for that steering group's assumptions to be looked at again and quietly made sure that at least three councillors would find themselves, well, embarrassed, if the plan was approved and passed on for further more detailed studies. That Mr Dangerfield would be pleased. Jack Trivet and his missus would be very pleased. And old Mr Rigg could live out his days undisturbed as landlord. Well done, Ern Copeman.

And that wasn't all. That was not his only good deed for the day, because he'd brought off what he had planned with respect to the Brinshore fishermen too. That had been easier, but he'd seen the opportunity and grasped it. Usually no one paid much attention to Councillor Mrs Lizzie Cheal's effusions. With her gins and tonics and diamonds set in platinum it was generally understood that Jimmy Cheal's posh sister-in-law was only on the Council as a line of communication back to TRICE, nothing improper mind you, just a convenience; but then he'd seen her committee's minutes and how she had gone on and on about how picturesque the old boats were, and did you know they actually mended their nets on the front and those funny baskets they catch lobsters in, and how she thought, well, if it was left to her, they should be encouraged not harassed.

Taking this as his starting-point, Ern had prodded and wheedled, made enquiries and dug out figures (a picture-postcard of Kevin Rammage holding up a lobster in front of the pier was the best seller on Brinshore Front), until that very afternoon he had managed to get it made official Council policy that Brinshore fishermen should be encouraged as they provided a tourist attraction, a piece of genuine local colour, were 'folkloric'. As a practical gesture in this direction it had been decided that the cost of providing a fresh water facility on the front, as required by paragraph ten, sub-section D, section three of the Marketing of Fish and Allied Trades Act, as amended in 1976, would be met out of the rates.

All in the day's work, thought Ern, and with the added satisfaction that both items would be in the weekend *Post:* a Council spokesman has said that ... we can now confirm that plans involving ... and so on. Well, perhaps he wouldn't go to the Athlone tonight, but leave it to tomorrow, when the news would be out, or even find an excuse for being in Brinshore lunchtime, yes that would be the thing. *The Post,* though nominally a Friday paper, was usually out by Thursday lunchtime, and no one would miss him at the Council offices – he'd just say he would be out in the afternoon looking at some site or other.

Round Abbott's Mere. That will be my next project, Ern thought, scotching that Sandra Black's petition. Proper little interfering busybody she is, and he thought back again to Frank's joke about the Department of Social Interference. Well, I've stopped two bits of that today, and it goes to show what I always say – it's not always the Council are instigators.

He pulled up outside his house to let Dot Green push her luxury baby carriage across his drive-in and he didn't notice how she cut him, ignored him completely. He pulled in after her as she turned the pram towards her own front door, and wound down his window.

'Hullo there,' he called. 'How are you and yours today?'

Dot Green stopped, looked at him. Saw the round face, the frothy halo of black and grey hair beneath the balding crown, the eyes that twinkled puckishly from between grey pouches.

'It's not your business how we are. Right? It's just not your business,' and with a near sob she rushed on up to the door, fumbling for her key.

Ern's face fell, his mood collapsed, for he had only wanted to be kind, and so rarely had the chance that he was always hurt by a rebuff, however undeserved.

20.42

Nick Green picked up the eighteenth exercise book. On the green cover: Frances King 4G1 English. He turned to the last used pages and picked up his red pen.

> Imagine You are a Neighbour of Silas's – How would You React to his Fostering of Eppie? How would you try to help him? You may imagine this story is happening now if you like.

man
slang/large
does

> Down our road lives this old geezer and he's a right one I can tell you, great staring eyes and an old coat like a sack. Well he doesn't do proper work, I mean he don't go out to work, he sits in

his front room all day and just weaves, making cloth like. But he does it well and the posh ladies over on old Merriedale where the posh houses are by his stuff and he makes a living. But that don't stop him being a real dirty old man in all senses if you ask me and not quite right in his head, especially since his money was took. Well, he said it was, he said he had tons there, all in gold, but no one had ever seen it like, so who knows, that's what I say. Anyway, like I said, he's not quite right in the head and gets into like trances all the time, when he just stands there like a post and don't see nothing nor hear nothing neither.

Anyway, the other day, like it was New Year's Eve actually, and it snowed and snowed till there were drifts all down our lane, what should happen but what a young girl with this baby comes stumbling along the lane and snuffs it almost on this old geezer's, Marner's his name, Silas Marner's doorstep. And the baby just toddles in past Old Marner because he's like having one of his fits.

This girl, the mother I mean, not the kid, is a junkie, and full of opium which is like raw heroin, well that's what comes out at the inquest, and no one knows who she is.

Well Marner takes a shine to the kid on account it's got gold hair like the gold he's lost, in fact when he comes out of his trance he reckons her hair is his gold come back, he being what they call nowadays partially sighted, but I'd say was nearer being as blind as a bat, but then he reckons it's a kid, and she, she's about two going on three she seems happy enough to stay.

But of course she can't, it wouldn't be right not nowadays would it.

First thing is they say he oughta go to the

council with it but he says I can't part with it, I can't let it go. It's come to me – I've a right to keep it. Then some tell-tale (there's one in every street my mum says) goes up the council and tells them and the next thing is he has the Health Visitor there, and the social workers, and meals on wheels and the doctor and the district nurse, till you can't hardly get in his house and they say the kid should be in a home. Who says so Marner says will they make me take her? Till anybody shows they've a right to take her away from me … the mother's dead, I reckon it got no Father: it's a lone thing – and I'm a lone thing. My money's gone, I don't where, and this has come from I don't know where.

So they go up the court, the health visitor and the social worker and all that lot to get a court order saying she's got to be in an home but the magistrate's an old-fashioned old codger and says why should she be a charge on the rates if old Marner will look after her so back they all come, the visitors and social and all and they get together all the evidence they can and it takes them more'n a year all told.

But this is what they get.

Old Marner don't change her wet clothes quick enough.

He ties her to his loom thing with a long linen band like she was a donkey or something.

He lets her play with scissors and lets her get in the Stone-pit which is dangerous and anyway he being partially sighted he can't find her.

He lets her play in the coal'ole and she gets all dirty.

He feeds her on nothing but brown sugar and porridge.

He takes her on his trips with him when he goes selling what he's been weaving.

He calls her Hepzibah which is a daft name, even though it's what his mum and sister were called.

But worst of all he's always cuddling and holding her and stroking her hair and putting on her under things like after she's had a bath, and that's not right, an old man with staring eyes and prone to fits and not related like, that's pedophilia the socials and all that lot say.

Another 'chatty' sentence!

Lazy expression

So when they all go back to the court this time the magistrate makes an order and they take this Eppie away from Marner and puts her in a home, and I shouldn't wonder but what she goes to the bad, becomes a scrubber and a druggie like what her mother was, most girls as go in homes ending up like that if what you read in the papers.

as

This needs a bit added

Marner's upset at this, especially when enquiries arising reveal he's not been buying his stamps or his VAT so now he's back at TRICE on nights like my Dad who went self-employed decorating but found too much paperwork and worry attached so gave up.

6/10 Quite good Frances, but try to write in a slightly less chatty way; I don't think that bit at the end about your Father was quite relevant, do you?

Two days later, when Frances got her book back, she added the following below Nick Green's comment.

Dear Sir,

that bit that goes 'It got no Father, it's a lone thing – and I'm a lone thing ect' I copied from the book as Ms George Eliot wrote it. So I think you were wrong to interfere with that bit.

VI
THURSDAY
Tragic News

BEEP-beep, beep-beep, tra-affic ne-yooos. Teresa, up to her elbows in hot water, pounded Jack's second pair of work trousers in the kitchen sink. Behind her Miriam poured from a kettle on to *Bland* – the smoother coffee drink. *Owing to a serious accident on the M 6 northbound carriageway, two lanes are now closed and there are long traffic tail-backs.* She added milk. 'Do you have sugar in this stuff, Mum?' 'Just one.' *Tra-affic ne-yoos from Radio One.* 'It's ready.' 'Right, I'll just wring these out.' *Beep-beep, be a safe-driver.* 'There. That'll do for the day. Can't wring them properly with my wrists, but they'll drip-dry on the line. I always try to do some each day, then it doesn't get on top of me.'

'Well, come and drink this before it gets cold.'

'Right. Turn that thing off, would you? It gets on your nerves after a bit, doesn't it?'

They sat opposite each other on either side of the narrow red-topped table. The kitchen was warm, steamy, the windows hazed with condensation. Outside the sky was grey.

'You know when it says "traffic news" like that, I used to think it was *tragic* news.'

'I expect it usually is for someone. I mean it normally means an accident, doesn't it?'

They sipped. Vague thoughts about tragedy went through Miriam's mind – an accident wasn't tragedy, but Raymond Williams (is that who I mean?) thinks it might be because of the socio-economic factors that make some accidents inevitable, and anyway they're tragic all right for the people who suffer them.

'You ought to get at least a spin-drier, Mum. A little one, second hand, cost nothing.'

But Tess was impatient with this conversation which recurred often enough. She did not want a spin-drier, and it was her privilege *not* to say why – nevertheless there was a complex of reasons: she would be frightened of the noise, and believed it would damage the clothes; she would operate it wrongly and it would flood the kitchen; she grudged the space in the small area and would resent the alien presence; she *liked* rinsing clothes . . . .

Miriam thought it was because she grudged the expense, not only the outlay but the extra on the electricity bill. Not much, a Guinness a week ...

'I've got to go into town this morning. Would you like to come?'

'Not really, Mum. I really must get some reading done before I start at TRICE.'

'It's your life. Anyway it won't be much fun. I thought I'd try to get to poor Trev Stevens' funeral. I don't suppose anyone else will and I don't like to think of Marge on her own.'

'When is it?'

'Two. Or half-past. It'll be in the paper.'

'It's not out yet, is it?'

'Jack'll bring it, with the money. He does every Thursday.'

Thursday mornings, since TRICE had insisted that all pay should be in cheques, Jack went down to the bank, drew the housekeeping and his expenses for the weekend, and called at the offices of the Brinshore *Post* on the way back, picking up a copy before it was distributed to the newsagents.

'But what will you do between getting down town and going to the funeral?'

'I have to see Doctor Ferrit for my back, and there'll be a bit of shopping to do. Then it'll be a bus out to Mudwick and the way they run now I'll have to get the one o'clock from the bus station to be at the church before two.'

'What about your lunch?'

Tess ignored this too. Her head went up, her back very straight. She pushed a cigarette in her mouth and lit it with a Ronson gas lighter Jack had found on his way home from fishing some months before. She would have her lunch, *if* she had lunch, at the Athlone, that is if she felt like it, and anyway it wasn't Molly's business or anyone else's where she had her lunch.

Miriam realised that this was what was in her mother's mind, realised indeed that it was a fair picture of her own thoughts, and tried to make amends.

'What I meant was, if you've got time, and it's not too far extra for you to walk, I wondered if you'd be able to go into the dentist for me.'

This was credible enough for Tess to relax without loss of face: anyway the dentist was in a side road just by the Athlone.

'And ask for those receipts again?'

'That's right. If you're sure you don't mind. It will save me the trip, an hour or more there and back, and I really must get down to it this morning. Tell them it was paid in December. Day before Christmas Eve it was.'

Half an hour later Tess was in front of the little mirror in the kitchen using a long-handled comb to adjust the tight half curls in her permed hair. She had changed into a black polo-necked jumper, black trousers, black shoes, and had replaced the mounted sovereign she usually wore on a chain for a filigree silver cross.

'That man's usually back by now,' she said. 'He'd better get a move on or I'll miss the ten-forty bus. It's no use going to the Health Centre after eleven. I expect he'll only give me twenty-five again this week. They're on short time up at TRICE. Still, it means he only works till one on Friday. Sometimes he's even earlier. Last week we got down to the George before closing.'

Miriam, who had stayed in the kitchen because it was warm and she didn't like to put on the electric fire in her bedroom, fetched a five pound note out of her purse.

'Here Mum,' she said putting it on the table. 'I'd have given it you earlier, but I didn't know whether or not I'd be able to afford it.'

'I didn't mean that. No way. I know you can't afford it. Now don't be silly, Molly.'

'I've got enough to last me a week. Then TRICE'll pay me.'

She had three pounds and forty-eight pence.

Without warning the back door opened and Jack came in.

'Hullo. Still here then?' He went to the kitchen table and counted down five fivers. 'There's the housekeeping. You're looking very smart, where you off to then? Lunch at the Park Hotel is it?'

'I thought I'd go to Trev Stevens' funeral.'

'Yes. Well. It's here in the paper.' He read slowly and carefully, in a voice a little louder than usual, just as old Mr Trim, who was still at the Comp, had taught him to in the Alma Street Elementary forty-three years ago. 'Private cremation at eleven-thirty, Rifedale Crematorium, it says private so you won't want to go to that, interment of ashes in St Richard's, Mudwick, half-past two. That'll be the public ceremony like. I ordered a spray at Blyth's, those lilies they'll be, the little ones. That's why I'm late. Tell Marge my sympathy and all that.'

'I must be off or I'll miss the bus.'

'Don't forget the dentist for me, will you Mum?'

'No dear. Receipts of twenty-third of December.'

'And I'll get Dad's supper if you're not back in time.'

Tess went out and Jack sat down opposite Miriam and automatically pressed the on-button of the old-fashioned portable he'd picked up cheap when minature trannies first came in.

Three people have been killed and two injured in a collision between a coach and an articulated lorry on the northbound carriageway of the M 6. The accident which occurred . . . ., Jack retuned to Radio Downland.

Miriam closed *Little Dorrit* over her finger. She knew her father would be off to bed in a minute or so – then she'd have the kitchen to herself until it was time to wake him.

Her father found music he liked, orchestral arrangements of old show music, and he unfolded the paper. 'Fire at The Club – damage estimated at fifty thousand pounds,' he read. Then: 'It says here the Council are going to pay for a fresh water facility on the south side of the front. Councillor Mrs

Cheal told our reporter that not enough has been done for our fishermen. They are a tourist attraction, she said, and help the front to retain a touch of the old Brinshore ... Your Kev'll be pleased to hear that.'

'He's not my Kev,' said Miriam.

Glad to hear it, thought Jack, but was careful not to say it out loud.

At the Health Centre Tess had to face long ziggurat-like ramps – designed for push-chairs, ideal for skate boards, they were necessary because the whole thing had to be on concrete stilts: only thus was it possible to make private parking areas available for the three doctors, three district nurses, eight clerical staff and four ancillary staff, plus visiting specialists who worked there. The result for Tess was pain. No doubt her sensibilities too were punished by the brutal concrete, the orange-red paintwork, the blood-orange carpeting (same as in 157 Spithead Road), and above all by the thick black line signs which everywhere replaced writing, were often obscure, (it's not always easy to tell whether an angled arrow means go sideways or up), and reduced humanity to pin-men without hands, feet or faces.

After a twenty-minute wait breathing filtered dead air, ignoring *Country Life* and *Yachting World* and the other people around her, she saw Doctor Ferrit. He gave her four and a half minutes, most of which was spent writing her prescriptions – sleeping pills and a powerful pain-killer. Doctor Ferrit was tired, harassed, suffered from writer's cramp, and lived nowhere near as close to reality as Dickens's Physician in *Little Dorrit.* Still he did his best.

Then down the long ramps Tess went, even more nervous now because she couldn't see what was coming down behind her. She averted her eyes from the patch of wasteland where she had once found some fulfilment in keeping a nice house clean and pretty before the Council pulled it down, and so out on to pavements where high solid steel rails fenced her off from where she wanted to go and funnelled her like a rat in a maze to the crossing where lights blinked and a high-pitched bleep, which in fact sounded like a danger signal, actually told her to cross.

At the dentists' it took twenty minutes of grim determination in the face of rude incomprehension to discover that the duplicates of Miriam's receipts had been sent to the Dental Estimates Board at Rackham, and a letter would have to be sent to get copies back. 'Who should write the letter?' asked Tess. 'Well, *we* don't need them,' said the lady in accounts. At which Tess gave up – Miriam after all would have to deal with it.

The Athlone was a restful harbour after such assaults.

'Guinness, dear?' asked Jane as Tess settled herself on her usual stool.

'Please.'

'You're looking smart today.'

This repeat of her husband's comment annoyed Tess, who rightly prided herself on always looking smart.

'Funeral, Jane.'

'Eh?'

'Funeral. I'm going to a funeral this afternoon.'

'Oh. I'm sorry. Whose is it? Not someone too personal I hope.'

'Trevor Stevens. We've known them – oh for as long as I can remember,' Tess gave a little flutter with her hand which signified suppressed emotion, a sort of I'm-suffering-but-there's-no-need-for-you-to-join-me attitude, which she would maintain now until the funeral itself.

'They were talking about it the other day. Sudden, wasn't it? That'll be thirty-two, dear.'

'Five pound note Jane, I'm sorry to say. Heart usually is sudden.'

'That's all right dear. Yes I suppose it is. You know I'd never thought of it like that before?'

She counted out the change and moved on to serve the next customer, a pensioner, small, fat, with protruding eyes and bald head, who always spent one pound every Thursday lunchtime.

Tess sat very upright and sipped her Guinness, smoked her

cigarettes, and played with her rings. She was beginning to wish she wasn't going to a funeral, was almost deciding that she wouldn't after all, but the thought of Marge on her own continued to upset her. The old man droned on to a crony: 'See what I mean?' he asked, 'and of course I was trained, I was properly trained. Not like nowadays.' He drank deeply at his mild and brown, wiped his mouth, and said with satisfaction: 'I thought you'd find that interesting.' His crony, even older, but tall and thin with wrists exposed by sleeves too short, said: 'There aren't half been some clever bastards.' Tess sighed impatiently. Bloody old fools, she thought.

Frank Dangerfield came in with that Pet Rogate.

'Hullo there, Mrs Trivet,' he said. 'Morning Jane. A half of bitter, and a slim-line bitter lemon, and Guinness is it, Mrs Trivet? Oh dear, you're in weeds by the look of it, looking very sombre.'

'Yes, Mr Dangerfield. The fact is I have a funeral to go to this afternoon.'

'Not, not someone, well ... '

'Trevor Stevens, Mr Dangerfield. He went last Sunday in the intensive care at Rifedale General.'

'Did you know him well?'

'Well, but not close, Mr Dangerfield. But I think it likely that Marge, his wife, will be on her own.'

'No family then?'

'There's a son. But he moved to Wolverhampton and he married a black, so he won't be coming. The daughter's in Australia. So. No family. Cheers.'

'Cheers. Well it's good-hearted of you to go. I'm sure she'll appreciate your support.'

Frank held a glass in each hand. Pet Rogate had moved off to sit at a table, but he hovered. There was something he wanted Tess Trivet to say – and he was quite surprised at the relief he felt when she did.

'I gave Molly your message. About how you were sorry you missed her on Tuesday.'

'That was sweet of you. Now, can I ask you to pass on

another? I just wonder if Miriam knows there is a disco tomorrow night at school. All past pupils welcome.'

'I think she does know, Mr Dangerfield, but I'll remind her.'

'Jolly good. I'm sure she'll have a good time if she comes. Just a pound a head and that includes two drinks – the usual way round the licensing laws, you know? Just beer or wine for the over-eighteens, coke for the rest.'

He moved off to the table. Tess heard Pet Rogate's high voice that carried: 'Who's that funereal woman you were talking to?' Then a whiff of cigar smoke made her turn to find that Mr Rigg had made his landlord's appearance, precisely at twelve-thirty, as he always did. Hands on the counter in front of him, his eyes moved over the bar checking that all was as it should be, cheroot in his mouth, very clean, very bright, very smooth, with the perfection that alcoholics do achieve in the hour or so run up to the first of the day. His white beard was perfectly trimmed, the ends of the moustache exactly even in their upward tilt, his bow tie immaculately knotted above spotless starched shirt. Only his hand, an old man's hand, shook as he raised a glass to the cognac optic.

'What do you think, Mr Rigg, of schools and such-like providing drinks at functions?' Tess asked.

'Not much Mrs Trivet. Not much. Let them be licensed or stick to soft drinks. But it's the spirit of the times – every law can be bent if you want to bend it, trouble is everyone seems to want to.'

'Thank you Mr Rigg. That's just what I think.'

The small bald-headed pensioner eyed her with his eyes popping like marbles – blood alleys. He had a huge paunch that so filled and tightened his trousers you could see what hung below pressed against the inside of the top of his leg, a sight lost to him several years since.

'Trev Stevens, is it then, Tess?' he asked.

'Yes Mr Twine. It is.' Normally she called him Ted, but today she resented his harmless ugliness, his innocent stupidity.

'I'd go myself, but the doctor wouldn't allow it. Of course if it was here in Brinshore ... ' Twine drank deeply. 'But he wanted it in Mudwick they say.'

'That's right Mr Twine. He was born in one of the cottages by the church.'

The tall thin crony cleared his throat – recalled that spitting on the floor in bars had gone out of fashion some years ago and employed a handkerchief instead.

'I knew old Ben Stevens,' he said. 'Trev's father.' He spoke with rich satisfaction at the thought of generations trodden down and he lived on.

The two old men now adopted a ritual posture – spreading their knees on their stools, facing the twinkling many-coloured radiance of glass bottles doubled up in the mirror behind, heads hunched forward a bit, and hands palm down on the bar on either side of their pots.

'I'm not a religious man myself,' intoned Ted Twine.

'Nor me, when it comes to church-going,' came the response.

'But that's not to say I don't believe in something.'

They drank. Mr Twine breathed in.

'I mean I don't care what they say there has to be something after all this.'

'You've got to believe in something. Wouldn't be any point in living if there wasn't anything else.'

'Well it stands to reason like really, doesn't it? I mean there has to be a Hereafter. What are we here for if there isn't a Hereafter?'

'It's like determined, to my way of looking.'

'The way I look at it is – we're here for a purpose, that's what they call pre-determined, like preparing for the Hereafter. When you're born it's all mapped out for you.'

Tess, annoyed with them, and against her own conscience which had been put together by a village priest not twenty miles from Cork and set going to last her her lifetime, said: 'It's going to be a crowded Hereafter. All those who've gone before'll have got the best places.'

Slowly their faces turned to her – one round, set with the eyes that looked as if they might fall out, the other long and chapfallen with a wet moustache. They were not shocked, reproving merely.

'Ah yes,' said the thin one, 'ah yes but. It's not like that.'

'No way,' said Ted Twine. 'I mean only those who are ready go on to the Hereafter. Very few at any time. I mean the rest come back again, go round again like.'

'Sort of what they call recycled.'

'That's it. The blacks and suchlike mostly.'

They drank up and waited, but Tess still had half a glass left and she wasn't going to rush it just so she could buy their drinks for them. At last they re-ordered for themselves.

Time dissolved in a warm fug of nicotine and alcohol. Tess watched it melt away. In five minutes, no four, she would have to get off her stool and make her way to the bus station if she was to get the last bus that would get her to Mudwick church in time. And once there there would be a fifty-minute wait before the ceremony. Her heart felt heavy in her, heavy with dread. If she had a Bell's, perhaps that would help ... ? Of course she could take a taxi later – for two pounds. Two pounds there and two back probably. Indecision drifted through her, stirred the scum on top of the dread.

She became aware that Ern Copeman had arrived, was sitting next to her.

'Hullo there Tess. Top off the top of a bottle of Guinness for you?'

'Thank you, Ern. You're a stranger here at lunchtimes.'

'Well you know how it is, Tess. Work brought me over to Brinshore this morning, had to have a look at how the Leisure Centre's progressing, and there's the Athlone, I said to myself, and why not? said I.'

'Why not indeed.'

Ern turned to the landlord. As he spoke he put the new *Post* on the counter by his glass of light ale. 'Have you seen the paper, Mr Rigg?'

'I have not.'

'Well, there's good news for you. The plans to pull this place down have been shelved. A new lot are to be got up preserving it as an old piece of Brinshore.'

'Is that so? Is that really so? May I see?'

'Of course Mr Rigg. Here it is. At the bottom of page one.' Ern was gleeful. His small dark eyes twinkled.

Mr Rigg took the cheroot out of his mouth, placed it in a spotless ashtray and reached for his reading glasses which were always placed by the till so he could read the till roll. He read the article in silence. Then switched back his glasses – both had thick black rims – picked up his cheroot and without a word padded slowly out of the bar. The dark depths of the town mansion that had once been Number One, The Terrace, flowed over the broad white expanse of his back, and his silver hair above it.

Ern was crestfallen: 'He didn't look pleased.'

'No. Why should he be?' said Tess.

'Whyever not?'

'He's a man of taste is Mr Rigg,' said Tess, 'and he wants to retire in ... in a way that, well, suits him.'

'So?'

'His only hope was to sell this place for a good price, and your Council was the only way he was going to get a good price. He can't retire till he sells it.'

'Oh dear. Oh.'

Tess looked at her watch, at her glass still a quarter full; at the untouched bottle of Guinness Ern had bought her. It'll have to be a taxi now, she thought.

'Ah well. Bad news for old Rigg perhaps, but good news for the rest of us.' Ern took a drink. 'Well, Tess, how are you? I hope all your black doesn't denote any bad news on your behalf?'

Tess explained yet again, but this time allowed the possibility of not going because she had left it too late for the bus, and felt taking a taxi out to Mudwick was going it a bit. Ern listened, head on one side. Then: 'No problem, Tess, no problem at all. I'll give you a lift out there. I'm not going back to the office today, I've decided that. They won't miss me and I reckon I do more harm than good when I'm there.'

An hour later they sat side by side in the front box pew at

Mudwick Church, Ern having stopped off on the way to change his tie for a black one. The church was empty and cold. Tess thought it plain and gloomy in comparison with Our Lady of Loreto in Brinshore, which was a much cheerier place; the fact that it was twelfth-century Plain rather than Late Victorian Decorated cut no ice with her. The only bit of colour, the hangings and upholstery round the altar beyond the choir, seemed to her to be in bad taste. They looked like someone's lounge, she thought.

A door far behind them clanged as if in a dungeon and soft footsteps approached up the aisle.

The moon face of the Reverend Shamcall beamed at them: 'Mourners for Mr Stevens?' he asked. 'They'll be along presently.' He looked at his watch. 'I make it only just gone twenty past.'

He moved around the choir and the skirts of his long black cassock, held in over his podgy tummy by a worn black belt, whispered over the flags. Silently Tess and Ern watched him bring a small wooden table which he placed on the chancel step and covered with a cloth of purple brocade. Then his feet hissed away back down the church to his vestry.

Time trickled down. Tess looked about her. She had been in this church only once before, for a wedding. She was surprised to see a banner of Our Lady up in a corner by the altar – she narrowed her eyes and made out the letters beneath the image: 'Mothers' Union'. What was that? Not a Trade Union, surely. There had been an organ before, she remembered. A proper organ. Now it had gone and there was one of those electronic things in its place. A large brass plate on the transept wall almost in front of her caught her eye. 'Lt. General Sir Arthur Abbott', she read. 'K.V.O. C.B. For Queen and Country.' Round the outside edge a long list of names, of places. *Vimeiro, La Albuera, Ciudad Rodrigo, Salamanca, Vittoria* – Spanish were they? Battles? Then more, which looked Indian, or eastern anyway.

The door clanged again, dank air breathed round them and they could hear voices, soft, at the back of the church, then footsteps.

Shamcall first, moving well in a mauve chasuble with a white surplice beneath. Behind him came poor Marge. He opened the pew door for her on the opposite side of the aisle from Tess and Ern, murmured something easily condoling, as gentle as any sucking dove, pointed out the prayer book and then went on to take his place on the chancel step facing them with the little table between him and them. Now a man in black, First Undertaker, came up to place a small deal box with mouldings that suggested the ecclesiastical, on the table. He gave it a brisk nod, to signify respect, turned and went into the pew behind Marge where he was joined by the Second Undertaker. Shamcall's head remained bowed in prayer – clearly he expected everyone else to do the same.

Marge looked up, across the aisle, her eyes wide and staring, the whites glowing in the gloom. She shook her head from side to side twice and her lip began to tremble. Tess looked round, saw there was no one else in the church. She turned the catch on her pew, just as Shamcall raised his head and cleared his throat, then slipped across the aisle. The Vicar's eyebrows rose – two black half-moons above his gold-rimmed specs, as Marge made room for Tess, who took the widow's hand and squeezed it and felt a squeeze, then another one firmer, in response.

'The order of service is on page three hundred and eighty-nine in the prayer book.' He paused. Ern Copeman and the undertaker's men fumbled, Tess looked a question at Marge and Marge shook her head, so they left their prayer books where they were. Shamcall waited, then he cleared his throat again: 'We brought *nothing* into *this* world, and it *is* certain we can carry nothing *out.* The Lord gave, *and* the Lord hath taken away; blessed *be* the Name of the Lord.' He moved on to the psalm, said antiphonally. The undertaker's men supplied the responses for him in clear but muted voices – much practised. Tess's attention soon wandered again. *Trevor Austen Stevens,* she read. It should be Aust*i*n she knew, because his mother had been an Austin. His name and dates were painted in black gothic lettering on the lid of the small box. With a little shock she realised she was looking at the ashes, then the shock turned to disgust. This is no way to do it, she thought.

After more sing-song intoning Shamcall invited them please to be seated. He was going to give a little talk, a little homily. Putting podgy white fingertips together under his chin he looked over them and down on the two aging women beneath him, and then up at the rose window in the west wall. In mellifluous tones he exhorted his small congregation to think of the life departed with gratitude. It had been a worthy, honest life, devoted to hard work, to innocent pleasure, to the joys and rewards of family life. On such bed-rock the whole of society is founded. As long as we can say that such lives are the norm amongst us, he said, so long we can hold up our heads among the nations of the world, confident that our dear country will weather all storms. He then said some verses, lovely they were, and beautifully spoken, about the short and simple annals of the poor.

What's he on about, thought Tess. The poor man only worked himself to an early death in a factory all his life, there's nothing special in that.

A hint of a smile twitched a muscle in Ern's cheek, like a small boy trying to get attention: he had remembered a school joke from forty years back – the short and simple *flannels* of the poor.

Shamcall got them to their feet again. With some awkwardness a little procession was formed – at the front, Shamcall, the First Undertaker with the box, next Marge and Tess, behind them Ern, and Second Undertaker took up the rear. They moved off at last down the aisle, out at the back of the church and into the churchyard, and so across the ill-kept squalid little field of stones, uncropped grass, rank weeds and decaying flowers to a little corner under a bramble bush – the spot reserved for interment of ashes. Marge stumbled amongst the graves and Tess had to support her. Under the bush a small rectangular hole – like the slit in a letter-box, Tess thought – gaped between mats of green plastic straw, simulated grass, that had been put down for them to stand on. There was a wait now while Second

Undertaker went back to the black car to fetch the floral tributes.

It was still chilly for June, though the cloud was beginning to break with a breeze off Mudwick Marsh behind them, and when the sun came fitfully through it was hot. Rooks cackled over their young in skeletal diseased elms, and a flight of large ducks, five of them, wheeled and then arrowed away beneath the clouds.

Marge said: 'He wanted it here. See, he was born in one of those cottages. Grandad were a labourer up on Church Farm. They're all here, the Stevens, hereabout somewhere.' She looked round her blankly.

An advertising executive weekended in the cottage now; his boat, on a trailer, filled the tiny front garden which had been cemented over. Trevor Stevens' mother had been the last tied tenant. All this Ern knew and wished he did not. The man was a florid-faced thirty-five-year-old who wore jeans and a heavily ribbed white sweater. His wife, the second, was skinny and loud and they drank noisily together in the Pilot Bar. To put them out of his mind he summoned up his vision of a Tiger Moth against a flaming sunrise. The aeroplane got smaller and smaller, more and more distant every time he thought of it. If I don't paint it soon, he thought whimsically, it'll be gone.

Second Undertaker looked monstrous, like some reveller at an oriental festival, dressed in a pagan costume of flowers, as he stumbled through the graves towards them. There were three wreaths and the Trivets' spray. The two largest wreaths were identical – one printed card said: 'With Heartfelt Sympathy from James Cheal and all the Management at TRICE': the other: 'In Warm Remembrance of our Loyal Brother from Branch 862 Associated Engineering Workers' Union'. The third wreath was from the Granby – the pub the Stevens frequented. Among all the arum lilies and forced-on glads, Tess thought the lilies of the valley and white carnations Jack had chosen looked very nice – they added a touch of something personal anyway.

'There's nothing from Wilf,' said Marge, and began to

weep again. Wilf was their son. Shamcall opened his prayer book. 'Man that is born of a *woman,*' he intoned, 'hath but a short *time* to live, and is *full* of misery.'

Then they all heard again, from a distance, just as they had the previous Saturday night, the two-note call of an ambulance siren.

Ern offered to give the two ladies a lift into Brinshore, but the undertakers were going back to their base in the High Street, and they kindly said they wouldn't mind dropping them off. In fact they were contracted to take Mrs Stevens back, but this wasn't mentioned.

They sat in the front and put the two ladies in the back. The seats were real leather and there was plenty of leg-room. Second Undertaker drove the slow silent car; First Undertaker offered them a rug: 'It's a chilly business, a funeral,' he said quite cheerily. They refused and wished they hadn't.

As they approached Merriedale Precinct they could see there had been an accident. Blue lights twisted and flashed on an ambulance roof, above a police Rover 3500, and on a small fire appliance. In the middle of it all was a yellow corporation dust-cart. One of the policemen, a young man Tess rather thought she knew, came towards them putting down orange and white rubber bollards. With leather-gloved hands he directed them into the right-hand lane. As they whispered by it was easy to see what had happened. Merriedale Precinct is a drab square of concrete, with drab flower plinths made out of drab inverted concrete cones. On three sides are shops and a bank. The fourth side is a layby for cars to park in. A blue invalid carriage had backed out of the layby and straight into the path of the dust-cart which had carried it on its high steel fender for five yards before shaking it free on a lamp-post. The fibreglass had buckled, torn and shredded. Firemen were using a small electric saw to cut through to what was inside.

The old song came into Tess's head: 'More Work for the Undertaker'.

'Nasty, very,' muttered First Undertaker, and then they

were past it all and murmuring down the long meads, leas, mews and drives of Merriedale, past blank windows and open-plan lawns, past roses and fuchsias and garages and woodwork painted magenta, purple, brilliant green and acid yellow, and so, slowly, back to Brinshore.

As they turned into Alma Grove Marge said: 'You'll all come in for a glass and a bite, won't you?'

First Undertaker answered firmly: 'That's very kind of you Ma'am. Very kind. But we shan't be able to stay long.'

'What about you Tess?'

'Oh yes Marge. I'll come in.'

The car slid into the curb and the purr of its engine faded and died. The solid smooth doors clicked behind them, then the thinner clang of the wrought iron gate. Four pairs of feet crunched four yards of gravel and Mrs Stevens fumbled in the keyhole beneath the oval, leaded glass light in her front door. She showed them into a tiny front room that was just about filled with a table in the window, a small three-piece suite in fringed brown moquette and a large black sideboard. The fireplace was orange-tiled and there was a clock in a polished wood case on the mantelpiece beneath a mirror. There were several ornaments, many of them presents from the Isle of Wight, a brass toasting-fork, and two bright pictures of oriental scenes woven in artificial silks. The table in the window was laid with plates covered with tea-towels, six large sherry glasses in simulated cut crystal and a bottle of Vintners Medium British Sherry. Marge removed the tea-cloths to reveal neatly cut sandwiches and a Dundee fruit-cake.

'Shall I do the honours, Ma'am?' asked First Undertaker.

'Please.'

He poured four glasses of sherry. For a moment they stood in the dingy little room, heads slightly inclined, ears tuned to the traffic and the hiss and pop of the gas fire which Marge had left on at economy rate to take the chill off a room that was almost never used.

Then they sipped.

'Went off quite well, I thought,' said Second Undertaker.

'Very well,' said Tess in a tone of unchallengeable conviction.

'Do you think so?' asked Marge. 'Do you really think so?'

'Very well indeed,' said First Undertaker.

'That's all right then. I'm sure I'm very grateful. Will you have a sandwich?'

'I don't mind if I do.'

'They're pressed tongue.'

'Of course.'

'It's not like it used to be,' said Marge. 'I remember when Dad went. My mother and Aunt Mabel laid *him* out. They don't let you do that now.'

'Times change, Ma'am, and we have to move with them.'

'And my uncle and his boy, my cousin Arthur, they dug his grave for him, a proper one that was.'

'And we must be moving too, Ma'am.' First Undertaker managed to raise an eyebrow at Tess who nodded, ever so slightly. 'Capital sherry, and capital sandwiches. A credit to you, and a credit to the departed, if I may say so.'

Tess saw them to the door where she reassured them that she'd be able to stay on a bit longer, and Marge stood at the window, lifting the lace curtain and giving a sort of half-wave as Second Undertaker turned to latch the gate. She was weeping again when Tess came back, because, she said, their little bit of privet needed clipping and Trev had been going to do it Saturday afternoon, but hadn't felt like it.

Tess managed to organise a move into the back room, which was the real living-room, and quite comfortable since Trev had built on the tiny kitchen behind it twenty years ago. There they were much cosier, sitting in low armchairs over the fireplace, eating tongue sandwiches and rich fruit-cake, and finishing off the sherry. Marge got out an old handbag stuffed with photographs and laboriously went through the lot; most were holiday snaps taken on the Island.

'You could get a boat, a Campbell's Steamer, from the pier, right here in Brinshore,' she said. 'It made a lovely day out.'

There were pictures of Rose and her husband and grandchildren Marge had never seen, sent from Sydney. 'Perhaps I'll go there now,' said Marge. And of Wilf who was now a laboratory assistant at a college in Wolverhampton. 'I don't know why he married that girl,' Marge said. 'He didn't have to, you know.'

'There's no saying about some things,' said Tess.

'Mind, I wonder sometimes. I mean they have charms and that still in those countries they come from. Trev wouldn't have her here. Not in this house. And I agreed with him. Well. I don't know. Perhaps we were wrong. I'd have liked Wilf here today, but not with her. He sent a photo. But I couldn't keep it.'

'I don't hold with mixed marriages,' said Tess, the Irish Catholic daughter of small-holders married to an English Protestant factory hand. 'No way.'

It was twenty past six when she got home. Miriam was at the tiny glazed sink washing up, but she stopped when her mother came in through the back door. It was a nice evening now – the sky had cleared, there was a lot of sunny daylight left, men back from work were out in their back gardens hoeing, tying up bean-poles, tending their early peas.

'Do you want a cup of tea, Mum?'

'I'd love one, pet.'

Miriam filled the kettle and the pipes throbbed and banged.

'Did it go all right?'

Tess shrugged, rather exaggeratedly. 'How would I know, pet?' she said. 'It was a funeral. That's all.'

'Many there?'

'Just me and Ern Copeman. That's all. And two men from Claypoles.'

'It was as well you went then.'

'I think so. It would have been a poor thing if I hadn't, when all's said and done.' She fumbled for her cigarettes. 'Your help yesterday was much appreciated.'

'Yesterday?'

'At the Department. Something about a Death Grant. I don't know all the whys and wherefores of it but that was the gist of it, and Marge said it was appreciated.'

'Oh yes,' said Miriam. 'I never told you about it,' and she told her then, while she made the tea; but Tess hardly listened. To tell the truth she'd had enough of Marge Stevens for one day.

'Dad get off all right?' she asked; and listened even less while Miriam told her about the baked pork-strips she'd done for Jack.

'I do them in the pan,' Tess said. 'It's quicker. Oh yes. I have a message for you from Mr Dangerfield. He was in the Athlone. He said to tell you there's a function, a disco, at the school tomorrow evening. And you're to write to Rackham, some board or other, I've got it written down, for your receipts.'

'Oh *no*!'

They watched the end of University Challenge, Emmerdale Farm, and an episode of some American epic. Tess drank two bottles of Guinness and went to bed at half-past nine. Miriam locked up, and turned out the lights – after she had finished *Little Dorrit*.

VII
FRIDAY
It's All Happening

1.

BY three o'clock on Friday the stink round the foyer and HAL's office had become insupportable. People who had to pass through the area did so with handkerchiefs over their noses; HAL's secretary with her two assistants walked out, if not off the premises then as far as the staff-room, which was in effect a walk-out since they had no means of continuing their work there; HAL himself, pale and twitching, sought places to hide from what seemed to him the disintegration of society around him, and ended up in his beloved library where he fidgeted, coughed, grunted and rattled keys in his pockets. The smell penetrated even there and soon the sixth-formers revising for A levels drifted away, leaving him twisting and turning in front of the immaculate shelves – the powerhouse of the school. Meanwhile the caretaker, who had been sent for, took his time whitewashing the sight-screen at the far side of the playing-field.

It was generally thought that the source was in HAL's private lavatory and this gave rise to countless witticisms about the quality of the commodity he turned out there. As news of the smell spread through the class-rooms, Friday afternoon fever became as acute as any member of staff could remember it and noise-levels began to rise. In some class-rooms gusts of laughter bumped about, often prompted by those teachers who followed the if-you-can't-beat-them line in circumstances of this sort; in others sullen martinets banged desks, organised detentions, and occasionally resorted to clouting ear-holes while the giggles spluttered in every corner except the one where teacher's attention was focussed. Hitler Armstrong, teaching 4CSE French in one of the language labs, heard exaggerated farting noises on his headphones and an anonymous voice told him that the tape-recorders were picking up interference from the foyer; but he was quick at this game and immediately identified the source of the joke, a heavy, dark lout of Greek parentage, who sat in the back row. Armstrong did a berserk and slapped the boy's face, the boy stormed out threatening civil action for assault, and the rest of the class went on silence strike. School finished at three thirty-five on Friday, and many felt the bell went only just in the nick of time. As it was a concerted cheer went up and most class-rooms emptied in a sudden storm of crashing chairs and tables as nearly two thousand children spilled out into the corridors without waiting to be dismissed. By three forty-five the school was virtually empty.

Friday was Frank's duty day and his last job was to check the senior end of the school to make sure the premises were clear and that all those still on them were vouched for – he was also meant to list any new signs of vandalism he came across and report them to HAL's office before he left, but this he rarely bothered to do unless he came across something so startling he could not possibly pretend he had not seen it. HAL found him in the sixth-year coffee bar flirting with the girls who were putting out covered trays of sausage rolls and the like for the disco.

'Are you coming tonight, Mr Dangerfield?' a particularly pretty girl with blond hair and china-blue eyes asked him.

'Only if you are, Gillian,' he replied. This girl wore thin blouses and her low-cut bra was clearly visible. Her breasts were small and perfect, and she manoeuvred them with a shy skill that made Frank sweat. The truth was, he was in a state – the day had been sunny and hot though now clouding over and becoming close, and his lunchtime patrol outside had taken him past row after row of similar girls in sheltered corners with their skirts about their waists exposing their thighs to the sun; and the last lesson of Friday he and Pet Rogate were free and he always spent it helping her unload the two kilns – warm work, where hands and thighs had touched, and her hair had swished across his mouth as she straightened in front of him with a tray of fired animal figurines.

'You'll have no luck with Gillian,' a nymphet just as gorgeous chipped in, 'she's bringing her boyfriend from Rifedale High, aren't you Gillie?'

'Well, I don't know.' Gillian stretched forward across the table towards Frank to adjust the corner of the napkin that covered the tray she had just put down. She smiled up at him. 'Given a little encouragement I can put him off.' There was nothing arch in the smile – it was entirely open and friendly and it hit Frank like electricity so that his diaphragm contracted and an acid, salt taste bloomed under his tongue.

'Ah. Frank. Old chap. Doing your rounds?'

'Yes, Headmaster.'

'I'll come with you.'

Laughter like spring water rinsed the air behind them as they went.

HAL led the way, glossy brown shoes slapping the vinyl tiles and then the rubber-edged stairs as they went up to the floor above. Frank loped behind. HAL flung open class-room doors, tutted, shook his head at chairs left on the floor instead of on the tables for the cleaners, at blackboards unwiped, at chewing-gum wrappers on the floors, and noted it all down in a black note-book. In the modern languages area they found little Hitler Armstrong putting up the chairs his pupils had left and all three looked suddenly guilty, awkwardly wished each other a good weekend, and then HAL passed on briskly to the boys' cloakroom area and toilets next door.

HAL counted the broken coat-hooks under his breath, thirteen, fourteen, fifteen, then stooped to pick up a Marathon wrapper – 'Marathon,' he said, a little louder, then, 'marathon, marathon, marathon.' He turned on Frank, his eyes wide, and a fleck of spittle in the corner of his mouth. 'It's escalating, old chap. It's an escalating situation.' It occurred to Frank that the man was going mad, not just mad as he had always been, but really mad.

Frank moved into the toilet area – a space with six urinals and four booths – and then came out quickly. 'I shouldn't go in there, Headmaster, I really shouldn't.'

HAL looked up at him, his eyes even wider, then flinched away. He pulled at his lower lip, smoothed his silvery hair, jangled his keys. 'Make a note of it. Make a note of it all,' he said, then turned quickly on his heel and his leather soles clicked away down the long corridor to the fire door at the end.

Frank went back. Across the wall above the urinals he read: 'Harte eats shit and shits educat ... ' Either the author had been interrupted or the fecal matter he was using as a medium had run out.

A different step behind brought his head round and he found he was looking down at Hitler Armstrong. The little man was grey, his eyes like chips of ice, and his thin lips compressed. 'I should say that Bright boy is behind this. Only people of his sort could stoop so low. And mark my words there's malice there and a twisted intelligence ... '

Suddenly Frank laughed, a hard bellow of a forced laugh – he had to do something, had to get out some of the surge of feeling that had spurted up in him, that or explode.

'You bloody fool,' he yelled. 'You stupid bloody fool.'

For a moment the two men faced each other and the urinals hissed behind them. Frank thought Armstrong was going to hit him, but he didn't, he just spat: 'I'll not be abused by you, Dangerfield. Not again. Mister Harte will hear of this. I shall want an apology,' and then he too was gone.

*

Dr Naylor-Prim was a tall thin man with deep-set eyes of a warm brown that glowed beneath bushy grey eyebrows. His hair was wiry iron-grey and a little longer than you'd expect in a doctor. His hands had long but strong fingers. He generally wore grey suits in a light tweed that was very expensive and he always talked very gently in tones from which every trace of region and class had been scrupulously refined. He was the nearest thing to a flesh and blood TV doctor one could imagine and clearly, had he followed his natural bent as a young man, he would have ended up as an actor playing just such a role. Children thought him wet, teachers found him ineffectual, administrators too clever by half, and most children's mums (who were, when all is said and done, his real customers) thought he was lovely. He himself suffered acutely and chronically from what he would have called, had he been sufficiently self-aware to make the diagnosis, excessive need affiliation. In plain terms he sought to be loved and more or less unconsciously judged his success or failure with his patients by the amount of 'love' he was able to extract from them. Children in our society are adept at this sort of contract – from the very earliest age affection is a commodity which is manufactured, bought, sold and exchanged for other commodities (sweets and toys on one side – silence, eating up, peeing in the right place on the other), and so Naylor-Prim generally found that his interviews ended in an atmosphere of unanimous self-regard that was rewarding to all concerned. And if the children lapsed into socially dysfunctional behaviour within hours of leaving him, well, that just showed how important his job was, how demanding it was in terms of skill, tact and understanding, how understaffed he was, and how essential it was that the Department should double the budget for the Child Psychotherapy Unit which he ran.

Friday afternoon was Brinshore Health Centre day and on this particular Friday he spent an hour from four to five, with The Club arsonists. For the first ten minutes he had them all together – Dorian, Mark, Jimmy, Linda Rose and Rose Linden, then he had five minutes with Linda, then five with Rose, and finally the three children on their own for the rest of the session.

The similarity in the names of the two mothers confused him, and he was also confused by the fact that Linda had, in her middle-class way, dressed *down* for the occasion and was wearing a sloppy sweater and jeans, while Rose had dressed up – in a smart brown suit with matching accessories. His records showed that one was married to a TRICE manager, the other to a skilled technician in a surgical instruments factory, and he decided that Rose was the former and Linda the latter. Moreover, young Mark had been wanting to go to the lavatory for over an hour – first his teacher at Woodcroft Primary had refused him permission since school was nearly over, then his mother had rushed him off to the Health Centre, saying bluntly that at his age he should be able to control himself till they got home. At times of stress, especially where her children were concerned, Linda often insisted on the virtues of restraint and discipline that her particularly bad private school had tortured her with, and which she never now applied to herself.

For forty minutes then Naylor-Prim talked in calm warm tones to three boys about whose identities he was confused, and occasionally listened to them as well. He sat in a low armchair of the Parker Knoll variety and encouraged the boys to do likewise; thus they could have what he called a cosy chat. Almost immediately his trained eye noticed a marked difference between their behaviour patterns. The eldest boy sprawled out, legs stretched, hands behind the back of his head, and maintained a laconic, withdrawn manner throughout – anyone but Naylor-Prim would have diagnosed an advanced case of dumb insolence not to say bloody-mindedness. The smallest boy was also withdrawn but sat hunched up, feet under him on the seat, and sucked his thumb. Apart from insisting that he had been 'on' on Junior Choice the previous Sunday and that no one believed that he had, he said nothing. This left the middle boy who Naylor-Prim quickly realised was the ringleader.

For a start this boy could not keep still. At first he fidgeted in his seat, later he got up without asking and walked nervously this way and that about the room. His answers to a little number test were quick and accurate, so he was obviously intelligent, while his answers to the verbal test were way off, and clearly showed advanced distractibility. Then while the other two gradually began to smile, and, following the drift of Naylor-Prim's questions, provided the answers he wanted (commodity exchange), no longer flinching away when he caressed an arm or a thigh, the middle one became more and more irritable and unco-operative.

In the end Naylor-Prim decided he was faced with a classic case of the pre-adolescent hyper-active child: more than normally intelligent, showing distractibility and unco-operativeness, constant motor activity, and, from the arson incident, clearly disruptive. Amphetamines are indicated in such cases as they stimulate the cerebral cortex and increase control over the rest of the brain. The contra-indications exist for anyone over twelve: in small doses they produce euphoria, and in larger ones the symptoms known as being 'spaced out' – unresponsive irritability and tenseness, and in cases where the tendency is already there, psychotic paranoia. But this boy was eight, nine at the most – Naylor-Prim with his experience did not have to look at the record to be sure of that. He wrote out a prescription. He then sent out the boys and called in the mothers. Mark Rose took the opportunity to go to the lavatory.

Naylor-Prim said he wouldn't keep the ladies long, and he didn't. He was especially warm to plump cuddly Rose whom he took to be the mother of Dorian and Jimmy, and the wife of someone in TRICE management – her children were obviously well-behaved, well brought up (near-silent boorishness often passes for good manners in middle- and upper-class children). He was only marginally less nice to Linda – he often found these rather skinny, slightly sluttish working-class wives highly attractive. Her posh accent didn't cause him to question his assumptions – he had written a monograph on the use of 'posh' and 'common' in working-class women with aspirations, and evolved an equation now much used in similar Centres, Units and Clinics all over the country. $T(wcD)/T(mcD) = NA$. That is: Time spent using working-class diction related to Time using middle-class diction provides a parameter to the Need Achievement of the subject.

So it was to Linda that he gave the prescription explaining that the red and white capsules should calm Dorian down a bit, as he seemed a very bright boy though rather overactive. He concluded with reassuring platitudes – none of these customers was a villain, they'd just need watching for a week or so, that was all, lovely children, no he really meant it, and he made appointments for them all to see him next week. They rewarded him with smiles of shy but open acceptance – for the relief he had sold them they were prepared to pay way above what they would ever give their husbands in esteem, gratitude, adulation. Thus Naylor-Prim accumulated the emotional capital he needed if he was to continue to perform the essential duties that society had laid upon him.

Only when she got to Boots did Linda realise the prescription was made out for Dorian Linden. However, it was a natural mistake, she decided, and she went ahead. To tell the truth, now the interview with the child shrink (once out of sight the adulation evaporated) was over, she had very little thought for anything but the evening ahead – miraculously, as if in answer to a prayer, Muriel White had rung her up that very morning and invited her and Timothy to dinner that evening. Ossie, she said, had found them such *sympathetic* people, and wouldn't it be nice if they could all get to know each other better.

Oh wouldn't it, thought Linda, never mind about baby-sitters, they're only three doors away after all, and 'I chose freedom' she carolled to herself as she dragged Dorian and Mark off to Saintrose's for the weekend shopping.

*

2p off. 3p off, 4p off, hullo Rose, hullo Sandra, fancy meeting you here, 6p off, 7p off, watch the super savers, shop for less where you see this sign, buy more and pay less, that's what I call economy.

Three tins of baked beans, they're on offer, and four tins of low-calorie soup, buy three and you get one free, they'll do for my lunches, that Linda is watching me, I'll have some of those foreign herring fillets in a spicy sauce and real mayonnaise, Jimmy do shut up, there's a good boy.

A kilo and a half of self-raising, what's that she's got? The stoneground wholemeal? Well, really, I don't see the point and it's 15p dearer, I suppose she's going to bake her own bread, well, I think that's daft, I really do, some people want to put us back in the stone age, three tins of potato salad, and three of Russian, George loves that potato salad, and there's ever such a good recipe using the Russian in *Family Hearth*, something to do with crumbling up digestive biscuits, must remember to get some of them. Jimmy stop it, please stop it, I don't care if the lady did bump you with her trolley, I'm sure she didn't mean it.

Only four in the delicatessen and patisserie queue, now five, excuse me, I'm sorry, excuse me, get out of my way you fat old bag, get out of the way, that tall man with sandy hair and a beard like that king on telly, he's there now, oh fuck this old woman in front of me, there, there, what'll I have. That shoulder looks nice, and not too dear and that pâté at 20p, save where you see this sign, I'll have a half of each, and a quarter no a half of the low fat cheese to follow the low-calorie soups, that man's buying those long thin sausages, cabanos, what are they like I wonder, don't know if you're meant to eat them raw and I don't like to ask. Anything else? anything else? anything else?

Yes. Three almond cream slices with fresh cream, no make it four.

Jimmy I'll smack your ear-hole for you if you don't belt up, I promise you I will.

Two old bags in my way gossiping, how can they go on like that, this is no place to gossip, aren't they from down our way, yes they are, hullo Mrs Roberts, hullo, hullo, yes I am in rather a hurry, come on Jimmy, Jimmy come on.

'Well I had to go to the doctor like this morning I mean I'd ever such a bad night with it. It was more the shock really, more the shock than the horror, I'm sure I'll have nightmares for weeks. Oh didn't you know? I thought everyone knew. I think I'll have two packets of them lemon creams, I like the lemon cream don't you? Well, there I was, just standing there, and she opens the window and says "Excuse me, can you see behind me, is there anything coming?" So I stands on my toes like and can see over the car next to her, and I says "hold on dear, there's a corporation dust-cart", and she says, and these are her very words, mark me, her very words as I said to the police after, they were: "I thought so," she says, then, "Right, here goes." That was them as true as I stand here. "Right, here goes," and back she shoots just like that, straight under his wheels, chocolate digestives I'll have, milk chocolate not plain. Well she had no chance. No chance at all. Died in the ambulance they say, though what I say is it's a miracle she lasted so long.'

6p off, 5p off, 4p off, save where you see this sign, give 'em meat, it's got the lot, sirloin, topside, rump and fillet, the blood leaking and collecting in the corners of the polystyrene trays and how about a pound of pigs' melts for the cat?

I won't bother with anything for tonight, thought Frank; I'll get some of those sausage rolls Gillian was putting out, oh dear, I wonder if she would ditch a boyfriend from Rifedale High, no, no, that way madness lies, anyway the *News of the World*, can I get green lentils here to go with the cabanos. Excuse me, excuse me, I say can I get lentils here. Left side of the next passage, dried goods. This is hell, it really is, just look at them all, must be hundreds crowded in here using their trolleys and baskets like weapons, and what they're buying, does that woman need two dozen bog rolls? Hey. Don't slap him. Slapping him won't stop him. It'll only make him worse. No. I'm wrong. It has stopped him.

Jimmy's face froze, fixed itself into a long, long thirty-second silent scream, then crumpled into soundless sobs.

Ten thousand pounds must be won, two de luxe Minis and a holiday in the south of France, use your skill to match the ... and answer this question in a witty and appropriate way. Why the fuck am I here? Today's man cares. He looks after himself. He cares about what he eats, and if he had any sense he'd buy a ton of cholesterol-free, polyunsaturate margarine, grease a telegraph pole with it, and stick it up Lord Saintrose's arse, which must be the biggest arse-hole in the world, all the shitting he does on us poor bleeders ... 5p off your packet of sunshine, now you can give them goodness in a cracker, and don't forget it's Father's Day on Sunday. We've got a gift for pleasing every Dad.

'Mind it's the driver I'm sorry for. The driver of the dust-cart. I mean he had no chance. No way. Those fore-hocks look nice, don't they, I like a bit of boiled bacon, don't you? And you should have seen him, his face white, white as chalk, I tell no lie. He was shaking too, it was shock, see, state of shock. And the thing is she done it on purpose, "Right, here goes," she said, I heard her say it, right as I'm standing here, "Right, here goes," she said, and drove the thing right under his wheels. Well, I think she might have had more thought, more thought for others before she done a thing like that, the poor driver, I'll have two of the marge, the one with flowers on it.'

Tight'n brief control, if you've got a slightly over-fed tum they'll give you a little extra hug, don't stay in the sun for as long as a girl who is using ... Jimmy, stop snivelling for Christ's sake, I wouldn't lie out on a beach like that absolutely in the all-together, well the sand would feel rough and think of the men, young men you get on beaches like that, and marital aids lightly textured to make it better for both, no need for those since he had his parky, but those pant-liners for complete freshness and confidence in those in-between times, they look a good idea, there's that tall fellow again, don't trust sandy-haired people, what's he doing here, looking at the knicker ads, lentils? lentils? That's dried goods right the other end of this passage, I thought only Paks and that ate lentils any more, that man gives me the creeps, sure he's following me.

3p off, 5p off, 4p off, Italian-style, Spanish-style, Chinese-style, why not give them cheese and anchovy dip? Why not indeed?

There's Penny Brown, and ooh yes, she's got Dave with her

too, there's talk of us going there Saturday and the Blacks'll be there, not a party exactly, but, well, you know, a get-together. Digestives yes, and a packet of those marshmallow things, make it two, I hope there's a nice bit of pork left, I fancy pork this weekend, I wonder if it will be a get-together. I wonder who I'll end up with, they say Sandra's already been with Dave, so I mean he might be looking for a change, I don't half fancy Dave. That Tim Rose was getting to be a pain in the arse, with his funny tasting brandy and soft music and then shooting off between my boobs, well I'm not surprised, that Linda's got nothing, nothing at all in front, and not much anywhere else. I must say George has been going much more since Sunday, we've done it twice, three times if you count ... Jimmy, do you want another smack? Do you want another smack? You've got another smack coming. That does seem a nice bit of pork, I'll get an apple-sauce mix to go with it.

Red lentils only, blast. Oh well, they'll have to do, there goes that plump woman, gave me a funny look just now. Perhaps she saw the look I gave her when she thumped her kid. What else? Spaghetti, parmesan, tinned tomato, fancy a camembert or a piece of stilton, so bloody expensive, never mind. Wonder what Johnny Manet wants. Note on the doormat. Come and hoist a pint. Sold your pictures for a thousand each, that'll be the day, but I shan't stay later than eight o'clock, I know Manet and he'll have me pissed, and I don't want to be pissed if I'm to get inside Pet Rogate's knickers tonight. And I am, you bet I am. My God. Duck. Talk of the devil, there she goes. Didn't see me.

I'd better not.

Really I'd better not.

She's as neurotic as hell. She'll be nothing but trouble. Trouble at school, trouble with HAL, trouble with her husband who is a prick.

Really I'd much better not.

But I will. Damn it I will. Ooops, sorry, am I in your way? I will hang one on the next person who hits me with a trolley.

I will assault the next greedy bitch who stops in front of me. I will ... I had better get out of here, I really can't stand it, what else do I need? God help me, I don't know. A bottle of Scotch. Yes. Why not? It's fucking Father's Day on Sunday, isn't it? Don't be vague, take it anywhere, a thousand pipers, Teacher's pet, no, no. 5p off, special offer, Saintrose's own, can't tell the difference, and I am not, I am not going to feel guilty, one man on his own with a bottle of Scotch to himself, anyway who says I'll be on my own, probably spend most of Saturday in bed with ... all she ever drinks is slim-line bitter lemon, three lunchtimes in the boozer this week and six bottles of slim-line hit the dust. Do I really want to get tangled with a girl who drinks nothing but slim-line bitter lemon? Do I? Really? There she goes in the queue. God she's thin.

'They came for the carriage very quickly, give them their due. Well they had to really. I mean it wasn't very nice all smashed up and there was blood, see. And her dentures. I always get Harry four lagers for the weekend. Yes. Horrible. Both sets on the pavement. By the lamp-post. Oh no. It was what they call a write-off. Anyone could see that. Fit only for the scrap-heap. And I like a glass of tonic wine, well it does you good, gives you a lift, doesn't it? Well, I tell you I had the funniest idea about that. I mean what if her carriage ended up in the rubbish tip just by what was in the dust-cart what hit her? What then? That would be ironic. That's what I'd call ironic, and no mistake. Funny how thoughts like that get in your head, isn't it? I mean I wonder where they come from? Funny old world really, isn't it? Funny old world.'

The man in front of me in the queue is over forty, has dark short-cropped hair that leaves his neck looking vulnerable. He has a light blue jacket in an odd sort of tweed, and now he turns I can see he has a neat black moustache like Clark Gable. Now I see he's older than I thought, and I think his hair is dyed. His wife is fat and going to seed quicker than him – dyed blond hair, finger-joints already a little swollen, fatter even than she looks, there's a lot of corset there. Those could be real diamonds, and that is a gold swastika amongst the other charms on her bracelet. She has twenty-pound notes in her wallet, five of them. She watches her husband as he unloads the trolley, no expression on her face or in her very hard eyes, but her tongue flickers across her lips every now and then.

They have: two avocado pears, four fillet steaks, a packet of frozen prawns, a jar of tartare sauce, two packets of half-baked rolls, a leg of pork, six frozen lamb chops, eight tins of cat food, twelve large cans of German lager, a bottle of Spanish sherry, a bottle of Scotch, and four bottles of hock, three packets of frozen vegetables and three packets of frozen crinkle-cut chips, a bottle of vegetable oil, two packets of face tissues, a large jar of vaseline, four packets of butter, two of lard, a dozen eggs, a half-pound of short-back, a bottle of pre-mixed salad dressing – Tahiti flavour, six desserts in plastic tubs consisting mainly of currant-flavoured trifle and fresh cream, two packets of battered cod (battered wives, battered babes), a large loaf of sliced bread, a packet of scented soap, a large greetings card figuring an enormous bunch of dark red roses and inscribed in embossed gilt 'To Darling Dad on his Day', a roll of kitchen foil, a small glass vase made in Taiwan, a shirt with black and white stripes made in South Korea, two cans of cling peaches from South Africa, two tins of pineapple from Indonesia, two tins of corned beef from Argentina, and four cartons of concentrated orange juice from Brazil. The tin in the tin-plate in much of the packaging comes from Bolivian tin-mines where the workers shop at the company shop and their lungs give out in their forties.

This man owns a small chain of greengrocery stores in the poorer suburbs of South London; all of them are managed for him by Asian immigrants. He has worked during the week – that is he has looked at the books in each of his shops, driving to them from Merriedale in a Swedish car. He has a VW van in his garage as well, but that is kept for holidays in Spain. The hours of labour, much of it intolerable, and carried out by people living in intolerable conditions, needed to produce the commodities in his trolley are incalculable, but probably exceed the hours of not quite such intolerable labour he has extracted during the week from his employees.

He has bought a paperback for the weekend. *Hitler's Children, the Story of the Baader-Meinhof Gang.* The title appealed to him. When he reads the book, he will find much in it with which he disagrees, but finally he will approve the basic assumptions – that western society is free and democratic and that consumerism reflects the will of the majority. It will go about as far towards satisfying his ideological needs as the plunder he has bought will go towards numbing his physical longings.

*

Ern Copeman paused at his garage door to watch Ossie and Muriel White unload their booty, three large cardboard boxes full, from the trunk of their Volvo – and so had one of his rare meetings with his daughter, Joyce. He heard her call – 'Bye Mum, don't wait up for me,' then the metal-shod tap of her heels down the crazy paving between garage and front door. She was wearing tight black trousers, high-heeled pink sandals, a loose top made of fine cotton and printed with large orange flowers on a black ground and she carried a shiny black plastic bag much hung about with silver studs and chains. Ern thought she looked a sight as she tipped and tapped past him without seeing him, but could not resist a cough to draw her attention.

She stopped and slowly turned. Her black hair was cut short and thin and brushed in a boyish quiff, she wore false eyelashes and her cheeks were rouged with orange – the effect, in the dull light beneath the cloud-filled sky, was garish.

'Oh. Hullo Dad.'

'Hullo Joyce. Off for the evening then?'

'Looks like it, don't it?'

'Yes.' When she had been a child, right through to her adolescence, Ern had been passionately fond of her, had ached with pleasure at her prettiness and cleverness (as he saw it), with dread at her illnesses, and had felt joy when she returned his love. Now he was bruised by her indifference. 'Yes. Yes it does.'

He made a tremendous effort to exclude any trace of curiosity from his voice, to allow nothing but the warmth and kindliness he felt to come through. 'New boyfriend?' he asked.

She tossed her head and earrings glinted.

'Not really. I mean, not really new.'

'Anyone I know?'

She shrugged. 'Yes. Actually. He sees you down the Athlone sometimes. Kev. Kev Rammage,'

'Young Kev. That's nice. He's a nice boy. Bring him here sometime, I'd like to see him up here.'

'He's all right.'

'He'll be pleased the Council are going to pay for his fresh water tap.'

'Eh?'

'You can tell him I had a hand in that.'

'I don't know what you're on about.'

'He'll know.'

She fidgeted sullenly. 'Can I go now? I'll miss my bus else.'

'Of course. Of course.'

She turned, tipped and tapped away down the pavement past the open lawns and low rose bushes at which she swung the jangling bag, scattering petals.

'Take care,' he called, but did not know if she heard him.

Ern now pulled down his garage door and passed through to his carpeted work-room beyond. He filled and switched on the electric kettle, flicked on the radio. Newsbeat.

'The Chancellor has announced that more money will be made available for prisons, community centres, and law enforcement ... '

Ern set out cup and saucer, dropped a tea-bag into the cup, and leant against his work bench, head on one side appraising the beginnings of his picture of a dawn sky with Tiger Moth. The news programme moved on. 'In a Pennsylvania court yesterday a fifteen-year-old was acquitted of murdering a neighbour, a woman in her eighties ... ' Ern reached forward to take a brush from the jar set near the canvas, then paused, have my tea first, he thought, and put it back.

'In his defence his lawyer pleaded the influence of violence on TV. His client, he said, had simply wanted to see if a real killing matched the incessant killings shown on television ... ' The kettle whistled, Ern switched off and lifted the chrome attachment from the spout. The hot water chased the bag round in his tea mug and the bag bled. A new voice was speaking: 'There is no evidence', it said, 'that TV violence is a cause of violence in adolescent boys; there is no cause for concern.' An interviewer intervened: 'So that American lawyer's defence was wrong. He was cheating?' 'I wouldn't go quite so far as to say that,' replied the sociologist. 'I can't speak for individual cases, you know.'

Ern added powdered milk and sugar and unwrapped a Milky Way. I won't go to the Athlone tonight, he thought. It'll only embarrass Joyce if Kevin takes her in for a drink. Now, who's that? A shadow had passed across the window, someone calling at the house, well, it wasn't his business, he wouldn't look. Above the radio – 'Meanwhile in Andover this morning a deaf and dumb man was remanded in custody for murdering his social worker' – he heard voices, then the front door shut. Almost immediately this was followed by a knock on Ern's door into the back garden. He found Nick Green from next door on the step.

'Mr Copeman. Can I have a word with you?' The young schoolteacher was white-faced, and his coarse dark hair stood up like an exclamation mark above his head.

'Yes, of course.'

'Not busy, are you?'

'Not at all. Come in. Just having a cup of tea. Would you like one?' Ern killed the radio.

'No thanks. I've had mine.'

'Quite sure? Well sit yourself down and tell me what I can do for you.'

'No. I mean I won't sit down. This won't take a minute. The thing is this. You're to stop interfering. I mean with Dot my wife. Oh I don't mean that. I mean not like that. I don't mean you've been *interfering* with her. I mean interfering in ... in things that don't concern you.'

'Honestly Nick, I have not the slightest idea what you're talking about.'

'Oh yes, I think you have. That woman, that social worker woman you sent from Rifedale. I don't mind telling you she upset Dot terribly. Terribly.'

Ern rubbed his pouchy eyes with the palms of his hands then pushed his fingers through the fine black and grey hair above his ears. He breathed in deeply.

'Look,' he said, 'I've no idea at all what you're on about, so you'd better start from the beginning and tell me all about it.'

It took Ern twenty minutes to convince Nick that he had not been responsible for Mrs Shiner's visit; then reconciliation after misunderstanding led to warmth. Nick praised Ern's paintings and admired the layout and comfort of his workshop/studio, and Ern asked solicitously after Dot Green's health and state of mind.

'Well, it's not bad, not good, you know, but better than it has been.'

'It's a shame she can't get out more.'

'Yes. Well. I mean there's this staff and past pupils disco at school tonight, but we've no baby-sitter. Trouble is round here there is a sort of baby-sitters' circle but they expect you to go to their parties and that and they're not really our scene, you know?'

Ern knew, thinking of the Roses, the Lindens, the Whites and the Browns, not to mention the Blews. He also thought of the evening ahead, how he'd banned himself from the Athlone because of his daughter, and perhaps he still couldn't quite face Mr Rigg's disappointment over the council's decision not to buy him out after all.

'I'll baby-sit for you,' he said.

*

Frank, tall, camel-like, paused behind the Health Centre by

the edge of the paddling pool in the middle of the 'Central Play Area'. This pool was shaped like the British Isles: that is to say it was perversely and completely wrong – for what is geographically land on a map was here water, and vice versa. Moreover, set into the concrete edge were mosaic names – London, Bristol, Southchester – firmly placed in what, on a real map, would be sea. It made him feel darkly angry – it was typical, he thought, typical of the whole absurd muddle that he was part of, typical of Brinshore, typical of ... and that was the question: how far did it stretch, was there a stop, an end to it? Was there a way out or a way through? In his pocket his hand clenched on Max Flash's letter, rescued from his bathroom floor. It would have to be answered this evening and only one answer was possible, there was only one answer he could afford.

Still angry he pushed on to the Athlone.

Johnny Manet, leaning against the bar, epicene, podgy, one hip pushed out beneath his tasselled and embroidered jerkin, waved to him and a gold identity bracelet flashed on his wrist. He looked an odd fish amongst the neat blazers and the tidy perms of the elderly shopkeepers and working people who made up Mr Rigg's clientele on a Friday evening. Frank, in a cream-coloured polo-neck that did nothing to hide the podginess round his middle, and well-pressed brown slacks, his beard trimmed to Mephistophelian neatness, looked less out of place as he padded up behind the artists' supplier and put his hand on his shoulder.

'Well done, Frank, what'll you have?'

'Pint please, Johnny.'

Manet raised a finger and Mr Rigg removed his cheroot and drew the beer. He respected Manet as a man of education – as well as a shop-owner of long standing in Brinshore.

They drank, then at Manet's suggestion moved to the last free table.

'Right Johnny, what's it all about? Let me guess. The Director of the Museum of Modern Art in New York happens to be in Brinshore, he wants my pictures and you're not sure if ten pounds is enough.'

Manet roared with laughter, put his soft plump hand with its ostentatious ring over Frank's and said: 'No, no, Frank, not yet. Athens in the time of Pericles Brinshore may be, but the world has yet to recognise the fact. Nevertheless, I've had a great offer for the one of the pier.'

'No! Really? An offer? How much?'

Manet leaned back and smiled – a fat cat just fed on cream.

'What would you say to one hundred and fifty guineas?'

Frank felt a great load fall away – even after Manet's one third commission that would go a long way towards paying off the rates arrears.

'Johnny, that's marvellous, truly marvellous. But how come? It's more than we're asking. Who is this patron of the arts, this Medici of the Southset coast?'

'Patroness, actually,'

'Go on, go on, tell me.'

'Mrs Liza Cheal. Our local industrialist's sister-in-law. *And* I think she has it in mind to have it hung in the Leisure Centre.'

'But that's *crazy*. Still never mind. She really is coming up with the loot, that's the main thing, isn't it?'

'She really is, Frank. She really is. Now drink up and have another.'

'No, no. I'll get these. Then you can tell me all about this ... this wonderful deal, and how you got her to raise the ante by fifty percent.'

At the bar his elation continued to blossom out, a wonderful combination of achievement and relief. He found he was grinning at everyone, at Jane the pouty barmaid who was busy with a large order, and at two old men, one tall with bony wrists and the other round with monstrous belly, sitting on stools beside him. However, they ignored him and as he waited he picked up their conversation and his euphoria leaked away a little.

'How about that Miss Barnacle then?'

'Miss Barnacle-Flavell. Yers. Terr'bl' wa'n' it?'

'Did it on purpose you know?'

'Yers. Terr'bl'. Driver had no chance. No way.'

'Why she done it, I wonder.'

'Incurable I'd say.'

'Yers. An incurable complaint like. But what a way to do it.'

'Still she was a lady.'

'Oh yers. She was a lady.'

Distracted, Frank carried the mugs back to the table and inevitably slopped them.

'Ooops. Sorry. I say, is it true about Miss Barnacle?'

Johnny Manet nodded. 'Yes it's true all right. She put that dreadful thing she drove in front of a corporation dust-cart. I'll miss her. She was worth all of ten quid a year to me. More. She used to buy pressed flower pictures that that Miriam Trivet did. Cheers.'

'Cheers.'

'Now there's a lovely girl. You must have known her, taught her?'

Frank looked away. 'Yes. Of course. Best pupil I ever had.'

'I can believe it. She was in my shop just the other day.'

'I heard she was around. I seem to miss her all the time.' Hope she doesn't go to the disco, he thought. Wouldn't want her to see me making my play for Pet Rogate. 'Come on now Johnny, tell me about Mrs Cheal and the amazing offer. You've no idea how this has bucked me up, no idea. One hundred and fifty quid.'

'Guineas.' Manet's eyes flinched away, then came back but warily. 'I insisted on it actually. You see . . . .'

'Go on.'

'You see Frank, well, it took a long time to get her round to it, I won't go into the whole shenanigans, the whole deal ... '

'Come *on,* Johnny. Cut the crap and tell me.'

'She just wanted the one. The one of the pier. And she would only take that on condition I took the other one, the one of the Leisure Centre and the shelter and the rude words out of the window. She thought the rude words applied to the Council ... '

'In a way they do.'

'Quite. Anyway she wants it out of the window and an undertaking from you not to exhibit it again. Anywhere. That's the extra fifty guineas.'

'Sweet Jesus.'

'Well. Yes. But think it over. You've made your point, that's the main thing. And you'll never sell that picture. Never. Come on Frank, be a good boy. Take the money and run.'

'You've agreed to this, haven't you Johnny?'

'Well yes. That picture's causing me trouble, you know. And you don't get on the wrong side of the Cheals in Brinshore, you know that Frank. Not if you can help it. Take the money and run. You've done well out of it. I have too. I've had a lot of people look in my window that don't usually bother and I dare say some have come in and bought. But that's it. That's enough.'

'Stuff your sodding little shop, Manet. Just give me ten p. I've a phonecall to make.'

'Frank.'

'Ten p. And you can stuff the deal. I'll come for my pictures tomorrow, OK? Now just give me ten p.'

Manet's eyes narrowed spitefully and his face paled. 'You're being a bloody fool Frank. You really are. And what about the framing? There's ten quid I put into those frames ... '

'Not guineas?' Frank sneered, and went to the bar to change a fifty-p piece at the counter. But fear of an insecure future, consciousness of commitments still unshed, however distasteful, fought with the anger that carried him to the nearest phone-box.

2.

Miriam's mood as she set out for the disco was contrarious – the clothes she wore expressed it. Despising both dressing-up, and conversely, slovenliness, she wore an old pair of black velveteen trousers from which much of the nap had been worn, an old black jumper and reversed pigskin bootees of the Hush-Puppie sort but actually bought in Spain – where she had hitch-hiked with a girlfriend, a student of Spanish, the summer before. Because the evening had turned gusty with warm rain on the wind, she wore a simple denim top, a jerkin with no buttons, zip or decoration which had to be pulled on over her head. All of these were extremely clean, well-pressed, and her long hair, for the moment tucked inside the jerkin, was also fresh and glowing, though quite untouched by lacquer or lotion or even scissors except across the ends which fell to a line just below her shoulder blades. Her only concession to fashion or vanity was that she had plucked her eyebrows into trim curves – but more for neatness than for the other reasons. She wore no make-up and the only scent about her was of Pears soap.

She did not expect to enjoy the disco but a perverse determination sent her cycling down the concrete roads through the council estate, a feeling that however awful the evening should turn out to be, it would be better than another evening at home, a determination to have some sort of fling before starting at TRICE on Monday. Also she expected to see Frank Dangerfield, to speak to him for the first time in nearly two years, and she hoped, contrariously, that this too would be a disappointment – a ghost would be laid if it turned out to be so.

Signalling broadly she swooped across the traffic and through the main school entrance (Headmaster: L. A. Harte . . . .is a shit, she read with grim amusement), placed her bike against the brick wall in the car-park, scorning the bicycle sheds further in, and chained and locked the back wheel. Straightening she glanced round the car-park. Not more than fifteen cars yet. None of them a beat-up Morris Oxford.

Nearby a side door into the main building was labelled *Disco, Way In.* A long blank corridor led past offices and class-rooms almost to the foyer, where a right-angle turn went on to the sixth form coffee-bar. At this angle a table and two chairs had been set, blocking off the foyer, and two girls, the same two that Frank had seen earlier laying out food, checked tickets.

'I haven't got one,' said Miriam as she came up to them. She felt relieved that she might after all be excluded.

'That's all right,' said the blond girl, Gillian, 'they're not all sold. One pound please.'

'A pound!' It was all she had brought, just the one note.

'There's food, Molly, and you get two drinks, plonk or lager, so it's quite a bargain really.'

'All right. Hey, what's that awful smell?'

The girls giggled, looked over their shoulders, leant forward conspiratorially.

'It's rotten fish. Someone put a whole load of fish in the cistern of Lah-di-dah's loo. They had an awful job getting it out because the cistern's up under the ceiling.'

The other girl chimed in: 'They had to have a plumber in and he had to take the cistern right out, cut the pipes and everything. He only finished half an hour ago.'

'Don't you mind sitting here?'

Gillian shrugged: 'We've no choice – it's the only place we can make sure no one gets into the rest of the building, and Lah-di-dah said unless we could be sure the rest was sealed off there'd be no disco.'

Miriam recalled the lay-out of corridors and the position of the coffee bar in it. 'Many here yet?' she asked.

'Only about twenty so far. But there's more than a hundred tickets sold.'

A second corridor, still terribly familiar even after two years, took Miriam along to the coffee bar. This was a large room which had several uses – it was where the Academic and Policy Meeting of the previous Monday had been held – but served for most of the school day as a common room for sixth-formers. It was furnished pleasantly enough with upholstered tubular chairs which had now been placed along the walls. At the far end from the door the apparatus of a travelling disco had been set up – projectors for the light show, speakers, amplifiers, turntable and so on. Decorations in the form of stylised flowers cut out of coloured card had been fixed to the four square pillars that supported the low roof and formed a sort of broad nave down the middle. This area had been left clear for dancing. Refreshments were laid out on tables near the door.

There was still the bleak feel about of a place where festivities are scheduled, but only a handful of guests have arrived: the question hung in the air – are we the *only* ones coming? Moreover the lingering day still cast a dingy light through uncurtained panes, and the music – intolerably loud – emphasised the chill hollowness.

Miriam exchanged half her ticket for a glass of Spanish Sauternes, then looked around, then looked around again this time for escape, any sort of escape, for the nearest people to her, until then half hidden by one of the pillars, were Kevin Rammage and Joyce Copeman. There was no way out of it, not even the sight of anyone else she could claim as an acquaintance.

'Hi,' she said, and sat down next to Joyce, but angling herself so she faced Kevin across the girl. 'I didn't expect to see you here.'

'Why not then? Past pupils isn't it? Didn't say nothing about you had to be a sixth-former.'

Miriam's back straightened and her head went back. She would no more let herself be put upon by this sort of thing than her mother would. 'You know very well I didn't mean that, Kev,' she said. 'I just thought you'd be out working.'

'Thought wrong, didn't you? Anyway, tide's not in till midnight.'

Joyce, whose hostility Miriam had feared rather than Kevin's, now looked up at her, her face white round the rouge patches, her eyes wide behind the false eyelashes. 'He's in an awfully bad mood,' she said, with a sort of awe in her voice.

Up to now they had been shouting above the racket, a disco sound in which few words were distinguishable apart from a refrain that seemed to say: 'We don't care, 'cos I'm the one, all we want to do is have some fun', but this now finished and the spotty, bespectacled DJ who had been in the sixth with Miriam, breathed an announcement into his microphone to the effect that Mike, his technician, was not quite satisfied with the teeter and woof or whatever, and there would be a short intermission while minor adjustments were made. 'A good chance to get at the scrummy-yummy goodies before they're all gone,' he added.

Miriam knew Kev's moods and felt sorry for Joyce, who, now Miriam allowed herself to see her as a person, seemed to be a rather simple, resourceless sort of girl.

'Oh, don't mind him. He'll come out of it given time.'

Joyce's eyes narrowed as she wondered whether or not to resent this as a claim of prior ownership from the other girl, but Miriam's face was so open and frank that she relaxed and leant forward with voice lowered – conspiratorial, we girls must stick together.

'But you see he's taking it out on me. 'Cos of my Dad. I told him it was my Dad got this effing fresh water tap for him and the fishermen, I thought to please him like, but he just blew up.'

Miriam, head quizzical on one side, looked across the girl again: 'Come on Kev. What's this all about? When I saw in the *Post* the Council was paying ... '

'That's just it, Moll. Can't you see? Surely you can see.' Joyce now did bridle – why should Miriam be able to see what she could not? But Kevin went on, face white behind his beard, hammering his red fist into the palm of the other hand. 'Did you see why? Because we're bloody picturesque. Like in this crazy exhibition they've got here in the foyer about us. All pretty pictures and diagrams. I even lent them a bit of old net for it. They're just making a sodding tourist attraction out of us, that's all.'

'If you swear in front of me again Kevin Rammage, I'm going home.'

Kev ignored this, went on, past Joyce, at Miriam.

'Five, six, seven times a week I go out in that bloody boat. To scrape a living. Fill in their forms, stamps, the lot. Only a gale keeps us in. Sometimes it's pissing so hard I reckon it's wetter in the boat than out. And I've seen ice form on the gunnels, no lie, ice on the gunnels. Nights. Nights cos it's better on account the cod come in closer. But to her dad, and all those toffee-nosed bastards on the Council, and the half-arsed teachers in this dump, we're just a tourist attraction. I tell you. I'm packing it in.'

'Good thing too if you ask me,' said Joyce. 'Get a proper job.'

'Piss off. Sod off.' Kevin spat these words out, then stood up, walked, no charged for the swing door which was about to open towards him as a new arrival appeared, but he smacked it hard with his open hand and sent it flying back with a bang.

'O-o-o-ooh. Why did he do that? What've I said now?'

'He reckons his job *is* a proper one.'

'O-o-ooh, he isn't half touchy. I didn't mean it wasn't proper. Just not regular. That's what I meant. Oh, Moll, what'm I going to do now?'

'Go after him I should think. Try to calm him down. And try not to let him drink any more.'

'Oh Moll. You are a brick. You were always so sensible,' and Joyce picked up her chain-hung bag and, arms flung out, legs swinging round each other, scampered out after him.

'OK,' said the DJ. 'Mike says he can see light at the end of the tunnel, so keep on truckin', how about this to get a few couples out on the floor. *Tonight you're mine completely, you give your love – so sweetly, tonight ...*

Miriam thought: Well, I might as well have something to eat, I've paid for it, then if nothing turns up (if *he* doesn't turn up), I'll go home.

As she reached for a sausage roll to put on her paper plate a soft Welsh voice said behind her: 'Well, it's the leading edge of the revolution, is it?' She turned, felt a lightening of her mood. 'Mr Davies. Fancy you being here.'

The little history teacher, neat in a tweed suit, reached out and took her wrist, giving it a squeeze since her hands were full. 'Why shouldn't I be? One must keep up with things, even at my age you know. Especially at my age. Come and sit with me and tell me all about life at Southchester. I was there, you know that? Only a college in those days. You remember I said I was there? Joined the Party yet? I did, I did, but that was a long time ago, just after the war. Me in my demob suit, first call to the bookshop, second to the Party. Seemed some point then.' He led her back to the side, near where she had been sitting with Kev and Joyce, with the pillars between them and the loudspeakers at the other end of the room. 'You're reading English, aren't you? Now why is that? You had a good mark in history, I remember it well, a proper appreciation of things you had, a real understanding, but never mind. How are things here? Oh much the same. The forces of history flow inevitably on to World Revolution and the Dictatorship of the Proletariat. But not in Brinshore. Not in Brinshore. But I tell a lie. Yes I do ... ,' and he went on to tell her of Martin Bright's essay borrowed from Karl Marx and read out by Mr Armstrong at Upper School Assembly. Miriam began to enjoy herself after all. Gwyn Davies was elfish, small, twinkling, malicious, gossipy, and in spite of the row, entertained her. 'You don't know him do you? New here since your time. He's Nick Green, new English teacher, got it all off pat, he has, creativity, self-expression, knows it all. Never teaches them grammar, you know? Now that must be his wife, never seen her before, kept her quiet he has, though I don't see why, do you? I mean no one's going to run off with her, are they?' and so on, anatomising all the new arrivals for her as they came. Later he danced with her, hopping from one foot to the other while she flicked and spun in front of him, and later still bellowed out at her his most recent thoughts on status consciousness as opposed to class consciousness. But for him she would surely have gone home.

*

Ern stood in the Greens' sitting-room window and looked out over the road and the low roofs at the slow development of the sunset, one of the best real life ones he had ever seen. Across the middle of the sky a front of purplish-black cloud, massed in battalions with pennants of white, scarlet and gold, was on the march towards him; beneath it columns of rain swept over the distant flat lands beyond Mudwick Marsh; above, a second rank of clouds, high cirrus, skirmished ahead and began to redden as he watched. A warm, almost hot wind gusted down the concrete road ahead of this army, tossing the rose-bushes, sending up tiny dust-devils over the flowerbeds and along the gutters, and carrying with it an occasional splatter of heavy raindrops from the low streaks of rolling mist that rushed black and smoking immediately above.

The strange house behind him was silent. The baby, in a cot in the back room, slept – Dot Green had been confident she would; 'She always sleeps when I have to be awake.' There was nothing on the television he felt like watching, and no books he wanted to look at. Apart from old stuff, classics and that, there was a lot of French and German, which he supposed must have been Dot Green's subjects at college. The rest was paperback fiction and Ern preferred biographies, what real people got up to, or anthropology and the like – Ardrey and Morris. But meanwhile he had the coming storm and the growing sunset.

A flicker of white behind a bed of tormented roses (Wendy Cussons and Elizabeth of Glamis – a cheerful combination) caught his eye three Scandinavian-style bungalows down, on the other side. By shifting his position to the end of the window he could see what it was.

Tina Rose, Linda's daughter, rising six, stood in a white nightdress against the purple garage door. She held, in both hands, a large old-fashioned teddy-bear. Fine sawdust bled out of a three-inch gash in its back and into the currents of the wind, and when the flow stopped she gave it a shake and set it going again. Her fair, almost white hair blew about her expressionless face and she ignored it, only turning pettishly away when the wind scooped the dust up higher than before and threatened her eyes with it. Between her and Ern the roses heaved, bowed, twisted and shook, but being hardly out of bud took no harm.

Linda appeared. She was dressed in a long kaftan-style gown, white and yellow, and as soon as the wind hit her she arched her back into it and her hair, almost as fair as her daughter's, streamed away from her face, subsided and rose again. She shouted at the child, stamped a gold sandalled foot, then reached out a long thin brown arm and grabbed Tina's wrist. She shook the child furiously then dragged her indoors.

Inside she pulled Tina along the passage and pushed her into her room closing the door with a slam; from inside Tina wailed: 'Dorian done it, Dorian done it with his knife, Dorian done it with his knife.' '*did* it, for Christ's sake,' screamed Linda, fists clenched at her temples. 'DID it, DID it, DID it.'

Timothy, her husband, murmured behind her: 'He did too. I'm almost sure he did.'

Linda turned on him. He was looking very smart, his absolute smartest in a lightweight grey suit, heavily skirted in the jacket, flared trousers, waistcoat with mother-of-pearl buttons. Normally he only wore it for weddings and the like.

'So? So?' she asked, 'and if he did?'

She hissed, her eye on the boys' door, not wanting them to hear, turned on her heel and strode to the living-room, forcing her husband to follow her.

'Well I think, I think, he's, well you know, disturbed.'

'So?'

'Well, honestly Kid, I don't think we ought to go out tonight. Especially not without a baby-sitter. I mean, honestly, it's not just breaking the law leaving them like this after last Sunday, it's practically flaunting it.'

She folded her arms and looked at him with a scorn so intense he felt shrivelled, as if every emotionally sensitive fibre inside him had been sprayed with acid. 'It all stems back from this, doesn't it, Tim Rose,' she said, 'you don't want to go to Ossie's and Muriel's tonight. You're frightened of them. That's it. You're frightened. At the end of the day it's as simple as that.'

'Of course I'm not frightened. Of course I'm not. Look, Lindy, I'll say it quite outright. We're civilised people and we ought to be able to put our cards on the table. I don't like the

Whites. I don't like all their views ... Oh, let me finish. No. Please. Let me finish. I don't like all their views, some sense in some of them I grant you, but he goes too far. But I'm not frightened of him. I'm sorry Lindy, but it's just silly to say that. Just silly.'

'Right. You've had your say. Now I'm going to have mine. No. I mean it. I'm going to have mine. And it's this. We're going out tonight, we're going to have dinner at the Whites. And whatever you think of anything he says that you don't go along with, you remember we're there as guests and you don't argue. Right? And you can stop making the children an excuse for not doing something I want to do for once. That's what I despise, Tim Rose. Making your own kids an excuse.'

'Lindy ... '

'There's no need to sigh.'

'Lindy. I'm not making Dorian's, well, his complaint ... '

'I see. He's ill now, is he? Your own son. Mentally ill.'

'No, Lindy, I didn't say that. But he is confused. Mentally confused, now you've got to go along with that ... '

'Listen, Tim Rose. You can't tell me about it. It was me, I, who saw the police, wasn't it? Went to see the Head-teacher? Had that social worker woman prying round here? It was I took him to the Child Psychotherapy Unit this afternoon, right?'

'Well, yes, of course.'

'So I think I know what I'm talking about. He's hyperactive, that's all, and the doctor has given us the pills to calm him down. That's all there is to it.'

'What he did to Tina's teddy didn't look calm to me.'

'Oh that's very clever. Now. Look. We're late. Ten minutes late. Why don't you just go in there', she pointed down the passage, 'and give him another of those capsules. Just to be on the safe side. And you can come back and look at them every hour on the hour if you want to. Oh, for Christ's sake Tim. It's only four doors away. Four doors. That's all.'

Five minutes later Ern, still enraptured with the Wagnerian sky, saw them go by. He wondered why they had not taken the Datsun until he saw them turn into the Whites. They looked smart, happy, on their way to a good night out. And in fact Timothy was relieved to be out of the house, just like that, felt he'd been a bit silly about it all. Dorian had seemed much calmer when he went in with a second capsule, had lost the flushed, lively air he'd had before, had stopped giggling. Indeed he had seemed sullen, preoccupied as he took the medicine and a glass of water. Tim had told him where they were going, how it was just down the road, said they could watch telly on the portable till ten o'clock, then they must go to sleep.

'They'll be all right, Kid,' he said as they turned on to the path to Ossie White's front door, and he squeezed Linda's hand.

'Of course they will,' she said.

The Librium was beginning to work. He had only had ten mgs, but he wasn't really used to it. They were on her prescription not his. She had had thirty mgs and was beginning to feel fine.

*

TRICE on a Friday night suffered the same sort of mood as afflicted the school on Friday afternoon; and on this particular June evening the mood was heightened by the fact that the factory was on short time and working only a half shift at the end of the week. The hands clocked on at eight and off at one o'clock in the morning, though nearly all had finished their stints by the allowed coffee-break at ten.

Friday night was always fiddle night.

Welders mended garden tools; sprayers in the paint shops painted panels from the second-hand cars they did up at the weekends; machinists and tool-makers turned spare parts for their motorbikes, fishing reels, or broken household appliances; and scrap was pressed and cut into brackets, repair-plates, and in one case, a piece of garden sculpture of modernist design suggesting a leaping dolphin. The artist, an Italian who was respected as a crank, hoped to make a fountain out of it.

Raffles and sweepstakes were run for old people, for the disabled, for the mentally handicapped and the spoils divided on a strictly quid pro quo basis, a quid for you, a quid for me, a quid for you, a quid for ... A shop-steward invited the night security guard into a store-room to see a Danish film (Danish Blue – get it?) and six TRICE washing-up machines were fork-lifted into a waiting lorry in the old railway siding where there was still a gate. This was of course padlocked but for a fiver the senior foreman would guarantee not to notice if the key went missing from his office for half an hour.

Meanwhile subdued lights were on in Jimmy Cheal's suite at the top of the square tower that stood in the middle of the factory. Present as his guests were the senior shop-steward, the senior quality control inspector, a truck-driver, a costing accountant, and the representative of the owner of a large chain of pull-in cafés and pie shops in the North-East. With cigars and Chivas Regal they were putting the finishing touches to a simple and common enough scheme. A run of sixty industrial washing-up machines, recommended retail price eight hundred and fifty pounds each, were to be made with a radical fault, rendering them useless. The union man would organise this; the quality control inspector would vouch for the nature and seriousness of the fault; the costing accountant would decree that it would be cheaper to scrap them than remake them and would enter the loss in the company accounts as arising from write-offs; and the truck driver would take them north and distribute them to the cafés where they would have a long and useful life – having cost their new owner two thirds of the asking price. Jimmy Cheal took twenty thousand pounds of the take in the form of a simple transfer of funds from the café owner's account in a Bahama bank to Jimmy's account in the same bank. Of the rest, five thousand went to the accountant and three thousand to each of the other men involved. Jimmy believed that generosity paid in deals of this sort – only the accountant would know how to launder his share, the rest could be exposed immediately if the deal was blown, and their loyalty was thus doubly assured. As Jimmy used often to say – anyone can be done in a TRICE.

Three floors below, with his cousin Bob King next to him, Jack Trivet, sitting on a piece of sacking, drinking orange squash and eating crackers and cheese spread was fed up. He knew where he'd rather be. He didn't want to stay until one o'clock: the tide would be out at dawn and he wanted to dig bait for night fishing on Saturday. He wanted to be down the pub, the Little George, with Tess – if he could get away now they'd have a couple of pints and a Bell's before closing, be snug in bed by half eleven, and that way he'd wake up fresh at first light. And, although he had done his full stint there was no way he could get off – he was paid hourly and the shift ran another three hours, with no work at all to be done in it. He could, of course, walk out, but he'd done that before on a Friday, and the Employee's Handbook was clear on the subject. Section Twelve – Penalties, para five: Leaving department or building without permission or reasonable excuse – reprimand to three days stand-off for first offence; dismissal in extreme cases. He could of course have a fit, take a turn, go dizzy ('If you should feel ill, report to your foreman. If you are not quite up to the mark, this is when an accident may happen ... '), but they'd only tell him to have a lay-down, and that's not what he wanted. Moodily he banged the cork into the squash bottle. Then looked at it, shook it, uncorked it, took another swig. 'Almost never', he said to cousin Bob, 'does it taste the way I want it – always it's too strong or too weak, no matter how I mix it before I come out.'

Mr Roberts, the charge hand whom, naturally, Jack Trivet hated, walked by, giving them a nod as he went – then he paused, turned and came back. They had been at school together, and if he had not done as well as Jimmy Cheal, their other class-mate in the building, he had done better than Jack Trivet or cousin Bob. Hard work, night shifts, proper apprenticeship, City and Guilds – they added up to a mortgage, first on a council house, and now that his children had left home, on a nice two-bedroom Scandinavian-style bungalow out at Merriedale. And only five years left to be paid off. Of course his wife was manageress of the hairdresser's at Mudwick Precinct (it was she had been the last to speak to Hilary Barnacle), and that helped.

'All right then, Jack? Bob?'

Jack grunted, wondering what was coming.

Mr Roberts, a large, stupid man, sat down beside them, hands spread out on his grey-flannelled knees. He didn't bother with work clothes anymore, not since they'd given him a little glass cubicle at the end of the shop floor, with a table, a high stool and rubber stamps to play with.

'Funny thing, Jack,' he said, 'forgot to tell you last night.'

'What funny thing then?'

'Got up for my tea, about three o'clock yesterday, and who do you think I saw, sitting in a car in the road just down from our bungalow?'

'Now how should I know who you saw sitting in a car in the road just down from your bungalow?'

The charge hand looked sidelong, not put out by the mimicry, knowing he had the surprise in store that would deflate old Jack Trivet. He didn't like Jack any more than Jack liked him, largely because he vaguely felt that with his weekend pubbing and his fishing, Jack got more out of life than he did from making rugs from kits and breeding goldfish.

'Well, I'll tell you who I saw. Tess Trivet it was, your good woman, sitting there cool as a cucumber in Ern Copeman's car. And then he came out of that place he's built on his bungalow, and drove her off. Not my business Jack, but we night-workers have to stick together, eh? And that Ern Copeman hasn't spoken to his own missus these five years. That's a well-known fact that is.' He stood up. 'Thought I'd let you know. Nod's as good as a wink. Nip the trouble in the bud before it goes too far, eh?'

Jack Trivet put the last mouthful of pie away, chewed, swallowed, uncorked his orange juice, took a final swig, and recorked his bottle. He thus had nearly thirty seconds to think things over in, as Roberts moved off down the harshly lit benches.

'Bob,' he said at last, 'Ern took Tess to ol' Trev Stevens' funeral, and very kind of him it was to do so. I know that. You know that now 'cos I've told you. But that nosey bugger, doesn't. Right?'

'Right.'

'So. Taking all in all, and remembering, if you don't mind, his exact words, I'm feeling very insulted.'

'Of course you are, Jack.'

'Very insulted indeed. So if you'll go and report the matter to the union rep, saying how very, very upset I am that nasturtiums should be put upon my wife by a charge hand, right here in public on the shop floor, and explain to him how hurt I am I wouldn't trust myself not to hang one on him like, I'll be off now.'

'Yes Jack.'

'Good man, Bob. Do the same for you sometime.'

As he rode out of the works entrance, richer by three hours of freedom, Jimmy Cheal's chocolate-coloured Rolls breathed out behind him, then ran alongside him for a moment. From inside Jimmy, richer by twenty thou, raised his hand to Jack and Jack outside raised his hand back, then the Rolls purred away into the windy rain, a tiny wisp of exhaust spinning beneath its tail-light.

What had Jack Trivet been up to to clock off early, Jimmy Cheal wondered, leaning back in the soft leather with his cigar going well and the whisky warm in his stomach. No trouble, he hoped – but it wasn't likely. Jack could look after himself. And how about his daughter, that Miriam? She'd made that assistant personnel manager, what was his name? Tim Rose? look a proper old charlie last Tuesday. Don't go much on that Rose and his toffee-nosed wife, thought Jimmy Cheal. Too many toffee-nosed bastards round the old business these days, taking all the fun out of it, not like it used to be when we started.

It had been a good racket then, in the old days, before the war with his mates, the two men who had started it with him back of a garage, taking apart an American dishwasher one of the big hotels had brought in for urgent repair. Well, the other two had pulled up stakes long ago, cashed in their chips and retired early to cheap booze and golf on the Algarve. Not my way, thought Jimmy, I'd die of boredom, I have to have something to do, something on the go. Like this deal tonight. Can't say I need the money, course I don't, but it's a laugh really, pulling a fast one over the other stock-holders (banks and the local building society for the most part now) and the snotty lot they're filling the place up with.

Take advertising. Old Mrs Jenkins, taught us to read in the Alma Street Elementary, she and old Trim, she wrote the copy of every brochure for the first twenty years, thought up 'It'll all be done in a TRICE', now they want to spend a hundred thousand quid getting a load of Oxbridge shysters from some London agency to do the same job. It'll be telly commercials next, and we all know what they cost. And these smart alecs, graduates, management trainees, stuff like that, like that Timothy Rose. What had he said? 'You've got to fit the men to the machines, Mr Cheal, fit the men to the machines.' Assistant Personnel Manager. What cock. Diploma in Industrial Psychology. When we started, thought Jimmy Cheal, I hired and fired, then the senior foreman did, and the dole queue was all the industrial psychology we needed.

Meanwhile, still with half an hour's drinking time in hand, Jack and Tess sat snug together in the Little George laughing with the Friday regulars, and the gusty wind threw handfuls of rain at the windows and the thunder rumbled over the Downs five miles inland.

*

'Delicious steak, er, Muriel, really succulent and tasty.'

'Glad you like it Tim, I'm sure. Perhaps, er, Linda would like to know how I do it, then she can do you one the same, sometime.'

Later, after coffee, Ossie will suggest games. Dressing-up perhaps. Muriel will take me to their bedroom, and she'll have one of those leather suits for me ...

'Linda?'

... black soft leather, like a sort of waistcoat on top, very low cut, first button just above my tummy button ...

'Linda!'

'Oh yes. Yes. What is it?'

'Muriel's going to tell you about the steak.'

'Oh thanks. Yes. So sorry, please go on.'

'Quite the little wool-gatherer, aren't you? Well I think the secret is the charcoal essence, that's what makes it distinctive, you just need a drop or two, but Ossie says it's the cut, the quality of the meat. I always let him choose the meat, of course ... '

... leather pants, very tight, short, contrast to the boots, tight too, but above my knees (Linda knew her knees were a wee bit knobbly), *and a peaked hat with that high bit in front.*

'Chilled, yes, frozen no. For beef that is. Nothing wrong with freezing lamb, but beef frozen loses texture-wise and flavour-wise. Of course, often they don't tell you, but I know what to look for. The fat must have that creamy, almost yellow look – it always loses that frozen, and the blood ... '

It'll be like charades to begin with, party games, me and Ossie against the other two. Yes, that's right, with forfeits. They'll lose of course, and we will start with quite fun forfeits, like drink out of the opposite side of your glass ...

'But you see Linda that's where we're so lucky, Ossie having his greengrocery business. I can really do special, very special side salads, knowing I've always got the best to put in them. This pineapple is fresh, you can smell that can't you? Oh I've got nothing against the tinned, no way, but ... '

Later we'll make the forfeits more interesting, like Tim will have to take off his trousers and I'll give him three, no six of the best on his bare bum, because Timmy dear, you were a wee bit naughty earlier this evening, six with a leather belt, or I expect Ossie will have a schooling whip somewhere, not a crop, gold-mounted ...

'Touch more of the old juice? Why not indeed. That's what I like about these German hocks, they go with anything, oh yes it's the real thing all right, none of your Yugo stuff here, they've got the weight, that's what it is, the body if you know what I mean. Chill's gone off now of course, but never mind, finish this, the next'll be all right, I popped it in the freezer.'

Then Ossie will get Muriel, fat cow she is, on her knees, over there by the music centre, and tie her wrists up to that wrought iron bracket, looks strong enough, mind you can never tell these days, probably plastic, and he'll ask me to rip that embroidered smock thing off, what did she say it was? Mexican Wedding Shirt? And he'll borrow the whip off me, first tenderly undoing her bra-strap so they fall all about like udders. He'll be dressed in those old-fashioned breeches, with a white shirt and gold medallion or charm nestling in the grey wiry hairs of his chest ...

'You see the way I see it is it's absolutely symptomatic of our society that the enemy is let into the camp. The lessons of history are there. Clearly. On the wall. And frankly I don't care which lot are in, Jim's lot or Maggie's. I mean, let's face it, they've got a job to do, there's a job to be done, that's the name of the game, that's where it's at. Linda do try this dessert, this sweet, it's fabulous, really Muriel, you are doing us proud, if I may say so.'

'But that's it, Timothy, that is it. You know their track record. You know the pitfalls. Things aren't like that any more. Now these union johnnies make all the running. All the running. And once we had a presence in every corner of the world. Now what? Nothing.'

'Right Ossie. Right. On the line.'

'So where does it get you? Nowhere. Well, that's the way it is from where I'm standing. From where I'm standing that's where it's at. Muriel, let's have that other bottle, there's a love. It goes well with this cheese too, you know. Emmental. Can't stick the blue stuff, can you? Never got used to it. Where was I? Oh yes. What it comes down to is this, and I say it without fear of trepidation, every which way you look at it, a new start is what is needed. And what I say is a new start is on the cards. Right now it's on the cards.'

Then when they're both blubbering and bleeding, yes bleeding in front of us, he'll embrace me, passionately, through the leather I'll feel his thing all hard and very big and he'll say let's go to the bedroom, and I'll say, no Ossie, let's do it here on the table in front of them and he'll say, by God Linda, you're a plucky woman.

'You see Tim, Linda, I'll be absolutely frank with you, put my cards on the table. Now I wouldn't do that if I didn't trust you absolutely, I can trust you, can't I? I mean I can sum people up right enough, at my time of life I should be able to, and soon as you first came here, nearly a year now isn't it? I said to Muriel, there's a couple who know where they're going, and a tuchaclass with it. The thing is this. I expect you know I own a chain of greengrocer's shops – Brixton, Clapham, Balham, Tooting, and I'm opening soon in Wimbledon, do it all kosher, seven outlets all told now and no more problems with cash-flow or liquidity, and capital depreciation properly adjusted – well I do have a bloody good accountant, Jew boy, they're always the best.'

'Ossie started at Brixton. The market. We're just ordinary folk, you know.'

'But I've made a go of it. No one can deny that, that's one thing they can't take from me. Anyway the point is this, now I need more time for my political work. The old country's done well by me, and the way I see it it's up to me now to do something for the old country. And John Trench, he's our Leader, he said to me, a month back, just before those pinkos trumped up those charges against him, he said, you know Ossie, if you could only find more time for the Movement you'd go far, but you must make the time for it ... '

Then he'll want me to lie on the table, but I'll say no Ossie, let me show you, you lie down. And then he will and I'll unbutton his breeches and underneath he'll have like a soft leather pouch, bursting it'll be, bursting ...

' ... so what it comes down to is I need a manager, and well, it seems to me you, Tim, you might have the right qualities I'm on the q. v. for.'

and I'll sort of ease it to one side so his big red thing pops out and up and I'll have my knees either side of him, and Tim and fat Muriel will stop blubbering, all wide-eyed on either side of the table and they'll be so they can see everything, and slowly I'll lower myself, because these leather pants I'm wearing'll have no gusset, they'll be open between, and I'll lower and wriggle ...

'Lindy.'

'Linda.'

'Linda, kid.'

'Lindy? Oh you are the wool-gatherer tonight, aren't you? What I was going to say was that being as our menfolk seem determined on business talk, would you like to help me with the coffee? I'm sure you'd like to see my kitchen, it's the Mayfair Luxury, you know, and we can have a nice old natter on our own, oh thank you dear, what a help you are I'm sure, there, if you'll put those down on that surface there we'll have it all in the TRICE, yes it's the new one, the DBXL 100, well, we don't like to think of anything less than the best for the Waterford, yes, it really is Waterford, lovely isn't it?, now if you'll just move the baby slicer to the side I can plug in the Perk-ee-one. There. Actually, dear, what John Trench said was, to Ossie I mean, was that he daren't let him go higher in the Movement while he's employing coloured in his shops, well seen to be. Well, of course that's all you can get in that part of London, they've taken over, so John Trench said get in a manager so no lefty's going to be able to say he's seen you chatting to a nigger ... Ooops. Oh dear. Yes. It's the front door chimes. Well who can that be at this time of night? Ossie. Oss-eeee. Someone at the front door. Well, I don't like to at this time of night. You answer it dear, there's a dear. You can't be too careful nowadays, can you?'

On the step was little Tina, still in her nightgown, still clutching the empty skin of her teddy-bear. She was wet, shivering and crying. Behind her, with the wind plucking at the tufts of hair above his ears, was Ern Copeman.

'She's been here sometime,' he said. 'She couldn't reach the bell.' Then he turned and walked briskly away into the noisy dark, already nervous for the Greens' baby left on her own for half a minute.

Once back in the Greens' house he couldn't resist staying at the window with the light out behind him to see what would happen next – the truth is he was now thoroughly bored. Had he not been he would probably not have seen Tina in the first place. Three minutes went by, then there went Linda Rose, clutching Tina in her arms, the hair of both of them blown together in the wind, the child's face peering over her mother's shoulder, green like the drowned under the street light. Ern waited. Three more minutes went by, then there went Timothy Rose, head down into the wind buttoning his suit jacket as he went. Ossie and Muriel White stood in their doorway and watched him go. Ern turned away, thinking the incident was over.

He was still listlessly punching buttons on the TV trying to decide which programme was the least stultifying when the bell rang. He thought it must be the Greens back, but on the step was Tim Rose again. The man was breathless, white-faced, with dark splashes of rain on his shoulders looking bizarrely like blood in the garish lamplight.

'You saw Tina, our girl,' he panted.

'Yes,' said Ern. 'But do come in.'

'No. No. What I mean is you saw Tina. But did you see Dorian and Mark? The boys? You didn't see them too, did you? On their bikes? They've gone on their bikes.'

'No. No, I didn't.

'Oh, my God. Oh my God.'

He turned, fled, and another squall rattled down rain, shiny where the light fell on it – bead curtains wildly shaken by a madman.

*

Love is where it's at – it has to be ...

Frank obediently jogged up and down in front of Pet Rogate.

Love is where it's at – it's what you are to me

Her dancing, she supposed, had style involving shaped gestures with the hands and small steps which brought her closer and tantalisingly away again. Frank was irritated by it, through it recognised that really he was not enjoying himself. The coffee bar was now full, lit only by stroboscopically flashing lights and projections on the ceiling of what sometimes looked like swirling blood, sometimes like molten magma. Fifteen years ago he had found such displays exciting, had in his last year at the Royal College created them himself with Max Flash for a student group that had achieved a brief glory soon faded. Now it all seemed old hat, though the youngsters about him – sixth-formers and students – seemed to be enjoying it well enough. The music was impossibly banal.

And now I see it clear, now I know the score
Now I've seen the start I know there must be more

And Pet Rogate, whose eyes had assumed the *de rigeur* zombie look, knew them all for she mouthed the words to every record. She must have Radio One on every minute of the day, Frank thought.

So make it with me baby, make it now or never
For Love is King, we just can't win, let it go for ever.

Too much beer already, Frank told himself, that's the trouble, and I'd have done better staying at home and getting properly plastered on Saintrose's Scotch, instead of coming here, behaving as if I was ten years younger than I am, and trying to get in this absurd girl's knickers.

Love is where it's at, it's written in the sea
Love is where it's at, and you know that love is free

she mouthed, and 'Number Twelve in the fun forty,' boomed the bespectacled DJ, and 'I'm not sure I altogether like fun,' said Frank, catching the girl's wrist, 'but I might like it more if I had something to eat.'

A few moments later they were sitting in the class-room next to the coffee bar which had been opened to cope with the overflow, eating sausage rolls and drinking the cheap wine.

'Hadn't we better ask you husband over?' Frank suggested.

'No, no, he's completely happy talking to his past pupils,

the bright and clever ones anyway. Oh Frank, you know he's becoming completely impossible. I told you how egocentric he's become, well it's more like a mania, you've no idea, most of the time he treats me as if I'm not there.'

But Frank wasn't having this, not again, not after three lunchtime sessions of it at the Athlone. He interrupted firmly, announced he had important news to tell her, and launched into an account of Max Flash's offer. She heard him out, interrupting only once to lean across the table and brush flaky pastry out of his beard, for the rest looking up at him with wide-eyed, intense seriousness, occasionally shaking her head very slowly from side to side.

'But you can't give up teaching,' she said, when he had finished. 'Oh no Frank, you can't.' She moved in and put her long thin fingers over his. 'You have so much to offer to these kids, to generations of them,' and she gestured broadly, 'so much that is truly wonderful. You know Frank, I'm sure you don't realise what an utterly wonderful teacher you are ... '

'Oh come on!'

'No, really Frank, I mean it. And such an inspiration to all of us in the department (she meant the other two art teachers), I mean that's where it counts, we're all so dependent on you.'

'Perhaps you shouldn't be. Perhaps ... '

'No but Frank. I mean you've done so much. And super things like The Living Past of Brinshore. I mean this has been *so* marvellous, bringing back the relevance of art teaching, even Nigel has come out of himself enough to notice what you've been doing (Nigel was her husband), you can't give it all up now, there's so much more to be done.'

Touching on the thing he currently despised most in his work, apart from chasing good exam results, didn't improve his temper, especially since on this subject his inarticulacy felt more than ever like a tide of thick oil in which he might drown.

'But this Southchester thing will be a sort of teaching,' he protested. 'Anyway I don't suppose I'll do it. I can't afford to for one thing, and it's too late in the term to give in my notice for another. I told Max I'd tell him definitely on Monday and

I expect I'll back down then. But I'm so sick of all this crap.' He gestured vaguely but comprehensively.

Pet Rogate shook her head sadly and wisely: 'You don't really mean all this. You're just letting things get you down.'

'But I bloody do mean it. We shouldn't be teaching art, you know. *How* to do it may be, but not *what.* Oh come on, you know what I mean.'

But she didn't; or if she did she found what he said repulsive. It was important to Pet Rogate, as it is to most teachers of arts subjects, to believe that what she was doing was meaningful, enriching, civilising. This sudden attack from someone who represented all this quite discountenanced her. But there was, of course, a simple explanation.

'Poor Frank,' she murmured, and leant yet closer. She was wearing a cotton summer dress with top buttons undone. Her breast bone was scrawny, her breasts beneath a flesh-coloured slip were wide-spaced and tiny; Frank lifted his head and blushed because he'd been so obviously peeping, but she seemed not to have noticed. Her eyes were now wide, wide, dark and moist. 'Poor Frank. You've been having such a rough time of it.' She alluded to his marital and financial problems – he had managed to tell her a little about these during their sessions in the Athlone. 'But you mustn't let it get you down, you mustn't let it make you hard and cynical. You're not a hard person, Frank, you're warm and considerate and understanding. If only there was some way I could help you to get back your faith in things ... '

Conscience, caution, a proper understanding of his best interests held him back – momentarily. Cynical despair, real cynicism, not the critical realism she had called cynicism, urged him on, and he made his pitch. 'Oh Pet,' he said, 'is there no way you can possibly arrange things to come back to my place tonight?'

'Oh Frank,' she said, 'I'll try. I promise I'll try,' and she led him by the hand back to the coffee bar where she danced very close to him in the noisy, flashing, beating, bumping dark, and the thought crossed his mind – she's even more of an armful of dry twigs than I thought she would be.

He drank as much of the wine as he could get hold of, but it wasn't enough, he wanted more. He pleaded the opposite complaint, disengaged himself, and made his way down darkened corridors to the deserted staff-room. There, in his upright narrow steel locker he had left his jacket, and in the inside pocket a used quarter whisky bottle refilled at home from the bottle he had bought at Saintroses. He took a long swig, then another slower but smaller one, swilling the sourness of bad wine and sausage roll mixture out of his mouth. He had reached the stage of drunkenness where neat spirits taste clean, refreshing, invigorating, when they give the illusion that they are waking you up, making a man of you. He screwed on the cap, replaced bottle in pocket, coat in locker, and said, aloud: 'And now gentlemen, I think a trip to the jolly old toilet really is indicated.' He pushed the door instead of pulling it and, 'Tut, tut,' he said.

The corridor was long and dark, the toilet he was heading for was round the corner at the end, next to HAL's private lavatory and opposite the library. The alcove occupied by The Living Past of Brinshore's Oldest Industry was between the two lavatories. There was one light only – the one actually in the foyer, over table and chairs where Gillian and her friend had sat earlier, checking the tickets. They had now gone, were supervising the distribution of food and drink in the coffee bar and the whole area was apparently deserted.

Frank went to the lavatory and as he came out the library door opposite swung shut, though the library itself was in complete darkness. He paused, head on one side, and listened. Distantly he could hear the Ian Dury record, *I could be the catalyst that starts the revolution, I could be an inmate in a long-term institution,* and at closer quarters a soft rustle, but just where he couldn't be sure. 'I ought', he said, 'to look into this. There is someone around I'm sure. Dr Watson, have you your revolver with you? Good man. Really Mr Dangerfield, it is grossly irresponsible of you not to check out these signs of intruders, but with no overtime rates why the hell should you?' He moved towards the foyer, turned and faced the Living Past of Brinshore's Oldest Industry.

'I should vandalise that. I really should,' he said, again aloud. 'What a load of Goddamn crap.'

Then he grinned, giggled. He had been told earlier about the rotten fish found in HAL's cistern, had realised, as he supposed HAL would, that they must have been those brought for the exhibition by the Rammage boy, the previous Monday.

'The very dead and stinking past of Brinshore,' he said. Then he stepped forward, hooked his foot round the leg of the table in the centre of the exhibit, and pulled. The gesture was so silly, so ineffectual, it infuriated him – he put both hands under the table-top and heaved it over, then, stooping, and with much more difficulty for they were built not to tip, toppled one of the mobile display stands that formed the wing of the cave and thus brought down the net roof and some of the display lighting. A bulb exploded, satisfyingly.

I chose to be the singer with a five-piece band
First night nerves every one night stand

Frank stood back, half appalled, half gleeful at what he'd done. At least none of the really quite good paintings had come to any harm.

What a waste, what a waste, but I don't mind.

He turned on his heel and moved briskly off down the corridor, not back to the staff-room, not back to the coffee bar, but out towards the side entrance, the way he had come in.

On the step he paused, sniffed at the rain-laden warm wind, felt in his pocket for his car keys.

'That', he said, thinking of Pet Rogate, 'was a near-run thing.'

He stepped down and moved towards his car.

'Hey. Mr Dangerfield.'

A girl's voice. He turned. The full moon, Queen and Huntress, darting from covert to covert of tumbled cloud, briefly lit her, standing by the wall, not far from the door.

'You don't remember me, do you?'

'Yes I do. Of course I do.'

He stopped, a yard in front of her.

'You're Miriam Trivet. The best. The best … '

She stepped towards him. Intense relief and intense excitement flooded through him as he put his hands on her shoulders and kissed her.

'I loved you,' she said.

'Why?'

'You made me think.'

This surprised him. 'I did?' Then he said: 'Shall we go to the Ring, or to the beach?' He was thinking of the wind, of high tide, of where the summer storm would most efficaciously drive through them.

'The Ring,' she said. 'I can drive, if you think you shouldn't.'

'I'll manage.'

Behind them, in the library, fire pounced and lit the faces of two small boys, one open-mouthed with terror, the other with clammy skin and staring cold eyes. They gripped each other's arms and watched the tongues licking and nuzzling at the books they had scattered like fallen birds for the flames to feed on.

3.

The Ring, a Stone Age town on the ridge of the Downs, is reached first by the main Rifedale road, then by a minor road that climbs through beech woods and passes over the hill only a couple of hundred feet from the top. Miriam was frightened on the way up. If Frank accelerated hard in top the engine jumped out of gear; the lights functioned only on dazzle – if a car approached them and he dipped, the road in front simply disappeared, and for as much as five seconds at a time only the oncoming lights gave any guidance at all. He wanted to have his left arm round her but she managed to persuade him to leave his hand on her knee.

They didn't say much on the way up.

'I didn't see you in the disco.'

'I thought you had but didn't want to speak to me.'

'Why ever should you think that?'

She remained silent, and he realised she had observed his preoccupation with Pet Rogate.

'But where were you?'

'Most of the time I was with Mr Davies. He's sweet. He even danced with me.'

'I wish I had.'

'Never mind. This is better.'

Or will be if we stay alive, she thought, as he squeezed her knee and the car raced on through the tunnel of tossing beeches.

'What were you doing in the car-park?'

'Waiting for you.'

'Waiting for me?'

'Yes. I saw you leave. You didn't come back. I thought I'd missed you, but when I got outside I saw this car was still here.'

'Missed me? What do you mean?'

'I only came to see you. To speak to you.'

This so transported him that he clapped both his hands above his head and hallooed. Miriam grabbed the wheel and the car lurched back to the middle of the road.

He stopped the car rather than parked it, jumped out, rushed round, opened her door. The wind buffeted her, threw rain in her face – the night was black, but filled with noise and wildness, rushing noises through grass and bushes, and roaring in the woods below.

'Where are we going?'

'To the top, to the top,' he cried.

But on the crest of the first turf rampart the wind and rain tore at them so furiously, penetrated their clothes so completely, forced such handfuls of wild air into their lungs, that they were grateful to slither then tumble down the short but precipitous slope into what had been the ditch beyond. There they cradled each other in the long wet grasses of June and the hubbub of the storm bellowed above them. After a time Miriam felt him shivering, fancied she could even hear his teeth chattering, and she wriggled until she was on top of him with her elbows on either side of his head. Fleetingly his hand passed up under her sweater over her bare back, then round and settled on her breast, then shyly moved on and she kissed him again, her wet hair about their faces.

He tried to move but she pressed down on him.

'What are you doing?' he cried.

'Trying to keep the rain off you,' she shouted back, 'you're freezing, you'll get pneumonia.'

'This is a bit mad, isn't it?'

'A bit.'

'Let's see if we can get back to the car.'

In the car she persuaded him to lie across the back seat, with his legs bent. She found an old rug in the boot which she spread across him; then she sat in the front seat and waited for the dawn to come. Frank stopped shivering, slept fitfully. She dozed. The storm blew itself out and she saw the moon set in a tranquil sky, sinking into a bank of cloud above the sea. They woke as the first beams of sunlight struck warm through the side windows.

The sky was cloudless, except for low banks of rose over the hills to the north-east, and cirrus already white, very high in the sky above them. With the dawn the last of the wind dropped, there was not even a breeze, and high above the ramparts a lark's song throbbed through every atom of the limpid air.

'Let's try again,' said Frank.

In the light it was easy to pick their way through where the ramparts were broken to form the mazy entrance of the citadel. On the third and last ridge which lies like a loose belt round the shallow dome of the ovoid hill they paused for breath and then decided to make the whole circuit, a narrow, irregular chalk path nearly more than a mile round. Rifedale Ring lies on a north-west south-east axis and they set off on the north-east side. Below them steep slopes dropped away to hawthorn bushes, their green still fresh and some still with the last of the may on them; rolling flinty fields with green corn rose beyond to beech-crowned summits or dropped to bosky villages and farms. The loveliest thing of all though was the grass at their feet which had not been grazed since early spring and was now knee high, a chalk garden of clovers, vetches and daisies with frequent spikes of orchids mauve through to pale lilac, and buttercups that brushed gold pollen on their shoes and trousers. Their feet and legs were wet, but with every second the sun grew warmer. Rabbits scampered about in the ditch beneath them, the larks sang on; distantly, way down in one of the combes, a cock crew, and the hawthorns and hazels round the base of the hill echoed with the shrill dawn chorus of blackbirds, warblers and thrushes.

Where the flowers and grass allowed they walked hand in hand; often they stopped and kissed. Miriam talked, chattered even – for the most part about Southchester, about the courses – some dull and mechanical, others exciting, and about the lecturers, who, she revealed, perhaps a little artlessly, all seemed to be in love with her. Frank could very well believe it.

'Don't mind my talking,' she cried out at one point. 'You know I'm not really a chatterer, I just have to talk now, I'm too excited not to.'

Frank was very happy to let her talk.

Time and the chalk track brought them round the north-western bend of the hill so they were facing south and west across the plain they had driven over in the storm. Thick woods lay immediately below them out of which plumes of steam were already rising; beyond, mist in layered banks collected above the River Rife and a heron flapped across the water meadows into which a herd of black and white Friesians were already turning out. Away from the river, cornfields alternated with pasture, orchards and market gardens, right down to the sea which glowed dully through the mist that gathered above it. From here they could make out the TRICE conglomeration, the Denham Tower of flats and even fancied they could mark a gleam of gold from the cupola on Trafalgar House. Beyond, the sun gleamed on wet sand stretching almost out to the line of black rocks just then melting into the rising mist.

'And it's all due to you, you know, all due to you,' Miriam exclaimed at one point.

'Oh come on. What did I have to do with it?'

'You made me think. You made me see the thought in art, you made me see the mind in Velasquez or Monet, and that made me see the same in Dickens or Hardy. None of the English teachers at the Comp could do that and precious few at the university; you made me see art as thought, something that can change you.'

Frank was already light-headed with exhaustion and exhilaration – this sudden affirmation of what he had come to doubt or wilfully suppressed now acted like an invigorating potion on him. Flight, soaring with the larks, would not then have been beyond him. But Miriam broke out of his embrace and still lightly, but briskly, switched the direction of the flow of her chat. 'Goodness,' she exclaimed, 'my watch has stopped. It must be well after six o'clock.'

'Does it matter?'

'Well yes. My dad comes home from work early in the morning, and if he finds me not there he'll worry, worry like anything.'

'Then we must get you back.'

'Do you mind? Do you really mind?'

And pulling his hand, and throwing the hair off her face with two small flicks of her head, she led him along the path to where they had climbed on to it, the sun well up now, warm, blood-warming, well clear of the mists.

*

Miriam had forgotten it was now Saturday, that her father should have come home at one not half-past six, and did not know that in fact he had left TRICE at ten o'clock the night before. And he was worried when on getting together the things he needed for bait digging he realised that her bike was not by his in the shed. He then checked that she was not in by going back upstairs and peeping round her door. He did not waken Tess; he did not even change his plan – there seemed to be no point. But then as he pushed his bike out on to the road he stopped to pass the time of day with the milkman, and learnt that there had been a fire at the school. Now he felt quite disturbed, though you would never have suspected it from the stolid way he pedalled along, with his bait fork strapped to his crossbar and his bait box on the carrier behind him.

At the school he found the worst was long over – the place now had the air of a debauched man sleeping off a night of riot. Pools of blackened water lay over the forecourt, a pile of smouldering books lay beneath the sightless windows of the library. A police patrol car, a white Rover 3500, was parked near the entrance. Jack Trivet went over to it, and the policeman who had been watching him since he arrived, lowered his window.

'Just the library was it?' asked Jack.

'Ay. Just the library.'

'Anyone hurt?'

'No, not that we've discovered. Two youngsters from Merriedale that probably started it nearly got asphyxiated, but one of the older lads here pulled them out.'

'I think my daughter was at some function here. She's not come home yet.'

'Well, she's not been caught in this, I can tell you that. It was all spotted in good time and there's no chance at all anyone else was anywhere near the fire.'

Jack was not easily reassured. He was almost certain that the bike he had seen leaning against the wall over by the side entrance was Miriam's. However, there was nothing else to be done so he pushed off from the curb and went on down to the front. By the time he got there he was agitated – angry and worried. She had not been in the fire; so she had spent the night out, with some fellow for sure. Jack knew of only one boyfriend she'd ever been serious about and that was Kevin Rammage. He dismounted between the broken pier and the hideous Leisure Centre, leaning his bike against the vandalised shelter, crossed the promenade and looked down over the shingle towards the fishermen's hut. Two of the four boats were pulled up above the high tide mark – neither of them Kevin's. So Kevin had gone out, in spite of the storm. For a moment Jack found this reassuring then his stomach went cold. She might have gone with him. She was crazy like that sometimes. And Kevin was bloody fool enough to take her. He narrowed his eyes and stared out to the sea which lay apparently dormant a quarter mile away beyond the flat wet sands. As he watched the lilac and gold, rose and yellow mist of early morning formed and the distant black rocks dissolved into it. Moaning Minnie, the Brinshore rocks lightship, mumured three times beneath the invisible horizon, then held her breath for another sixty seconds.

Down on the beach, where the shingle joined the sands, beyond the pier but visible through its barnacled rusty old girders, a figure moved with a metal detector. Arthur King. Jack tramped down through the stones towards him revolving in his mind how he would ask his cousin if he had seen anyone, seen anything untoward. He must do it carefully, not let on Miriam had been out all night – Tess would never forgive him, nor Miriam neither, if it turned out he'd needlessly set gossip going.

'Lovely morning, Arthur.'

'Lovely. But it won't last.'

They looked wisely at the mist and the sky.

'Found anything then?'

'Only this.' The thin, sad-looking man pulled something out of the duffle bag that hung from his shoulder. It took some effort – the object, a woman's handbag, was almost too big for the opening.

'Funny thing. I found it just below the high tide mark, but it's not been in the sea. Just rainwater. So it were dropped early this morning.'

Jack's heart beat faster. The bag was black, shiny, hung over with silver chains. He was sure he had never seen Miriam with anything like it, it certainly wasn't the sort of thing she ever bought. But one couldn't be sure. Suppose it was a present?

'Anything in it? I mean to show ownership like?'

'No Jack. A purse with about two pounds in it. A bus ticket. Make-up and that. Lipstick and that stuff they put on their cheeks.'

That sounded even less like Miriam.

He turned to go back up the shingle. He'd get his bait fork and box down after all. The noise of his feet in the stones drowned, to his ears, the very faint and distant knocking of an empty boat, bumping against the veiled rocks, a full half mile away. But he was still angry with Miriam. He wouldn't tell her off when she turned up, that would only start a row. But he'd let her know how he felt. Yes, he'd do that.

*

In the car-park – more a gravelled space set in a patch of briars, Frank plucked a spray of ramblers for Miriam and then a handful of honeysuckle. In the car the fragrance swam gently over the smells of wet clothes and tiredness. He was exhausted and she looked pale and wan too, yet there was one thing he had to ask her before he set the car going again.

'Miriam. Have you seen my pictures? I mean the ones in Johnny Manet's window?'

'Yes.'

'What do you think of them?'

'I liked them. A lot. Especially the one of the pier. The other one, of the vandalised shelter and the Centre, not so much.'

He waited.

'Do you mind what I think?'

'Of course. But I want to know.'

'Well. The one of the Centre, it seemed ... I don't know, sort of arrogant. And yet "so-what-y", passive. Ironic, which I liked, but impotent.'

He listened to lark-song, noted the prismatic flashing of sun through raindrops on the briars in front.

She went on: 'You mustn't make art, that sort of art, a get-out. Art should never be something to resort to. Not even a last resort. Let it be a beginning.'

He smiled at her. She had put the flowers between her thighs, where they glowed on the shabby black napless velveteen.

'Do you mind?' she asked.

He shook his head. She smiled too and sighed, put her head on his shoulder, and he started the motor.